COME NOVEMBER

COME NOVEMBER

Katrin van Dam

SCHOLASTIC PRESS
New York

Library of Congress Cataloging-in-Publication Data available

ISBN 978-1-338-26842-3

10 9 8 7 6 5 4 3 2 1   18 19 20 21 22
Printed in the U.S.A.   23
First edition, November 2018
Book design by Abby Dening

For Tony Fross—
As a turtle its shell,
So will I carry you
And live in your shelter
. And be at home.

AUGUST

one

Mom lost her job today.

Maybe that's not quite the right word. *Lost* makes it sound like, if we just looked hard enough, her job would turn up somewhere, maybe under a sofa cushion or in the back of a drawer. The only thing she *lost* is her mind, but that's not exactly breaking news. So what happened today, if we're being strictly factual, is Mom got fired.

And really, it shouldn't have come as a huge surprise to any of us. Her supervisor at the day care had been telling her for months that she couldn't talk to the parents about the Next World Society, but I guess Mom just couldn't hold it in anymore. So this morning, one of the dads was dropping off his kid and Mom slipped him a pamphlet. And that was that.

When I get home this afternoon, she's sitting at the kitchen table, logged on to the NWS site as usual. As she explains why she's not at work, I look for some sign that she's freaking out, but she just stares at me with those huge gray eyes and smiles. "I was going to quit next month anyway," she says, and I can feel my ears getting hot. "Now I'll have that much more time to prepare."

"Mom," I say, as calmly as I can. "Have you thought about where you're going to get another job?"

"Sweetie, please just trust me," she says in her breathy little-girl voice. "I don't need another job. Departure is only three months away."

I don't really remember when Mom became a Next Worlder. I do remember the day the divorce was final, exactly five days before my tenth birthday. I wonder, sometimes, how long it took Dad to realize that she had gone off the deep end and she wasn't coming back.

"Mom," I try again, keeping my voice low and even. "What about money? What about food, and rent, and . . . electricity and stuff?"

She blinks up at me. "Oh, Rooney. I know it's hard for you to accept, but none of those things matter anymore."

And that's when I know I won't be quitting the Java Connection.

I shut myself in the bathroom and glare at my reflection. Long brown hair frizzing in the humidity, hazel eyes blazing, neck and cheeks flushed red, broad shoulders clenched with rage. "Way to go, Mom," I mutter under my breath. "Way to take care of your family." Griping about it is kind of satisfying, but it's not going to put food on our plates, so I take a deep breath, splash my face with cold water, change into a clean shirt, and head out.

The one good thing about the house we live in now is that it's a pretty short walk to the center of town. Sure, it's tiny, and Mom has to sleep on the living room sofa. The wallpaper is peeling, and the heat doesn't work so well in the winter. There's no air conditioning, either, but it doesn't get that hot in Vermont any-way. At least it's not supposed to, although this summer, no one seems to have pointed that out to whoever's in charge of the weather.

Crossing Maple, I spot Mercer in the window and wave. As he waves back, he sticks out his lower lip and blows a floppy brown curl out of his eyes.

The bell jingles as I pull the door open. "Hey, what are you doing back here?" Merce asks. "Did you forget something?"

"No, I just need to talk to Maddie," I say. "Is she in back?"

"Yup." He's still looking at me curiously. "Everything okay?"

"Long story. I'll tell you later. I'm just hoping she hasn't hired anyone for the fall yet. I need to pick up more shifts."

Mercer raises his eyebrows but keeps his mouth shut as I walk past him into the back room.

Maddie barely glances up from her calculator. "What's up, Rooney?" she asks.

"I was wondering, are you still looking for someone to fill those afternoon shifts?"

That gets her attention. "I thought you said you wouldn't have time to work once school starts."

"There's been a change of plan." Her eyes are scanning mine for more details. "I could use the cash" is all I say.

Maddie nods. "How many days can you do?" she asks.

"As many as you need," I tell her. I might as well. My senior year is ruined at this point, no matter what.

"You walking home?" Mercer asks when I come back out. It's after three, and Amber, the girl I'll be replacing when she goes back to college, has started her shift. Mercer drops his apron in the back room and we head out together.

Merce and I have known each other since the day I moved to

Stonebrook. The first house Mom rented was just down the street from his. We were close to the town center then, too—we pretty much have to be since Mom doesn't drive—but on the other side of Maple. Mercer would never say "the better side" but you don't have to be a genius to notice that the houses where we live now are smaller and crappier and a lot closer together.

"You have a minute?" he asks as we walk down Main. "Come get some tomatoes. They're getting a little out of control."

For as long as I've known him, Mercer has had a garden. When we were little, it was just a few square feet, but at this point his yard is more garden than lawn. When we get to his house, he pulls the screen door open and we both brace ourselves as Mingus comes barreling toward us, curly black fur flying, nails scrabbling on the kitchen tiles. Mercer bends down to scratch the dog behind the ears, then hands me a couple of mesh bags. "You can give them back later," he says as Mingus and I follow him out into the backyard.

"Whoa, you weren't kidding!" The garden looks like a jungle, with vines sprawling everywhere. "This thing's going all Jurassic Park on you!"

"Yeah, the neighbors aren't crazy about it," Mercer admits. "But seriously, what's so great about lawns?"

He quickly fills one bag with veggies, and the other with the little orange cherry tomatoes he knows I love. Then he sits on the bench under the one big shade tree. "So. What's the deal?" He pats the seat next to him. "Why are you taking that after-school shift?"

It would be nice to just let the world keep going as if nothing has changed. But not telling him about Mom would be like trying to keep a secret from myself. Mercer is my best friend. Or more like my only friend these days. I'm not a total recluse or anything. I'm not that girl who sits alone in the cafeteria, scribbling stories about everybody dying in horrible accidents. I'm more like the girl who flies under the radar. Way, way under.

Back in middle school, I had more friends. I used to go to other kids' houses, hang out, talk about safe stuff like music and which boys I thought were cute. But by freshman year, Mom was getting more and more wrapped up in the NWS, and I started keeping a low profile. When girls in my class invited me to hang out, I told them I had to work or take care of my brother. I let them think it was just because we were poor, living on Mom's salary from the day care. It didn't feel great, but it was better than telling them the whole truth.

Eventually, people stopped inviting me, and I slipped into a social gray zone. Working on the *Stonebrook High Sentinel* was a perfect way to hide in plain sight. It gave me a crowd to blend in with, and writing articles let me stay on the outside without making people uncomfortable. Asking people to talk about themselves is a great way to deflect attention.

These days, when it comes to letting people see the real me, or what's going on in my life, it's strictly on a need-to-know basis. Mercer's the only one who gets an all-access pass.

"Mom got canned today," I tell him.

His brow creases with worry. "So you're going to pick up the slack until she gets another job?"

"Oh, she's not getting another job," I say airily. "She seems to think the bills are just going to pay themselves."

His jaw tightens. "No. That is *not* okay. It's your senior year!"

"Yeah, well, it's not the end of the world . . . or IS it?" I say in my best movie-trailer voice.

Mercer lets out a snort and I stand up. "Listen, I need to go. Daniel will be home soon and I want to be there when Mom tells him."

"Rooney," Mercer says, grabbing my arm. "This is serious. You can't quit the *Sentinel*. You totally earned that editor title. And besides, you need it for your applications."

"Believe me, I know. But what am I supposed to do? Someone needs to pay the bills."

"Yeah, but it shouldn't have to be you," he starts again. "That's what parents are supposed to do."

"You're right. It's messed up. But don't worry, okay? I've already started my college essays. Nobody is more focused on getting out of here than me."

He shakes his head again, a frustrated look on his face. "It's just not right. This whole thing is crazy."

"I know it is," I say. "Thanks for the veggies. I'll see you tomorrow."

When I get home, Daniel is already there, and I can tell from the way he's sitting that Mom hasn't wasted any time sharing her big news.

"You okay, Bug?" I ask him. Daniel shrugs, not wanting to talk about it in front of Mom.

"Do you two mind having dinner by yourselves tonight?" she asks as a car horn sounds outside. "I'm going to a planning meeting with Susan. I don't think I'll be late."

"It's fine, Mom," I tell her. It's easier when she's not around anyway.

"Super!" She stops flitting around just long enough to kiss us both and tell us she loves us, and then she's out the door. As soon as she's gone, I rub the kiss off my forehead.

Daniel and I scrounge around in the kitchen cabinets, looking for something to eat. "Looks like it's PB and Js again," I say, sounding as cheerful as I can while silently cursing Mom for never buying any food.

"That's okay, I don't mind," Daniel says.

While Daniel makes the sandwiches, I dole out Mercer's cherry tomatoes, slice up a cucumber, and put the rest in the fridge. Hopefully, we can make it last a couple of days.

Daniel's pretty quiet over dinner. I ask him about his day, and he tells me about his enameling project at the Y, but I can tell his heart's not really in it, and after a while, I tell him he can read if he wants. I don't know what to say about Mom's job, and I can tell he'd rather bury his nose in a book than have a conversation anyway.

At bedtime, though, we stick with our usual ritual. "So, what are they up to?" I ask as I angle the window fan to bring a little cool air into Daniel's room.

He opens his sketch pad and shows me one of the careful pencil drawings inside. "Okay," he begins, "they've found the road to the Cloud Castle, but it's blocked by giant stones . . ." For the next fifteen minutes, I make the right noises and ask the right questions. But inside my head, I'm thinking about rent and the grocery list and calculating how long I can make my paycheck last.

two

Mom's already on the computer when I come downstairs early the next morning. I wonder whether she's slept at all. The couch shows no obvious signs of use. Not that Mom makes much of a dent—she and Daniel are both bony little bird-people. Clearly, I got my genes from the other side.

She looks up like she's surprised to see another human in the house. "Oh, Rooney! Come sit with me, sweetie."

I empty a carton of OJ into my glass and make a mental note to buy more after work. Then I sit next to her, glancing at the screen. No big surprise, she's on the NWS website. Just once, I'd love to catch her shopping for clothes or checking out a dating site. Anything that meant she was living in the world with the rest of us.

"We had such a wonderful meeting last night," Mom begins. "We heard the whole plan for the New York trip!"

I can tell we're heading into the same conversation we've been having for months, and right on schedule, she goes into her pitch: "Rooney, I really want you to come to New York—you and Daniel. I just know when you meet all the others, you'll understand how important this is."

Going to New York with a bunch of Next Worlders sounds like about as much fun as setting myself on fire, but after lying awake for most of last night worrying, I've already made up my mind. Even if it means I have to do something I swore I'd never do. "Okay, Mom, I'll think about it," I tell her.

She doesn't even seem to hear me. She just keeps going with her usual script: "There's so little time left . . . You and Daniel are all that I care about . . ." Blah, blah, blah.

"Mom," I say again. "I'll think about it."

She stops then, her mouth open. "You will? Oh, Rooney, that's wonderful. And I know you can convince Daniel. He looks up to you so much—"

"No," I interrupt. "Mom, even if I go, Daniel needs to stay here. He's too little."

"But . . . sweetie, it's August already. If he doesn't go now, it's going to be much harder for him to learn what he needs to know later."

I shake my head. "You need to drop it, Mom."

Her shoulders slump. "All right," she says. "For now." Then she seems to perk up. "I'm just so happy you're coming."

"Mom, I said I'd *think* about it," I start to say, but it's no use. She only hears what she wants to hear. And besides, it's not like I have another plan.

I run to my room and muscle open the top drawer of my dresser, which always sticks in the humidity. I root around until I find a small white card underneath my socks and shove it into my pocket. As I head down the stairs, she's already back at her computer. I'm glad Daniel eats breakfast at camp, since she probably wouldn't remember to feed him anything. "I love you, sweetheart!" she calls out as the screen door thumps shut behind me.

When I get to the Java Connection, Maddie and Mercer are setting up for the morning rush. I grab an apron from the back room and yank my hair up into a ponytail. "Hey," Mercer calls out, "you want to take the first shift on the register?"

"Sure," I call back, and start ringing up orders as he heads over to the line of cups he's got set up.

Once the rush ends, Maddie goes back to tally the morning's receipts and Mercer starts spritzing the plants in the window. It's hard to believe they're the same dusty, scraggly specimens that Mercer got his hands on in June. *Don't get too comfortable, plants,* I think to myself. *He's going back to school in a few weeks.*

"Listen, Merce, I need to ask you a favor."

"Sure. What's up?" he asks.

"I need to make a call. Can I use your phone?"

"Still determined to be the last person on earth without a phone, huh?"

"Yeah, you know me," I deadpan. "Total rebel."

He hands over his phone. "It's all yours. But if you want to call China, you'll need a special code."

He's smiling, waiting for me to smile back at his quasi-joke. But the solidity of the phone in my hands makes this suddenly seem so real that my stomach lurches. *Is this really a good idea? Maybe I shouldn't rush into anything. But if I don't call now, I may be too late . . .* I pocket the phone. "Thanks. Mind if I take my break now? You can leave me half the tables to clean."

"Don't worry about it. But are you going to tell me who you're calling? What's the big mystery?"

I pull out the sweat-creased card and show it to him.

His eyes widen. "Wow . . . Are you sure?" he asks.

I shrug. "I'm not sure about anything. But I don't have a better idea."

"Do you want me to come with you? For moral support or whatever?"

"Nah. Stay in here where it's cool."

"Okay," he says uncertainly. "Good luck."

I cross the street toward the park. The air feels like the inside of a dog's mouth, but at least no one can hear me out here. I find a bench in the shade and study the card again. *Does he even work there anymore? Will he take my call?* My hands are shaking a little, so I take some deep, slow breaths before I dial.

"Department of Housing, Peter Harris's office," a woman says into my ear. "Can I help you?"

"Is he in?" I ask, half hoping that she'll say no.

"Who's calling, please?"

Deep breath. "It's . . . Tell him it's his daughter, please."

"Oh! Just a moment, dear." She sounds surprised. Does she even know he has a daughter?

A few minutes go by, and I start to wonder whether he'll pick up. Maybe he doesn't ever want to talk to us again. *Keep cool,* I tell myself. *Remember why you're calling. Feeling bitter is a luxury you can't afford right now.* Finally, there's a click. "Marina? Is that you?" he says. He sounds like he's in a hurry.

"Um, hi. Yeah. It's me." *Don't let him hear your voice shaking.*

"Are you all right? Did something happen?" he asks, and now I wonder whether that's actually worry in his voice.

"I'm fine . . . Dad." The word feels strange in my mouth. How long has it been since I've said it out loud? "I just . . . I'm going to be in New York in a few weeks, and I was wondering if we could get together."

"Oh! You're coming to New York? That's great," he says. "Are you . . . looking at colleges?"

"Not exactly. I'm just going to be there for a day or two. With Mom. But I thought maybe we could . . ." *Could what?* Across the street, Mercer is framed in the window of the Java Connection. ". . . get coffee or something."

There's a long pause. "You and your mom?" he asks stiffly.

"Oh! No. I meant just you and me."

"I see." Then, after another pause, he says, "Danny isn't coming?"

So weird. No one who knew Daniel would ever call him Danny. "Oh, um . . . Daniel's staying home."

I tell him the dates of the trip. "I'm free Thursday night," he says. "Is dinner okay?"

"Sure." I don't know how I'm going to explain that one to Mom, but I'll worry about it when the time comes.

"Good. Would it . . ." He pauses for a second, choosing his words. "I'd like to invite Carol to join us. Is that all right?"

Great. That's not going to complicate things at all.

"Sure," I tell him. "That's fine."

"All right," he says. "So I'll see you in a few weeks. Is downtown all right? Carol is . . . It's better for her if she doesn't have to travel too far." He gives me an address and then, as I'm about to hang up, he says, "Marina?"

"Yes?"

"I'm really glad you called."

"Okay," I say. "I've got to go."

When I hang up, I'm sweating like I've just run five miles. And not because it's ninety-five degrees out.

That afternoon, Mom is even more fluttery than usual. I've barely made it through the door when she's all over me. "Sweetie! Have you thought about the trip? Will you come?"

I hand her the bags of groceries that I've just dragged home. "How about you unpack these, Mom? There's stuff that needs to go in the freezer."

"Thanks for going to the market," she says. "I don't know what we'd do without you!"

I'm pretty sure I know the answer to that one: starve in the dark.

Mom starts to unpack the cold stuff, but instead of putting it in the freezer, she dumps it on the counter and then just stands there looking lost. Obviously, she's not going to be able to concentrate on anything until I answer her question.

"Okay, Mom. I'll come to New York."

She jumps on me then, squeezing me with her scrawny little arms. "Oh, Rooney! You don't know how much this means to me. It's going to change everything, you'll see!"

I let her hang on to me for a few seconds, then pry her loose and start putting away the frozen food. As I brush past her, I notice that her eyes are bright with tears. Well, at least I didn't get full-on sobbing. I guess that's something to be grateful for.

I glance at Daniel sitting at the kitchen table with his book. He looks back at me, big question marks all over his face. *I'll explain later*, I try to tell him with my eyes. *Just trust me*.

For the rest of the afternoon, she's all sweet and attentive. She helps make dinner, and even eats a few bites instead of going straight to her computer. As I'm washing the dishes, she turns it on, but I can tell she's not really looking at what's on the screen. She keeps sneaking glances at Daniel. Finally, she comes over and pushes herself up onto the counter next to me, her legs dangling. "I'm so glad you're coming, Rooney, but . . ."

Here it comes.

"Don't you think Daniel should come, too? He belongs with his family now more than ever."

I shake my head. "Mom, he's nine years old," I remind her.

Daniel looks like he's wrapped up in his book, but I can tell that he's listening. So can Mom, I guess. She hops down and goes over to him, staring until he looks at her. "Daniel, honey, wouldn't you *like* to go to New York with us?"

Daniel looks back at her and I hold my breath. "I'm not sure, Mom," he says. "Can I think about it?" I breathe a silent *thank you* and turn back to the dishes.

At bedtime, Daniel isn't interested in talking about his drawings. "What's going on, Rooney?" he asks the second I close his door. "Why are you going to New York with Mom? And why don't you want me to come?"

It hadn't crossed my mind that he'd be mad about it. "I'm

sorry, Bug," I say. "I kind of made a snap decision. I should have talked to you about it first."

"Yeah, you should have," Daniel says, but I can tell that he's already losing steam. He doesn't have much stamina when it comes to being mad. Not like me.

"I know. But listen, it's not that I don't want you to come. I mean, I don't want you to come, but I don't want to go either. I just have to."

I've spent the day trying to decide what to tell Daniel about Dad. The thing is, we never talk about him. If it weren't for Mom leaving me no choice, I never would have called Dad. I don't know whether Daniel even thinks about him. And the last thing I want to do is stir up a bunch of uncomfortable questions for him.

"Why do you have to go?" he asks.

Looking at him, I make another snap decision. I'm not going to tell him about Dad. Not yet. Why rock his world if nothing is going to change? So I settle for something that's at least partly true. "You know how I want to apply to Columbia?" Of course he knows. We talk about it all the time. Planning for the future is basically the only thing that keeps me sane these days.

"Yeah," Daniel says. "I know."

"Well, Mom will never let me go visit the campus, since she doesn't see the point. I figure this is probably my only chance to check it out before it's time to apply."

"Oh," Daniel says. "That makes sense." He's quiet for a little while, thinking. Then he says, "I think it's good that you're going. You can keep an eye on Mom. She seems like she's getting worse."

I can't even pretend I don't know what he means. Mom's definitely been getting weirder and weirder. And I can't imagine this trip is going to calm her down. After all, November is just a few months away.

The next two weeks pass too quickly. Mom and Susan meet almost every night, and every day Mom seems more wound up. Half of the time, she's hugging us and telling us how much she loves us. And the other half, it's like she has no idea we exist. She spends most of her time staring at the computer with big, empty eyes. When Daniel tells her he's decided not to go to New York, she just nods. But a few minutes later, I hear her crying in the bathroom.

I'm wiping down the cappuccino machine during my last shift before the trip when I hear a voice behind me. "Well, Madame Editor-in-Chief. I was hoping I might see you here."

I don't have to turn around to know who's talking: No one else in Stonebrook has that warm spice in their voice.

I haven't seen Mrs. Fisher, my adviser at the paper, since the spring. And now that she's standing here in front of me, I know I've let her down. At the end of the school year, we agreed to meet over the summer to start planning our back-to-school issue, and now it's almost September. She must be wondering why I haven't been in touch. I kept thinking there was plenty of time, and then Mom did her Mom thing, and all my plans got thrown in the dumpster. And since telling Mrs. Fisher would mean it was absolutely and finally true, I haven't said anything.

"Are you looking forward to getting back to work?" she asks, and I'm surprised to see a look of uncertainty cross her face, like she wishes she hadn't asked the question. Normally, every word she speaks feels as deliberate as if it were coming from the

Earth itself. "Of course, you have been working all summer, haven't you?" she adds.

"Yeah, it's been pretty intense," I admit. I know I need to fill her in, but this isn't the time or the place. Luckily, the bell over the door jangles and Mrs. Fisher glances over her shoulder as two customers come in. "I see you're busy. I shouldn't trouble you at work," she says. "But perhaps you could drop in sometime so we could begin discussing our plans for the year?"

"I'll come next week," I promise. "There are some things I need to talk to you about."

"All right, then. Until next week."

"Thanks for stopping by," I call after her, my throat tightening. Then I turn to the new customers and take their order, blinking away the stinging feeling behind my eyes.

The night before we leave, I help Daniel pull together his sleepover bag. I've arranged for him to stay at his buddy Max's house while we're out of town. Max's mom, Stefanie, is super nice about it. I think she feels sorry for Daniel, and probably for me, too.

"Maybe just take two books," I tell him. "We're only going to be gone a couple of days."

"It's going to be weird with you gone. I wish I was going, too."

"Nah, you're the lucky one," I say. "I bet Max has air conditioning!"

"Yeah." Daniel shrugs. "I'd rather be hot at home with you."

I push the hair up off his warm, sticky forehead. "We'll be back before you even have a chance to miss us. I promise."

Mercer calls after dinner, and I tell Daniel I'm going for a walk. Mom doesn't look up from the computer as I slip out the door.

It's still crazy hot out, but at least there's a breeze. When we get to the park, we sit on a picnic table. "Here," Mercer says, pulling a cloth bag out of his backpack. "You can take them with you on your trip."

"Thanks, Merce." I reach in and pop a little orange tomato into my mouth. It's still warm from the sun, and when I bite into it, the seeds squirt all over his T-shirt.

"Oh, no! I'm sorry!" I say, but we're both laughing too hard to take the apology seriously.

"Nice," he says, wiping his shirt. He reaches into the bag and hands me another one. "You want to try again? I think you missed a spot."

"Nah, I wouldn't want to waste it," I tell him. "Seriously, I hope it won't stain."

"Rooney, don't worry about it," Mercer says, and suddenly he looks serious. "Listen, I've been thinking: I know you don't feel like you have a lot of options right now. But your dad . . . he hasn't exactly been the most reliable person in your life. I just don't want you to end up getting crushed again."

"I know. But what am I supposed to do? My paycheck barely covers the groceries."

"I don't know. I wish I had a better idea. This whole trip just sounds insane to me. I still can't believe you're going on a Next Worlder recruitment drive."

"I know, right?" I say. "It may be ninety-eight degrees in Vermont, but it's a cold day in hell, my friend."

Mercer barely smiles. "Just promise me you won't get sucked in by Everett and his Next World nuts," he says. I trace an X over my heart and then hold up my hand in a mock salute.

He bursts out laughing. "What is that? Some kind of gang sign?"

"I don't know, isn't that what Scouts do or something?"

"Beats me."

There are still a few seeds clinging to his shirt, and I reach up to brush them away. The solid ridge of muscle under my fingers doesn't track with the skinny torso I saw about a million times at the Y pool when we were younger. "Whoa, check you out! When did you get all ripped?" I prod his chest, feeling the outline of his pecs, then reach over and squeeze one of his biceps.

"Quit tickling!" he yelps, twisting out of my reach.

"Ooh, sorry, Buffy McBufferson." I pull my hand back. "Did you start lifting while I wasn't looking?"

"Just gardening." He grins and flexes for me. "It's the weeding workout."

"Sweet. You should have a YouTube channel."

We sit there for a little while longer, enjoying the breeze. I'd love to just stay here with Merce, with the sun going down and the night sounds swelling around us, but it's almost Daniel's bedtime. I pick up the bag of tomatoes. "I should get going. Thanks again for these. And for, you know, taking care of me."

"Well, *somebody* has to," he says, serious again. He jumps down, his feet landing in the dusty pine needles. Then he turns around and reaches out a hand to me. "Have a good trip," he says. "Borrow a phone and call me if you need to talk. And take good notes, okay? Sounds like this is going to be a pretty juicy story."

SEPTEMBER

one

Early the next morning, Susan and her husband, Roger, pick us up. They're driving a huge white van with vinyl banners on both sides that say NEXT WORLD SOCIETY. I don't know why they rented something so massive, since Susan's Ford is plenty big enough to hold us. Of course, those giant banners wouldn't fit on her car.

We leave Daniel at Max's house, then head south. Mom is talking too much, the way she does when she's overexcited. Susan, in the front seat, keeps laughing her big horse laugh. I take the opportunity to study Roger. I've seen plenty of Susan over the last few years, but Roger is never with her when she comes to pick Mom up. Even sitting down, I can tell he must be about five inches shorter than Susan. He seems quiet and kind of nerdy, but nice enough. I wonder what he and Susan have in common, aside from the fact that they're both Next Worlders.

Pretty soon we're on Route 91. "Brattleboro is first, and then we'll pick up the Garcias in Hartford and have some lunch," Susan announces. "It's a good thing you don't take up much space, Anneliese—it's going to be a tight squeeze!" Another big laugh.

That explains the van. I'm actually glad there are going to be other people on the trip. It will dilute the Susan effect a little.

Our first stop is a little house with peeling paint and one shutter dangling at a crazy angle. When Roger beeps, an old couple in matching white sneakers and pleated khaki shorts comes out. Mom introduces them to me as Mr. and Mrs. Andrews. "No, dear," the woman says as she hauls herself into the van. "You just call us Fred and Alice."

We drive for a couple more hours and everyone in the van is talking like kids on a field trip. Everyone but me, that is. I'm in the back, doing my best to maintain a cone of silence. Every now and then, I pop one of Mercer's cherry tomatoes into my mouth, each one like a juicy little dose of normalcy. Just past Hartford we pull off the highway into a strip mall, and I follow the group into a diner. There's a big table already set for us, and a girl in an apron who looks a few years older than me rushes over and starts hugging everyone. "I'm Anjelica," she says when she reaches me. "You must be Rooney!" I'm afraid she's going to hug me, too, but she settles for a handshake.

Anjelica takes our orders, and pretty soon we're all eating burgers, fries, and milk shakes. The food is so good that Mom even eats half a burger, which is practically a miracle. Anjelica keeps swinging by to chat with everyone and refill water glasses, and I start to piece together the situation. Her parents own the restaurant, and she and her brother, Francisco, both work there. She points out her father behind the grill, and her mother expediting orders. "Are they ready to go?" Susan asks. "We'll need to get moving soon."

"I'll go check on them," Anjelica says, and disappears for a few minutes. When she comes back, she's got her arms around her parents and is sort of steering them toward us. They've taken off their aprons, and I notice they're both dressed a little too formally for working in a diner in the middle of summer.

Francisco and a man who looks a lot like Anjelica's father come out of the kitchen, too, and watch us unsmilingly as we leave. "See you in a few days, Tio!" Anjelica calls, but her uncle is already heading back into the kitchen. Francisco says something into her ear and I see her face cloud over with anger, or maybe sadness. But she gives him a kiss and moves away.

Once she's got her parents safely in the van, Anjelica makes her way to the back. "Mind if I sit with you?" she asks, squeezing in next to me.

After just a few miles, it's obvious my cone of silence isn't going to work with Anjelica—she's way too friendly. Mom and Susan are basically the only Next Worlders I've met before today, so it's strange to see someone close to my own age in the group. And while I didn't come on this trip to make friends, it's hard not to like Anjelica.

"Francisco and I, we went to Catholic school," she tells me. "For him and my parents, the Church has all the answers. For me, it was different. I always felt like the Church ignored a lot of what was going on in the world."

"So what made you join the Next World Society?" I ask. I sound like I'm interviewing someone for the *Sentinel*, all detached and impersonal, but I'm genuinely curious. I can't help wondering how someone like Anjelica ended up in this van.

"Well, I was a freshman," she tells me. "I was thinking about becoming a social worker or a teacher, but I was also interested in activism. So this one day, I was researching different environmental organizations, and I found the NWS website. It was like everything suddenly made sense for the first time. So this past spring, I decided to leave school. I spent the summer working at the restaurant and helping the NWS with their online outreach. My parents are still hoping I'll go back." Her eyes narrow as she looks at them sitting a few rows in front of us.

"How do they feel about the NWS? And . . . November?" I ask her.

"Well, like I said, they're Catholic, so this is way outside their comfort zone. We're definitely not on the same page about November yet. That's why this trip is so important. I think if they can just listen to what Everett has to say, it's going to click for them, just like it did for me."

It's the same thing Mom has been saying to me for years, but for some reason, when Anjelica says it, it doesn't make me mad. I actually feel kind of sorry for her. "Well, good luck," I tell her, not sure what else to say.

"Thanks," she says, then lets out a sigh. "The thing is, Francisco is totally closed off to it. He said even if it was true, he'd rather stay here. So he volunteered to help my tio look after the restaurant." For a second, I'm worried she's going to start crying, but she forces a little laugh and shakes her head. "So all the pressure is on this trip. If I can just get my parents on board, I know Francisco will come around."

Maybe she realizes she shouldn't talk to me about trying to brainwash her family, because she changes the subject abruptly. "So. Is Rooney your real name?"

"Oh, no. It's Marina. But most people don't call me that."

"How did you go from Marina to Rooney?"

I grimace, embarrassed. "It's kind of a lame story. My little brother couldn't pronounce my name so he'd call me Reena. And then that morphed into Reena-Rooney. And Rooney just kind of stuck."

"That's not lame," she says. "It's sweet."

"Well, I'm planning to change it anyway. When I go to college, I'll probably go by Marina."

She gives me a puzzled look. "College? But it's . . . November is less than three months away."

Crap.

"Yeah . . ." I say. "I'm not . . . so sure about November."

"Oh! I just assumed, you know, since you're here with your mom . . ." Anjelica's voice trails off and she shrugs. "Well, look, the important thing is, you're here. It'll give you a chance to see things firsthand."

She's starting to sound a little too much like Mom again. "You know, I didn't get a lot of sleep last night," I tell her. "I'm going to take a nap."

"Sure," she says, and pulls out a copy of Everett's book. "I need to do some studying anyway."

I close my eyes and lean my head against the window, but I don't fall asleep. There are too many things on my mind. I wonder what it will be like to be in New York again after all these years. I wonder how it will feel to see Dad and meet his new wife. But mostly, I wonder what I've gotten myself into, and how I'm going to get through the next couple of days of Next Worlder hard sell.

———

NWS headquarters is a building in Washington Heights that looks like it used to be a school. We step out of the van and are instantly wrapped in the hot, wet blanket of a New York City heat wave. I had forgotten just how steamy it can get here.

A businesslike African American woman named Janice greets us and leads us upstairs. There are two big rooms set up with cots, one for the men and one for the women. I haven't had to share a bedroom since we moved to Vermont, and now I'm going to be bedding down with a roomful of strangers. The whole setup makes me feel like I've been sent to juvie.

I put my backpack on a cot at the far end of our room, hoping that will give me a little privacy. "Mind if I set up next to you?" Anjelica asks, and I nod. Maybe she'll be too focused on her parents to pay attention to me. Anyway, better her next to me than Mom. Or Susan.

"What about your folks?" I ask her.

"We have a cousin who lives near here, so they're staying with her."

Orientation is in what looks like an old gymnasium. We all fill out HELLO, MY NAME IS _____ stickers as we walk in, then sit on metal folding chairs. There are over a hundred of us in the room, including the nine from our van. I'll say this for the Next Worlders: They're a pretty diverse group. There are men, women, couples, single people, old people, teenagers, every skin color and accent you can imagine. A few people even brought little kids. I'm glad I convinced Mom to leave Daniel at home.

There's a buzz in the room, and everyone is looking around. I think they're expecting Everett to walk in, but Janice switches on a big TV monitor and Everett's face fills the screen. His chin-length silver hair is tucked behind his ears and he's smiling the same pompous smile he's got in all his pictures. Can I really be the only one in this room who has the urge to slap that smile off his face?

"My friends," he begins, "I wish that I could be with you in person tonight, but please be assured, I am with you in spirit. And soon, we will all be together."

He takes a long pause, his eyes barely blinking, like a lizard. "The survival of our species hangs in the balance tonight. In the little time that remains, the key to humanity's future is in your hands."

Everett keeps talking, but I stop listening to his words. I'm more interested in the way his hair is lit up. It makes him look glowy, like he's got a flashlight inside him. The effect reminds me of something from a bad movie about the Bible. His voice sounds actor-ish, too—sort of English or something. That accent makes him sound like he *knows* things, like everything he says is *extra meaningful*. I'd bet a hundred bucks it's fake.

I'm obviously in the minority, though. All around the room, I can see people happily falling under Everett's spell. There's something familiar about the scene, but I can't quite put my finger on it. Then it clicks: a cartoon I used to watch when I was little. A man in a turban is playing a flute, and a snake is rising up out of a basket in front of him, weaving and swaying to the music.

I look down and squeeze my eyes shut. Now would not be a good time to laugh.

Everett's still going on. "We can't save our beautiful planet. But we have a chance for a new beginning. And in the brief time we have left, it is our duty to let the world know that they can choose to perish with the past or Depart with us and begin anew. Tonight I'm asking you: Give everything you can. We can't take it with us. We must give our all to persuading the world that Departure is upon us."

With one last piercing look from Everett, the screen goes dark and Janice starts passing out stacks of pamphlets. "Everett said it best," she says. "The future of our species hangs in the balance. We're fighting for survival, but not with guns, or bombs. We're fighting with words, with ideas. We are here to open people's minds. And it's my job to make sure that everyone has all the tools they need."

I look down at the pamphlet in my hands. On the front, there's a picture of Everett. The headline reads, "The Future of Humanity: A Lecture by Everett Nichols, PhD," and then, at the bottom, "The Town Hall, NYC. Friday, September 3rd."

"For the next few days," Janice says, "we're going to be spending a lot of time together. Well"—she gives a little chuckle—"not *just* for the next few days!"

Everyone chuckles back.

"As you all know, our job this week is to Activate as many new members as possible," Janice continues. "Remember, there's room for everyone, as long as they're committed to living in Balance. They may not want to stop and listen to you, but don't be discouraged. Just remember what's at stake. Are you really going to worry about rubbing a few people the wrong way when the survival of the species is on the line?"

People are nodding in agreement.

"Now, the people in this room, we all share something very important. What do we have in common? We got Activated."

More nods.

Janice clicks at her laptop, and a slide comes up on the screen with the word *heuristic* on it. "Now here's a little piece of psychology for you. Is anyone here familiar with this word?"

Anjelica raises her hand. "It's kind of a shortcut for making decisions."

Janice gives her a warm smile. "That's exactly right. Most of the decisions we humans make aren't based on deep thinking. We use shortcuts. And you know what the most common shortcut is? *Identity.* We say to ourselves, 'What do people like me do in this situation?'"

Janice walks over to someone sitting in the front row. "Tell me, Michael," she says, glancing at the man's name tag. "Are you the kind of person who worries about the destruction of the rain forest?"

Michael nods.

Janice moves down the row. "Hi, Shirley," she says to a woman with frizzy gray hair. "Are you the kind of person who is concerned about rising sea levels?"

"Yes, I am," Shirley replies.

"And how about you, Jean? Are you the kind of person who cares about the future of the human race?"

"Of course!"

"And do you feel helpless to fix these problems?" Janice asks them, and they all nod.

"You see," Janice says, smiling, "I've just established common ground with these folks. We care about the same things. Now here's the tricky part."

She stands for a second, like she's deep in thought, then

addresses the three in the front row again. "Since you're concerned about these things, how about leaving behind everything you know and joining a bunch of strangers on a one-way mission to outer space?"

She's clearly expecting a laugh from the audience, and she gets it. She grins and nods at us. "Too soon, right?" She brings up a new slide: FOOT IN THE DOOR.

"You can't rush this. It's too hard for people to get their heads around. Some of you have had years to make this decision, but we have less than three months now. So how do we speed up the process? How do we help more people Activate faster? Well, let me ask you: Which is easier to open—a door that's locked tight or a door that's open a crack?"

Without waiting for an answer, she gestures behind her to the screen. "So here's what we do. We identify people who are already concerned about the planet. And then we get that foot in the door: We invite them to a free lecture about something that speaks to that identity. Just by agreeing to come to the lecture, they're opening the door a crack. And then you know Everett will open it wide!"

I have to admit, Janice's techniques make sense. The story she's selling is still ridiculous, but the Next Worlders aren't exactly what I was picturing. I expected a bunch of trippy-dippy flower children like Mom. But a lot of these people seem totally normal. Which is probably even scarier.

As Janice walks us through a detailed process to Engage, Enlighten, and Activate the people of New York, I look over at Anjelica. She's writing furiously in a notebook while her parents sit with their arms folded tightly over their chests. She probably should have let them skip this meeting. Nobody likes to see how the sausage is made.

I'm not meeting Dad until seven tomorrow night. I have no idea how I'm going to spend my time until then, but one thing is clear: I need to get away from the group. *I really need a plan.*

Three men carry in big platters of sandwiches, and Janice tells us we can take a little "bio break." As I'm washing my hands, Anjelica walks into the ladies' room and gives me a big smile. "I'm so excited for tomorrow," she says. "Our team got assigned to Times Square!"

I look down at my hands and pretend I'm extremely concerned about getting all the soap off. I'm hoping she can't see the panic in my eyes, but I probably don't need to worry. She seems to be on such a high from the meeting that she's not noticing anything.

As I walk out of the ladies' room, Mom comes over, wearing an NWS T-shirt. The size small hangs off her, making her look even more waif-y than usual. "Pretty spiffy, huh?" she says, spinning like a kid modeling a new dress. The shirt is green, with NEXT WORLD SOCIETY in big white block letters on the front. "I grabbed yours for you, sweetie. I don't think we've ever had matching outfits before!" She giggles, then slides an arm around my waist and gives me a little squeeze. I try not to let her feel my body stiffen as I slip out of her grasp, and she doesn't seem to notice.

There's no way I'm going to be able to slip away from the group dressed like a walking billboard. And the only way to blend in with them is to go along with the recruitment drive. But how can I? What if I follow Janice's instructions and actually manage to convince some poor sucker to go see Everett speak? What if they go home afterward and start acting the way Mom has these last few years? What if they quit their jobs? How am I supposed to live with that?

Maybe I can just hand out pamphlets and let everyone else do the talking. It's still a pretty gray area, morally, but at least I won't be actively selling the lie. It's not much of a plan, but it will have to do for now.

At bedtime, I brush my teeth at the big communal sink and get changed in one of the bathroom stalls. I'm studying the NWS pamphlet when Mom comes over and sits on my cot. Her hair is pinned up for the night, and the breeze from the vent over my bed is blowing stray wisps around her face. I remember how much I used to love helping her braid her hair when I was little. Back then, it didn't have gray streaks in it.

"I'm surprised they're using the air conditioning," she whispers in my ear. "It's so terrible for the planet."

"It's like a hundred degrees out," I point out. "And we're crammed in here like sardines. We'd probably all die without it."

"I guess that's true," she says with a little laugh. "My brilliant girl is right again!" Then her face turns serious. "Sweetie, I need to ask you something. Please don't say no right away. I really need you to think about this."

Whatever it is, it can't be good. She hasn't even told me what she wants yet, and she's already bracing herself for the no.

"I want you to talk to your father," she says.

All the air in my lungs goes whooshing out in one big breath. "You . . . what?" I stutter.

"I know, I know. But please just hear me out. Your father is still very angry, but, Rooney, I've never stopped hoping he'll come around. November is less than three months away. I think you may be the only one who can reach him. And if you don't, he's going to be left here after we Depart, and you'll never see him again." Mom's got her feet pulled up under her nightie now, her arms wrapped around her knees. "He's flawed, Rooney, but he's still your father. When we get ready to Depart, I don't want you to have a single regret in your heart."

For once in my life, things almost seem too easy. Now I won't even have to lie about where I am tomorrow night. I take a minute, look like I'm turning the thought over in my head, then nod. "You're right, Mom. I think I should talk to Dad."

Mom actually claps her hands. "Oh, Rooney! That's wonderful! Once you get him through those doors on Friday and he hears what Everett has to say, I'm sure he'll finally understand!"

Well, that's more like it. Of course it's not going to be easy.

"I don't know about Friday, Mom," I waffle. "I'll talk to Dad, but I can't promise he's going to come to Everett's lecture. That's just . . ."

"All I'm asking is that you do your best. Just like you always do." She kisses me damply on the forehead. "Thank you, thank you, thank you! I'm so glad you're here."

I watch Mom drift back to her cot, then I pull up the sheet, punch my pillow a few times, and curl up on my side. The last thing I see before I close my eyes is Anjelica going over her notes.

two

They wake us up early by piping New Agey music into the dorm rooms. Once everyone has showered, we meet in what must have been the school cafeteria. Everyone digs in to their cereal and eggs, and then Janice hands out little maps of the New York City subway system and prepaid MetroCards.

I still can't quite believe I'm here. Of course, this isn't exactly *my* New York. Washington Heights and the Upper West Side may be only a few miles apart, but this place is so unfamiliar, I might as well be on a different planet. Still, it's the same subway, which means home is just a MetroCard swipe away. Except it's not my home anymore. I wonder whether I'd even recognize it.

"Have a great day, all of you," Janice tells us. "And remember: Get that foot in the door, then Engage, Enlighten, Activate!"

Our group from the van gathers by the main stairwell to pick up our pamphlets. Susan does a quick head count. "Let's see, there are only seven of us. Anjelica, where are your folks?"

Anjelica shakes her head. "They're not coming. They decided to go to church instead."

"Sorry, kiddo. Maybe tomorrow, huh?" Susan says, patting Anjelica's shoulder. "So we're a team of seven today. And lucky us, we have two actual New Yorkers to show us the ropes!"

"Well, Rooney was only ten when we left," Mom points out. "You probably don't remember that much about the city, do you, sweetheart?"

"I don't know. I guess we're about to find out."

It takes a while to get the whole crew to the subway, since Fred and Alice need to rest every block or so, and can't manage stairs very well. By the time the downtown local pulls into the steamy station, they're both looking pretty wilted. I wonder how they're going to manage a whole day in Times Square.

The train starts and stops its way downtown and I watch the stations pass without recognizing anything. And then we pull in at 116th Street, and in big letters, it says COLUMBIA UNIVERSITY. It's not like I didn't know where it was. But to have it right there, staring me in the face, is like getting a little electrical shock. I look at the open subway doors, and a voice in my head yells, *Run for it! Go! It's where you belong!*

But I don't move. People push onto the train, the doors close, and we pull out of the station. As the letters on the wall glide away, I make a silent promise to myself. *I'll be back. Soon. And without all these crazy people.*

A minute later, we pull into the Ninety-Sixth Street station. I look up and see Mom watching me. I don't ask the question, but she nods anyway. This was our stop. Across the platform, another train is pulling in. "Hey, the express is coming," I hear myself say. "We can switch here."

Susan squints at a little piece of paper. "No, kiddo, my notes say to take the 1 train all the way to Times Square." But Mom is already on her feet. "No, Rooney's right," she says. "The express would be faster."

So I guess there's some stuff I haven't forgotten. The train stops, the doors bang open, and Susan barks, "Well, you heard the lady. Let's move, everybody!"

We grab our tote bags and push onto the 3 train, which is crowded with commuters. Maybe I'm imagining it, but I think I see a woman notice our matching shirts. She covers her mouth and whispers something to the man next to her. *How am I going to get away from them?* I wonder again.

Two express stops later, we pull into our station. The platform is about a thousand degrees and packed with people. We let the crowd push us up the stairs and then we're in Times Square, in our stupid green T-shirts, wondering what to do next.

It wouldn't be hard for me to slip away now. Susan, Mom, and the others are standing like a bunch of field mice, completely overwhelmed by the crowds and the traffic noise. It would probably be at least a minute or two before anyone even noticed. I take a few experimental steps away from the group, but immediately spot three cops on horseback posing for pictures. The last thing I need is to be hunted down by the cavalry while my mother freaks out in the most public place in the universe. For the time being, at least, I'm clearly not going anywhere.

Now that I'm resigned to that fact, I have to wonder who thought it was a good idea to meet in New York in late summer. Even this early in the day, I can feel the heat coming up from the sidewalk, and the only people who don't look like they're in a hurry to get inside to the air conditioning are the tourists who aren't really sure where they're going. Like us.

Finally, Susan's take-charge attitude revives. "Let's get set up," she hollers, and barrels into the crowd, with the rest of us trailing after her. It doesn't take long to figure a few things out. First of all, it's pretty much impossible for a group of seven people to walk through Times Square together. Second, Fred and Alice probably shouldn't have signed up for this mission. Even with us carrying their stuff, they can't keep up, and they keep getting separated from the group.

We've barely made it half a block when Susan decides we need a new plan. She rounds us up into a bunch so we're blocking the sidewalk. Now it's not just our T-shirts that are drawing attention— I can see the dirty looks from the commuters who have to detour around us to cross the street. But Susan is oblivious.

"Folks, I think we need to break down into smaller groups," she says. "Sort of a divide-and-conquer strategy." She points to some people wearing vests with the name of a tour bus company. "Like them. See, they're in teams of two and three. Makes them more flexible."

Susan's made up her mind, and the group seems more than happy to let her lead. "So, let's see. Fred and Alice are a team. Anjelica and Rooney, do you want to pair up, and Anneliese can come with Roger and me?"

Instantly, I perk up. Getting through this hellacious day is going to be a lot easier without Mom fluttering around me like an anxious hummingbird.

"Oh, I think Rooney and I should be together," Mom protests.

Susan actually looks surprised, like it hadn't crossed her mind that Mom might want to stay with me. "Well, it's up to you," she says. "I just thought the kids would have an easier time Engaging folks their own age if they didn't have us dinosaurs hanging around." For the first time in my life, I feel a flicker of gratitude toward Susan.

Mom's got little frown lines on her forehead. "Do you think it's safe? Two girls on their own in Times Square?"

"Anjelica's twenty," I point out. "And I'm almost eighteen. There are a lot of people our age here by themselves."

"I have a phone. Rooney can use it whenever she needs to," Anjelica offers.

"Well, all right . . . Whatever you think is best." Mom gives me a big smile, but I hear that little hurt-feelings quiver in her voice. If I were a nicer person, that voice would probably make me feel guilty. Instead, it makes me want to kick her.

We all agree to meet up at lunchtime, and the teams head off in different directions. "I love you," Mom calls to me as Susan takes her arm and guides her across the street. I respond with a feeble wave.

Anjelica and I stop in front of a tall office building and watch the crowd pushing along the sidewalk and spilling out into the street. It's like being inside an ant farm. "I think Susan's strategy makes sense," Anjelica says. "We should probably try to Engage people who are close to our own age."

I can't just run off and leave Anjelica, but the idea of stopping people to talk about the Next World is making my skin crawl. "Have you ever done this before?" I ask, stalling for time.

"Not exactly. I've done some social networking stuff. But never actually face-to-face." At first I think she looks nervous, but then I realize she's actually excited. "It's going to be so amazing to reach out to people and help them Activate!"

"But don't you worry what people will think?"

Anjelica shakes her head. "It's like Everett and Janice were saying yesterday. About the stakes being so high?"

"What do you mean?"

"Well, maybe you think it's not polite to bother people. But if their house was on fire, you would tell them, right?"

"Of course."

"Well, this is basically the same thing. Only, instead of their house burning, it's the whole planet. They don't smell the smoke yet, but by the time they do, it will be too late. So I have a responsibility to let them know, now, while they can still do something about it."

She's looking at me with her wide brown eyes, and I can see that she's deadly serious about this. Suddenly, I'm starting to feel like a jerk for coming on this trip. Recruitment has always seemed obnoxious to me, but if she honestly believes that the planet is about to go up in flames, I can understand why she feels like she has no choice. If I believed what she believes, I'd be running through Times Square with a megaphone, shouting at the top of my lungs. The problem is, I don't believe it. "I'm not that comfortable with all of this. Do you mind if I spend some time just watching?"

"Sure," says Anjelica. "Take all the time you need." She gives me a long look. "Rooney . . . ?"

"Yeah?"

"I'm just curious. Why did you come on this trip? Were you even considering Activating?"

And there it is. The question that I obviously couldn't avoid, but was hoping to all the same. And she's just so nice that I can't imagine lying to her. So I don't.

"No. I came on the trip because I need to see my father, and it was the only way to make that happen." I feel better the second I say it out loud.

Anjelica's eyes widen. "And your mom doesn't know?"

I shake my head. "Not exactly. Mom wanted me to come, and I agreed to it. She's hoping it will change my mind, and I didn't go out of my way to tell her that wasn't going to happen."

"Wow. So you're not convinced about Departure or the Next World . . . or any of it?"

I shake my head.

"And your mom has told you all about it?"

"She talks about it all the time."

"But you . . . ?"

"I don't buy it. Sorry. I know you believe Everett. But I just . . . I honestly don't know how anyone can."

"I understand," Anjelica says. "It was hard for me to believe at first. But do me a favor, okay?"

"What?"

"Promise me that you'll listen with an open mind on Friday. Give Everett a chance to lay the whole thing out for you. And then if you're still not convinced, we never have to talk about it again."

I shrug. "I'll listen, but I really don't think it's going to change anything."

As I bend down to pick up my tote bag full of brochures, a short woman with spiky blond hair practically mows us down. "It's called a side*walk*," she growls. "If you want to *stand* somewhere, move out of the way!" She doesn't even hear us apologize as she darts through the building's revolving door.

"Maybe we should move over there, out of the flow of traffic," I suggest to Anjelica, pointing to the side of the building.

But she isn't done with the conversation. "Can I ask, what do you think about climate change? Doesn't it worry you?"

"I know it's a problem. But right now, I have more important things to worry about."

"More important?" She shakes her head. "If you don't believe it's possible to start over, how could anything be more important than the planet you live on?"

"Well, okay, maybe not more important. But more . . . urgent. I can't worry about what's going to happen in a hundred years when I'm not sure we're going to have anything to eat tomorrow."

Anjelica studies me with gentle eyes. "I sure hope Everett can get through to you on Friday. Because I really want you to Depart with us."

I desperately want to change the subject. My eyes fall on the pamphlets. "Maybe we should . . . ?"

She gives her head a sharp shake like she's shooing away a fly. "You're right," she says. "Let's get to work."

—

We spend the next few hours being ignored by ninety percent of the people who pass us. When someone does stop, it's inevitably someone you wish would keep walking. Some people give us dirty looks, but most people don't even seem to see us, which is a relief in a way, but also strangely exhausting.

Anjelica never seems to get discouraged or tired, no matter how rude people are to her. She just keeps trying to connect. She doesn't even seem that bothered by the heat, despite the fact that our clothes are soaked through and I'm starting to develop a rash.

"I can feel the air conditioning coming out of that building every time someone opens the door," I say to Anjelica. "I wonder if they'd let me stand in the lobby for a minute."

Anjelica shrugs. "You can give it a try."

Just stepping into the revolving door, I can feel the temperature drop. I spin into the lobby and stand there fanning myself with a pamphlet until a security guard makes me leave.

I drag myself back outside and hand out a couple of pamphlets, but all I want to do is hide. I hate knowing that people are thinking I'm one of Everett's groupies. Still, as the morning wears on, it does occur to me that I'm hardly the most freakish character in Times Square today. The girls posing for pictures in G-strings, feathers, and body paint are maybe a little more out there than I am. If I had a phone, I would snap a photo of them for Mercer, but I settle for taking a mental picture.

When twelve thirty finally arrives, we trudge over to our meet-up, an open plaza between Broadway and Seventh Avenue with tables and chairs on it. The sun is beating down hard and everyone looks a little ragged. Alice, Fred, and Roger are sitting and fanning themselves with pamphlets, and Susan is drinking from a huge plastic water bottle. "I can't believe she's drinking that," Anjelica mutters under her breath as we approach the group.

"What?" I whisper.

"Bottled water! She might as well just carry a big sign that says, 'Screw this planet!'"

Mom hurries over, linking her arm through mine. I let her hang on me only for a second before I pull away. "Too hot, Mom."

"How did everyone do this morning?" Susan asks. She eyes our bags of pamphlets and clucks her tongue. "Looks like you've still got a lot in there." I can feel my face getting even redder, and Mom leans over to whisper in my ear, "Don't worry, sweetie. I'm sure you're doing your best."

I look down, feeling like a fraud, and Mom asks, "Can we have lunch together, just the two of us? I found a place I want to take you to."

"Sure. What is it?"

"It's a surprise," she says with a little mischievous smile. We make plans to meet up with the group in an hour and she steers me down the street and around the corner. We stop in front of a restaurant and Mom points to the words on the glass doors. "See? Real New York brick-oven pizza!"

She opens the door, the smell hits me, and I instantly time travel. Mom, Dad, and I are sitting in the pizza place we used to go to every Sunday night. In my memory, Mom is pregnant, and she's laughing at something Dad is saying. I'm laughing, too, as a string of cheese stretches off my slice and slaps me in the nose. It's the last memory I have of the three of us being together and happy.

I look up to see her studying me with a strange expression. Disappointed, I think. "Is this . . . okay?" she asks. "We can go somewhere else if you don't feel like pizza."

I push away the memories and pull my face back into neutral. "No, it's great. Pizza is great."

We gulp down two tall glasses of water. The air conditioning is starting to dry the sweat on my neck, and I realize that I'm starving. When the pizza arrives, I grab a slice, fold it in half the way Dad used to do, and bite down. I have to hand it to Mom: It's insanely delicious.

She uses her fork and knife to cut a tiny wedge and pops it into her mouth. Her face lights up. "Oh! Yummy!"

I smile back at her, almost against my will. She looks exactly like Daniel.

When I've downed three slices and Mom's about halfway through one, she puts her fork down and looks at me. "Rooney, have you given any more thought to what we talked about last night? About your father?"

"Yeah . . . I'm going to have dinner with him tonight." As long as I leave out the details, it's not even a lie.

"Oh, Rooney, that's wonderful! Do you want to practice together? I can help you work on what to say!"

"I think I'm just going to wing it," I say quickly.

"Oh, gosh. Are you sure?" She's forgotten all about her pizza now. "This is such a big burden I've put on you. Won't you let me help?"

"It's okay, I don't mind."

"Where are you meeting him? Do you want me to go with you? I could wait outside for you; he'd never even know I was there."

There's nothing in the world more conspicuous than Mom trying to blend in. "You don't need to go with me. I'll be fine."

She shakes her head. "Sometimes I can't believe how grown-up you are. I don't know where you find the courage."

"It's no big deal. It's not like I've never been to New York." The truth is, I am a little nervous about finding the restaurant, and even more about seeing Dad. But Mom's "help" would only make everything much, much worse.

When the check comes, I reach for my wallet, but she stops me. "I've got it, sweetie." Ten different sarcastic responses start to form on my tongue, but I swallow them all down and settle for a note to self: Apparently, she's still got pizza money stashed away somewhere.

Back at the pedestrian plaza, Susan, Roger, and Anjelica are waiting. There's no sign of Fred and Alice, and I hope they decided to take a little extra time in the air conditioning. As I start to walk toward Anjelica, Mom reaches for my hand. "Meet me later. I'll make sure you get on the right train."

"I can find it myself. You don't have to worry about me."

Mom blinks a couple of times, her eyes bright. Then she nods and kisses me. "Of course you can, sweetie." The residue of her kiss is hot on my skin.

"Okay, everybody, enough chitchat," Susan bellows. "It's time to Engage!"

On the way back to our spot, Anjelica and I pass a huge store with its doors wide open. A blast of arctic air hits us, and I stand there for a second, enjoying the temporary break from being roasted alive. But Anjelica doesn't look relieved. "It just hurts my heart," she says. "It's so wasteful. I don't understand how people can do this."

"They do it because it feels good," I say. "It probably makes people want to come inside and shop."

"Of course, but it only makes things worse. The planet's getting hotter because of people using things like air conditioners. And now they're just letting it pour out into the street."

"I guess, but . . ." I look at her, wondering if I should say what I'm thinking.

"But what?"

"Why do you care? I mean, if you're going to Depart in November anyway, why not just let people use their plastic bottles and waste their air conditioning?"

"Because of Francisco," she says. "And maybe because of you, too."

"How do you mean?"

Her forehead creases. "My brother's not going to Depart. Even if I can convince my parents, he'll probably never agree to it. In November, I'm going to have to leave him behind. It's going to be terrible on Earth—if not right away, then soon. But maybe, if people start living more balanced lives here, now, Francisco can still have a good life."

The look she gives me is so intense that I have to pull my eyes away.

The rest of the afternoon is pretty much a slo-mo replay of the morning. Around three o'clock, a guy comes and stands ten feet away from us. He's wearing a signboard that says JUDGMENT DAY IS COMING on the front. On the back, it says, AND AS YE GO, PREACH, SAYING, THE KINGDOM OF HEAVEN IS AT HAND. He seems to be taking the "preach" thing pretty seriously, waving his Bible and shouting at people to repent. He's so loud, he's completely drowning out Anjelica. I feel bad for her, but at the same time it's kind of hilarious. Eventually, Anjelica realizes she's been out-crazied, and we move up the street to a quieter spot.

By the time five thirty rolls around, I'm about to lose it. Even Anjelica looks like she's had it. Her face is bright red and her voice has gone hoarse. I bet right now she wouldn't argue if someone tried to hand her a bottle of water.

"I just don't know if any of them will come on Friday," she sighs as we stuff the leftover pamphlets back into our bags. "No one cares that the world is dying. They just want to buy stuff."

She wanders off to meet the group, and I head back to the pizza place to get a soda. I need to mentally prepare for tonight. And I need to change out of this stupid T-shirt.

three

I leave myself about forty-five minutes to get from Times Square to the restaurant, and it still isn't enough. I guess my New York sense isn't so sharp after all, because I'm halfway to Queens before I realize I'm going the wrong direction on the R train. So by the time I get to Prince Street, get my bearings, and run to the restaurant, I'm about ten minutes late, my heart is racing, and the back of my clean shirt is soaked through.

There's a crowd of people outside the restaurant, and I have to push my way to the front of the line, where I can see a woman holding a pad. I ask her if she's got a reservation under Harris. "We don't take reservations, but there's a Harris party of three on my list. Have a look inside."

For the second time today, the smell of pizza engulfs me. There's no time to dwell on the irony of that, to ponder how two people who hate each other so much can think so much alike. Instead, I will my heart to stop pounding and scan the crowded room, not quite sure what I'm looking for. I haven't seen Dad in over five years, and the only picture I have of him was taken way before that. Over by the bar, I see two people holding drinks. She's got her back to me, so all I can see is short, curly hair and a flowered dress. He's got on a rumpled suit, and he's checking his phone. His hair has gone all salt-and-pepper, but I'd know him anywhere.

"Dad," I call out, suddenly noticing how dry my mouth is. He looks up and the woman turns toward me and smiles. I start to walk toward them, then stop in my tracks. Now that she's facing me, there's no way to miss it.

She's wearing a maternity dress.

They sidestep their way through the crowd toward me, and I stand there like a statue, too stunned to move. He reaches me first, and we do a stiff little dance, part handshake, part hug. Then he steps back and puts his arm around the woman. "Marina, this is Carol. Your . . . stepmother."

However awkward Dad and I are around each other, Carol seems determined not to let it faze her. "I'm so happy to finally meet you," she says, and wraps her arms around me. I can feel the curve of her belly pushing against me. If she notices how sweaty my back is, she doesn't let on. After a long squeeze, she takes a step back and peers into my eyes, her hands cupping my shoulders. "God, you look just like your dad," she says, laughing. "The photos we have of you are so old, I didn't expect you to be such a grown-up!"

Dad clears his throat. "So, let me just check and see if our table is ready. I'll be right back."

Carol waits until he's a few yards away, then whispers in my ear, "Poor guy. He is *so* nervous."

"Yeah," I mumble. "I guess neither of us really knows how to act around each other."

"Well, worst-case scenario, we can always talk about the weather. Hot enough for you?" She has tiny dimples on both cheeks.

I try to smile back at her, but part of me wishes she would stop talking so I could get my thoughts together. It's hard enough figuring out how to act around Dad without the extra complication of a pregnant stepmother.

Across the room, I see Dad beckoning us. We follow him to a smaller room with just a few tables. "This is perfect, Pete," Carol exclaims as she eases herself into the chair he's holding out for her. "Nice and quiet."

"I hope you still like pizza," Dad says. "I remember how much you used to love pizza night."

I think about telling him about the memory I had earlier, but then I'd have to tell him what reminded me of it. "Sure, pizza's great," I say for the second time today.

Dad is picking at the corner of his menu, where the two halves of the lamination are peeling apart a little. "This place is famous . . ." he says, pointing at the menu, which says "America's First Pizzeria" across the top.

"Cool," I say. I know I'm not holding up my end of the conversation, but "I desperately need your help" isn't the kind of thing you just announce over garlic knots.

Finally, Carol breaks the silence. "What do you say we order so we can get to the good stuff?"

Dad and I nod like puppets.

Carol flags down a waitress and we order a large pepperoni pie, plus a small one with mushrooms and olives and double anchovies. She looks at us apologetically after the waitress walks away. "I know, it must sound gross. For some reason, I've been craving salty food lately."

I laugh a little too loudly. "For some reason?"

Carol glances at Dad and her cheeks turn pink.

"Right," he says slowly. "I guess we should probably talk about the elephant in the room."

Carol pretends to look offended. "Elephant? Hey, I may have put on a few pounds, but . . ."

Dad gives her a lopsided grin and drapes an arm around her but doesn't seem to know what to say.

"So when is the baby coming?" I ask to fill the silence.

"She's due in late December," says Carol, happily patting her round belly.

She. "Congratulations."

Carol gives me another one of her dimpled smiles. "Thank you, Marina. I can't wait to introduce you to each other."

I like her, I realize. It's interesting to finally meet her, this woman I've spent so much time imagining. Even when she was a blank outline with a question mark inside it, I never blamed her for the way Dad faded out on us. Not really. I was just a kid, but I knew that if he'd wanted to be in our lives, he would've found a way, no matter whom he was married to. But I did think about her a lot, and wondered why he'd chosen her instead of us.

Watching her now, I don't have to wonder anymore. This meeting must be just as awkward for her as it is for Dad and me, but she seems . . . serene. Like the exact opposite of Mom. Just being around her, I feel a little calmer myself. If I'd had to choose between bubbly Carol and dark, depressed Vermont, I probably wouldn't have visited much either.

For the last few weeks, when I played out this scene in my head, it usually involved getting Dad alone somehow. But now that I've met Carol, that doesn't feel right. Dad has a new life, a new wife, and a new baby on the way. I've known for a long time that we weren't a family anymore. But seeing him with Carol definitely drives the point home. Maybe I should just forget about this whole thing.

Like she's reading my thoughts, Carol says, "So, Marina, I asked your dad what brought you to town, but he said he didn't know."

I guess that's as good a lead-in as I'm going to get. "Mom was coming for a Next World recruitment drive, and I needed to talk to Dad. So I tagged along," I say.

They exchange a look. "I had a feeling," Dad says. "They've been advertising some big lecture at Town Hall."

"Right. Tomorrow night." I take a sip of water, hoping it will help ease this wicked case of dry mouth.

"So, did you come here to recruit us?" Dad asks. His voice sounds like he's cracking a joke, but there's a hard look in his eyes.

Carol says softly, "Honey, Marina came all this way to see you. I think that's pretty wonderful, don't you?"

His expression softens microscopically. "Of course. Thank you for coming. It's good to see you."

"You too."

Dad looks down, shaking his head.

"What?" I ask.

"Did you . . ." He drags his eyes up to meet mine. "Did you and Danny get my cards?" he finally asks, and I swallow hard, on the spot.

For the last few years, the cards have been the only contact from him, aside from the money he was paying Mom. One on our birthdays, one at Christmastime. Always with a check inside and a little note that said something like "thinking of you."

"Yeah, we did. Thanks." I think about adding, "The money helped a lot," but can't decide whether it will help or hurt me when I finally get to the reason for this visit.

He raises his eyebrows. "Ah. I wasn't sure if you got them. I mean, the checks got cashed, but I thought maybe your mother . . ." Carol glances up at him and his voice trails off. "I guess I was just hoping I'd hear from you."

It's true. We never wrote back. What was there to say? "Thanks for the check. Hope you're enjoying your new life!"?

When we first moved to Vermont, Dad came to see us pretty often. I remember him strapping a car seat into his rental car and driving us to the diner for breakfast. Sometimes we'd hang out with him in his motel room, or if it was sunny, we'd go to the park. The last time he visited, he told us about a nice lady named Carol. He hoped we'd get to meet her soon. He was sure we were going to love her.

And then the visits just stopped. I'd sometimes hear Mom yelling on the phone, and I was pretty sure she was talking to him. But he never asked to talk to us, and we never saw him after that. We got letters for a while and then just the cards twice a year, and those monthly envelopes for Mom. Then a couple of years ago, Mom told us that he had married Carol.

"Sorry," I say now. "We should have sent thank-you notes. I guess we just thought you had kind of, you know . . ."

He shakes his head. "No, actually I don't. That I had what?" The edge is back in his voice.

I know I should keep things light, make him comfortable. But there's something in me that wants to push it, to let him know exactly how it felt. "We thought you weren't interested in being a dad anymore. After you guys met, and then you didn't invite us to the wedding."

It's oddly satisfying to see him react like I've punched him in the gut. His mouth drops open, but no words come out. When he finally speaks, his voice is all strangled. "Didn't *invite* you? Is that what she told you?"

I try to remember what Mom said. I don't recall actual words, only the feeling. "I'm not sure if she said that exactly," I admit. "That was definitely what we thought. We never got invited, anyway."

There's another soundless pause, and then Carol reaches for his hand. "It's so good that we have the chance to clear the air on this," she says calmly. "It seems like there have been an awful lot of misunderstandings."

"Misunderstandings? How about flat-out propaganda?" I can practically see steam coming out of his ears. "Marina, I begged your mother to let you and Danny come to the wedding. I told her I'd fly there and pick you up myself. I even offered to pay for her to come with you. Flights, hotel rooms, whatever. She told me you were upset that I was getting remarried, you didn't want to talk to me. I kept calling for months, hoping you'd just talk."

This is all new information, but the second the words are out of his mouth, I know they're true. "I didn't know," I mumble.

"Of course you didn't," Carol says soothingly. "You were just a kid. None of this is your fault, Marina."

Dad closes his eyes and pinches the bridge of his nose. When he speaks again, it's like something has loosened up inside him. "All this wasted time . . ."

A busboy appears and sets a metal rack on our table, and our waitress follows a minute later with the pies. The pizza looks amazing, but I can't imagine eating with this big knot in my stomach.

Carol looks from Dad to me. "Guys, I'm sorry, I know this is bad timing, but if this baby doesn't eat soon, things are going to get ugly." She reaches across the table and lifts a slice onto her plate. "There's no point letting it get cold, right?"

Dad lets out a big breath. "You're right, honey. Here, Marina, hand me your plate."

As we chew on our pizza, I shake every memory of Dad out like a sweater, then try to put it into one of two piles: things Mom told me, and things I actually saw or heard for myself. Until now, I've only known one version of the story. It didn't exactly make sense, but it was all I had, so I accepted it. Sort of. But all along, there was a part of me that couldn't believe Dad had just stopped wanting us in his life.

And now . . . ?

Now I know that the whole time I was mad at Dad for leaving, I really should have been mad at Mom. Or, I guess I should say, madder. I've been mad at her for her crazy ideas, for making us live in our dumpy house, for being unreliable, and for a million other things. But none of that even compares to this. If she deliberately kept us from having a relationship with Dad, I'm never going to forgive her.

After she's put away a couple of slices, Carol folds her hands over her belly and looks at me. "Marina, you said that you needed to talk to your dad about something."

I nod, wiping my mouth with my napkin.

"I was thinking you two might like a little privacy. Why don't I meet you back here in, what? Fifteen, twenty minutes?"

She pushes herself up from the table while Dad and I have synchronized panic attacks. "Oh, that's all right . . ." I blurt out as Dad says, "No, honey, you don't have to disappear . . ."

But she waves us both off. "I don't mind at all. My legs are a little crampy and I could use a stroll. Make sure they wrap up the rest of the anchovy, okay?" Dad looks concerned, but she holds up her phone. "Don't worry, I won't go far. And you know how to reach me." She rests a hand on my shoulder for a second and then she's gone.

I can feel my heart starting to thud again. "She's great," I finally manage to say. "I'm glad you invited her."

"Yeah, she is. She's always wanted to meet you and Danny." I try not to let it show in my face, but he catches me. "What?"

"It's just . . . no one calls him Danny. Since he was, like, four years old, he's been Daniel."

"Huh. He was so little when . . . I really never got to know him."

"And while we're at it, no one calls me Marina, either."

This time, he actually looks pissed. "Oh, for God's sake. Why didn't you say something? What do people call you?"

"Rooney."

He raises an eyebrow. "Really?"

"Yeah. Mostly."

"Is that what you want me to call you?"

Once he's asked the question, I realize that I don't. "No, I kind of like it that you call me Marina."

"Okay, Marina it is. Just as well, since I'm not sure I could get used to calling you Rooney. And Daniel . . ." He pronounces it slowly and deliberately. "What's he like?"

"He's . . ." All the words that come into my head—*smart, sweet, gentle, creative*—they just seem like words. The best I can come up with is "He thinks deep thoughts."

"Did he . . . I guess he's not interested in seeing me?"

"He didn't know I was coming. I didn't tell him in case it didn't go well."

"I see. Well, how would you say it's going so far?" His eyes are like two lasers on my face.

"I'm not sure. I haven't gotten to the hard part yet."

He nods slowly. "Well, there's no time like the present. Might as well dive in."

He's right. It's now or never. Part of me is still leaning hard toward never, but if I won't do it for myself, I have to do it for Daniel. "I just . . . I wanted to say, I didn't know Carol was pregnant when I called you."

"Well, of course not. How could you have known that?"

"Right, I mean, I wouldn't have bothered you if I'd known."

He shoots me an impatient look. "Do you honestly think you're bothering me? Look, Marina, I'm nervous, and this is awkward. But there is nothing I'd rather do than talk with the daughter I haven't been able to see for five years. Nothing."

I hope he still feels that way after I tell him why I'm here. "I need to ask you a favor. It's a pretty big one."

"Okay, I'm listening."

"I wouldn't ask, except I don't know what else to do."

"Go ahead. It's all right." He folds his arms and sits back.

The way he's looking at me, it almost feels like there's a stop-watch ticking in his hand. So I fill him in as quickly as I can. And then I just come out and ask him: "If you could help just until November is over . . . I can pay you back. And by the time the baby comes, I'm sure we'll be back on our feet." I'm not even breathing, just trying to get it all out before I lose my nerve.

Dad holds up his hand like a stop sign. "Wait, slow down. Your mom quit her job?"

"No, she got fired."

"Jesus H. Christ. A woman with her brains can't even keep a job in day care?"

"I guess not."

"Sorry. That was . . . I shouldn't put you in the middle." He blots his forehead with his napkin. "Look, I'll do whatever you need me to do. And please don't talk about paying me back. That's out of the question."

Relief flows through my body like cool water. "Thanks, Dad. Really."

"But there are some things I want to ask you, okay?"

"Sure." I clutch my napkin in my lap, trying to dry my sweaty palms.

"You said your mother is convinced that you're going to . . . take off in November. It sounds like you disagree. Is that right?"

"Of course."

His eyebrows twitch. "Well, it's not a foregone conclusion. I mean, your mother must have tried to teach you about the Next Worlders and what they believe."

"Yeah, she tried."

I see Dad smile faintly as he absorbs that. "And what about Danny—sorry, Daniel. What does he think?"

"He thinks what I think: that Everett is full of crap."

He lets out a sharp laugh. "Okay. That's good to know." Then his face gets serious again. "But listen, Marina, if you're expecting your mother to just snap back to some kind of 'normal' on November eighteenth, you may be setting yourselves up for a big disappointment."

I know what he's getting at, but right now I can't even think about November 18. There's way too much to get through between now and then. "I just hope it won't take too long. I'm so ready to be done with this."

"I understand. But you have to remember, she's got so much riding on this, after all this time. It's not going to be easy for her to accept that Everett was, you know . . ."

"Full of crap?"

"Yeah." As his smile fades, I can see that his eyes are worried.

Just then, Carol comes up behind him. "Am I back too soon?" she asks.

"Was there anything else, Marina?" Dad asks.

"No. That was it."

"Good! Then who's up for dessert?" Carol asks.

—

As we walk out, Carol stops. "Hey, wait. I want to get a shot of the two of you. We need an updated photo for the living room."

"Why don't we take one of the three of us?" I suggest.

"Oh!" She looks surprised. "I'd love that. Are you sure?"

"Yeah. If it's good, maybe you could email it to me? So I can show it to Daniel?"

Her dimples sprout again. "Sure! That's really nice."

She hands her phone to Dad. "Here, hon, your arms are longer. Make sure you get the restaurant sign." We squish together and Dad snaps the pictures, then Carol scrolls through them, inspecting. "This one is pretty good. I look like Shamu, but you two look great."

"I'm glad we got together," Dad says. "I feel like we cleared away a lot of cobwebs tonight."

"I'm glad, too," I say.

"I'd like to keep talking. Maybe we could video-chat when you get back home?"

"I don't have a phone. But I could maybe borrow Mom's computer."

"You don't have a . . ." This time he stops himself even before Carol's hand reaches his shoulder. "Well, we'll figure it out. Where are you staying? Maybe we can share a cab partway."

"Oh, it's way uptown. Near the 181st Street stop."

He looks at me sharply. "You're staying in Washington Heights?"

"Yeah, at NWS headquarters."

"And your mother thinks it's all right for you to find your way back on your own?"

"I have a MetroCard. I got here fine."

Dad shakes his head. "Unbelievable. Look, for my peace of mind, would you please get in a taxi?" He takes out his wallet, pulls out all the bills, counts them, and hands them to me. "Thirty should cover the cab, and the rest should tide you over until next month's check. Okay?"

"Thanks, Dad." I pocket the money and give him a quick hug. "And thanks for, you know, for everything."

"Thank *you* for calling," he says. "I mean it."

"When do you go back home?" Carol asks. "School must be starting soon."

"Yeah, next week. We leave Saturday morning, I think. After Everett's lecture, anyway. Which reminds me," I say, turning back to Dad. "I promised Mom I would talk to you about coming. How about if I just give you one of these pamphlets so I can say I did my best?"

He takes the pamphlet. "She asked you to talk to me about this?"

"Yeah. She says she doesn't want me to have any regrets when we Depart."

"Regrets? What kind of regrets?"

"Not trying to save you, I guess. I know it all sounds crazy, but . . ."

"But she's your mom," Carol finishes for me. She hugs me again. "I'm so glad I finally got to meet you. Will you come back after the baby is born? Please? And bring Danny, too?"

Dad rests his hand on her arm. "Apparently, it's Daniel nowadays. Or so I'm told."

"Fine, bring Daniel, then. Just come, okay?" Carol looks from me to my dad. "It's time for this family to stop harping on the past and start looking to the future."

"I'd like that," I tell her. "Maybe we could come in the spring sometime. After things . . . settle down."

A taxi pulls up and Dad opens the door for me. "So we'll be talking?"

"Yeah." I hug him again, a little less awkwardly this time, and they wave as the cab pulls away. Once they're out of sight, I pull out my subway map. "Can you take me to the closest 2/3 stop?" I ask the driver. New York isn't going to feel like home unless I act like a real New Yorker, and the subway will probably be faster anyway. Besides, I might as well save the thirty bucks, since Everett already paid for my MetroCard.

four

By the time I reach HQ, people are settling in for the night. Mom spots me the second I walk in, like she's been lying in wait for me. She waves me over and I sit at the foot of her cot, trying to preserve a little personal space in spite of the close quarters.

All the way uptown on the subway, I played out my options. I could confront her as soon as I got back to HQ. Call her a liar in front of her friends, cause a big scene, make everyone here hate me and then . . . *what*? It wouldn't change the past, and it definitely wouldn't make the rest of this trip any less awkward.

Or I could fake it, like I've been faking it for years. I could act tired and tell her the bare minimum about my visit with Dad. I could muscle through the next two days and go back to Vermont, and then keep finding every excuse to distance myself from her until graduation.

And ultimately, that's the goal, isn't it? To just survive until I'm free? So I pack away my anger and all my questions and act like nothing has changed. It isn't even that hard. Practice something enough and you're bound to get good at it.

"Did you see him?" she asks.

"Yup. I gave him a pamphlet."

"And? Do you think he'll come to the lecture?" She's so wound up she's practically vibrating.

I know it's not nice to enjoy someone else's disappointment, but tonight I'm not feeling very charitable. "I seriously doubt it, Mom."

Her face falls, and she twists her braid around her hand. "Well, it's his decision. Thank you for trying, sweetie. The important thing is, you did everything you could."

"Yup," I say. *Liar*, a voice hisses in my head, but I'm not sure if it's for me or for her.

"What was it like, seeing him?" she asks, peering into my eyes.

It was like opening an envelope marked "Top Secret." It was like someone lifting a big rock off my chest. It was like an atom bomb of truth. "It was fine," I say. "So what's the plan for tomorrow?"

"Well, in the morning, there's a Harmonization workshop for the recently Activated." She untwists the braid and reaches for my hand. "It would be really good for you to go. It's a very important technique."

"But you said it was for the recently Activated."

Mom lowers her voice, like she's sharing a secret with me. "It is, technically. But this is an incredible opportunity to learn from an amazing, skilled practitioner. If you wait, you may not have access to teachers like this."

"I'll think about it," I say, just to shut her up.

"Oh, that's wonderful! Thank you! And then in the afternoon, we'll be together again for more Engagement. I think this time our group will be around Columbia."

I wonder if Mom sees me catch my breath. All my hopes for the future are attached to that word. But the idea of going there tomorrow doesn't exactly thrill me. Yes, it opens up all kinds of possibilities. I could sneak away from the group and walk around campus. Maybe even find the admissions office and get someone to talk to me. But to be there with the NWS, handing out their pamphlets, wearing their T-shirt . . . The last thing in the world I want is for anyone there to see me that way.

"I'm wiped out," I say, standing up. "I'm going to get ready for bed."

"Sweet dreams, sweetheart."

I dump my NWS shirt in a laundry bin and head for my cot. Anjelica is sitting up in bed, writing in her notebook.

"How was it?" she asks.

"It was good. Confusing, but good."

"Why confusing?"

"Long story. So what's been happening around here?"

She puts her notebook down. "We had some drama, actually. Fred and Alice had to go to the emergency room this afternoon. Apparently, Fred has a heart condition and he's supposed to avoid getting overheated. He's okay, but everyone was pretty scared."

"Why did they go out with us if he's supposed to avoid over-heating? It's like an oven out there!"

"I know. But Departure is very important to them." She lowers her voice. "They're hoping they can fix his heart in the Next World."

Of course. Departure is going to fix everything.

"And what about your folks?" I ask, hoping she didn't catch the look on my face.

"They spent the day praying for me. It's ironic, right? I spent mine thinking about how to convince them, and they spent theirs praying for me to come back to the Church. I guess we'll have to call it a draw."

"Sorry. I know this is important to you."

"Yeah. It is." She picks up her notebook and flips absent-mindedly through it. "You know, my parents have no trouble believing all kinds of things that are pretty hard to swallow if you look at them logically. I mean, the virgin birth and miracles, all that . . . To them, that's normal. That's just what faith is. But life-forms from other planets? That's crazy."

I know I should probably bite my tongue, but my inner journalist can't let it go. "So the aliens and the spaceships and the secret coded messages . . . that doesn't seem at all far-fetched to you?"

Anjelica looks at me thoughtfully. "Have you ever thought about how huge the universe is?"

"You mean, like, the whole infinity thing?"

"Exactly. In all that space, do you think it's possible that there are other life-forms? That it's not just us on our tiny planet . . . and then nothing but lifeless rocks until infinity?"

"I guess it's possible. I don't know. I mean, I'm not a scientist."

"Right, but tons of respected scientists are convinced that there's other intelligent life in the universe." She pulls out her phone. "I could do a search and probably pull up twenty or thirty examples."

I should have left it alone. Because it's not so much that I don't believe alien life-forms could exist, it's that I'm one hundred percent confident that Everett is a liar. And now I'm worried that the only way I can end this conversation is by saying something rude.

Anjelica must notice me struggling, because she puts the phone away. "Look, I'm just saying, listen to what Everett has to say tomorrow. Okay?"

During breakfast, Janice taps on the microphone to get everyone's attention. "This morning, some of you will be getting your first introduction to Harmonization. And there's also a leadership training session on the third floor. If you're attending either session, please eat a light breakfast." I look at the piece of dry toast sitting untouched on Mom's tray. If she ate any lighter, she'd float away. My own tray is loaded up with pancakes and eggs. I'm not even that hungry, but I'm determined to eat as much as I can on Everett's dime.

"The rest of us will be hitting the streets again," Janice continues. "I heard so many wonderful stories of Engagement yesterday, and I want to thank all of you for the incredible effort you're making."

So I can either spend the day out on the street again, or take my chances in a Harmonization workshop. I figure the workshop has to be better than harassing strangers, and at least there will be air conditioning. Plus, I have to admit, I'm a little curious to know what goes on in there. It would make a pretty interesting story for the paper—if I still worked on the paper, that is. And if I wanted to expose all the demented details of my private life to the entire school.

There are mats laid out on the floor in the Harmonization

classroom. I'm expecting my classmates to be mostly young people like me, but again, it looks like someone reached into a bucket of assorted people and pulled out a random handful. There are even a few senior citizens sitting awkwardly on their mats. I'm thinking about Fred's visit to the emergency room and wondering how he's feeling today when the room goes quiet, and I see that the teacher has arrived. He's wiry, with a shaved head and almost freakishly light blue eyes. He's wearing some kind of thin cotton pajama-type pants and a T-shirt, and his feet are bare.

"Hi, everyone, I'm Patrick," he says. "Welcome to our Introduction to Harmonization workshop. Let's get started, shall we?"

Patrick sits cross-legged on a mat at the front of the room. "For those of you who have experience with certain types of meditation or relaxation techniques, a lot of this is going to feel familiar. But if you've never done anything like this before, don't worry. For today, I'm going to assume that you're all blank slates."

He has us take off our shoes. "Find a position where you can lie comfortably, and close your eyes." He turns out the lights, and I can hear him moving around the room as he talks.

"I want you to focus on being present." His voice is soft and warm, and I think that if I'm going to focus on anything, it will be on not snoring when I fall asleep. The mat I'm lying on is more comfortable than my cot in the dorm.

"And I'm also going to ask you to put judgment aside," Patrick says. "Not just for your own sake, but for the sake of everyone in this room. Judgment is the enemy of Harmonization. So now, with every breath, try to let your judgment go."

Right now, I'm manufacturing enough judgment to power a small city. I'm glad my eyes are closed, since I'm pretty sure if Patrick could see what was in them, he'd ask me to leave the room.

The room fills with the sound of our breathing. As Patrick counts through cycles of ten, the people around me inhale and then hum like a hive full of giant bees.

Lying there, with no one watching me, I can't decide whether to hum along or stay quiet. No one will ever know if I just tune Patrick out—nobody but me, that is. But that thing he said about judgment is nagging at me a little. It's not that I believe that Harmonization is for real. But I do sometimes wish that I could turn off that voice in my head, the one that's always analyzing and criticizing everything around me. It's the thing Mrs. Fisher is always saying about being a journalist: You have to start from a place of objectivity.

"Now I want you to take an inventory of your body. Are you holding tension anywhere?" Patrick's voice is coming from right above my head now. I look up at him, and he gestures with two fingers for me to close my eyes. "Anywhere you find tension, just breathe into it. Tell that body part that it can let go." I try to do what he's saying, and realize that I'm holding tension pretty much everywhere. I'm not sure there's enough air in the room to breathe into all those places. I decide to start by unclenching my hands.

Patrick tells us to think of ourselves as trees, with roots growing out of our feet. "The roots grow deep down into the Earth. And your arms are branches, stretching up to the sky." I start to move my arms, but Patrick tells us to keep our bodies still and just move with our minds. I wonder whether he's talking to me, since his voice is coming from the other side of the room now. Maybe I'm not the only one doing it wrong.

Once we're all feeling like trees, Patrick tells us to feel the Earth's energy moving through us. We're supposed to absorb it through our feet and pull it up through our bodies until it exits through our fingers and the tops of our heads. I'm concentrating so hard I can feel my face scrunching up. I try to relax it, and after a while I notice that my fingertips are starting to tingle a little, like I can actually feel energy moving through them. I would never admit it to a living soul, but it feels sort of cool.

"You're all doing great," Patrick says. "I can really sense how rooted you are to the Earth. Now, if those roots are ready, they can choose to let go of the ground. I want you to picture new roots starting to grow out of your chest and your hands and your head. Your hair is growing and twisting into thick, ropy coils. And as you release the Earth, without fear, these new roots are pulling you upward. Let them lift you up into the blue sky."

Just try to picture it, I tell myself. *Don't think, for once. Just feel.*

"These new roots you're growing aren't like your old roots. These roots can intertwine with the roots of other beings to create one giant, interdependent organism. All those interconnected roots will form a raft of energy to take you to the next plane."

I've never felt this combination of sleepy and alert before. Patrick's voice hums inside me, and I'm starting to see the things that he's describing, not so much with my mind, but in my body. The tingling feeling travels up to the top of my head, and I can almost feel my hair pulling upward and twisting into long, gnarled roots. I let the feeling migrate to other parts of my body, and now the roots feel like they're growing all over me. The feeling is strangely peaceful, not scary at all.

What happens next is hard to describe, and even harder to explain. As I'm lying there on my mat, I suddenly realize that I can't feel the floor anymore. I actually feel like my body is rising, and even though my eyes are closed, I can see a bright light behind them. It's so strong I'm afraid to open my eyes. I feel my body pulling away from the Earth, and all around me I can feel roots snaking around me, lifting me faster and faster.

I'm going too fast, I think. *I'm not ready!* Suddenly, my stomach lurches like I'm in free fall and my eyes pop open again. I'm still lying on my mat, gasping for air like a fish that's been pulled out of a lake. Patrick is standing over me, smiling down into my face. "Good," he says in his soothing voice. "Very, very good, everybody."

As he leads everyone out of the visualization, I lie there trying to bring my heartbeat back down to normal and wondering what the hell just happened to me.

I'm lying on my cot, replaying the Harmonization workshop in my mind, when Mom gets out of her leadership session. She practically floats over to me. "So? How do you feel? Was it amazing?" She looks the way she sometimes does when she comes home from meetings, her eyes huge and her cheeks flushed like she's got a fever.

"I feel fine," I say. "Just kind of sleepy."

Mom looks sympathetic. "Harmonization can be exhausting, especially when you're just starting out."

This is not a conversation I want to have with her. "I wasn't exhausted. Just bored."

"You were bored? Patrick told me you have a real gift for Harmonization. He thinks you're a natural."

"I don't know why he'd think that," I say like a reflex. "I almost fell asleep." Sometimes the only way to keep her out of my space is to crush her a little.

"I guess Patrick must have been wrong. Well, don't worry, sweetie. I'm sure you'll get it." She gives me a brave little smile. When she walks back to her cot, I notice she's not floating anymore.

This afternoon's group is smaller than yesterday's, since Fred and Alice decided to rest until tonight. Just like Mom thought, we're assigned to the area around Columbia. Anjelica and I set up right in front of the main gate. I thought yesterday was stressful, but somehow this turns out to be even worse. It feels like every person walking by could hold the key to my future. *Is she a professor? Could he be on the admissions committee? Is that a student?* I don't even dare open my mouth for fear of saying the wrong thing to the wrong person and ruining my chances of going here forever.

Being this close, peering in through the gate at the big, beautiful buildings, I want this life for myself so badly it makes my chest tight.

Anjelica catches me watching and her face clouds over with concern. "Are you okay?" she asks. "You look worn-out."

"I guess I am," I say, wishing I had a better poker face.

"Why don't you take a little break?" she suggests. "I can handle things here."

Nothing sounds better right now than walking away from all this and disappearing into the crowd. "Thanks," I say. "That would be great."

"It's no problem. Are you sure you're all right?"

I don't really feel all right. I feel overwhelmed. Ever since I got in the van back in Stonebrook, nothing has been what I expected. Times Square yesterday. Dinner with Dad and Carol. The Harmonization workshop. And now being here, at Columbia . . . I don't even know which way is up anymore. "Do you think I could borrow your phone?" I ask. "I can pay you back."

She hands it over with a sad smile. "Don't worry about the money, Rooney. I have plenty to get me through the next three months."

"Right," I say glumly. "Well, thanks. I'll be back in a couple minutes."

I don't know whether I'm allowed to walk through the big gate and onto the campus. People are streaming in and out, and they just look like regular people. I wish I could change my shirt, but there's nothing I can do about that. I'm here, and I'm not going to leave without at least seeing those buildings up close. *If someone tells me to go, I'll go*, I decide. I take a breath and cross the invisible line, and no one tries to stop me. I'm standing on the Columbia campus, and nobody even seems to notice that I don't belong here.

There's a big white building not far away, with groups of people sitting on its steps. I make a beeline for it and dial Mercer's number.

"Hello?" His voice sounds cold, suspicious.

"Hey, it's me. Rooney."

"Oh! Hey!" I can hear the smile flood into his voice, and my shoulder muscles start to unclench. "I thought you were a robocall. How are you?"

"I'm okay, I guess. This is one strange trip I'm on."

"I bet. So what's going on?"

"Too much. I can't even tell you right now. I just wanted to hear your voice."

"Well, give me something! A ten-second version?"

"Okay," I say. "Guess where I am."

There's a tiny pause, then, "Are you at Columbia?"

"Ding! Nailed it. I'm sitting on the library steps."

"That's awesome! How did you pull that off?"

"We got assigned here. To recruit."

"Oh, no!" I can picture him settling back, his ankle on his knee, his elbow resting on the top step of his back porch. "Are you wearing a bag over your head? Or maybe a ninja mask would be cooler."

"I wish I'd thought of that." I feel a thousand times more myself than I did a minute ago. It's not even anything he's saying, it's just hearing his voice. He's the only person in the world who can snap all my pieces back together when I start to come undone.

"So? Is it the way you pictured it?" he asks.

"It's kind of amazing." I look around at the people clustered on the steps. "I know it sounds dumb, but it just feels like I'm supposed to end up here. Does that make any sense?"

"Sure it does," he says. "So, who's A Garcia?"

"What?"

"The phone number," he says. "That's how it comes up on my phone."

"Oh, right. A friend," I say. "Someone I met here."

"What's he like?" There's an unfamiliar prickle in his voice. I could swear it sounds like jealousy, but there's no reason in the world for Mercer to be jealous. So it must be something else. Protectiveness, maybe?

"She." I correct him. "Anjelica. She's nice, actually."

"Is she like you? Did her parents drag her there?"

"Nope. She's a true believer."

"Wow," he says quietly. "So is everyone trying to convert you?"

"Not everyone. Some of these people are actually really sweet. I almost wish I hadn't met them. It makes all of this a lot harder to laugh at."

"Right. I guess it's all starting to get pretty real, huh?"

I pluck at my sweaty green T-shirt, trying to fan a little cool air onto myself. "This is all so strange, Merce. I don't feel like I understand any of the rules anymore. Every time I think I've got my footing, it's like the ground slides out from under me again."

"Hey," he says gently. "This is seriously hard stuff you're deal-ing with. You're going to get through it."

"I know," I say, not very convincingly. "I wish you were here. I swear, it feels like I've been gone for weeks. What's going on at the Connection? Do you miss me?"

"Of course I do. But you know who misses you more?"

"Who?"

"Clara Jacobs. She called the foam on my cappuccino 'unim-pressive.' She told me she can't wait till you get back."

I laugh. "Well, tell Clara I'm coming home tomorrow."

"Good. I don't think my ego can take much more abuse from her. Oh! I didn't even ask—have you seen your dad yet?"

"Last night."

"And . . . ?"

"And you were right. It's a pretty juicy story. I'll tell you everything when I get back, I promise."

"Oh, man! Are you seriously going to leave me hanging?"

"I'll see you soon."

"I can't wait. Take care of yourself, Rooney, okay?"

"I will. Thanks, Merce. Really."

"Anytime. Really."

They should sell Mercer pills, I think as I head back to Anjelica. *The world would be a happier place.*

Back at HQ, there's a weird, nervous electricity in the air as we gather in the assembly room. Looking for Mom, I spot Alice and Fred. They're both dressed up for their night out, and he's wearing a sport coat that looks way too warm for this weather. His face is red, and I hope he isn't going to overheat again.

Just a few days ago, the Next Worlders were a bunch of gullible weirdos who were ruining my life, but now that I've met them, I can't stop worrying about them.

Alice waves at me. "How are you, dear? Excited for tonight?"

"I'm all right. It's still awfully hot outside. Will the two of you be comfortable in those clothes?"

Alice winks at me. "I guess you heard about our little scare."

"Anjelica told me there was some trouble with the heat," I admit.

"Oh, we're fine," Fred says with a chuckle. "That was all just a lot of hoo-ha."

"That's right, he's just fine," Alice says, patting him on the knee. "You're sweet to ask, but there's not a thing to worry about."

Times Square is even more crowded than it was during the day. It takes us almost ten minutes to walk the two blocks to the Town Hall. Outside the entrance, there's a cluster of people carrying signs and chanting. One sign says NEW YORK SAYS NO TO NOVEMBER NUTS and another reads LET'S FOCUS ON FIXING THIS WORLD! A strong breeze has picked up, and the air is a little cooler on my sweaty arms. It feels like a storm is coming.

The lobby is full of people. I recognize a bunch of them from HQ, but there are a lot of strangers, too, and more are filing in every minute. Each door into the auditorium has a guy with a metal detector stationed in front of it. We all line up and shuffle through, opening our bags so they can check them. It seems kind of over-the-top, and I wonder what Everett is so worried about. It's hard to believe anyone takes him seriously enough to want to hurt him.

The first few rows of the auditorium are already starting to fill up with NWS members. We were instructed to fill in the front. Janice didn't say why, and I assumed she just wanted to make sure the room looked full. But now that I've seen all the security, I can't help thinking maybe we're supposed to be some kind of human shield between Everett and the world.

Anjelica leads her parents to the front row, and Alice, Fred, Susan, and Roger fill in on either side of them. Mom goes to follow them, but I steer her toward seats a few rows behind them.

Hopefully, that puts us far enough back that we won't get picked if there's any audience participation. Mom gives me a questioning look, but goes along with it. "Thank you for coming, sweetie," she whispers. "And for talking to your dad. It's not your fault that he didn't come."

"I know, Mom." I should feel like a big phony right now, except I'm pretty sure I could have begged Dad on my knees and he still wouldn't have come to Everett's lecture.

five

Finally, around ten minutes past eight, the lights start to fade out. Pulsing music comes on over the speakers, and huge projections appear on screens around the stage. First, there are photos of a desert and a group of little kids with swollen stomachs and scrawny legs. Then there's a scene of a tropical forest being cut and burned down. Then a polar bear floating on an iceberg in the middle of the sea turns into an aerial picture of a flooded town. More and more images pile up as the music swells and then crashes into silence.

When the lights come up, Everett is standing onstage. He's wearing a dark gray suit and a white shirt that I'm sure he chose because it shows off his silver hair. If I didn't know anything about him, I'd be impressed. He looks like a movie star, or maybe some bazillionaire inventor. "Good evening, ladies and gentlemen," he begins in his deep voice. "I'm Dr. Everett Nichols, and I'd like to thank you for coming here this evening."

Mom is looking up at the stage like a twelve-year-old at a boy band concert as the first three rows break into frenzied applause. Everett waits for them to quiet down again, then continues. "The people in this room accepted an invitation. You chose to attend this event because you're concerned about a planet that is dangerously out of balance." He gestures to the screen behind him, which is now covered with a collage of the photos we just saw. "You've all read the news. There isn't a serious scientist in the world who denies that climate change is the greatest threat facing humanity today. Atmospheric carbon dioxide levels are climbing so fast that our computer models can't keep up. Droughts from Russia to California to Africa are causing catastrophic crop failures and food shortages. Alpine glaciers and the polar ice caps are melting away, and we're regularly seeing the kind of floods that used to take place only once in a hundred years."

He pauses and gestures toward the doors. "This very city has been brought to its knees by the rising waters. We're seeing record-breaking temperatures right now, right here. The Earth is convulsing. These are her death rattles. And all the while, the number of human beings occupying this planet continues to grow."

Everywhere, heads are nodding. So far, this is all sounding a lot like a documentary on PBS. You would never guess that this man, with his beautiful voice and well-cut suit, is a complete nutjob. "Scientists call this epoch the Anthropocene," Everett continues, "meaning that mankind's actions created these desperate conditions. And yet we now feel powerless to change our future. Civilizations have found themselves on the verge of collapse before, but never on this scale. It's not just one corner of our world; it's the entire planet that hangs in the balance today."

Under the stage lights, Everett's eyes glitter fiercely. "Tonight, I'm going to extend another invitation to you. I can tell you with certainty that only a few of you will accept. You see, to accept is to commit a great act of will, to say good-bye to everything you have known. But it is also a new hope for humanity. A chance to begin again."

Here we go, I think. *Next stop, Crazytown.* Mom is taking deep, gulping breaths, like she's trying to drink Everett in. The pictures on the screens shift again, and now there's a photo of a huge library behind Everett. "But before I can speak about the future, I must explain how I came to possess the knowledge I will share with you this evening. My story begins some thirty years ago, in a most unlikely place. The Vatican Library, where I was engaged in research for my doctoral dissertation.

"My field of endeavor was linguistics, and more specifically, dead and extinct languages. One fateful afternoon, I came across a document tucked inside an obscure volume that had not been opened for centuries. I was immediately intrigued, as it was written in a language I had never encountered in my many years of research."

Everett points at some strange-looking writing on the screen. "This mysterious document became an obsession for me. From the moment I discovered it, I dedicated my life to deciphering it. I sensed from the start that it contained something of great import, but it resisted all my efforts to unlock its secrets. Finally, after years of struggle, I made a critical discovery. The writer or writers of the document had cleverly embedded within it the key to its decryption. After that, the work of translation possessed me, and I began to unravel its mysteries."

This last part is new to me. I've always wondered just how Everett explained it, what could make all these people believe something so absurd. Now, finally, I'm hearing it for myself. Everett is putting on quite a show tonight, his voice swooping and soaring, and I'm enjoying the performance a little in spite of myself.

Behind Everett, the words *The Hwaral* appear on the screen. "Contained within this document, which I will henceforth refer to as 'the Writings,' is the history of a highly advanced extra-terrestrial race." Everett pauses for a second as a rumble of voices fills the room. He holds up a hand, waiting for them to quiet down, then continues. "They referred to themselves as the Hwaral—the Voyagers. According to the Writings, these voyagers have come to Earth numerous times over the millennia. And they will return one more time." Everett takes a long pause, and then says clearly into the microphone, "On November seventeenth of this year."

As soon as the words are out of his mouth, all hell breaks loose in the auditorium. There are gasps and loud explosions of laughter and a bunch of people stand and head for the exits. Everett doesn't seem to be bothered or surprised by any of it. He stands still on the stage, his expression completely neutral.

When the room has settled down again, he smiles. "Well, now that we've separated the wheat from the chaff . . ." The first few rows of the audience join him in a self-congratulatory chuckle, but I can see a bunch of people around me with tightly folded arms and expressions that say, *Go on. I dare you to keep talking.*

Everett raises his microphone again. "As I was saying, on November seventeenth of this year, the Hwaral will return one last time to the Earth. But before we speak of that visit, it's important that you know about the Hwaral's history with our species."

At this point, a guy sitting a few aisles over stands up, waving his hand to ask a question. Everett gestures for him to take his seat. "We will have plenty of time for questions at the end of my presentation, I assure you." The man sits back down, looking frustrated, and Everett goes on with his story.

"The Writings do not document the specific dates and locations of the Hwaral's previous visits, but I have deduced that the first one dates back over five thousand years." A map of the world appears on the screen. A red dot starts to glow on the western edge of Europe, and then dots appear all over the map. "They first encountered man in the area that we now call England. Later visits were likely made to Egypt, Southeast Asia, Peru, and Easter Island. Stonehenge, the Plain of Jars, the Nazca Lines . . . all unexplained for so long. Now, in the light of the Writings, they resolve into obvious human attempts at communication on an interplanetary scale. The people of Earth were trying to reach the Hwaral. Perhaps they were trying to summon them back."

Someone behind me lets out a hiss of air, and Everett taps a finger on his temple. "I can see you thinking, 'Surely, if the Earth had been visited by a highly advanced alien civilization, there would be some record of it, would there not?' My friends, I puzzled over this myself for many years, until at last I came to understand the threat that the Hwaral and their ideas posed to our human power structures. Our religions, our economic systems, our governments would all disintegrate if we were to adopt the Hwaral's way of life. So is it any wonder that you've never heard of them? That through the millennia, those in power have done their utmost to bury the truth?"

The audience starts to rumble again, and more people head for the exits, but Everett just raises his voice and keeps going. "What is this way of life that is so threatening to so many? Ladies and gentlemen, it is the simplest thing in the world, the most obvious, intuitive, and yet, today on Earth, the most controversial of ideas. It is the notion of living in Balance. An equilibrium between inputs and outputs, taking out of the system no more than we put in. Replacing every life with no more than one life. Refusing to participate in the senseless push for growth."

Everett's eyes drill into the audience. "What is the goal of every religion? Expansion. What is the goal of every economic system? Expansion. From birth, we humans are programmed to expand, to colonize, to absorb the energy of other life-forms until we have dominated and destroyed them. My friends, what does that sound like to you?"

A voice from the front row calls out, "A virus!"

"Correct!" Everett practically shouts. "And unless it is kept in check, the human race will overwhelm its host, just as a virus does. The strain on our planet's immune system is already evident. Everywhere you look, systems are breaking down. Soon there will be no more fish in the oceans, only jellyfish and rubbish. Forest fires rage out of control because of our misbegotten efforts to dominate nature. The bees are dying off, and no one knows why. These are not acts of God, ladies and gentlemen. These are acts of man. One species alone will be responsible for the death of all the others. Why? Because it could not learn to live in Balance."

Everett takes out a dazzlingly white handkerchief and mops his forehead. "We disappointed the Hwaral time and again by failing to learn their lessons. At long last, they came to recognize that the Earth would not survive the human onslaught. But they did not cast us aside. In their infinite generosity, they left us a prescription, in the form of their Writings. For those humans who would commit to renouncing the wasteful, destructive practices of their brethren, there would be a new beginning. Not here on Earth, but on a new planet, distant and nameless, that can support a small but committed colony of humans. And on November seventeenth, those of us who have made that commitment will Depart with them, to find the Next World, and to ensure the survival of the human race. Because, despite our many failings, the Hwaral believe"—he clasps his hands to his chest more or less where his heart ought to be—"and *I* believe that humanity is worth saving!"

Again, the front rows break into wild applause. Mom jumps up and claps like she's trying to break something. I look back at the rows behind us. There's still a trickle of people leaving, but others are staring at Everett wide-eyed. I can't tell whether it's rapture or disbelief on their faces. Everett waits for everyone to settle down again, then points into the aisles, where three people are holding microphones.

"I promised you I would leave time for questions," he says. "I believe this gentleman would like to begin?" A woman with a microphone scurries over to the guy who was waving his hands before.

"So you're saying aliens are going to land their spaceship on Earth, and you want us to climb on board and go colonize a new planet. Is that about right?" he asks, then hands the microphone back and folds his arms over his chest.

Everett smiles patiently. "Not precisely. The process for Departure is a bit more complex than simply walking up a ramp onto a flying saucer. The Writings provided very clear instructions for how the committed will indicate their readiness to Depart. It involves an act of focused mental projection to signal a person's agreement to the principles of Balance. We are conducting workshops in this technique, which we call Harmonization, for all interested parties."

More hands shoot up, and the microphone gets handed to a young woman wearing a tank top and big, dangly earrings. "What do the Hwaral look like?" she asks. "Are they the humanoid type of alien? Or reptilian?"

Everett shakes his head. "Alas, I cannot tell you. The Writings contained no reference to any physical characteristics whatsoever. My personal theory is that the Hwaral are unconcerned with physical appearance, and lead lives that are centered on intellectual pursuits."

Nice one, Everett, I think to myself. The guy is smooth.

This time a woman with bushy white hair takes the microphone. She speaks in a New York accent so thick it sounds like a joke. "So these Hwaral. They've found us a new planet to move to, right?" Everett nods patiently. "So why are they gonna just give us this planet? Why don't they colonize it themselves, if it's so great?"

"Ah, madam, that is a superb question," Everett says. "Thank you for asking it, as I fear I have not been sufficiently clear about the concept of Balance. Let me first say that the Hwaral did not always live a balanced life themselves. Long, long ago, in their own early history, the Hwaral came perilously close to tipping the balance on their own planet. Like us, they bred heedlessly and overpopulated their planet. They used resources without thought to replacing or regrowing them. Their ecology suffered, and had things continued as they were, their planet would have become a wasteland.

"Fortunately, for their sake and our own, the Hwaral experienced an awakening. Through wise leadership and extraordinary discipline, they instituted policies of Balance. They stabilized their population, until there were only as many individuals on their planet as it could easily support. They became careful stewards of their lands, taking no more than they replaced. And so the simple answer to your question is, the Hwaral have no need for another planet. All their needs are met by their own."

The bushy-haired lady is still holding the microphone. "So, what? They're just letting us have this planet out of the goodness of their hearts? What's in it for them?"

Everett is grinning now. "Another excellent question," he says. "The Writings don't provide an explicit answer, so I can only tell you what I believe. Based on my interpretation of the Writings, I would say that the Hwaral feel about us much as we feel about the art in our libraries and museums. We humans are part of the cultural heritage of the universe. As an evolved society, the Hwaral believe that we are worth preserving."

"What, like animals in a zoo?" the lady with the microphone asks. "No, thank you!" Around her, the audience is laughing and a few people clap loudly as she sits down.

Everett's voice is mild, but his eyes aren't twinkling anymore. "That's not how I would characterize it, of course. The principal difference is that animals have no choice about living in a zoo. No one is forcing you, or anyone in this room, to Depart. I am merely inviting you to make a conscious choice: You can help to take the human race forward into a new plane of existence. Or you can stay behind on a doomed planet. Next question, please."

In the front row, Susan's hand shoots up. Someone gives her a microphone and she jumps to her feet. "Thank you for coming here tonight, Dr. Nichols," she says in a voice that sounds abnormally high-pitched. "My question is, have there been any threats to your safety because of what you know?"

Mom nods and leans into me, her eyes never leaving Everett. "He's had to make so many sacrifices," she says under her breath.

Everett is looking serious now. "I alluded earlier to the threat that the Writings pose to our human power structures. If humans were to live a balanced life, we would eliminate poverty and greed in a single stroke. There would be no more need for war. As an idealistic young man, I couldn't imagine anyone wanting to prevent such an outcome. Wasn't peace the highest goal of all humans?" He shakes his head sadly. "I was terribly naïve. In speaking publicly about the Writings, I unleashed a firestorm. I had to go into hiding for many years, and my life was threatened repeatedly. As the sole witness to the Writings, I was a threat to church and state alike. To this day, I cannot appear in public without protection."

A man's voice comes from the back of the auditorium, loud and strong without any microphone. "And why, exactly, are you the sole witness, Mr. Nichols?" There's something familiar about that voice, but I'm too interested in Everett's response to turn around.

"Because the Writings were destroyed," Everett says. His eyes are closed, and he steeples his fingers before he speaks again. "When I realized their import, I risked great personal danger to remove them from the Vatican, and hid them where I thought they would not be discovered. It was a grave error on my part. One night while I slept, my apartment was set ablaze. I barely escaped with my life, and all my possessions were incinerated, and with them, the scrolls. The authorities concluded that the fire was accidental, the result of a neighbor smoking in bed. But I know differently."

I look over at Mom. Her whole body is rigid. Before I have a chance to wonder what's up with her, the man's voice comes from the back of the room again, this time amplified by the microphone. "Well, isn't that convenient?" it says drily. Even before I turn around, I know why the voice is familiar.

I look back at Mom. "He came," she whispers. She looks like she's about to pass out. I know how she feels.

We sit there for the rest of the Q&A period, but my mind isn't really on Everett anymore. All I can think about is Dad. What is he doing here? And what's going to happen when the lecture is over? I wonder if there's a way to keep Mom away from him. Nothing good can come of the two of them meeting tonight.

Up on stage, Everett is still answering questions, when a commotion breaks out in the back of the auditorium. I turn around to see a woman holding one of the microphones. In her other hand, she's got a cardboard sign. She must be one of the protesters from outside.

A bunch of the HQ people try to drown her out, but Everett silences them. "My friends, everyone can have their say. We have nothing to hide," he tells them.

"I'm glad to hear you say that, Everett," the woman says. "As a former member of the NWS, my question for you is, what's going to happen to all the money you collected from your followers? On November eighteenth, are you going to return all that money to them?"

The audience erupts with people standing up and shouting. I look back toward the woman with the microphone just in time to see one of the doormen hustle her out of the auditorium. So much for everyone having their say.

Everett looks calm. "She's right about one thing. I owe a great deal to the thousands of Next World Society members around the world. Without their support, for instance, tonight's free event could never have taken place. And so I want to thank them now for their remarkable dedication. I could not have chosen a more wise, generous, and gifted group of people with whom to begin the human race anew. Not everyone is cut out for this mission. The commitment to live in Balance is too great for any but the most evolved of humans, and so I need to thank the young woman who just spoke up. It is fortunate that she recognized her own limitations before it was too late."

He checks his watch. "Ladies and gentlemen, I fear that is all the time we have this evening. I'm sorry I wasn't able to get to all your questions, but this conversation will continue on our website." He walks to the front of the stage and looks out at us one last time. "I know that my invitation is not an easy one to accept. But if you feel you are ready to make a commitment to a life in Balance, and to the preservation of our human culture, I urge you to act without delay. Take a pamphlet, email us, stop by our headquarters. November is just two months away. Thank you."

As soon as he's gone, people start to file out of the auditorium, but Mom doesn't budge. She just sits there, staring straight ahead and gnawing at her cuticles. I guess I didn't have to worry about her going after Dad and making a scene. Finally, they start flicking the lights and she lets me steer her up the aisle and out of the empty lobby. The storm has hit and rain is pelting down on the last few stragglers, who squeal and cover their heads with their programs.

As we turn toward Broadway, a couple steps out of the shadows and my stomach clenches. Not just Dad, but Carol, too. A full-on nightmare. Right on cue, a massive thunderclap lets loose from the sky, and I feel Mom flinch next to me. I assume she's spotted them, but she's looking down, trying to navigate around the puddles. Maybe there's still hope of avoiding this disaster. I look at Dad and try to send him a telepathic message: *Please just let us walk by.* But I guess my mental projection skills still need some work, or Dad is too fired up with his own thoughts to be able to read mine. "Anneliese," he says, stepping in front of Mom. "We need to talk."

Mom looks up, startled, and for a second I think she's actually going to run away. Then her shoulders slump, and she whispers, "Peter." She was so desperate for me to convince him to come, but now that he's here, it's like he's the last person in the world she wants to see. Carol clears her throat and puts a hand on my shoulder. "Um, maybe Marina and I should give you a little privacy. I'm sure you have a lot to talk about."

Mom looks up sharply, noticing Carol for the first time, taking in the hand on my shoulder and then the unmistakable bump. Her mouth drops open, but no words come out. Carol steps forward and holds out her hand. "Hi, Anneliese, I'm Carol." When Mom doesn't take her hand, Carol rests it lightly on her stomach. "I'm sorry, this must be a lot for you to process. I think maybe you could use a little time . . . Marina, do you want to grab an ice cream or something? We can find someplace dry to wait."

As the words come out of her mouth, they seem to activate something in Mom. Usually, she looks like prey, a baby gazelle or antelope all alone on the grassy plains. But now she looks more like a lion. "You're not taking my daughter anywhere," she snarls, pulling me away from Carol. Then she turns to Dad. "If you have something to say to me, you can say it in front of Rooney. She's staying right here."

Dad turns to me, looking exasperated. I shrug. There's no way I can defuse the bomb that's ticking in front of me. "Sorry," he says to me. "I didn't mean to put you in the middle of this." The sky cracks with thunder again and he looks at Mom. "Could we . . . go somewhere? Sit down and have a reasonable discussion?"

Mom shakes her head furiously. "No, Peter. You chose to come here, to ridicule me and Everett and everything I value. So why don't you just say whatever it is you want to say?"

"Now wait a minute," Dad says, his voice getting louder. "Who asked Marina to talk to me? Who pushed that pamphlet down my throat? You were the one who wanted me to come tonight!"

"But to listen! Not to sit there . . . judging and mocking!" I squeeze her hand, trying to get her to lower her voice, but at this point, she doesn't even seem to know I'm there. Suddenly, I'm slipping back in time again, back to our old apartment. I'm kneeling next to Daniel's bouncy seat, trying to distract him with a toy while Mom and Dad scream at each other in the next room.

Mom bursts into tears, and Carol pulls a packet of tissues from her purse. She hesitates, then passes them to me, gesturing with a tilt of her chin at Mom.

Dad is standing with his head in his hands. When he speaks, his voice comes out muffled, and I can barely hear him over the sound of the rain. "Look, Anneliese, I didn't come here to fight with you. Let's please not make this about Everett or the NWS. I think we've already talked that one to death. This is about our kids."

"What about them?" Mom asks. She steps in front of me, like she's protecting me from Dad. For a second, I want to laugh. I'm towering over her, and so is Dad, but she thinks I'm the one who needs to be protected.

"I'm their father," Dad says in a low voice, "and I'm not going to let you keep them away from me anymore. I'm going to be in their lives, even if I have to get a court order."

Mom lets out a hard, sharp little bark of a laugh. "You want to be in their lives? Well, I guess you'd better start going to Harmonization workshops right away, Peter. Because eleven weeks from now, they'll be gone."

"Oh, for Christ's sake, Anneliese!" Dad says, his voice rising. "Will you grow up? When are you going to realize the spacemen aren't coming to rescue you from the big, bad world? You're responsible for our children, and you can't even hold down a job! What judge would deny me custody?"

"Custody?" Mom shrieks. "Why would you want custody? You don't need them!" She jabs a finger toward Carol. "You're already replacing them!"

Dad darts an apologetic look my way. "Of course I'm not replacing them," he says, more calmly. "Yes, Carol and I are expecting a baby. And Marina and Daniel have a right to know their little sister."

Mom is laughing wildly now. I almost think she's enjoying the drama. "Do whatever you want, Peter. None of it matters. We're Departing, and there's nothing you can do to stop that. Yes, I wanted you to come tonight. I hoped that you could finally be convinced to do what's right. For your family. But now I see you're just as unenlightened as ever. You'd have to be totally oblivious to want to bring another life onto this planet now. There's no hope for you, Peter. Good-bye."

She grabs my arm and starts to pull me away. Dad tries to stop her by taking my other arm, but Carol grabs his free hand, and suddenly we're stretched out like a human chain on the sidewalk. The rain is sharp on my face and shoulders. For a second, we're all trapped, and then Dad drops my hand. "I'm sorry, Marina. This isn't how I meant for it to go." Mom drags me toward Broadway. She's not even trying to avoid the puddles anymore, and the rain instantly soaks through my shoes.

"This isn't over, Anneliese," Dad calls after us. "You're not going to keep us apart anymore!" As we turn the corner, I look back through the sheets of rain. Dad and Carol are standing under an awning. She's got her arms around him, and his head is buried in her neck.

Six

After the long, strained drive back to Vermont, the first thing I do is go to Max's house to pick up Daniel. Max's mom, Stefanie, comes to the door, and I expect her to call upstairs to the boys, but instead she offers me a seat in the kitchen. "Was everything okay?" I ask. "I hope Daniel wasn't any trouble."

"Oh, Daniel's never any trouble. He's a great kid," Stefanie says.

"Oh, good," I say. And then, when she doesn't say anything else, "Should I go get him?"

"Rooney, there's something I just wanted to mention to you. I don't think it's a big deal or anything, but I walked in on the boys last night and they were looking at a website . . ."

I don't say anything, but my mind starts racing. What kind of website would a couple of nine-year-old boys be looking at? Violent games? I can't imagine Daniel or Max getting into anything much racier than that.

"It was . . . that group your mom belongs to? That New World, um, group?" Stephanie says. *How does she even know about Mom?* I think, fighting down a sudden wave of panic. *Does everyone know?* "They were watching some lecture about . . . I don't know, about aliens or something. I'm not sure because I asked them to shut it off when I found them."

I clear my throat. "I'm really sorry, Stefanie. I'll tell Daniel to stay off that site. But I hope you'll still let Max hang out with him."

Her eyes widen. "Oh, gosh, of course I will. I thought you'd be upset with me. I should have been supervising them more closely. And I just thought you should know about it, in case it comes up later. I think Daniel may have been a little . . . intrigued by it."

"Thank you for letting me know."

"Sure." She studies me for a minute. "Rooney, have you told Daniel that he maybe shouldn't talk about . . . about your mom's interests at school?"

"Oh, I don't think he'd do that. He's a pretty private kid."

"I just thought . . . Well, you know how mean kids can be. I'd hate to see him having problems because of . . . you know."

"Sure. Thanks, Stefanie," I say again. "I'll just go up and get him now, okay?"

I wait until we're about halfway home before I ask Daniel, "Hey, Bug? Stefanie said that you and Max were on the NWS website. What were you looking for?"

Daniel looks quickly away. "I just wanted to watch the speech. I thought maybe I'd see you and Mom in the audience."

It's natural enough that he'd be curious, but I can't help thinking he isn't telling me everything. "So . . . what did you think about it?" I ask. "Everett's speech. Pretty nutty, huh?"

Daniel shrugs, looking down at the sidewalk. "It wasn't what I expected. I thought he would seem more . . . I don't know. More crazy, I guess."

That's the whole problem with Everett. He doesn't seem crazy at first.

"Daniel, does Max know all about Mom? Does he know what she believes?"

"Max knows everything."

My heart sinks. "Are you sure that's a good idea? I mean, you don't want all the kids at school to know, right?"

A frown puckers his brow. "Max is my best friend."

"I know."

"Why wouldn't I tell him? I tell him everything. Doesn't Mercer know all about Mom?"

I nod, feeling out of my depth. "Look, Daniel, I'm not saying you shouldn't talk to your best friend about stuff. I'm just saying you should be careful. We don't want everyone talking about our family."

Daniel looks up at me. "Are you mad at me for something?"

I put my hand on his shoulder, then pull it away again. Everything feels awkward. "No, of course I'm not mad at you."

"Good. Because you seem kind of mad."

"I just think we need to be careful. Things are hard enough without everyone knowing our business."

Daniel doesn't say anything more. It's almost a relief that he doesn't want to talk. I haven't decided what to tell him about seeing Dad and Carol, and I'm still not sure how to bring it up without admitting that I lied to him about my reasons for going to New York. So for the rest of the walk, I don't say anything. I figure I'll tell him tonight at bedtime, or maybe tomorrow.

—

Late that afternoon, Mercer and I sit in his room with the windows wide open and a fan going at top speed. Mingus is on the bed between us, his tongue hanging halfway down to the floor.

"So your dad . . . What was he like?" Mercer asks.

"He was like I remembered, only not as tall."

He laughs. "No, seriously, what kind of person is he?"

"I don't know. He seems kind of . . . normal. You know how Mom looks out of place everywhere she goes?"

"She definitely stands out," Mercer says diplomatically.

"Well, he's the opposite. He seems like he could blend in anywhere."

"So you're saying he's boring?"

"No, not boring. He seems smart. And nice. He's definitely got a temper, though, if you push his buttons."

Mercer raises an eyebrow at me. "Sounds like someone I know."

"Yeah, maybe," I admit. "We might have one or two things in common. Hey, let me borrow your tablet, okay?"

"Sure."

I check my email and find the picture Carol sent of the three of us outside the pizza place.

"Wow. You look a lot like him," Mercer says, studying it. "I always thought it was strange how you didn't look anything like your mom." He points at Carol. "And . . . that's his new wife?"

"Yup. Carol."

He leans in closer to the screen and his eyebrows go up. "Is she . . . ?" He wiggles a finger at her belly.

"She's due around Christmastime. A girl."

"Wow. How do you feel about that?"

"I'm happy for them. Dad seems really excited. And Carol is sweet. I think that baby will be lucky."

Mercer shakes his head. "I don't get it. Your dad basically abandoned you guys. I keep waiting for you to be mad about that."

"That's the thing: I don't think any of that is true. I haven't exactly had all the facts." I tell him about dinner, and what Dad said about Mom not letting him see us. When I get to the part about the wedding, Mercer's jaw drops, and he's still gaping when I finish describing the horrific scene after the lecture.

"That's crazy! Do you think he was serious about custody?" he asks. "I mean, you're a senior. He's not going to shake everything up now, is he?"

"I doubt it. I think he was just trying to scare Mom."

Mercer absentmindedly strokes Mingus, a worried look on his face. "But what if he *was* serious? Would you . . . Would you want to go live with him?"

"I don't know. I'd love to get Daniel away from Mom, but I can't imagine just picking up and starting over now. Anyway, school's about to start."

"Well, I know you'll end up in New York eventually, but you'd better wait until we graduate. You can't go ruining my senior year by leaving."

He says it in a joking way, but I know he kind of means it, too, which makes me happy. "I wouldn't lose any sleep over it," I tell him. "I think I'm about as likely to move to New York this year as I am to be abducted by aliens."

He smiles and lies back on the bed, resting his head on Mingus's side. "Good," he says.

I start to lean back, too, but something about the way the light is coming through the window brings me up short. His features have always been kind of delicate, but they've changed since the last time I really looked. I've known Mercer for so long that at some point, I sort of stopped thinking of him as a boy. He was just my friend. And now, I realize with a shock, he's crossed over some invisible line into manhood. My eyes travel up the line of his body, and it's like looking into a trick mirror that shows the past and present at the same time. He still has a boy's slender waist, but he has a man's hands. His jaw is a man's jaw. I lean in closer, wondering whether it's just the angle, and find myself staring at his lips. Did they always look that soft?

"What?" he asks, brushing his hand across his mouth. "Do I have something on my face?"

"What?" I say guiltily. "Nothing. I mean, no. I should go." I jump off the bed. "See you tomorrow."

Mom has a meeting tonight, so we're on our own for dinner as usual. At bedtime, Daniel picks up his sketch pad, but he doesn't open it. He just sits on the bed with the closed pad on his lap.

"So what's the story about?" I prompt him. I don't mean to rush him, but I need to get downstairs and use Mom's computer. My conversation with Mercer planted a thought in my head and I want to do something about it before I lose my nerve.

"Well, it's not exactly a story," Daniel says.

"Okay, what is it, then?"

"Well, I tried drawing . . . them. You know. The thingies. From the lecture." He lets the pad fall open on the bed. There, carefully sketched in colored pencil, is the last thing in the world

I want to see. Daniel imagined the Hwaral with long, delicate limbs and fingers, and big, dark eyes. Their faces look peaceful and kind, not quite human, but not creepily alien, either.

"Daniel, why are you drawing those things?" I try to say it calmly, like it isn't important, but when he looks up, his eyes widen for a millisecond. "Have you been thinking about them a lot since you watched the lecture?"

"No, not really. I just thought they'd be interesting to draw. It doesn't mean anything."

I've watched Daniel lie about little things before, his eyes sliding off to the side, his shoulders slumped. But he's never lied to me. Not about anything that mattered, anyway. Not until now.

"Well, do you want to tell me a story about them?" I ask as casually as I can.

"No. They were just something to draw." He closes the pad and puts it on the floor next to his bed. "I'm kind of tired, Rooney."

He curls up with his back to me, and I turn out the light.

I'm so focused on what I'm about to do, I'm not even hurt that Daniel doesn't want to talk. I sit down at the kitchen table, open up Mom's laptop, and start typing out a response to Carol's email.

OCTOBER

one

Just five weeks until November 17.

It's all Mom talks about. And now that she's counting the weeks instead of the months, it's starting to seep into the rest of the house, too.

Before September, Daniel and I were always a team. It was the two of us against the world. But after New York, something changed. I didn't realize it right away, but as the weeks passed, I started noticing that Daniel was spending more and more time with Mom. Sometimes, I would come home from work to find the two of them sitting at the kitchen table, and they'd stop talking when I came in. And even though I still made him dinner and put him to bed when Mom went to her meetings, there was something different about Daniel. He wasn't cold, exactly, he just seemed kind of secretive.

But if Daniel had a secret, he wasn't alone. I still hadn't told him about Dad and Carol. I wanted to talk to him about it, but I kept telling myself it was better to wait until the plan was more definite. There was no point getting him all stirred up about moving to New York next year if it wasn't going to happen.

Sometimes, I wondered if it was my own guilt that made me think Daniel was keeping something from me. Other times, I told myself that he was just growing up, that it was normal for a kid his age to want some privacy. But whatever the reasons, one thing was clear: Things were different between us.

Once I was back at school, I didn't have time to think about Daniel so much. I was too busy getting used to my new schedule, trying to squeeze homework and college applications in between school and work. My hands were so full, I didn't even have time to feel lonely, except the first time I saw the *Sentinel* staff heading into an editorial meeting as I was leaving for the Java Connection. But even as I was thinking about them laughing and working without me, there was a part of me that knew it was probably for the best. The fewer friends I had, the less risk there was of the whole school finding out about Mom and the Next World.

It wasn't even that hard telling everyone I was quitting the paper. Except Mrs. Fisher, of course. When I went to see her after the trip to New York, I was worried she'd be disappointed or even mad. She had pushed so hard for me to get the editor position, and now I was messing up all her plans. But she only looked concerned. "I'm sure I don't need to point out that this is a very important decision. Are you absolutely certain this is what you want?"

"Oh, it's not what I want," I said quickly. "I love working on the paper. But I have to make money."

"Has something changed at home?" she asked, leaning back in her chair. Mrs. Fisher was one of the few people in my life who knew about Mom and the NWS.

I checked to make sure the door was closed. "My mom lost her job."

She nodded slowly. "I see. I'm very sorry to hear that, Marina."

"Thanks. It'll be all right. But I am really sorry about the *Sentinel*."

"Well, your colleagues there and I will certainly miss you. But at the moment, I am more concerned about your college applications."

"You don't need to worry. I'm all over it. But I was wondering . . ."

"Yes?"

"Would you read my essay before I send it out? I can't exactly ask Mom."

"Of course, I'd be delighted. So you're still planning to apply early to Columbia?"

Mrs. Fisher was the one who had first suggested it, back when I was in her sophomore English class. After that, it was like I'd always known that was where I'd go. "It's my first choice," I said. "I just hope I can get in."

"Well, I am impressed that you are so far ahead of the deadline. Well done!" She flashed me a bright smile, and I realized how rare it was for her to do more than lift the corners of her mouth in approval.

"Thanks," I said, drinking in the praise. "I'd better run. I'm going to be late for my shift."

"One last thing," she said. "Even though you can't be on the staff this year, I hope you will still find the time to write a few articles for us. The *Sentinel* will not be the same without your point of view, Marina."

"Thank you. I'd like that." I didn't know when I'd find the time, but I was glad she'd asked.

Now, whenever I see her, she checks up on me. I think she wants me to know that someone's paying attention. First, it was reviewing my Early Decision application. Then she wanted to know if I'd started applying for financial aid. When I told her I wasn't sure how much money I was going to need yet, she pursed her lips and shook her head slowly. Maybe she's right to be concerned, but it's kind of hard to ask Mom about my college fund when she doesn't even know I'm applying. And with the countdown clock ticking so loud, it's not a conversation I want to have right now. It can wait until after November 17.

The Java Connection is empty, and Mercer and I are sitting at one of the café tables. He's been hanging out with me a few times a week after Jazz Band rehearsal. Maddie doesn't mind, since it's so quiet in the afternoons, and at least he always buys a cup of coffee and a bagel. Plus, without him watering the plants, they'd all be dead by now.

Mercer is working on his Vassar application, and I'm trying to focus on poetry for AP English. I flip through the pages in my Yeats book until it falls open to "The Second Coming." I don't exactly know what the poem is about, but I'm pretty sure it's the end of the world. The language is full of blood and fear and confusion. It's kind of terrifying, and kind of awesome. "Can I ask you something?" I say to Mercer.

"Course," he says, closing his screen.

"Do you think we're the only planet with life on it?"

"Well, if you look at it statistically, it seems pretty unlikely. Why?"

"I don't know. Just thinking."

"About Everett?" he asks.

"More about Daniel. I'm a little worried about him."

"Why?"

"He just seems a lot less skeptical about Departure than he used to be. Like he's starting to think it wouldn't be such a bad idea."

"Maybe it's just Pascal's Wager," Mercer says.

It takes me a second to remember what he's talking about. "You mean that thing from Comparative Religion last year?"

"Right. Since you can't prove that God exists, Pascal said you should just act like He does. Then if God does exist, you win, but if He doesn't, you haven't lost anything."

"So you think Daniel's decided to wager on the existence of aliens?"

Mercer shrugs. "Why not? If he believes in them and they turn out to be real, he gets to go on this incredible adventure. And if they turn out to be a giant hoax, it's no big loss."

"I guess that makes sense," I say a little grudgingly. I'm not so sure about the "no big loss" part.

Mercer checks his phone. "I need to go. But before I forget, do you have to watch Daniel Friday night?"

"I don't know. Probably. Why?"

"A bunch of us are going to a party at Eric Wurtzel's place. You should come."

"A party?"

"Yeah. It's this new thing with music and snacks and people having fun. Maybe you've heard of it?"

I roll my eyes at him. "You're hilarious. I'm just not into being around a lot of people right now. I don't want to give anyone a reason to talk about me."

"Don't you think that's a little paranoid?"

"Paranoid? Remember what happened with that picture of Sonia Bartlett last year? People are still calling her Boobie Bartlett behind her back."

"Okay, that's a ridiculous comparison," Mercer says, laughing. "That was way more interesting than your mom being in some cult."

"It's not a cult!" I snap.

Mercer holds his hands up defensively. "Okay, it's not a cult. My point is, it's just not that big a deal. Anyway, don't you think you deserve to have some fun for once? You're never going to be a senior again."

"I'll think about it."

"Good!" He hoists his backpack and oboe case. "You need help closing up?"

"Nah. I'll see you tomorrow."

When I get home, there's no sign of Mom or Daniel until I wander upstairs and hear their voices coming from Daniel's room.

"Does it feel like flying?" Daniel is asking.

"I think it's different for everybody," Mom says. "For me, it's more like feeling super peaceful, and then floating up into the air."

I rest my hand on the doorknob and hold my breath, hoping against hope that they're not talking about what I think they're talking about.

"I didn't feel anything like that," Daniel's saying, his voice small and disappointed.

"That's okay, sweetie! You just keep practicing. I know you're going to get it!"

"But what if I don't?"

"Then I can do it for you, remember? I'll Harmonize for both of us." The word hits me right in the chest, and for about the millionth time, I wish I'd told Daniel about Dad the day I got home from New York.

I hear a sniffle. "What about Rooney? Can you Harmonize for her, too?"

"We don't need to worry about Rooney. She'll be just fine." I wonder whether Mom looks as uncertain as she sounds.

"But what if she doesn't want to go? Or if she doesn't try? Can we still take her with us?"

"It's all going to be okay, sweetie."

I never told anyone about what happened in the Harmonization workshop. I didn't even tell Mercer. Not because I thought he'd judge me, or think I was crazy. It was more that talking about it would make me *feel* crazy. I'm not the kind of person who imagines stuff like that. I'm the one who always brings things back to reality. I know I probably dreamed the whole thing. But it felt so real that I still sometimes think I could do it again in a second if I chose to.

But I don't choose to. I just keep reminding myself of that. I choose to keep my feet on the ground. Not just for myself, but for Daniel.

I tiptoe back downstairs and open and close the front door with a bang. "Hello?" I yell. "Who's ready for dinner?"

At bedtime, Daniel's room is freezing, so I go get his old comforter from the closet. As I shake it out and spread it over his bed, he says, "Mom says you're really good at Harmonization."

"Excuse me?" I've been wondering all evening whether to tell him I overheard them.

"Harmonization. Mom says you're a natural." He traces the pattern of primary-colored trains and cars with his finger. "Do you think you could teach me?"

"How do you know about Harmonization?" I ask, sitting down next to him. "Did you and Mom talk about it?"

"She's been teaching me how to do it."

"Since when?"

"A couple of weeks, I guess. But I'm not so good at it. It just makes me sleepy."

"Did you ask her to teach you? Or was it Mom's idea?"

Daniel's eyes flick up toward mine. "I asked about it. I read about it on the NWS website. I wanted to try it, but I was scared I might get sucked into outer space or something. So I asked her to help me."

"Why didn't you tell me before?"

Daniel lets out a little snort. "Because I knew you'd say it's all a bunch of crap."

"But, Daniel, that's what you always said about it, too," I point out.

"I know." The fringe of his eyelashes is casting a dark shadow on his cheek.

"So did you change your mind? Do you believe Everett now?"

"No. I don't know. I just wanted to know about it, just in case."

"In case what? In case it turns out to be true?" *Maybe Mercer was onto something.*

Daniel won't look me in the eyes. "I know you think it's stupid. But what if Mom is right? What if the Hwaral really are coming? What happens if you and Mom go with them, and I get left behind?"

"Well, first of all, they're not coming. But even if they were, you know I wouldn't leave you behind. And neither would Mom."

"So will you teach me?"

"Bug, I slept through that workshop. I don't know why Mom thinks I know anything about it."

"Fine. Never mind."

I pick up the book that's on the crate by his bed. "So you're reading about Easter Island? What's up with those big stone heads?"

"I don't know. I haven't gotten to that part yet. They're still canoeing across the ocean."

His voice is sulky, but I pretend not to notice. "Across the ocean? In canoes? That's pretty amazing."

"Yeah. I'm going to sleep, okay?"

I can see he's shutting me out, and before I have a chance to think it through, I do something a little desperate. "Wait," I say. "There's something I want to tell you. About the trip to New York." He rolls over and looks at me and I pause, trying to give my brain time to catch up with my mouth. I can't screw this up—it's too important. "I saw Dad when I was there."

His expression doesn't change. His eyes are a total blank. "I know," he says, and I realize I've made a massive mistake.

"You knew? How?"

"Mom told me."

"When?"

"When you guys got back. Weeks ago."

"So you've known this whole time? Why didn't you say anything?"

"Why didn't you?"

The words hit me like little daggers. "I'm sorry, Daniel. I should have. I was waiting for the right time."

"Why is this the right time?"

I shake my head, knowing that anything I say right now will only make things worse, and he turns stiffly away from me.

"I'm sorry," I say again to his back, but he doesn't make a sound.

Well played, Mom, I think as I creep downstairs. *You totally won that round.*

two

On Tuesday, I walk in the door after work and Mom is all over me. "Sweetie, I wanted to talk to you about Friday night. Daniel and I have a super-special plan and we really need your help."

I fold my arms across my chest. "Let me guess: You're practicing Harmonization, and you want me to join you."

"Oh my gosh! How did you know? That's exactly what I was going to ask you!"

"Lucky guess," I tell her, and just like that, I decide that Eric Wurtzel's party sounds like a pretty awesome place to be on Friday night. "Sorry, Mom, but I have plans."

"Plans? Are they important? Daniel was really hoping you would help him."

"I don't know what makes you think I could help him. And besides, you can Harmonize for him, right? So why does Daniel even need to learn?" I realize a second too late that I only know that from eavesdropping on them, but Mom doesn't seem to notice.

"It's important to him," she says. "He wants to learn."

"And this is important to me. I just want to have a normal life for once. Maybe you can handle the Harmonization on your own."

Mom looks kind of stunned. "Well, if that's how you feel. But Daniel is going to be so disappointed."

For the next couple of nights, Daniel is borderline sullen with me. At bedtime, when I ask him what he's reading, he answers in one-word sentences, then says he's tired. When I try talking to him about Dad again, he shuts it down hard. "I don't want to talk about him. He doesn't care about us."

"That's not true, Daniel. He does care. He wants to get to know you."

"Then why did he leave?" I can practically hear Mom's voice whispering behind his words.

"It's complicated," I try to say, but he just turns away. I can't tell whether he's mad at Dad for leaving us, or at me for lying, but either way I don't bring it up again.

As we're finishing up the dishes on Friday, I hear a beep in the driveway. Mercer usually rides his bike everywhere, but I'm glad he borrowed his dad's car tonight. Eric's house is a couple of miles away, and it's pretty cold out. Still, it feels strange to be sitting in a car in the dark with Mercer. Almost like . . . a date. The second the idea comes into my head, I give it a hard push.

Walking up Eric's front steps, we pass a couple of kids from school smoking. I glance at them, hoping to see a friendly face, and recognize Brandi Chilton from PE freshman year, and Trevor Buck from Chem. But they stare at me with the same blankly hostile looks as the others. I don't belong here.

I want to tell Mercer I've changed my mind, but it's too late: He's already pulling open the door. It's dark inside, and the music is so loud I can feel it pounding in my chest. This is not the kind of party we used to go to a few years back, with somebody's mother putting out snacks, and parents lining up around the block at ten o'clock to pick up their kids. As we squeeze past a couple of girls in sheer blouses, I look down at my own ratty sweater and wish I'd thought to put on something more flattering. Not that I'd have many options. I've barely bought any new clothes since I stopped growing in freshman year.

Two seconds after we get through the door, Mercer is surrounded by half the horn section from Jazz Band. I've known most of these guys since we were eleven, but I can't remember the last time I had a conversation with any of them. "Hey, Rooney," Eddie Scott says when he spots me. "What are you doing here?"

Mercer cuts him a look. "I invited her, you idiot."

Poor Eddie looks mortified. "No, I mean, it's good to see you. What are you up to?"

"Nothing," I say, a little too fast. And then we just look at each other uneasily until he excuses himself.

I should have trusted my instincts. If you don't want to talk to people, you should definitely avoid parties. But I can't duck out now. I'm just going to have to blend into the woodwork until I can get Mercer to take me home.

A girl I don't know makes a beeline for us. She's wearing a short skirt and boots, and her long blond hair is loose and wavy around her face. "You came!" she says, beaming at Mercer.

"Yeah. Hi." Mercer smiles down at her, then seems to catch himself and turns to me. "Do you guys know each other? Skyler transferred here this year. She plays killer flute. Skyler Jamison, meet the great Rooney Harris." He makes a gesture that I guess is supposed to whisk away the awkwardness in the room, but only serves to sweep it up higher.

Skyler turns to me with a thousand-watt smile. "Oh! Mercer's told me about you. It's so nice to meet you!"

"You too," I mumble, wondering what, exactly, Mercer has told her.

More and more people are packing the room, and I gradually let myself get pushed toward the doorway. Mercer is still talking to Skyler, but he keeps looking over and waving. I wave back, but I don't try to push my way back to him. Eventually, I slip into the next room and someone hands me a cup of punch. It smells flammable, and I think about abandoning it on the coffee table, but it's good party camouflage, so I hang on to it.

I'm considering hiding in the bathroom for a while when I notice the door to the basement is propped open. The TV is on down there with no one watching it. I help myself to some fluorescent orange cheese puffs from a big bowl and click around until I settle on a dumb comedy Daniel and I used to love, back when we still had cable. The punch doesn't taste so bad when it's paired with cheese puffs.

I settle into the movie, and pretty soon the punch and about half of the puffs are gone. When a commercial comes on, I head back upstairs to see if I can pry Mercer out. I'm feeling a little fuzzy in the head, and I've seen enough middle school health videos to know what that means. I should quit now while I'm still in control. I look for Merce in each room, but all I see is more and more of the popular crowd from school. I'm willing to bet none of them even know whose house they're in, but it doesn't matter to them. Word of out-of-town parents gets around fast.

Finally, I spot Mercer, still talking to Skyler Whatshername. The two of them are standing awfully close together, his lips practically brushing her ear as he talks, and there are about a million people between me and them. It's a lot easier to reach the punch bowl than to swim through this crowd, so I refill my cup and go back downstairs.

I'm getting my third or fifth cup of magic punch when Mercer finally intercepts me. "Hey, where have you been?" he half shouts over the music.

"Oh, sorry. I didn't want to bother you." The connection between my brain and my mouth doesn't seem to be working at its normal speed. Plus, it's taking all my concentration not to slosh punch all over myself.

Mercer gives me a concerned look. "Whoa . . . You've had a few of those, huh?"

"Yeah. One or two. Ish."

"Ish?"

"Yeah, more or less-ish," I say. This strikes me as incredibly witty. "I've also had a *lot* of cheese puffs. They may be the most delicious substance known to man." At least, that's what I try to say, only the second part gets a little mangled.

"Okay," Mercer says. "I think it's time to take you home." His face looks so serious that I can't help laughing.

"No, come on. You told me I needed to have more fun! So now I'm having fun. You want to dance?" My body feels loose and relaxed, and for once I'm not responsible for anyone or anything. It seems like the perfect time to dance.

"I'll take a rain check, thanks," Mercer says. Then he takes the cup out of my hand. "Let's just leave this here."

I sing along with the music, and try to dance in a little circle around Mercer, but my feet aren't obeying orders that well, and I end up kind of lurching toward him. He grabs me before I tip over, then takes me by the shoulders and looks into my eyes. "Rooney, I need to get you home."

"No, come on," I say. "All these people are still having a good time." The room is loud with laughter, and there's a couple making out in the corner. Seeing their tongues writhing around makes my stomach do a little flip, and I look away quickly. "I'm not ready to go home now."

Skyler Whoozis floats over to us. "Is she okay?" she asks Mercer.

"I'm fine," I say, pulling myself up straight and speaking very clearly.

"I'm going to take Rooney home," Mercer says. "I'll see you in school, okay?"

As we step into the cold air, I shiver and lean into him. He puts an arm around me to stabilize me, and I can feel his wiry frame pressing against me and the taut curve of his waist. The curls have fallen over his eyes, and I reach up to try to push them aside, but I miscalculate and it throws me off-balance. "How about we just focus on getting down the stairs, all right?" Mercer asks. "Let's do the right foot first. No. The other right foot."

The two of us stagger down the stairs and then stop at the bottom, steadying ourselves. The light from the porch is casting sharp shadows on his face. He may have a man's jaw now, but his eyes are still like a girl's. Those eyelashes are too long for a man.

"That Skyler girl is pretty," I say.

"Yeah."

"Do you know her well?"

"Not really. She only moved here a few months ago."

"She looked like she wanted to know you a lot better." It's supposed to be teasing, but it comes out more like taunting.

"Come on, let's get you into the car." He opens the door for me and I potato-sack myself onto the seat. Once Mercer's made sure I'm buckled in, he says, "So I'm going to ask you a favor, okay?"

"Anything." My voice sounds too loud in the car.

"If you need to barf, can you give me a heads-up so I can pull over? My dad loves this car."

I burst out laughing, but Mercer just shakes his head at me. "I promise," I tell him when I catch my breath. "You'll be the first to know."

We drive slowly, the streetlamps making yellow streaks on our frosty windshield. By the time we reach my house, the inside of the car is just getting warm. I'd give anything to stay here and sleep, but Mercer comes around and hauls me out of the car. It feels so nice to have someone else carrying my weight that I don't do much to help him. We stagger up the driveway, and for once, I'm glad that it never occurs to Mom to replace a lightbulb. The one over the front door burned out months ago.

"Are you going to be all right?" Mercer whispers to me. "Try to drink a couple of glasses of water. That should make you feel a little less terrible tomorrow."

I try to whisper, too. "You're the best friend ever." I put my arms around his neck and lean my cheek against his, breathing in his clean smell. Then I turn my face and kiss him on the cheek. His skin is soft and warm, and suddenly I picture him whispering in Skyler's ear. I wonder what his lips feel like. If anyone should know the answer to that question, if should be me, not Skyler Perfectskin. I kiss him again, still on the cheek, but a little closer to his mouth. *Kiss me!* He doesn't move, so I kiss him a third time, my lip just grazing the corner of his mouth. And then I think, *Oh, what the hell,* and smash my lips onto his.

For a second, everything freezes. He doesn't move and neither do I. And then I feel it, a tiny change, so small you could miss it. He's kissing me back. His lips are pressing against mine softly, and then not so softly. We stay like that for a second or two, neither of us moving, and then he pulls away from me and steps back.

"Okay," he says, his breath clouding the cold air. He puts his hands on my shoulders and looks into my eyes. "Rooney, you are very, very drunk. And because I am the best friend ever, I am sending you inside to drink some water and go to bed before things get really weird. Good night." He kisses me lightly on the forehead, then pushes the front door open. Before I can say a word, he's in his car.

I watch until the headlights disappear, and then I step into the kitchen.

The first thing I see is Mom sitting at the table.

She's not on her computer or anything, just sitting in the dark. "Did you have fun?" she asks in a low whisper.

"It was okay." I reach into the cabinet for a glass. It takes me a couple of tries because it's kind of high and I'm not very steady. I fill the glass and head for the stairs, walking carefully so I don't spill the water. I probably shouldn't have filled the glass so full.

"Rooney." Her voice is like a hand on my arm, pulling me back into the room. "Come and sit with me for a minute."

"I'm pretty tired, Mom," I say. "Can it wait until tomorrow?" Even just getting those two sentences out takes a lot of effort. The nice, floaty feeling in my head is starting to feel more like a thick fog. All I want to do is go upstairs and lie down and try to make some sense of what just happened.

I turn to go, but she stands up and walks over to me. "Are you . . ." She sniffs at me like a dog. "Have you been drinking, Rooney?"

I don't even bother lying. "Yup. I'm pretty trashed."

"Oh, Rooney. Was Mercer drinking, too?" Somehow she manages to sound babyish and disapproving at the same time.

"Of course not," I say. "He was driving."

"Well, thank goodness one of you was behaving responsibly."

It takes a second for that to sink in. "Wait. Are you saying I'm irresponsible?" I ask slowly.

"Well, what would you call it?" Mom asks. "Your family needs you, but you'd rather go out and get drunk with your friends?"

It's like she's flipped a switch in my head. I feel my face getting hot and the air around my ears starts humming. "Really, Mom?" I say. "Maybe you shouldn't throw stones."

"Excuse me?"

I know I should just shut up, but my brain can't seem to get the message to my mouth. I put the glass down a little too roughly, and half the water sloshes onto the table. "You want me to spell it out? Fine. You probably shouldn't accuse me of being irresponsible when you're basically the least responsible person I know."

Mom's eyes open wide. "I . . . You don't talk to your mother like that!"

"If you want to be treated like a mother, maybe you should try acting like one." She opens her mouth to say something, but I'm unstoppable now. "When we need groceries, and when Daniel needs help with his homework, and when the bills need to be paid, where are you? You're in outer space!" Half of my words are garbled, but I can see my meaning is sinking in anyway.

"I never asked you to do any of that. And I pay the bills," she says, waving her hands to shush me.

I laugh much too loudly. "With Dad's money! You can't even keep a job. Oh, but you're happy to take money from your own daughter."

"You shouldn't say such cruel things," Mom says, her lower lip quivering.

"I can say whatever I want!" I'm shouting now, and Mom is starting to cry, but I don't care. The words have been building up inside me for so long that nothing's going to stop them from coming out. "I earned it! Working at the coffee shop and taking care of Daniel while you hung out with your Next World buddies. What kind of mother does that?"

Mom drops back onto her chair, her head in her hands. "You don't understand," she whimpers. "You and Daniel are all I think about. All I care about is your future."

"Forget about the future, Mom!" The room is starting to spin, but I stay standing, towering over her. "We're in trouble *now*. I can't keep holding us together. It's not my job."

"But you don't need to worry about any of that!" The words are pouring out of her on a river of tears and snot. "It's only a month away. We just have to make it to the seventeenth and then none of this will matter anymore. I'm not asking you to work. Quit your job, quit school tomorrow if you want to! I'm just asking you to believe in me and start getting ready!" She tries to reach for my hand, but I jerk away, knocking over the water glass. It falls on the floor and smashes, but I barely notice.

"But I *don't* believe it, Mom!" I yell. "I don't understand how *you* can believe it. It's pathetic! And now you've got Daniel believing it, too."

Mom doesn't seem to have any response. She's just opening and closing her mouth like a fish now. Which is kind of perfect, since I feel like I'm underwater. And then my mouth goes salty like the ocean, and I realize I'm about to throw up. I stumble upstairs and reach the toilet just in time. A fountain of bright pink punch and orange snack food splashes into the bowl while I cough and gasp and try to claw my hair out of the way. I stay there for a while, waiting to see if more is coming. Then I hear a sound and look up to see Daniel in the doorway.

"Are you okay?" he asks, his eyes wide.

I nod, turning away so he can't see me. "Yeah. I just ate something nasty."

"I heard yelling. Were you and Mom fighting?"

I take a deep breath and try to speak clearly. "Go to bed, Bug," I tell him. "It's okay."

He stands there for a few seconds, then I hear his footsteps padding back to his bedroom.

I think about crawling to my own room, but I'm not sure I'm done barfing yet. It seems like a better idea to just lie down on the cold tiles and wait for the spinning to stop.

When I wake up, the sun is just starting to come in the bathroom window. I'm still curled up on the floor, but someone's put my quilt over me. My mouth tastes like garbage, so I brush my teeth and scrub my tongue before I crawl to bed.

The next time I wake up, it's almost eleven o'clock and Daniel's peeking into my room. "Mercer's on the phone," he says. "And guess what! Mom made pancakes!"

I try to focus on him, but it hurts to open my eyes. "I'm still not feeling so great, Bug. Tell him I can't come to the phone."

"Don't you want pancakes? They're really good!" Daniel sounds surprised that Mom actually knows how to cook.

"I'm not hungry. You go ahead and eat mine, okay?" I pull the covers over my head and lie there, breathing slowly and wondering what I'm supposed to do about the giant mess I made last night. Making a move on Mercer was pathetic. Letting Daniel hear me screaming at Mom was maybe even worse. At a minimum, I'm going to have to do a whole lot of apologizing today. It might be better to just stay under the covers for the rest of my life.

I know I should be thinking about what to say to Mom, since I'm sure she's waiting to pounce on me. But all I can think about is how it felt to press my lips against Mercer's. When I close my eyes, I can almost feel the warmth and softness of it. I even press my lips against the back of my hand to try to re-create it. The second I do, I feel like an epic dork, and that's enough to snap me back to my senses.

Focus.

Mom. What do I say to Mom?

The way I see it, I have two choices. I can own up to the truth and hope that it's somehow going to change everything, or I can pretend I don't remember last night and act like nothing happened. And the more I think about it, the more the choice seems clear. Nothing's going to change around here until November 17 is behind us, so why stick my neck out?

Without a doubt, the lie wins.

Once I've made up my mind, it's not even that hard to go downstairs. Mom is sitting at the kitchen table as usual, staring at her computer. The circles under her eyes are darker than ever. She looks tired and vulnerable, the way Daniel looks when he wakes up from a bad dream. Seeing her, I don't even feel mad anymore. I mostly feel sorry for her.

She hasn't noticed me yet, and for a split second, I almost change my mind. Maybe there's some way we can get things back on track. Maybe I should at least try. But then I look at the screen of her laptop and see Everett's face, and I know I might as well tell the easy lie. She's not going to change.

Mom looks up. "How are you feeling?" she asks quietly.

"Not so great," I tell her. "I think I may have gotten sick last night."

"You don't remember?"

I shake my head. "Not really. Someone must have spiked the punch at the party." There's one big advantage to having a mother who's completely checked out from life on Earth. Any other mother would already have called Eric's parents to scream about serving alcohol to minors. At least I don't have to worry about that.

Sure enough, Mom doesn't even mention the alcohol. Instead, she says, "So you don't remember what you said yesterday?"

"Nope."

"I think . . . maybe we need to talk about it anyway," she says uncertainly.

I sigh. "Okay, go ahead."

Mom looks down, winding her braid around her hand. "You told me you felt like I had failed you and Daniel, and put all the burden of parenting on you. That was really hard for me to hear. But the more I thought about it, the more I realized that you were right to feel that way. I have depended on you a lot because I've been so busy." She looks up at me, her eyes slick with tears. "But, Rooney, being a parent to you and Daniel is all I think about, every day. Once we leave here, the things that seem so important right now just aren't going to matter anymore. But other things, things you probably haven't even thought about, are going to be really important. And then you'll see that I truly have been thinking about our family all this time."

She turns her laptop toward me. "Look. I want you to see what I've been working on." She clicks on a folder labeled DEPARTURE PLANNING. There are dozens of documents inside, all with titles like "Final Cleanse," "Plan for Day 1," and "Six-Month Plan." She starts opening one document after another and showing them to me. The one titled "Hwaral: Questions" includes headers like "Zero-gravity issues," "Sustenance," "Education," and "Travel time," and then each of those has a bunch of bullet points below it. As my eyes flit across the pages, I can feel the hairs standing up on my arms. This is so much crazier than I had even imagined.

I never thought about what she was doing on her computer all that time. I figured she was just surfing around the NWS website and maybe chatting with other Next Worlders. But as she opens up all these documents, I realize what she's saying is true. She may not be helping much here on Earth, but if there actually was a Next World, she'd probably be named Mother of the Year there.

There's a tiny part of me that aches for her. The colossal wasted effort, the misplaced hopes, the life destroyed . . . my throat feels raw with it. But a bigger part of me wants to grab her by the shoulders and shake her until she comes to her senses. Her life isn't the only one she's ruined.

"You see?" she says, snapping me out of my thoughts. "All I do is work to make sure you and Daniel have a future. I'm sorry if I've lost track of the present, sweetie, but you have to trust me. You'll see. After the seventeenth, it will all be worth it."

"Okay, Mom," I say, exhausted. There's no sense arguing with her. In her head, she's already living on a different planet. It would be like trying to argue with a Martian.

"I'm sorry, Rooney," she says again. "I didn't know you were so upset. But now that I know, I promise I'm going to do better. You don't have to be the parent anymore. I'm going to take care of everything." Suddenly, she gives an excited little gasp. "That reminds me," she says, and practically skips over to the oven. When she turns around, she has a plate in her hand and she's beaming at me. "I saved you some pancakes! See, I can do both. I can plan for our future and be a better mom here on Earth, too. It's just for a few more weeks, but I promise I'll do better. Okay?"

She hands me the plate and watches as I fork a bite into my mouth.

Daniel's right. The pancakes are delicious. He's too little to remember, but for me, one bite is all it takes. Sunday mornings in New York. Daniel sitting in his high chair, his face covered in syrup, his sticky hands reaching for the fork as Mom laughs and steers another bite into his mouth. The happy, safe feeling of being home, and everybody getting along, even if it's only temporary. So different from the way it is now, it's hard to believe we were even the same family.

By the time I finish the pancakes, Mom is back on her computer. She barely looks up when I leave the room.

three

A few hours later, the doorbell rings, and my heart starts pounding. There's only one person that could be: the person I've been thinking about all afternoon instead of doing homework. Sure enough, a few seconds later, Mom calls upstairs, "Rooney, Mercer is here!"

I was hoping I wouldn't have to deal with this until Monday. I don't have a clue what I'm going to say to him. Lying to my mother was one thing, but lying to Mercer is another story. If I fake my way through this, he'll just be another person who doesn't see the real me.

Plus, there's something else: If I pretend the kiss never happened, it will probably never happen again.

"Rooney?" Mom calls again. "Did you hear me? Mercer is waiting for you."

I check myself in the mirror on my way down the stairs. *Stop being such a freak*, I tell myself. *It's only Mercer.* But after last night, I'm not sure what that means anymore.

"Hey." Mercer smiles unconvincingly and something crumples inside me.

"Hey."

"Want to go for a walk?"

"Sure." Grabbing my coat and scarf from the hall closet gives my hands some time to stop shaking. "I'll be back in time to make dinner," I tell Mom.

"Oh, no, sweetie, don't worry about that," she says. "I'll make dinner tonight! I promised, remember?"

"Okay. See you later, then."

Out of habit, we head toward the park, our feet shuffling through the dead leaves on the side of the road. The longer we walk without saying anything, the more the awkwardness starts to weigh me down. Finally, I can't stand it anymore. "Thanks for, uh, getting me home last night," I say.

"Sure," he says. "How are you feeling?"

"Not too bad. I got lucky and puked most of it up after the screaming fight with my mom."

Mercer raises his eyebrows. "What happened?"

"Oh, she tried getting all parental with me when she figured out I was drunk. And then I let her have it."

"What did you say?"

"I basically told her she was a terrible mother. And then she cried, and I went upstairs and hurled."

"Wow. Sounds like a mess."

"Pretty much."

He nods his head thoughtfully. "You know what? Good for you."

I look at him, surprised. "Seriously? I get drunk and scream at my mother and you're congratulating me?"

"Okay, maybe not for getting drunk. But you've been mad at her for years, and you never say anything. Maybe now that she knows how you feel, things will get better. She said she was making dinner tonight. That's a start, right?"

"I guess."

It's a beautiful afternoon, clear and crisp, and the park is glowing orange, yellow, and red. The long, slanting light is making all the angles of his face stand out in a way that sends a sharp pain right into my chest. *Get a grip, Rooney*, I tell myself. *It's not happening.*

"Anyway," Mercer says as we climb onto a picnic table, "I'm proud of you for telling her how you feel. Maybe next time you can do it sober."

"Thanks for the support, pal." I give his arm a light punch, and instantly feel self-conscious about touching him.

A woman pushing a stroller smiles at us, and I can tell she thinks we're a couple. Everybody has always assumed that about us. I used to think it was funny, but suddenly, it doesn't seem like a joke.

"Listen, Rooney, there's something I need to ask you." He looks just as nervous as I feel.

"Is it about the . . . about me kissing you?" I ask, trying to just get it over with.

"Well, sort of. Skyler and I were talking last night, and . . ."

Her name hits me with a nasty little jolt. "Yeah, you two talked for a long time." *How could I have been so stupid? Of course he didn't want to kiss me. He'd just spent the whole night talking to Skyler. He probably didn't even want to leave the party, but I ruined his plans.*

"Yeah. Anyway, what I wanted to know was . . . did the kiss . . . you know, mean anything?"

"You mean, am I in love with you?" I say, too fast and too loud. I sound spiky as hell. *Why am I acting like this?*

"No, I just mean . . . I didn't want to . . ."

Oh, God, is that pity in his eyes? "Don't worry about it. You saw how drunk I was. I barely even remember it. Okay?"

The words come out in a rush, and Mercer watches me, quietly appraising. "Okay," he finally says.

And then, with all the vicious voices in my head egging me on, I proceed to put the cherry on top of this humiliation sundae. "You know what?" I say, my teeth clenched in a terrible imitation of a smile, my eyes burning with held-in tears. "You should totally ask Skyler out. She's obviously into you. You two would be perfect together."

"You think so?" He's not even making eye contact with me anymore. "And you wouldn't mind?"

"Why would I?"

When I get home, Mom is standing by the stove stirring a pot of something. She's even wearing an apron, for God's sake. "It's just pasta and sauce from a jar tonight," she says apologetically, "but I'll go shopping tomorrow and make something really yummy."

The last thing in the world I feel like doing is eating, but she looks so desperate to please that I don't have the heart to say I'm not hungry. She and Daniel keep sneaking looks at me as we set the table. I manage to hold it together through most of dinner, and even tell her the food tastes good, but in my head I'm just counting the seconds.

I've almost made it through my plate of spaghetti when Daniel turns his enormous eyes on me. "Are you all right?" he asks, so gently that it completely undoes me.

"I'm fine," I manage to gasp out, and then I drop my fork on the table, bolt up the stairs, slam my door, and proceed to cry my face off.

On Sunday, I spend much too much time thinking about what I should have said to Mercer, whether things might have turned out differently if I'd been honest with him. But every time I think maybe there's still a chance to turn things around, I picture him whispering into Skyler's perfect little shell of an ear, and another tidal wave of mortification crashes over me.

By Monday I've decided that the only way to survive this is to act completely normal. When I see Mercer carrying his tray over to me at lunch, I force myself to smile and wave just like any other day. It feels like hell.

"Hey," he says as he slides in across from me.

"Hey."

If this were a normal day, we'd start joking and he'd make his carrot sticks dance or something, and next thing we'd know, lunch would be over. But today I can't think of a single thing to laugh about, and he seems just as uncomfortable. I'm practically choking on my sandwich when Skyler appears out of thin air. "Hey, guys!" she says, flashing her toothpaste-commercial teeth. "Mind if I sit with you?"

"Great," Mercer says, making room.

"Great," I echo.

Skyler squeezes in next to us. "How are you feeling?" she asks me. "You looked like you were hurting pretty bad on Friday."

"I'm fine," I say with as much finality as two words can hold.

"Oh, good! I was worried about you." She gives me another dazzling smile, and then turns to Mercer. The two of them start talking about something hilarious that happened during rehearsal last week, and I try to nod and laugh when they laugh, but all I want to do is run away.

"I just remembered," I say at the first break in the conversation. "Mrs. Fisher asked me to help her with something before next period."

"With what?" Mercer asks.

"Oh, it's not important. I'll see you later." By the time I'm five steps away, they're laughing again. I doubt they even remember I was there. The last thing I see before the cafeteria door closes behind me is Skyler looking at Mercer like he's a giant slice of birthday cake.

I spend the last ten minutes of lunch period in a bathroom stall with a wet paper towel over my eyes, trying to fight off the red blotches that sprout all over my face when I cry.

After that, it seems like wherever Mercer goes, Skyler's sure to follow. Instead of two of us at lunch, now we're a threesome. Mercer still comes by the Connection to study every now and then, but it feels like he's only doing it to prove a point. I know he'd rather be with her.

Lying in bed at night, I compulsively inventory all the ways Skyler is the exact opposite of me. Her honey-colored hair. Her tiny frame and cute little clothes. Her "killer" flute. The way she's always smiling. I can't even blame Mercer for choosing her. She's like human sunlight. But that's not even the worst part. The worst part is, Skyler Jamison is really . . . *really* . . . nice. Like, toothachingly nice. A total sweetheart.

I want to choke her.

NOVEMBER

one

Eight days until D-Day.

As far as I'm concerned, it can't come soon enough. I keep telling myself: Just a few more days until I get my life back. Just a few more days until November 17.

When I get home tonight, the kitchen smells like roasted chicken, and Mom and Daniel are sitting at the table, waiting for me. I know I should be happy that she's finally acting like a mom, but it just makes me even madder.

It doesn't help that she and Daniel have been getting chummier with every passing day. It's not just the meals, although even I have to admit Mom's cooking is a whole lot better than my canned soup and sandwiches. It's things like bedtime. Daniel never shares his stories with me anymore. Now he and Mom shut themselves in his bedroom and listen to lectures on the Next World site. I know because I can hear Everett's voice coming from under the door.

I sit down at the table and Mom makes a big show of serving up a whole chicken, potatoes, squash, and salad. She probably didn't even notice she spent a week of my pay on one meal. *Just eight days to go.*

I take a few bites of chicken, but my mouth is so dry that I can barely chew it. I'm about to clear my plate when Mom says, "Guys, there's something I need to talk to you about. Tomorrow night, I have to go to one last meeting, so I won't be able to have dinner with you. But I'll make something for you before I go."

"I can handle dinner," I say, but she shakes her head.

"No, sweetie. I should never have asked that of you. And I promise, after this meeting, I'm all yours. This next week is incredibly important, and I want you to know you're going to have my full attention."

Great, I think, but Daniel looks like he just won the lottery.

"There's something else we need to talk about," Mom says. "Tomorrow is going to be your last day of school . . ."

"Tomorrow's only the tenth," I interrupt. "We still have over a week to go."

"We have a lot to do to get ready."

I shake my head hard. "I have two tests on Friday. I can't screw up my grades. And Daniel can't skip school either."

She and Daniel both look at me with wide eyes. "But you have to," Mom says. "You need to prepare."

I push my chair away from the table. "You can prepare," I say. "We're going to school."

Her voice is getting higher and higher. "But I showed you all those lists. We need to focus now. You can't be distracted by your friends, and classes . . ."

I carry my plate to the sink and turn on the faucet without looking at her. "Forget it, Mom," I say. "You can do whatever you want, but Daniel and I aren't going to mess up our whole year for you."

I hear a chair scraping the floor, and Daniel shouts, "You can't talk for me, Rooney!" I turn to see him standing with his fists clenched, his face a white mask of anger. He runs toward the doorway, then spins around to shout at me. "Maybe you don't want to Depart, but I do! And I'm staying home with Mom so I'll be prepared!" He pounds upstairs and slams the door to his room.

Mom and I look at each other, then we both run after him. I get to the door first. "Daniel, can I come in?"

"Go away!" he yells.

I lower my voice. "I'm sorry, Daniel. I shouldn't have spoken for you. Can I please come in and talk about it?"

"I don't want to talk to you, Rooney. I only want to talk to Mom!"

It's as simple as that, and it takes the wind right out of me. Mom puts a hand on my back, and I'm so stunned that I don't even shake it off. "He doesn't mean it. Let me talk to him," she says, and slips into Daniel's room. I stand there, shaking, wondering if I should listen at the door. My first thought is to call Mercer, since he'll know what to do, but then I remember that Mercer's not exactly waiting around for my calls these days. So I go to my room, lock the door, and shove my face into my pillow.

Breathe, I tell myself. *Calm down. He doesn't mean it.* But as the seconds turn into minutes, I feel myself getting sucked deeper and deeper into the darkness. Daniel and Mercer have been the two most important people in my life for as long as I can remember. And now Skyler's taken Mercer away, and Mom's taken Daniel, and there's nothing left for me. There's no one left in the world for me.

It takes a solid twenty minutes of self-pity before I realize that's not entirely true. When I finally creep out of my room, I can still hear voices down the hall, so I go grab Mom's computer and lock myself back in my room. If she's going to steal my lifeline, she can't blame me for borrowing hers.

Since September, Dad and Carol have been keeping up a steady stream of emails. Reading them has been like getting news bulletins from the Island of Normal People. It's given me hope that there are better things ahead for me and for Daniel. I open a few of the emails now and read them again, trying to rekindle what I felt the first time I read them, but the magic has sort of worn off. Tonight, I need more than words on a screen. So I click CALL.

After just a few rings, Dad's face fills my screen. "Marina? Is everything all right?"

"Hi, Dad. Yeah, I'm okay."

"Oh! Good! Well, I'm glad you called." His eyes flick downward. "You know, I can't see you. Is something wrong with your computer's camera?"

"It doesn't work. It's pretty old."

"Oh, well, that's all right. We'll just kick it old school." He looks uncertain for a second, like he wishes he could take back his lame line.

"Maybe next week I'll send you a telegram," I offer, and he grins and looks more comfortable.

"Thanks for your emails," he says. "Carol and I have been thinking about you so much. And Daniel, too, of course . . ."

"Yeah. Things have been . . . interesting around here lately. How are you guys doing? How's Carol?" I ask, easing gratefully into the safe harbor of small talk.

"Do you want to talk to her? I know she'd love to hear your voice!"

"Sure. That would be nice."

"Come on, let's go find her," Dad says. His face disappears as he starts walking with the computer. The room he's in looks like a tiny library, with shelves full of books and a comfortable-looking leather chair.

"Nice room," I say.

His face peeks around the side of the screen. "Oh! Yeah, this is . . . Well, this is the extra room. It's small, but you know, we could fit a bed in here if . . . well, depending on how things go."

Since my first email, neither of us has ever come right out and used the word *custody* when we've talked about Daniel. I think Dad likes the idea as much as I do, but I don't want to push now, with everything up in the air. Better to wait until after the seventeenth, after the baby comes, after things settle down. There's no rush. I'm not going anywhere until next year anyway.

"So . . . Where's Carol?" I ask.

"Right!" he says briskly. "Let's go find her. I'll give you a tour." He walks us down a hall and into another room. "Here's the living-dining area. And the kitchen's back there." He stops in front of a half-closed door. "This will be the baby's room, but we're taking our time setting that up."

He taps lightly on another door. "Honey?" The door swings open and the first thing I see is Carol lying on a bed with her back propped up against some pillows. There's a book resting on her stomach, which is probably twice as big as it was in September. "I have a surprise," Dad says. "Guess who I've got here."

She puts the book down. "Mom, you have to click the button for the camera, remember?"

Dad laughs. "It's not your mother," he says. He looks into the camera. "Say hello."

"Hi, Carol," I say. "How are you feeling?"

Her eyes light up. "Marina? Is that you? Why can't I see you?"

"Webcam's out," Dad says. "She can see us, though."

"Oh, it's so great to hear your voice," Carol says.

The camera jostles out of focus, I hear Dad say, "Hang on," and then I'm looking at the two of them sitting side by side. The room looks bright and warm, and familiar somehow. Then I realize they're sitting on Mom and Dad's old bed. I can't believe I didn't recognize that massive wooden headboard right away. I once got in big trouble for scratching a little *M* into it with a nail file I found in Mom's bedside table. I don't know why he would keep that bed, even if it is a family heirloom.

"So how are you?" Carol asks. "Your dad and I were just talking about you."

"I'm okay," I lie, determined to keep this part of my life clean and untouched as long as I can. "How are you? How's everything with the baby?"

"Well, aside from the fact that I'm big as a house, the baby and I are both doing great. Although she's been kicking me a lot lately."

"What does it feel like?"

She rests her hand on her stomach, looking thoughtful. "Really hard to describe. I guess the closest thing would be someone poking you."

"Like this?" Dad asks, poking her gently in the belly.

"Sort of, only from the inside," Carol says, laughing.

People always talk about pregnant women glowing. I never understood that. Mostly, they look big and kind of uncomfortable to me. But Carol really does seem like she's lit up from inside. It takes a minute to dawn on me: She looks happy. I guess I haven't spent a lot of time with happy people.

Watching the two of them makes me hopeful and sad all at once. The bubble they're in is so bright and shiny that I can almost feel it around me, too.

Almost, but not quite.

"So, Marina, how are you doing, for real?" Carol asks gently. "It's only a few more days now, huh?"

Instantly, my throat tightens again and my eyes start to sting. Good thing they can't see me. I pinch the bridge of my nose hard and stare up at the light on my ceiling. When I'm pretty sure I can talk without my voice shaking, I say, "Things are all right, I guess. School is going okay. Home is weird, but that's nothing new."

"Can you say more about that? What's going on with your mother?" Dad asks.

The last time I clued Dad in on my life, he and Mom ended up screaming at each other on Forty-Third Street. But right now, I just want someone to be on my side. So I tell them about Mom's lists and Daniel's new obsession with Harmonization. By the time I get to the part about staying home from school, Dad is scowling and Carol's looking worried.

I start to tell them what Daniel said tonight, but my throat tightens up again, so I just say, "I think Daniel has it worse than I do. He really wants to believe all of this."

Dad and Carol exchange a look. "Is there anything we can do to make things easier for you?" Carol asks. "I know you don't want us to go there, but maybe you could come stay here next week?"

For a half second, I actually let myself consider it. I would love to run away to New York, but I can't leave Daniel behind. He may not be talking to me tonight, but next week, someone's going to need to pick up the pieces. "Thanks," I say, "but I don't think there's anything you can do right now. We just have to get through it."

Dad's mouth is pinched down at the corners. "I swear, Marina, I'm not looking to make things harder for you, but I can't just sit here and let your mother turn your lives upside down. I feel like I'm failing the two of you all over again!"

"Honey," Carol says quietly, "we've talked about this. The last thing Marina needs is you getting Anneliese even more worked up. We're just going to have to let this play out for now. And then later, after the baby comes . . ."

I nod, then remember they can't see me. "Carol's right," I say. "Dad, I appreciate that you want to help, but you talking to Mom is just going to make things worse."

Carol suddenly looks like she's remembered something. "What about Thanksgiving? Why don't you come spend it with us? You and Daniel, I mean."

"Thanks. It's hard to know what things are going to be like in two weeks. But I'll definitely think about it."

"Sure," Dad says. "No pressure. We just want you to know that you're welcome here."

"Always," Carol adds.

Dad clears his throat. "Listen, next week is going to be rough. I don't know what we can do to help you and Daniel get through it, but if there's anything you need, we're here for you. Anything at all. Okay?"

"Thanks, guys," I say. He's right: There probably isn't anything they can do, but knowing that they're there does make things a tiny bit better. "So, uh, I guess I'll talk to you in a couple of weeks. Unless they don't have video-calling in the Next World, that is."

Dad's eyebrows twitch, but Carol laughs. "Sounds like a plan," she says.

Dad looks into the camera. "Good luck, Marina. We love you." And then they're gone.

"I love you, too?" I say to the blank screen.

Is it true? I have no idea. More than ever, I feel like I don't even know what love is. I love Daniel, and he won't talk to me. I love Mercer, and he's with someone else. Mom is constantly telling me she loves me, and I'm supposed to love her back because she's my mother, but generally I just want to scream at her.

As far as I can tell, love is mostly a big mess.

But I'm still glad he said it.

Hours later, I'm woken up by a sound like an animal howling, high-pitched and wild. I go over to the window, but the sound isn't coming from outside, so I open my door and listen. It's coming from Daniel's room.

When I tap on his door, the sound cuts out like someone hit MUTE. I tap again, then open the door a crack. "Daniel?" I whisper. "I'm coming in, okay?"

"Go away, Rooney," he says, his voice choked.

"No, I'm not going away. You can be mad at me tomorrow if you want, but right now you have to talk to me."

I step into his room. Daniel sniffles loudly. "Wow, that was pretty juicy. Hang on." I go get a wad of toilet paper from the bathroom and hand it to him. "Here, blow your nose."

After he does, I hold out his trash can for him, then sit on his bed and put a hand on the bump that must be his shoulder. He gives a little twitch, like he's trying to shake me off, but it feels pretty half-hearted, and I leave my hand where it is. "What's going on, Bug? What's with the tears?"

"Nothing," Daniel says, his voice muffled under his blanket. "You'll think it's stupid."

"Well, why don't you tell me anyway?"

"It's just a book," he says.

"What book?" I scan his crowded bookshelves, then notice one on the floor near the bed. "This one?"

Daniel lowers the covers an inch and gives a tiny nod. "Can I have more toilet paper?"

"Sure, hang on." This time I come back with the roll and balance it on top of his head. I'm hoping I'll get a laugh out of him, but he just grabs it, unwinds a few sheets, and blows his nose again.

I look at the cover of the book. It's about Easter Island, but it's not the one from a few weeks ago. That one looked like an adventure story, but this book is definitely not for kids. I flip through the pages to a section in the middle with black-and-white pictures, a lot of small type, and some charts. It's hard to see how this book could make anyone cry, unless it was from boredom. "So what about the book?" I ask him.

"I told you, you'll think it's stupid," he says, but he turns over and sits up a little.

"I don't think anything about you is stupid. Just tell me, okay?"

He's quiet for a little bit. Then he wipes his nose on another piece of TP and mumbles, "It's complicated."

"That's all right. We haven't had a book talk in a while. So it'll just be making up for lost time." He glances over at me, and I wish I hadn't brought it up. "So this is your second book about Easter Island, right?"

"Yeah," he says without looking at me. "Miss Klein found it for me."

"Well, last I heard, they were canoeing across the ocean," I remind him.

He takes a deep breath. "Okay. Well, they found the island, and everything was good. There were tons of trees, so they could build canoes and go fishing, so they had plenty to eat. And the different tribes settled on different parts of the island, and then they'd compete with each other by building these big stone statues."

I point to a grainy picture. "Like these?"

"Yeah."

"Okay. So far, that doesn't sound so sad."

Daniel shakes his head. "No, that's not the sad part."

"So what happened?"

"They just did what people do. They fished for their food, and they had a bunch of babies, and the tribes got bigger and bigger. And they kept building the statues, and they cut down the trees to build more canoes and stuff . . ."

"Uh-huh . . ."

"So they were just like us." He stops and looks at me like he's made an important point.

"How is that like us? We don't build big stone heads."

"No, but if we lived there, we'd do what everybody else was doing."

"Okay, so let's assume we'd be fishing and building statues. What would be so bad about that?"

Daniel opens and closes his mouth a few times and his eyes fill with tears again. Finally, he says, "People . . . We use everything up, and we take everything over. And we think we won't run out. But they ran out."

"Ran out of where?"

"No, they ran out . . . of everything. They used everything up, and then they didn't have any more, and . . ." Daniel's voice cracks.

"Bug, slow down," I say. "I don't get why you're so upset about this."

"They *ate* each other!" Daniel whispers. The tears start pouring down his face again, and he scrubs at them with a wad of toilet paper. "They ran out of food, so they ate each other."

It's so out of left field that I almost laugh. "Is that what you're so upset about? You've read about cannibals before. What about that pirate book a few years ago?"

"That was just a dumb story. But this actually happened. To *people*."

"But it was a long time ago. And a totally different place. It's not like that could happen here."

"How do you know?"

"I just know, okay? Look, I promise, no matter how hungry I am, I won't eat you." I squeeze his arm. "There's not enough meat on you to make a decent meal anyway. You're barely a snack."

But Daniel doesn't laugh. He doesn't even crack a smile. "You just want to make jokes! But you don't know. Maybe it could happen again! Maybe it *is* happening again, and we just can't see it. Like they couldn't see it. They just kept chopping down trees until there weren't any left, and it was too late!"

The neck of his pajamas is turning dark with tears. When he was little, I just had to distract him or get him laughing and he'd forget whatever was upsetting him. But this is different. This isn't a scraped knee or playground teasing, and I don't know how to fix it.

"I'm sorry, Daniel," I say. "I didn't mean to treat it like a joke. I just don't understand why you're worried about this now. But I'm trying, okay? Can you explain it to me?"

I pat his back while he blows his nose again. Eventually, his breathing steadies. When he finally speaks, his voice is flat. "I know you don't believe Everett. But Mom and I want to go with the Hwaral. I don't want to stay here and wait for all the trees to get cut down."

Everett. If he was here right now, I'd punch him in the nose. "Look, Daniel," I say, "I know the world is kind of a mess. But we'll figure it out before it's too late. People always do."

"No, they don't! That's just what people tell themselves so they don't have to worry about it. The Easter Islanders didn't figure it out!"

"I guess I just believe something different. I believe everything's going to work out all right."

"How? How is it going to work out?" Daniel asks fiercely.

"Smart people like you will come up with solutions. And they'll plant more trees before it's too late."

"It's not just the trees, Rooney! And anyway, Everett says it's already too late."

"Well, that's just one man's opinion."

"No. It's not. Mom and I believe it, too, and so do lots of other people."

"But lots of people *don't* believe it, Daniel!" I hear my voice rising, and I try to get myself back under control, but I can feel the irritation leaking out all over the place. "Just like you didn't use to believe it. So why are you getting yourself so worked up about this?"

"Because I want to Depart!" He's crying so hard, there's snot bubbling out of his nose. "And if you won't come with us, then we can't go. Mom says you'll change your mind, but I know you won't! And I don't want to go without you!"

And just like that, all my irritation is gone. I haven't lost Daniel. Not by a long shot.

"Shhhh, it's okay," I whisper, putting my arms around him. "It'll all be okay. You don't have to go anywhere without me." I'm not even sure what I'm saying. I just want him to stop worrying.

"So you'll Depart with us? You'll Harmonize with us and everything?" Daniel asks through hiccuppy little breaths.

"I'll tell you what," I say. "I promise you that . . . if you and Mom Depart, I'll go with you. All right?"

"And will you stay home from school so we can all prepare together?"

Now he's pushing it, and he knows it. I put my hands on his shoulders and hold him away from me a little so I can look him in the eyes. "No. I'm going to school next week. And you should, too. But I won't give you a hard time if you decide to stay home."

"But what about the seventeenth? We all have to be together so Mom can Harmonize for us."

"Fine, Daniel. I'll stay home on the seventeenth. That's my best offer. Take it or leave it."

He looks up at me, his little face blotchy and tearstained, and all I can think is *This is just the beginning*. The next week is going to be brutal. But at least Daniel is talking to me again. And once the seventeenth is over, maybe we can finally start figuring out our future.

two

Seven days until D-Day.

Lunchtime has gotten so bad that I don't even go into the cafeteria anymore. Mrs. Fisher has been letting me hang out in her classroom during lunch period. It's a huge relief not to have to watch Mercer and Skyler drooling over each other, or fend off any more of Skyler's endless attempts to "include" me. I'd much rather be alone than be their third wheel. Still, sitting in an empty room studying while everyone else in the world is laughing, gossiping, and flirting doesn't feel that great either. I even think about asking to sit with some of my old crowd from the *Sentinel*, but with Departure Day looming over my head, I just don't have much small talk in me.

I know I can't hide in there forever. I'll deal with it after the seventeenth.

Mom and Daniel look up from the computer when I walk in tonight, and Mom gives me one of her panicky little smiles.

"Oh! Rooney, I'm so glad you're here! We were just talking about you," she says. "Guess what I made for dinner tonight!"

"I don't know, Mom."

"Lasagna!" Either she's totally oblivious or she's deliberately ignoring my mood. "And Daniel has something he'd like to show you."

"What is it, Bug?" I ask, dropping into the chair next to him.

Daniel turns the laptop toward me. "We're working on our good-bye lists," he says, his voice almost as breathy and nervous as Mom's. "Do you want to do one?"

"Good-bye lists?" I repeat, even though I should know better.

"All the people we need to say good-bye to before we Depart."

I reach over and brush his bangs out of his eyes. "Daniel, have you been saying good-bye to everyone at school?"

He nods.

I look at the screen. "Who's Jennie at the Y?"

"She was my enameling teacher last summer."

"And Miss Klein . . . She's the kids' librarian, right?"

"Yeah."

"So you've kind of been telling everyone in town we're leaving, huh?"

"Not everyone. Just my friends," he says a little huffily.

Mom reaches for my hand. "You should tell your friends, too. They're going to miss you."

I get up from the table. "I don't have any friends. Call me when dinner's ready."

Three days until D-Day.

Daniel's supposed to spend Sunday with Max, but he's back home after only a couple of hours. When Daniel climbs out of the car, he and Max don't even look at each other. I'm guessing the good-bye scene didn't go so well. Stefanie waves apologetically as she pulls out of the driveway.

That evening, I'm expecting another "greatest hits" meal, but Mom tells us we're starting a pre-Departure cleansing regimen. She puts a plate of steamed broccoli in front of each of us. I wait for her to put out the rest of the meal, but she and Daniel just start eating.

"So . . . All we're having for dinner is broccoli?" I ask.

"Oh, no!" Mom says with a little uneasy laugh. "There's grapefruit for dessert!"

I'm about to ask her if she's completely lost her mind when I catch sight of Daniel's face. He's frozen with his fork halfway to his mouth, looking at me pleadingly. As usual, it completely deflates me. Instead of yelling at her, I shovel the broccoli into my mouth as fast as I can.

By ten thirty, my stomach has started making crazy gurgling noises and I feel like I might pass out from hunger. I tiptoe downstairs, hoping Mom's asleep. I bought a big box of crackers and some peanut butter a week ago, and I open up the cabinet where they should be, but there's nothing in there. I open a few other doors, just in case they got moved, but they're all empty, too. I look in the fridge and it finally hits me: Mom's tossed all my food. There's only grapefruit and vegetables, and some strange packets with the NWS logo on them in one of the drawers.

Now I don't care if I wake her up. In fact, I'm sort of hoping I do. I go through the cabinets again, slamming the doors as each one turns up empty. That does the trick: A few seconds later, she's in the doorway blinking up at me.

"What is it, sweetie? Why aren't you in bed?" she asks.

"I'm too hungry to sleep," I tell her. "Where's all the food I bought last week?"

Mom puts her hand to her mouth. "I had to throw it out," she whispers. "That's the protocol before the cleansing regimen."

"You threw out all the food I bought?"

"It's the protocol," she says again, her voice quavering.

"But, Mom, I bought that food with my own money."

"I'm sorry, I should have told you. Everett says that any food that isn't on the cleansing regimen presents too much of a temptation."

"Great. What else is on this protocol, Mom?" I ask, my voice just barely below a shout. "I'd appreciate it if you'd fill me in on the whole plan. Like what are these things?" I drop the mystery packets on the counter in front of her.

Mom shows me the labels with shaky hands. "Those are for tomorrow and Tuesday. To help us cleanse our bodies and focus our thoughts."

"My thoughts are already focused. On how hungry I am."

She grabs my hand in both of hers and squeezes it. "I know, sweetheart, the first day is really tough. But I promise, by Wednesday, you'll feel so light your body will want to float up all on its own!"

I stomp out of the kitchen. I can't buy more crackers at this hour, so I just go back upstairs and listen to my stomach rumbling until I finally fall asleep.

Two days to go.

Since there's nothing in the house for breakfast, I decide to head to school early on Monday to buy something in the cafeteria. As I'm putting on my coat, Mom intercepts me.

"Wait, Rooney, you can't leave yet," she says. "You need to do the next step of the cleanse." She dumps one of the DAY 1 packets into a glass, stirs in some water, and holds it out to me. I'm staring at her, thinking I might throw this orangey-brown witch's brew in her face, when I hear footsteps coming down the stairs. Daniel's still in his pajamas since he's not going to school, and his hair is sticking up in clumps all over his head.

"Oh, good, we can all do it together!" Mom fills two more glasses. "Down the hatch! Try to do it all in one long drink, like this." She takes a deep breath, gulps it down, and forces a smile.

"Let's do it on the count of three," Daniel says.

The stuff smells like Indian food, but not in a good way. I was hungry a minute ago, but now the smell makes me retch a little. "God, Mom," I say. "Are you seriously asking us to drink this first thing in the morning?"

"It's not so bad," she says unconvincingly. "Just toss it back as fast as you can."

Daniel gives me another imploring look. "Fine," I say. "One, two . . . three!" Even with my nose plugged, I almost gag as it hits my tongue, but I manage to choke it down.

"You guys did great," Mom says, hugging Daniel. "The next one should be super easy!"

There isn't going to be a next one, I think as I yank on my coat.

"Are you sure you won't stay home with us?" Mom asks.

"I'm going," I say. It would actually be a giant relief to avoid the social black hole of school, but I'm not about to tell her that. As I walk toward the door, Mom hands me a paper bag. She hasn't packed lunch for us in years, so at first I don't realize what

I'm holding. But then I look in the bag and discover another grapefruit and a bag of raw spinach.

"This is very important," she says. "You need to drink eight glasses of water today, and this is all you can eat. I'm sorry, sweetie, but it's only for a few more days. And, Rooney?" She waits for me to look her in the eyes. "If you change your mind about school, Daniel and I will be right here waiting for you. Okay?"

I wait until I'm around the corner, then chuck the spinach into the bushes. By the time I get to school, the burning in my throat has started to fade away, and a huge helping of French toast dippers from the cafeteria wipes out what's left. I eat every last bite, then get a waffle for good measure. I feel disgusting afterward, but it's worth it for the satisfaction of knowing that I've totally canceled out the cleanse.

Dinner tonight is even more pitiful than last night's. We each get a glass of some green drink that tastes like dirt, plus a bowl of steamed beets and kale. The only way I manage to swallow it is by thinking about the grilled cheese sandwich I had for lunch. I look over at Daniel, and I can see that he's struggling to clean his plate. He looks pale and he keeps blinking like the light is hurting his eyes.

"He needs some real food, Mom," I say. "Is this cleanse even safe for kids?"

That perks him right up. "I'm fine, Rooney," he says, and eats another beet. "Don't worry about me." I know for a fact he hates beets, but now he has something to prove. Well, so much for trying to stand up for him. We eat our grapefruits in silence, and as soon as he's finished, Daniel goes up to bed.

As I'm clearing the table, Mom plants herself in front of me. "Have you spoken with your father?"

"Why?"

"I just thought you'd want to say good-bye to him."

It's hardly worth the time to wash the dishes, considering how little food actually touched them, but it's a good excuse to avoid looking at her. "I've talked to him, yeah."

"How did he sound?"

"Normal."

She comes over and perches on the counter next to me. "Do you think he . . . has any regrets?"

"What do you mean?"

"You know. About not going with us. With you, I mean."

"I don't think so."

She sighs, then heads into the dark living room. A second later, I see the glow of the computer screen.

I wake up around midnight with a sharp pain in my gut. I try to go back to sleep, but the pain just gets worse. Then my stomach lets out a rumble and I realize I probably have about thirty seconds to get to the bathroom. By the time I'm through in there, the French toast, the grilled cheese, and everything else I've eaten in the last month has exited my digestive system. I guess the cleanse got the last laugh after all.

The last day.

In the morning, Mom watches as Daniel and I gulp down the DAY 2 drink. My stomach is so empty that my jeans feel loose, and Daniel is starting to look like a little scarecrow, but Mom doesn't seem to notice. "This is going to give you so much clarity," she says. Then she comes over and rests her sharp little chin on my shoulder. "I can't believe it's our last day. Try to remember every minute, sweetie. These will be your last memories of Earth."

Her fear, anxiety, and excitement are written all over her face. It's just so sad. She hasn't even been living her life here, just waiting to start over somewhere else. Before I can start to feel too bad for her, though, she hands me another brown paper bag. I can feel the weight of the grapefruit inside. As I walk out the door, she calls out, "And don't forget, sweetie. At least eight glasses of water, okay?"

I don't know whether it's the DAY 2 cleanse or starvation or what, but by the time I get to school, I'm feeling light-headed and unnaturally sharp. It's like the opposite of being drunk, like everyone but me is moving in slow motion. I feel like I could catch flies with my bare hands, or outrun the captain of the track team. In first period, I know the answer to every question, sometimes even before the teacher asks it. The feeling lasts until about lunchtime, and then I crash hard. I eat three slices of miserable cafeteria pizza in Mrs. Fisher's office and spend the rest of the afternoon fighting to stay awake.

At the end of the day, Mercer stops by my locker, alone for once.

"Where's Skyler?"

"She went ahead to practice."

"Is she allowed to do that by herself?"

Mercer plays it classy and pretends not to notice what a snot I'm being. "So tomorrow's the big day, huh?" he asks.

"Yup."

"Well, it's been great knowing you. Send me a postcard from the Next World when you get there."

"Ha, ha."

"Sorry. How are you, seriously? I feel like we haven't talked in weeks."

"Maybe because we haven't," I say, closing my locker door just a little too hard.

"Yeah, okay, I've been busy. But I'm not the only one, Rooney. I feel like you're always running off somewhere."

"Well, sorry. It just seems like you and Skyler don't really need any company."

Finally, I get a rise out of him. "But that's all you," he argues. "Skyler wants to spend time with you."

"Why?"

"What do you mean, 'why'? Because you're my best friend, dumbass. She wants you to like her."

Best friend. The words feel about as comforting as a knife in the back. "Why does she need me to like her? She already has you!" My voice echoes off every locker in the hall as Mercer gapes at me. "I have to go." I jam my books into my backpack and flee.

"Good luck tomorrow," he calls after me.

When I get to the Java Connection, Maddie starts getting ready to take off as usual. "You remember that I'm not coming in tomorrow, right?" I ask her.

"Yup," she says. "I remember." She doesn't put on her coat, just waits for me to finish ringing up a customer. "So," she says when the shop's empty.

"So," I say back. "What's up?"

She hesitates, and for a second I'm worried she's going to cut back on my shifts, since the afternoons have been so slow. But she says, "Look, I know it's none of my business, but I wanted to say . . . good luck tomorrow."

The deepest conversation Maddie and I have ever had was probably about ordering more skim milk, so at first I think she's just saying it because I'm taking the day off. But instead of her usual cheerful-but-tired expression, Maddie's looking at me with something an awful lot like pity.

I can feel the blood rushing to my face. "How did you know?"

"One of my girls goes to the day care where your mom used to work. Word kind of got around." She starts to pull on her coat. "Sorry, Rooney. Maybe I shouldn't have said anything. I just didn't want you to feel like you had to keep it secret."

"That's okay," I tell her. "I guess it was stupid to think people didn't know."

"Oh, sure, people know," Maddie says, then bites her lip. "I mean, it's no big deal. It's not like people talk about it all the time or anything."

Which obviously means exactly the opposite.

"So I was just wondering," she says with badly feigned nonchalance. "You only mentioned that you'll be out on Wednesday. But what about after that?"

"What do you mean?"

"Well, if your family is . . . leaving, I'll need to find a replacement for the afternoon shift."

"We're not leaving!" I sputter. "Look, my mom has some crazy ideas, but it's all going to be over tomorrow. And I definitely need this job. I have to take tomorrow off, but that's all."

Maddie raises her eyebrows. "Okay, sorry, I just wasn't sure. You don't need to worry. You've got this job for as long as you want it."

"Thanks," I say. "I definitely want it. I'll be back on Thursday."

"Okay." As she heads out the door, she calls, "Good luck, Rooney."

People keep saying that, but I don't see what luck has to do with any of this. I guess "good luck" is what people say when there's nothing else to say.

"Oh, thank goodness you're finally here," Mom says, even though it's exactly the same time I always get home. "I was so worried you'd be late. We're leaving any minute now."

"What do you mean?" I ask. "It's still the sixteenth. I thought nothing was supposed to happen until tomorrow."

"Not to Depart," Mom says. "Susan's coming to pick us up."

"What are you talking about? You didn't say anything about Susan."

"I didn't?" She looks flustered. "I was sure I had mentioned it to you. Well, that's not important now."

"But why is Susan picking us up?"

She looks at her watch. "We're spending the night at Susan and Roger's. Since we don't know the exact Departure time, we need to be in place a little early."

I've never once asked Mom about Departure Day. I didn't want to encourage her by talking about it. But when I did think about it, I just assumed we'd be at home. I even brought home a bunch of schoolbooks to keep me busy tomorrow. "I thought it was just going to be the three of us," I say. "Can't we stay here?"

"Oh, no. That would never work. We all need to be together, to combine our energy."

"Who's 'we all'?"

"The whole Northeast Chapter."

"So we're going to be spending the day with a bunch of strangers?"

"No, silly, they're not strangers. These are the people we're going to be spending the rest of our lives with!" Her voice is getting higher and tighter. "I'm sorry if I forgot to tell you, sweetie, but there's no time to discuss it now. Just leave your bag and go change into some comfortable clothes." She flaps her hands toward the staircase. "Go on, scoot!" A pair of headlights sweeps across the window. "Oh! She's here!"

"Hurry up, Rooney," Daniel urges.

I know in the end I'll do whatever Daniel asks, so I go up and change into sweatpants and a hoodie without arguing.

As the three of us walk out the door, I notice that Mom's left her little silver watch on the kitchen table. She told me that watch was a gift from her parents when she graduated from college. I don't think I've ever seen her without it before. And right next to it, the house keys are sitting in a sad little pile.

"Aren't you going to take those?" I ask.

"Why?" she asks. "We're never coming back here."

three

There are strange shapes on the lawn outside Susan and Roger's house, and at first I think they haven't put away their lawn furniture for the winter. But as the headlights sweep across, I can make out a couple of sofas, some big padded chairs, a coffee table, and even an ottoman.

"Why is there furniture outside?" I ask.

"Oh, we had to make room for the mats," Susan says, like this is the most natural thing in the world.

"So you put your furniture on the lawn?"

"Well, sure." She gives one of her barking laughs and squeezes out of the car. "We weren't going to put it on the roof."

"But what if someone takes it? Or what if it rains? It'll get ruined." Those couches are made of leather. They couldn't have been cheap.

Mom looks at me like I'm a very slow student. "Sweetie, what does it matter? It's not like Susan and Roger can take it with them!"

There's really no way to argue with any of this. *Just a few more hours*, I tell myself.

"Have any of the others arrived yet?" Mom asks after she's introduced Daniel to Roger.

"No, they'll mostly be coming early in the morning." Susan checks her watch. "Well, I reckon it's time for the last cleanse."

In the kitchen, she mixes up five packets of FINAL CLEANSE and passes them around. "Bottoms up, everybody!" she bellows. The powder this time is light pink, and smells sort of fruity. It crosses my mind that it might not be safe to drink it. I can just imagine the headline: "Mass Suicide in Suburbia." But I'm so hungry I almost don't care if it's poisoned. It's thick, and tastes a little like strawberries, so I try to imagine it's a milk shake.

"Mmm! That was tasty, wasn't it?" Mom chirps. "And it will maintain our electrolyte balance."

"What about food?" I ask. "I feel like I'm going to pass out."

She shakes her head and whispers, "Sorry, sweetie, no more food for us on this side. It's normal to feel a little light-headed. Don't worry. It will actually help you if you can just give your-self over to it." Susan is looking over at us, and I wonder if Mom's whispering because I've embarrassed her in front of her friend.

"Well, that's it for now," Susan says. "Why don't you all make yourselves comfortable?"

I follow Mom into a big room that was probably pretty nice when it had furniture in it. Now it looks more like a yoga studio, with a bunch of exercise mats lined up. Each mat has a name card on it. I find Mom's on one of three mats in the middle, and mine and Daniel's on either side of hers. I see a card for Anjelica, too, and Alice and Fred, the nice old couple from the trip.

"So we're all sleeping here tonight? On the floor?" I ask.

"It's just for a few hours," Mom says. "Sweetheart, this is our final preparation time. I really need you to be present now."

"I'm here, Mom," I say. My voice sounds whiny, but I don't care. She should be grateful I agreed to come along at all.

"I know you're here, physically," she says. "But I'm talking about being here mentally. It's time to stop judging and give yourself over to this. We have a little time before people get here. Won't you let me teach you some techniques for breaking those earthly ties?"

"I don't need any techniques."

She blinks up at me. "Oh, Rooney, I wish I could help you see through my eyes."

And I wish you could see through mine, I think.

I look at the mats again. "Why are Daniel and I on opposite sides? Can't we be next to each other?"

"It's because of the energy flow," Daniel pipes up. "Mom needs to be between us so she can Harmonize for us."

Of course Mom's going to be between us. It would have been nice if Daniel had at least wanted to be next to me. I lie down on my mat and close my eyes. Maybe if it looks like I'm asleep, everyone will just leave me alone.

Over the next hour or so, a few more people trickle into the house. Fred and Alice are among the first to arrive, wearing matching gray sweatpants. They both hug me, and Daniel, too, even though they've never met him before. I wonder who was on their good-bye list, whether there are kids and grandkids they think they'll never see again.

Anjelica is the next to arrive, alone. I don't ask her about her family. I was already pretty sure from reading the names on the mats, and now the look on her face tells me all I need to know. I try to beam *I'm sorry* messages at her with my eyes, but she's mostly staring at the floor.

Around ten o'clock, Susan brings in a pile of blankets. "You should all try to get some sleep. Fred, Alice, I'll show you up to your room. And remember, everybody, no more water from now on."

When everyone has a blanket, Mom turns off the lights. "Sweet dreams, everybody," she says. "Try to rest your minds. We have a lot of work to do tomorrow."

I lie there listening to the breathing of the people around me. Back in September, I thought the dormitory at NWS headquarters was the strangest place I'd ever slept, but the floor of this suburban living room leaves it in the dust.

It feels like I've been asleep for about fifteen minutes when Susan's voice is in my ears again. "Time to rise and shine, everybody," she says. "It's almost time for the Departure video!" It's still pitch-dark outside, and the light burns my eyes when she switches it on. I squint at my watch: four thirty in the morning. My mouth tastes like rotten cheese. I wish I'd thought to bring a toothbrush.

A few more carloads of people arrive and Mom and Susan show them to their mats. Alice and Fred come down looking kind of crumpled. Finally, when there are twenty-three of us crammed into the room, Roger fires up a laptop and Susan says, "Well, folks, it's good to see all your faces here this morning. Look around, everybody! This is going to be your family from now on. Any of you who haven't met yet, make sure you introduce yourselves after the Departure speech."

Roger clears his throat. "It's time," he says. An image comes up on their big TV screen. At first, all I can see is a plain room with a desk and a chair in it. But then Everett walks in, takes a seat, and stares into the camera.

"Good morning, friends," he says. "Wherever you are, it is early morning on November seventeenth. I so wish that I could be with each and every one of you today, but of course that's not possible. And for the safety of our movement, my location needs to be hidden, even from you, my family, on this all-important day."

His voice is just as smooth as ever. To me, it's like the feeling of something with too many legs crawling across my stomach. But I look over at Daniel, and for the first time in days, his cheeks are pink and his eyes are sparkling. It's the same look he used to get when I read him a story he loved.

"In the past year," Everett continues, "some of you have endured personal hardship, even ridicule, in order to spread Enlightenment in your communities. For that, you have my gratitude. But more importantly, you have the knowledge that you have given others a chance at salvation."

The camera zooms in so his face fills the screen. Even this close up, you can barely see a wrinkle in his skin. "In the short time that remains, I ask you to focus your thinking." He puts his fingers on his temples and his eyes drill into the screen. "Banish all thoughts of what you are leaving behind so that you may concentrate fully on where we are going. Whatever ties are keeping you on Earth must be severed here and now. Anyone whose past holds them back threatens to hold back the entire group."

I hear a sniffle across the room. Anjelica has her eyes closed and tears are dripping onto the yoga mat between her folded legs. I bet she's going to have to work harder than most people in this room to banish all thoughts of what she's leaving behind.

Everett is still talking, but I can't pay attention to what he's saying anymore. I feel terrible for Anjelica, plus my stomach is rumbling so loud I'm surprised people aren't staring. I wish I'd thought to grab something before I left work last night. Right now, even a stale bagel would seem like a feast.

Everyone in the room applauds, and I look up to see Roger turning the computer off. Then Susan says, "I don't know about you, but that just gave me chills! I can hardly believe Departure Day is finally here!"

She looks at her watch, then takes it off and puts it on the fireplace mantel. "Well, we have about an hour before sunrise," she says. "That should give everyone time to share any last thoughts with the group. I'm going to go ahead and start the ball rolling by saying that I am so honored to have been the head of the planning committee for the Northeast Chapter all these years, and I can't wait to go on serving you all in the Next World. And now let's hear from my fellow Harmonization Leaders. Mark, Anneliese, what would you like to say to the group?"

A shaggy-haired guy with a nice face waves from his mat in the middle of the room. "I guess I just want to ask everybody to be patient. We don't know how long it will be before we're called up, and that type of uncertainty can be pretty hard to deal with. If you start to get impatient, or lose your focus, just be gentle with yourself, and bring your attention back to the breathing. That's the most important thing."

"Anneliese? Anything you want to add?" Susan prompts.

"Thank you, Susan," Mom says, and I notice her voice doesn't sound high or shaky—she actually seems calm and relaxed for once. Daniel is staring up at her, looking so proud it almost hurts.

"It's hard for me to believe that it's finally today. I'm so full of emotions." Mom puts her hands on her chest. "I feel excited, and scared, and just . . . awestruck by this amazing opportunity. But most of all, I feel ready. And that's what I want to talk about."

She looks around the room. "Today, we'll succeed or fail together. As a group. Just like Everett said, if even one person is holding on to the Earth, our whole group could fail. It's not easy to let go of your whole life. But that's what we all have to do now."

She's not looking at me, but I know she's aiming every word straight at me. "Whatever it is that's holding you here, please, for all of our sakes, let it go now. Let go of the past. Step into your future."

"Thank you, Anneliese," says Susan. "Now let's open it out to the rest of the group. Does anyone else have any final thoughts to share?"

A heavyset woman with faded blond hair and pink cheeks raises her hand. "I'd like to just thank the Earth for the life it gave all of us," she says as tears start spilling down her cheeks. "I'm sorry we can't save you, Gaia. I promise we won't squander this second chance." Someone puts an arm around the woman's shoulder, and there's a lot of head nodding and murmuring.

An Asian man raises his hand next. He's sitting cross-legged on his mat, and his daughter is sort of draped over one of his shoulders. She looks so tired that her whole body has gone floppy. "I want to say," he says, "that my daughter and I are so grateful for this new beginning. Things were very difficult for us after her mother passed. But this community has become like family for us. Thank you all for giving us a reason to be hopeful again."

Next, Fred clears his throat. "A lot of people might not have wanted to take a chance on a couple of old codgers like Alice and me. But I want you to know that after they fix my ticker, we'll work just as hard as everyone else to build our new world. So what Mr. Lee said goes double for us."

When no more hands go up, Susan says, "Thank you, everybody, that was wonderful." She walks over to the mantel and looks at her watch. "We have just enough time for a potty break. Remember, this is your last chance before Departure. After this, no one can leave the room, so go now, whether you need to or not."

I feel like I'm in kindergarten, walking upstairs to take my turn. As I leave the bathroom, Mom and Daniel are waiting for me. "I just wanted to check in with you two," Mom says. "We won't be able to talk once Harmonization starts. I want to make sure you both feel ready."

"I think I'm ready," says Daniel. "And everybody will be sharing their energy with us, right? In case I can't do it?"

Mom puts her arms around him. "That's right, sweetie. Just send as much energy up as you can, and I'll be there to help you both."

She looks at me. "Rooney, do you have any questions? Is there anything at all you want to know?"

"Actually, yeah. What did that guy Mark mean about uncertainty? Don't you know what time we're supposed to Depart?"

Mom looks surprised. "Didn't you listen to Everett's speech?"

"I may have zoned out a little toward the end," I admit.

Daniel's eyebrows go up in worried little arcs. "Rooney, you should have listened," he scolds.

"I did. I just missed a few sentences!"

"It's all right," Mom says. "We don't know the exact time. The Writings say that the Hwaral will come to us within the sun's

177

passage. So it could happen anytime from the moment the sun rises until it sets."

"That's why we need to start Harmonizing before sunrise," Daniel says. "We have to be in a prepared state."

"That's right," Mom says, patting Daniel's shoulder.

"So you're saying that it could take all day?"

"It's possible."

This is going to be a long day, I think as we follow Mom downstairs.

Daniel is moving kind of slowly, and I wonder if he's crashing. "You doing all right, Bug?" I whisper to him.

"My stomach feels funny," he says.

"I know, you must be so hungry," I say, but he shakes his head.

"I'm not hungry. I'm just . . . nervous, I guess."

"How can you not be hungry? You haven't eaten any real food in days."

"That's not true, I . . ." He stops and looks away from me. "I ate all the cleanse stuff. Mom says that's all I need."

"Okay, whatever you say." I brush past him and head back into the living room. I know I shouldn't be annoyed with him, but I wish he'd stop acting like such a perfect little Next Worlder. As I pass Susan, she points at the earrings I'm wearing.

"Honey, you need to take those off now," she says. "Anneliese, didn't you tell her not to wear any jewelry?"

Mom blushes like a guilty kid. "I forgot to mention it," she says. "Sorry, Rooney, I should have told you earlier. You'll need to take off your watch, too."

"Why?"

"Metal can interfere with the waves," Susan says. "We don't want anything slowing us down, now, do we?"

I shrug and start to put my watch and earrings in my pocket, but Susan waves a finger at me. "No, hon, not anywhere touching your body. You can put them on the mantel with mine. I'm sure someone will find them there."

"Or I could put them outside on the coffee table," I say, but nobody so much as cracks a smile. "That's okay. I'll just leave them next to my mat." Susan looks ticked off but keeps quiet for once.

I see Daniel looking at me and fight off an impulse to grab him and run. A few months ago, I think he would have let me. But he'd never leave with me now. There's not much comfort in being right if it means you have to be alone.

Mom comes and sits on the mat between us and grabs our hands. "This is it," she says. "I love you both so much! Don't be scared, okay?"

"Sure, Mom," I say. I lean over and whisper, "See you later," to Daniel. He gives a little nod. Then I lie down and get ready to take an epic nap.

"I'm going to turn off the lights now," Susan says. "This is it, everyone. The next time I look at your faces, we'll be on our way to the Next World!"

four

The room goes dark, and Susan starts talking in a low voice. A low voice for her, I mean, since Susan's whisper is louder than most people's shouts. All around me, people start to hum, and I think back to the Harmonization workshop in New York. Sometimes when I'm lying in bed drifting off to sleep, I remember that feeling of floating up off the ground.

I still don't understand what happened that day. It wasn't like I believed I was actually flying up into outer space. I mean, I didn't believe it in my mind. But it was almost like my body did believe it, just for a little while. I've heard that you can hypnotize people and make them believe that they're a chicken or can speak a different language or whatever. Compared to that, it would probably be easy to make someone believe they were floating a little. Maybe that's all that Harmonization really is.

If that's true, I'm pretty sure I can resist Susan's hypnotic skills. Even though she's following more or less the same script as Patrick did in New York, her voice isn't the kind you want to let inside your head. It's the kind you want to shut out.

As she starts going through the sequence to get us to relax our bodies, I let my mind wander off. Most of the time, I'm so busy keeping everything from falling apart that I don't have time for daydreaming. But today, I've got nothing but time. And even though I would never choose to be in this room with these people, it doesn't completely suck to just lie here with nothing to do and nowhere to be. When I feel myself starting to drift off to sleep, I don't bother to fight it. We're going to be here all day, so I might as well give in. Nothing in the world feels better than that moment when you let go.

I wake up to the sound of humming. I'm not sure how long I've been asleep, but the room is bright now, and my stomach is growling for lunch, so I'm guessing it's about eleven thirty. I slowly move my hand over to my watch and sneak a peek at it.

It's only eight fifteen. I stifle a groan and put it back down on the carpet.

Another round of Harmonization starts, this time with Mark leading. I guess they'll just keep looping through the whole sequence until it's time to give up. I honestly don't know how anyone can focus on anything but sleep and food at this point. Even with cheating, I'm so hungry it hurts. The rest of them must be about to collapse.

I hear a soft rustling sound and push myself up on my elbows to look around. Everyone is lying still, but one little boy across the room is tugging at his mother's yoga pants. She rolls over and points at his mat. He crawls over to her and whispers in her ear. She shakes her head, but he starts to bounce up and down and I realize the poor kid has to pee.

Finally, the two of them tiptoe out of the room. When they slip back in, the mother notices me watching, and a guilty look crosses her face. But then her expression hardens. She's probably worried I'll tell on her or something. Little does she know, I'm the last person she needs to worry about.

In spite of the yawning pit in my stomach and the dryness in my mouth, I manage to nod off again. When I wake up, I sneak another look at my watch. Still almost six hours until sunset. I try counting backward by threes to get back to sleep, but it's hopeless. I'm too hungry and thirsty, and my brain is wide awake. Plus, my back is getting stiff from lying on the floor.

Mom is leading the Harmonization now, and because there's nothing else to do, I just lie there and listen. Not that it's any big compliment, but she's way better at it than the other two. She's not just saying the words, she's painting a picture with them. She always was good at telling stories. That's another thing Daniel gets from her.

Except for her voice, it's so quiet that it's easy to imagine she's the only other person in the room. I remember how it felt to be a little girl, with Mom tucking me into bed and singing in her soft, breathy voice. Before I started being annoyed by everything that came out of her mouth, I remember thinking she had the sweetest voice in the world. Sometimes she would sing this song about ducks, and she'd pause so I could do the quacks. It probably wasn't such a good bedtime song because it always made me laugh so hard, but I loved it. She never sang that song anymore after she and Dad split up.

"Your body has no weight," she's saying. "The slightest breeze could lift it into the sky." The way she says it, her voice light as air, I can almost feel the breeze. It sounds peaceful, like floating on a cloud. No worries, no responsibilities, not a problem in the world.

I know it's not real, this feeling. I know she's just building pretty castles with words. But it's almost like I've been wired to respond to her voice. As she describes the energy field inside us, I'm not so much thinking her words in my head as feeling them in my body. It starts like a flicker of warmth in my stomach. Not like the hollow burn of hunger that I was feeling before, but like a gentle, spreading light. She keeps talking and slowly the warmth moves into my chest and down my arms.

I know I could open my eyes now and everything would stop. I could decide to come back to reality, and that would be the end of it. But the warmth feels so good, so much better than reality has felt for such a long time, that I let her voice take me away.

"Think about sending your energy out to the other people in this room," she says. "Not to their physical bodies—those aren't important anymore. Reach out to their energy, and feel their energy coming back to you. Send your energy out through your fingers and the soles of your feet. There's light shining out of the top of your head. Open up to the light!"

It's like I don't even have to try. As she says the words, they just feel true to me. My hands and feet are charged with electricity, and there's light pouring out of the top of my head and surrounding my whole body. And it's not just me. I actually feel the light coming at me from all directions. I let my eyes open a crack and the light in the room is so blinding that I shut them again. My brain knows it's just the sun coming in the windows, but my body is just as sure that the light's not coming from the sun, it's coming from us.

I'm not thinking about my stiff back anymore. I'm not thirsty or tired. And for once, I'm not mad. All these strangers in the room are generating an energy that I can feel through my whole body. Even before Mom tells us about our energy joining together as one, I can feel it happening. All this energy is surrounding me and reaching into me and pouring out of me, and it feels incredible.

I can feel my cheeks getting wet, and I know I'm crying. But not because I'm sad, or angry. I'm crying out of joy. I can't remember ever feeling so happy.

And then Mom says, "It's time! Let your energy rise up to meet them!" My heart starts pounding, and every nerve in my body is tingling. I'm shaking and I can feel the energy in the room pulling me upward. Slowly at first, and then faster and faster, I float up, not toward the ceiling but into the sky. The air is rushing by my face, and the energy from everyone around me is pulling me up. *Oh, my God*, I think. *It's actually happening! I'm ready!*

And then . . .

. . . And then . . .

. . . Nothing changes.

Absolutely nothing.

I keep waiting for a blinding flash of light, or a sound, some sign that they're here.

I'm ready, I tell them again, but nothing comes.

I keep breathing and focusing, and the seconds tick by, and slowly the floating feeling drains out of my body, and with it everything hopeful that was left in me.

I don't know how much time passes, but bit by bit all the electricity just fizzles out. The tingling in my arms and legs stops, and I can feel the hard floor under my body again.

There's no bright light, no long-fingered green men, no floating disk in the sky. I never wanted them, but now I know they're not coming, know it deeper than ever before, and it feels terrible. All around me, people are breathing in unison, desperately wanting something they can't have. Daniel's eyes are scrunched shut, his hands reaching out stiffly like a paper doll's. I can see how hard he's trying, how hard everyone is trying. It would be ridiculous if it weren't so incredibly, brutally sad.

I don't think I've ever felt this empty in my life.

The rest of the afternoon moves as slowly as a glacier. Every hour or so a cycle ends, they switch leaders, and the whole thing starts again. And as the hours pass, a new understanding dawns on me. Harmonization, the NWS, all of Mom's crazy ideas, I feel like I finally get it. It's about wanting something so badly that you're willing to forget everything you know. Maybe all these people wanting the same insane thing actually does create some special energy. An energy that makes them feel things they would never feel alone. But there's not enough wanting and energy in the world to create a race of aliens to save us from ourselves. Wherever he is today, I bet Everett is having a good laugh at all of them. All of us, I mean.

Sometime after four, the sun goes down, and as Mom finishes up another round, I find myself thinking about those emergency room TV dramas, where someone says, "Call it!" and they note the patient's time of death. This has to end eventually, but the minutes keep ticking by, and no one's saying anything. Susan gets everyone to hum and intertwine their energy, and another hour passes. And then Mark takes another turn. And I just keep lying there as the streetlights come on and Susan and Roger's neighbors come home to their bright houses and their hot dinners and their nice, normal families.

It must be almost seven thirty and Mom is saying, "Let your focus come back to the room," when a woman to my left says, "It's over. The sun set hours ago. It's not going to happen." In the half darkness, I can see someone sitting up on their mat. It looks like the heavyset blond woman who talked about Gaia before. "It's over," she repeats, louder this time, and it brings Mom to a full stop.

"We have to keep going." Mom's voice is a little hoarse from all the talking, and I can hear the edge of desperation in it. "There must have been some minor misinterpretation of the Writings. We just need to be patient."

"No, we need to face the facts."

Now Susan's voice breaks in angrily. "Meredith, you're disrupting the group's energy. We need to maintain complete concentration. If you're not able to do that, then I need to ask you to step away."

Other people around the room shush the blond woman, but another voice says, "Meredith is right. Everett said it would happen before sundown. The sun set hours ago."

Mom is still lying on her mat. "Please, everyone. It can't be much longer. If we lose focus now, we lose everything. I know you're tired and hungry, but we can't lose sight of what's at stake. We owe it to ourselves, and to all the others who are waiting for us."

She goes back to her script, and just as I think people are going to settle back down, the boy who had to pee earlier says in a voice that travels across the room like a bell, "Mommy, I'm hungry. When can we eat?" A few people shush him, but more people are sitting up and looking around now. It feels like the room is splitting in two.

And then Mark sits up and kneels next to Mom. "They're right," he says quietly. "The Writings were clear. The sun has set, and we're not going to Depart. It's time to stop."

It's like he's taken a cork out of a bottle, and now all these voices are pouring out. Half the people are telling everyone else to be quiet and leave if they're not going to keep Harmonizing. Other people are humming loudly, like they can block it all out. Even in the dark, I can tell that a bunch of people are crying. And then, suddenly, a high-pitched, urgent voice says, "Freddie?" I see a silhouette crouched over another silhouette as I recognize Alice's voice.

"It's his heart," she screams. "Somebody call an ambulance!"

Someone jumps up and hits the light switch as he runs into the next room. The rest of us squint and blink like cave dwellers in the sudden light. "The phone is unplugged. Just hang on," Roger calls out. A few more seconds, then: "We need an ambulance. Hurry!" As he gives the operator the address, Anjelica climbs over to Fred's mat. "I know CPR," she says. "It's going to be okay. Fred, can you hear me?" She shakes him as Alice hovers over her, making sounds like an anxious golden retriever.

Anjelica starts pushing at his chest while the rest of us watch uselessly. After what feels like half an hour but is probably only a few minutes, we hear sirens and then the EMTs burst through the door and wade through the sea of yoga mats. Two of them hook Fred up to some machines. A third EMT looks around and asks, "Is this some kind of exercise class?"

"Not exactly," Roger says. "Please, is he going to be all right?"

"Too early to tell," the EMT says. "We'll do our best, though. Does he have a history of heart issues, do you know?"

Roger nods.

"So what kind of exercise was he doing? Strenuous? Like aerobic stuff? Or like yoga?"

"More like yoga," Roger says quietly.

They start wheeling him out of the room with Alice hobbling along behind them. "Do you want me to come?" Anjelica asks.

"No, dear, you stay with the group," Alice tells her. "Maybe there's still a chance for the rest of you."

The kitchen door bangs shut, and we're alone again. The room has a different kind of energy now, the kind that makes people not want to make eye contact. We all look down at our feet, waiting for someone to take charge.

Naturally, Susan is the one who jumps in. "We all feel terrible about Fred, but there's nothing we can do for him now. We owe it to him and Alice to keep trying, as long as it's still November seventeenth." She goes over to the mantel and looks at her watch. "It's only eight thirty! There's still more than three hours to go. Maybe the whole sunset thing was just a . . . a bad translation or something. We need to go back to Harmonizing!"

"But that's not what the Writings say," Mark says. "If the sun is down, it's over. And besides, there's been too much disruption to the group's energy. No one could possibly Harmonize effectively after what's happened."

"Well, what do you think, Anneliese?" Susan asks, turning to look at Mom. In all the commotion, I sort of lost track of her, and now my heart gives a little lurch when I see her sitting with

Daniel's head in her lap. For a panicky second, I think he's passed out, but then I see his shoulders heave as he takes a big, shuddering breath.

Mom bites her lip and doesn't say anything. "Anneliese?" Susan says, louder this time.

"I don't know what to do," Mom says, and her voice has gone all quavery again. "I could go on Harmonizing forever if I thought it would help. But people are so tired, and I think Mark may be right about the sun. I just wish Everett was here to tell us."

"Well, maybe he is," a guy with a hideous man bun says. "We could check the NWS website for updates."

Around the room, people are nodding. Susan looks around and sighs. "Fine, let's make this quick."

Roger gets the laptop and in a minute the big TV screen starts to glow. I expect the NWS homepage to come up, but there's just a message: Page Not Found.

A murmur goes around the room. "Type the address in there again," Susan says.

Roger retypes it, and the same message comes up again.

"He's gone," someone says. "I knew it."

"But why is the website gone, too?" someone else asks. "What does that mean?"

"Maybe there are technical difficulties."

"Should we check the news?" a man asks. "The New York papers must be writing about it."

A second later, we're all looking at a headline that reads "Astro-NOTS."

"I'm not sure the *Post* is the most reliable source," Mr. Lee points out. "Maybe try the *Times* instead?" His little girl is sitting next to him, her eyes dark and watchful. I don't think she's made a sound the entire time she's been here.

"We could try calling one of the other chapters," Mark suggests.

"They'll have unplugged their phones, just like we did," Susan says. "Look, we're wasting time. If there's still a chance, we need to get back to Harmonizing right away. Who's with me?" She looks around the room, and a few people raise their hands, but most are shaking their heads.

Roger puts his hands on her shoulders. "It's time to let it go, love," he says gently. "You gave it everything you had. It's over."

Susan looks up at him, and at first I think she's going to yell at him. But then her shoulders slump and she buries her face in her hands. "Damn it!" she moans, her voice muffled and ragged. "Damn it, damn it, damn it, damn it!"

Roger wraps his arms around her. "I know," he keeps repeating. "I'm sorry. I know."

I turn away from them, but everywhere I look, someone's personal tragedy is playing out. It's all just too much. I'm about to get up and go outside for some fresh air when I hear Daniel squeak, "Mom?" and turn to see her slumping onto her mat.

"I'm all right," she says weakly as I run over to her. "I'm just feeling a little dizzy."

Mark comes over and takes her pulse. "Let's get her to one of the rooms upstairs," Roger says, and then he, Susan, and Mark half carry her out of the room. "She'll be fine," he calls over his shoulder. "Sorry, everyone, we'll be right back."

I slide over next to Daniel, but he doesn't look at me, so we just sit there waiting. After a few minutes, Roger comes back in the room, and I feel Daniel stiffen next to me.

"Is she okay?" I ask.

"She will be. Susan and Mark are keeping an eye on her. She needs to eat something. Actually, we all do." And just like that, Roger takes charge. "I know there's a lot we need to talk about, but until we've had something to eat and drink, we can't make any rational decisions. Can someone come with me?" Three people follow him out the door. "We'll be back soon. Everyone should have some water," he says, and then they're gone. I don't think I've ever liked anyone more than I like Roger right now.

As we wait in line to fill cups at the kitchen sink, I feel a tug on my sleeve, and turn to see Daniel looking up at me. "I need to talk to you," he whispers.

"Okay," I whisper back. "What is it?"

"Not here," he says. I follow him down a dark hallway and we sit on the floor in a corner.

"What is it, Daniel?" I ask again. "Are you worried about Mom? I'm sure she's just dehydrated or something."

He says something so quietly that I have to ask him to repeat it.

"I know why we're still here," he says a tiny bit louder. "It's my fault."

"That's ridiculous. It's not your fault."

"You don't know what I did!" he hisses.

The last thing I want to do right now is fight with him. "Okay, Daniel. You're right, I don't know. Do you want to tell me what happened?"

Without looking at me, he whispers, "I ate a cracker."

"You ate a cracker? When?"

"Yesterday. I opened the kitchen cabinets, just to see if they still smelled like food. But then I noticed a cracker way at the back. And I was so hungry that I . . . I ate it. And now we're all stuck here and it's my fault!"

Looking into his red-rimmed eyes, I don't know whether to laugh, cry, or hit someone. "Daniel, it doesn't matter that you ate a cracker. I promise, it's not your fault that we're still here," I say as I gather him up in my arms. And then the two of us just sit there in the dark hallway until Roger comes back with the food.

"Well, the furniture's gone," I hear him say as he comes in the front door. "Jeff, will you get the folding chairs from the basement? Can someone help me with the sandwiches?"

I pull Daniel to his feet. "Come on, Bug," I say. "Let's eat."

I can't remember a turkey sandwich ever tasting better. At first, Daniel doesn't touch his, but I lean over to him and say, "Bug, there's no point holding out anymore. Everyone is eating. You can't help anyone by starving yourself."

"What about Mom and Susan and Mark?" he asks. "Should we bring them some food?"

"Roger will bring them something." Daniel finally takes a little nibble, and pretty soon he's wolfing his sub down along with the rest of us. By the time the juice and chips have followed the sandwiches, I'm feeling a lot more human and a lot less worried that Daniel's going to topple over.

A few minutes later, Mark and Susan come back downstairs. Daniel runs over to them. "Is Mom okay?" he asks.

Mark puts a hand on Daniel's head. "I'm going to bring her something to eat, and she needs to get some rest. But she's going to be all right."

"Can I go with you?" Daniel asks. "I want to see her."

"Sure. Why don't you pick out a sandwich for her?" Mark takes some food, too, and then the two of them disappear back upstairs. Susan gets herself a sandwich, and Roger gives her his seat at the card table. She eats a few bites, then clears her throat to get everyone's attention.

"I'm sorry to be the one to tell you this, but we've decided to stop trying," she says in the quietest voice I've ever heard her use. "I still don't feel right with it. But Mark and Anneliese both feel sure that the window has closed for us. And unless the group sticks together, we won't have enough energy to Depart." She lets out a big sigh. "I'm sorry, everybody. I just can't understand what went wrong."

A few people move to console her, but I notice some faces in the group that don't look so sympathetic.

"I felt like our energy was off from the start," the blond woman, Meredith, says. "I could just tell we weren't going to make it."

A man sitting next to her lets out an angry puff of air. "Great. That's just great," he mutters, looking away from her.

"What?" Meredith asks sharply.

The man stares at her for a few seconds, then says, "Nothing. Forget it."

"No, what?" Meredith insists. "You might as well say it."

"Fine," the man says. "I was thinking, maybe *that's* why we didn't make it."

"What do you mean?"

The man looks right at her. "I'm sensing a lot of negative energy from you, and we all said we were letting go of that for the sake of the group!"

Meredith's face flushes a dark red right up to the roots of her hair. "How can you say that?" she says to the man. "I have very positive energy. I put everything I had into Harmonizing!"

Now the dark-haired woman with the kid pipes up. "I think certain members of the group weren't really trying. I saw you looking at your watch. The metal probably interfered with our energy!"

I'm so busy trying to be invisible that it takes me a second to realize she's talking to me. I'm about to tell her to mind her own business when someone else says, "And who got up to use the bathroom? Did you think we weren't going to notice that?"

"Please, everybody!" Roger says. "This is no time for blame. Especially since we don't know anything yet. Let's just handle this rationally. The first thing we need to do is find out if we're the only ones."

"I think we should try to contact the Southeast Chapter," Mr. Lee suggests. "They're in the same time zone as us."

Roger gets a contact sheet from the kitchen and dials a number. "It's not going through," he says.

"They must be gone," someone says. "All the others must have Departed."

He tries a few other numbers, but no one picks up. "Let's give it some time," Roger says. "We'll try again in a little while."

five

The room has divided up into little groups of people again. One group is staring at the computer screen while Mr. Lee types on the keyboard. I look around for his daughter and finally spot her curled up in a corner, sucking her thumb. Meredith and some other people are whispering in another corner, and a few other people are like me, on their own, watching and waiting. I wish Mom and Daniel would come back downstairs so we could get the hell out of here. It's getting late, and I'm so ready to be done with all of this.

The phone rings and Susan runs to pick it up. "Hello? Who is this?" There's a pause, then she says, "Sharla, calm down. Yes, I know. Us too. Have you spoken to anyone else?" When Susan finally hangs up, she doesn't look at anyone in the room. "That was the Southwest Chapter. They had a huge group out there in New Mexico. They threw in the towel about thirty minutes ago."

"But Southeast still isn't answering, right?" the guy with the man bun asks. "So they must have gotten out!"

Susan shakes her head. She looks like she's shrunk about a foot since this morning. "Sharla was on the phone with Southeast just before she called us. They're still here, too." She stands up slowly. "I'm going to talk to Mark and Anneliese. Roger, if the phone rings I'll answer, okay?"

She goes upstairs, and a few minutes later, Daniel comes back down. "They said they needed to talk," he says, sitting on the mat next to me. He wraps his arms around his shins and rests his chin on his bony little knees.

"How's Mom?" I ask. "Do you think she'll be down soon?"

Daniel shrugs unhappily. "I don't know. Mark got her to drink some juice. And she had a couple of bites of sandwich. But she seems . . ." His voice trails off, and I don't make him finish the thought. It's not hard to imagine how she seems.

Almost an hour passes, and the phone keeps ringing. With every call, the mood in the room gets darker. You'd think they'd be relieved to know they're not the only ones who didn't Depart, but I guess they'd still rather believe Everett was telling the truth than accept the fact that they've all been had.

Finally, Susan, Mom, and Mark come downstairs. Mark is supporting Mom's elbow, but she's walking under her own steam.

"Any news about Everett?" Meredith asks.

Susan shakes her head. "No. But we've heard from all the other national chapters. They're all still here." And then she just kind of crumples onto one of the chairs by the card table.

Roger goes over to her and pats her back until she shakes his hand off. "Listen, everyone," he says slowly. "I know none of us were prepared for this, but we have to start making plans for what happens next. If you have nowhere else to go, you're welcome to sleep on your mats again tonight. But those who can, I think you should go on home. We'll call you when we have news."

So that's it. The end. I look around the room, expecting

people to get up and head for the door, but nobody moves. Maybe they think that if they don't leave the house, it won't really be over. But I'm through with waiting around. It's time to move on, and if no one else is going to acknowledge that, then I guess it's up to me. I crouch down next to Mom. "Let's go home," I say in her ear. "We're all exhausted, and Daniel and I need to get up for school tomorrow."

"School?" she says, like it's a word in a foreign language.

"Yeah, Mom. We have to go back to our lives now." She looks at me, but I can tell she's not hearing me. I soften my voice, hoping to get through to her. "I'm sorry, I know it's been a hard day. But Daniel needs to go home. He needs to get back to his real life."

She just sits there, her eyes huge and empty. "Real life," she repeats. This is going nowhere.

"Stay with Mom," I tell Daniel. "I'll be back in a few minutes." I go over to Roger. "Can I talk to you?"

He nods, and I follow him into the kitchen. "What is it, Rooney?"

"Sorry to bother you. Could you please call a car to take us home?"

"Oh," Roger says, rubbing his forehead. "Yes, of course. I'm sorry I can't drive you myself, but I can't leave Susan to cope with everything here."

After he makes the call, I look for Anjelica, to say good-bye. I find her still sitting in the same spot she's been in since the ambulance left.

"Hey," I say quietly. "We're going home."

She looks up at me bleakly. "That's probably a good idea."

"What will you do?" I ask her.

"I have no idea. I can't even think about it right now."

"Will you stay here?"

"For tonight, I guess. I don't have anywhere else to go."

"What about your parents?"

Her eyes well up, and she shakes her head wordlessly.

"Are you that mad at them?"

She rubs her eyes with her palms, a quick, angry movement. "No, I'm . . . Don't you see, Rooney? I left them behind. I chose Everett over them. As far as they're concerned, I might as well be dead."

"That can't be true," I say. "Your parents would want to know you're okay." She looks so miserable that I just want to say something to make her feel better. "Do you want to come home with us? It's not that nice or anything, but at least it would be a place to stay while you figure things out."

"Thanks," she says, but shakes her head. "I think I'll just stay here tonight. Maybe tomorrow . . ."

She seems completely lost. *Stinking Everett*, I think to myself. I put an arm around her shoulders and we sit there until I hear a car horn out in the driveway.

"The car is here," I tell Mom. "Come on, let's go." But she doesn't move.

Mark steps forward and takes her arm again. With him supporting her, she walks down the hall like an old woman, taking tiny, slow steps. It's as if all the life has drained out of her body, leaving just a person-shaped shell behind.

At the door, Roger says, "Please call and let us know how you're all doing. Or if there's anything you need."

"I will," I say. "Thanks."

Mark helps Mom into the passenger seat, Daniel and I climb into the back, and we ride home without talking. When we finally pull up in front of our house, it's after midnight. The driver tells Mom the fare, but she doesn't move, and I remember that she's not carrying a purse. "Sorry, hold on," I tell him.

As I run up the porch steps, I fight off a little wave of panic, but everything is just like we left it. Thank God our house is too much of a dump for anyone to bother breaking in. Her purse is still in the kitchen, but of course there's no money in it, so I run up to my room and get the envelope out of my sock drawer. The ride is costing me more than a week's worth of groceries, but at least we're finally back home.

And it's November 18.

"Is she all right?" the driver whispers, giving Mom a worried look. "She seems kinda . . . out of it."

"She's just tired. Could you help me get her inside?"

We drag Mom into the kitchen with poor Daniel trailing along behind us. The house is freezing, so I go turn on the thermostats. When I get back, Mom has gone from sitting at the table to collapsing on it, her head on her arms. Daniel looks terrified and his teeth are chattering.

"Okay, guys, it's late," I say in my best "responsible adult" voice. "We all need to go to bed. Daniel and I have school tomorrow. And, Mom, you need to buy groceries. All right? I'll leave money on the table for you."

I give her a few seconds, and when she doesn't answer, I put my hand on Daniel's shoulder and try to steer him out of the room. "Maybe we should bring her over to the couch," he says.

"She'll be fine," I say, and gently push him toward the stairs. "You can skip your teeth tonight if you want. Just get under the covers and get warmed up."

"Wait," says Daniel. He gets Mom's blanket from the living room and drapes it over her shoulders. "Here, Mommy. So you won't get cold."

She still has her face buried in her arms, so when she speaks, her voice comes out muffled.

"What, Mom?" I say. "We can't understand you."

"I'm so sorry," she whispers. "It wasn't supposed to happen this way. I'm so sorry."

"I know," Daniel says, patting her on the head. "I'm sorry, too."

"Get some sleep," I say. "Let's go, Daniel."

Daniel insists on brushing his teeth, and then, once he's changed, I pull the covers up over him and turn to go. "Rooney?" he says as I reach the door.

"Yes, Bug?"

"I can't go to school tomorrow."

I sit on the chair next to his bed, pulling my knees up under my hoodie. "Daniel, you have to go. You've already missed too many days."

He shakes his head. "But we can't just leave Mom here all alone. She needs someone to take care of her."

"That's not your job, Bug. Your job is to go to school. Mom's a grown-up. She can take care of herself."

"No, she can't, Rooney. You know she can't."

He's kind of got me there. But I'm not about to stay home

and play nurse, and I'm not about to let Daniel sacrifice himself anymore.

"Look, how about we don't worry about it tonight?" I suggest. "Do you think you can sleep?"

"I don't know," Daniel says. He looks away from me. "Are you going to say it?"

"Say what?"

"That you were right. That Mom was wrong. That I was stupid to believe her."

"Oh, Daniel . . . I would never say that."

"Why not?" He looks up at me, and for the first time all day, I see anger in his eyes. "It's true, isn't it?"

"Of course not. I mean, yeah, Mom was wrong. But it's not your fault that you believed her."

"Can you turn the light out?"

There's nothing I can say that will make him feel any better. "I'll leave both our doors open in case you need me, okay?"

Lying in bed, I keep expecting to feel some sense of relief. The worst day has finally come and gone, but I still have the same knot in my gut that's always there. I'd like to send Dad and Carol an email to let them know that we're okay, but I'm afraid Mom will try to talk to me if I go down for the computer. Safer to wait and do it at school tomorrow.

A sound wakes me up in the middle of the night. I tiptoe down the hall to Daniel's room. He's closed the door, but there's no way to miss it. I think about going in, but he's made it pretty clear he doesn't want my company right now. Poor kid. I hope this is the last night he has to cry himself to sleep.

When I tap on Daniel's door in the morning, he doesn't answer. "Daniel? Time to get up." No response. I walk in to find him sitting up in bed. I wonder whether he's gotten any sleep at all.

"Kiddo, you need to get ready for school."

"I'm not going," he says. "I told you."

"Because you're worried about Mom?" He doesn't answer. "Daniel, I know things seem bad right now. But there's nothing you can do for her. And you need to get back to school."

"I can't go back there. I already said good-bye to everyone."

"You think they're going to make fun of you?"

"I know they are."

I sit on his bed. "Look, you're probably right. They're going to be mean about it. I know it sucks, but you have to tough it out. I'll ask your teacher to look out for you, okay? And in a few days, they'll get bored and move on." I'm not sure I believe that last bit, but it's not like he can stay home from school for the rest of his life to avoid getting teased.

I hold my hand out. "Come on. If you get in the shower now, we can walk to school together." He gives me a mutinous look, then drags himself out of bed and shuffles toward the bathroom like his feet are made of lead.

When I go downstairs, Mom isn't on the couch, and for a hopeful second, I think maybe she's gone to buy groceries. But no, she's still slumped over the kitchen table with the blanket over her shoulders. She lifts her head and stares at me when I walk in. Her eyes have huge dark circles under them, and her chin is even pointier than usual, like all the flesh is sliding off her bones. She looks a little scary, but I know she just needs some rest and a decent meal. Still, I don't want Daniel to see her like this and get even more worried. "Mom, you need to get some sleep. How about moving to your bed?"

Without a word, she stands up and drifts into the living room, looking like a Halloween ghost with that blanket draped over her. "And don't forget to pick up groceries later on," I call to her. "You need to eat something."

I leave a grocery list and a twenty-dollar bill on the table and take Daniel to school. He walks the whole way like he's being escorted to the electric chair, and I'm starting to feel like a big bully. Maybe I should have let him stay home, just for another day or two until he's less shaken up. But there's no time for second-guessing. I'm already late for class.

Daniel's teacher steps out of her classroom to talk to us. I feel a little better when she gives him a big hug and tells him she's happy to see him. With Daniel standing right between us, I don't go into a lot of details, just ask her to watch out for him.

"Of course." She stoops down a little so she's looking right into Daniel's eyes. "Ready to go in, Daniel?" she asks. He gives a tiny shrug, then lets her steer him toward the door. Just before it closes, she turns back to me and mouths, *He'll be okay!*

I hope she's right.

Walking into school, I feel like I've been gone for a month, but no one even asks where I was yesterday. I've gotten so good at invisibility, I'm not sure they'd even notice if I never came back.

During my free period, I go to the library and check my email. It's mostly spam, but there's one message I'm happy to see. "Congratulations!" it says in the subject line. "If you're reading this email, then you're probably still on Earth!" The rest of the message says, "Carol and I are thinking about you, and hope that you and Daniel got through yesterday without too much drama. I'm sure it must have been a very difficult day for you. We're here if you feel like talking. Love, Dad (and Carol). PS Have you heard anything from Columbia yet? We're keeping our fingers crossed."

"Still here," I write back. "Yesterday was pretty bad, but at least it's over now. Time to get back to normal! No word from Columbia yet. Should hear in a couple of weeks." I pause for a minute, then type, "Love, Marina."

At work, Maddie lingers instead of heading straight home to her kids. "So, what was it like? Were there special rituals?"

"Not really." I'm kind of missing the old days when Maddie and I didn't talk.

"But how were the aliens supposed to find you?"

"Everybody just kind of concentrated."

"Everybody? You mean the three of you?"

I've already said more than I wanted to, but I don't know how to get out of this without cutting off my boss. "Actually, we went to Mom's friend's house. There were a bunch of people there."

Maddie's eyes get wide. "So was it a whole cult meeting?"

"They're not a cult," I say, suddenly feeling defensive. "They're just people who wanted to live in a better world."

"What's the difference?"

I honestly don't know. Until Mercer used the word *cult* a few weeks ago, it had never crossed my mind that the Next World Society might be one. "Well, they weren't all living together and stuff. They weren't brainwashed."

"But what about the leader guy? What's his name, Evan? He seems pretty shady."

"Everett," I correct her. "Yeah. He's shady." That much is undeniable.

"Has he turned up? I read in the paper that he disappeared with everyone's money."

I haven't even had time to read what the papers are saying about Everett. "I don't know. It's my mom's thing, not mine." I turn away and start checking the sugar containers, even though I'm pretty sure she's already done it.

Maddie gets the hint and puts on her coat. "Sorry, Rooney. I shouldn't pry. I'm just so used to nothing ever happening around here."

Just as my shift is ending, Mercer walks in. It all seems so normal that I smile at him automatically before I remember that nothing between us is normal right now. He doesn't smile back. In fact, he's got an expression on his face that I don't think I've ever seen before.

He stands in front of the counter with his hands jammed deep in his coat pockets. "So . . . Were you ever planning to tell me how everything went yesterday?" he asks, and even though his voice is steady, I realize what that expression is. He's furious.

"Sure. I was just . . . busy today."

"Busy? Rooney, we've both been waiting for this day for years, and now you don't even want to talk to me about it? What the hell?"

There's something so satisfying about seeing him this mad. I know if I apologize, he'll forgive me, and that will be that. But I don't want to apologize. All I want to do right now is see how far I can push him. "I just figured you had other things on your mind," I say, not even looking at him.

"So this is about Skyler?"

"There we go! It was about time someone said her name. I mean, we've been talking for at least thirty seconds and you haven't mentioned her once . . ."

He makes an exasperated sound in his throat. "This isn't about her. You're the one who's been acting like you might catch something fatal if you get within ten feet of me."

"Oh, sorry if I didn't want to be a witness to your epic love story. I had more important stuff going on, you know?" My voice is pure acid.

"God, Rooney!" he finally snaps. "You can be a real jerk sometimes." He turns around, shoves the door open, and storms out, leaving the bell over the door clanging wildly.

Nice work, Rooney. Are you happy now? Instantaneously, I feel sick to my stomach. Mercer's right: I am a jerk. I can't let him leave. Not like this.

I grab the keys to the shop and run out the door after him. I'm only wearing my button-down uniform shirt, and the cold wind slashes at me. "Mercer, wait," I shout. "I'm sorry!" He's half a block away and moving fast. "I can't leave the store unlocked. Please come back!" His steps slow, and then he stops.

"Just give me a minute!"

He doesn't answer, but he doesn't move, either. I run back inside, grab my things, and close up in record time.

He's still standing in the same spot, a dark, hunched figure under the streetlamp.

"I'm sorry," I say again, out of breath from racing after him.

"What is your problem?" he demands. "You've been acting like a psycho for weeks. Is this all because of yesterday? What happened, Rooney?"

I ran out here to apologize, but now I'm not so sure I want to. "It wasn't that. I just hated being around you and Skyler."

"Yeah, you made that pretty clear. So why did you tell me to ask her out in the first place?"

"I don't know," I sputter. "I didn't mean it. I wanted . . ." *Am I really going to tell him this?* "I wanted you to be my person. Not hers."

"I've always been your person, Rooney. Since we were, like, twelve years old." The words are sweet; his tone is anything but.

"No . . . That's not what I mean." I shove my hands in my pants pockets, trying to steady my legs, which are suddenly shaking uncontrollably. *Just say it!* "I mean, I wanted you to be mine . . . *that* way."

He looks at me, unblinking. "Yeah. *That* way."

I stare back at him blankly. "What?"

"I've been your person—*that* way—forever." He pronounces each word slowly and carefully, like he's talking to someone very stupid.

In the dead quiet of the street, my heart is pounding so hard I wonder if he can hear it. "You never told me."

"Because you were never interested in me that way."

"That's not true! I . . . I kissed you!"

"Only because you thought I was into someone else," he says.

"No! That's not why!"

"It's not?" He crosses his arms over his chest.

"No!"

Even in the dark, I can see his eyes glinting. "Prove it," he says.

We stare at each other for a full ten seconds before I work up the nerve to tangle my fingers in the back of his hair and pull his face down toward me. When his lips are a fraction of an inch from mine, he pulls away from me, and my heart skips an anxious beat. Then our eyes meet, he breaks into a grin, and before I can take another breath, he's kissing me so deep it feels like it might cause a rift in the space-time continuum.

We don't let go of each other until a car turns onto the street, and then we jump apart like wild animals.

After the car passes, we look at each other, not sure what to say. And then Mercer starts to laugh, and I join him, and the laughter feels almost—but not quite—as good as the kiss. We howl until we're breathless, and then he grabs my hand. "Come on. Let's get you home," he says, and we walk the rest of the way with my hand clasped in his.

Mercer leaves me at the door and I step into the dark kitchen. The house feels abandoned—no smell of food, no voices. I want to run after him and follow him home. I'd do anything to keep feeling all warm and melty inside, but I know I can't escape my real life for long. I find Daniel in his room, writing in a notebook. "Hey, bud, how was school?" I ask.

"Bad," he says without looking up.

"Where's Mom? Did she say anything about dinner?"

"She's on the couch," he says. "She's not really saying anything."

"She's on the couch again?"

"She's on the couch *still*. I don't think she got up today."

"Is she sick?" I ask. "What's wrong with her?"

"Why don't you ask her?" he says robotically.

He must have had a truly crappy day. I think about apologizing for making him go to school, but I don't know how much good it would do at this point. It's not like I'm going to let him skip tomorrow.

Mom's got the blanket pulled up over most of her face. "Mom?" I say in a low voice in case she's sleeping. When she doesn't answer, I put my hand on her shoulder. "Mom, are you okay?"

She rolls over and looks up at me wordlessly.

"Are you sick?" I ask. "Do you need aspirin or something?"

"I don't need anything," she says, her voice barely a whisper.

Suddenly, it occurs to me that, if she's been in bed all day, there's still nothing in the house to eat. "Mom, did you go to the store?"

"I couldn't."

Immediately, the blood starts pounding in my forehead, but I keep my voice low. "You couldn't, or you didn't?"

"I'm sorry, sweetie," she breathes, then rolls back over onto her side.

"That's great, Mom," I say between clenched teeth. According to my watch, the general store is still open for another twenty-three minutes. If I hurry, I can make it.

"Daniel, I have to go to the store," I shout, snatching the money off the kitchen table. "I'll be right back."

As I run, the sharp cold pierces my chest with every breath. By the time I get to the store, I'm wheezing, but at least I still have time to grab some groceries.

Walking home, I can feel the last traces of happiness from

earlier in the evening disintegrating. Just once, I wish Mom didn't have the power to turn my whole life to garbage.

She's still lying on the couch when I get back. I dump the groceries out on the table as noisily as I can and heat up a can of soup. I call Daniel, then stand in the doorway to the living room. "Dinner's ready. Are you coming?"

"I'm not hungry."

"Fine. I'll leave a bowl for you." I'm not about to beg her. If she wants to act like a five-year-old, that's her choice.

I try to ask Daniel about his day over dinner, but he just shuts me down with one-word answers. I guess he's seen me use that technique on Mom enough to know how the game is played. After he goes back upstairs, I stand in the living room door again. "I left a bowl for you on the table. Can I borrow the computer?" I ask.

"You can have it," Mom says.

"For tonight?"

"You can keep it. I don't need it anymore."

I go to my room and shut my door, then search for stories about Everett. Most of the articles are profiles and interviews of NWS members. Most people seem sad and confused, but some are still insisting that there was a Departure, and that Everett is with the Hwaral now. There are a couple of articles about people who gave him their life savings. I guess it's a good thing we didn't have any money in the first place. I'm sure Mom would've given Everett everything if he'd asked for it.

As for Everett himself, no one seems to know where he is. There's a whole lot of speculation, but not a single fact. Wherever he is, it looks like he got away scot-free.

Figures.

Before I go to bed, I check my email and find a message from Mercer.

"I just talked to Skyler," it says. "She was amazingly cool about it. Said she always knew the two of us belonged together. I hope you have sweet dreams. I know I will." I reread it four or five times, trying to store up the Mercer feeling someplace safe and untouchable.

When I finally click the CLOSE button, I see there's an email from Carol a little farther down in my inbox. "Hi, Marina," it says. "Glad you made it through in one piece. Have you given any more thought to your Thanksgiving plans? Your dad and I would love to have you (and Daniel, too) join us in New York. Just say the word and we'll buy the tickets. Lots of love, Carol."

Thanksgiving is a week from today. I picture Daniel and me sitting around a table with Dad and Carol, laughing and talking about the dumb parade. I can almost feel the warmth in the room and taste the food. I bet Carol makes really good pie. And then I think about Mercer's lips, and remember the electric jolt of his tongue finding mine, and all I can think is that I want to be wherever there's going to be more of that.

"Hi, Carol," I write back. "Thanks so much for the invite. I think things are still too crazy here for me to leave. Hopefully in the spring! Xoxo, Marina."

Six

In the morning, the soup bowl is still sitting untouched on the table. That's a dollar I could have saved. "We're leaving for school in a few minutes," I tell Mom. "There's cereal for breakfast. And I brought the laptop back down so you can start looking for a job."

This time, when she rolls over and looks at me, I have to catch my breath. In the dark last night, I didn't think she looked so different from usual, but today, her skin is gray, her lips are dry and cracked, and the circles under her eyes are enormous.

"God, Mom, you look awful," I blurt out. "You need to pull it together. You can't let Daniel see you like this."

I get her a glass of water and a bowl of cereal from the kitchen. "Drink this," I say, pushing the glass into her hands. She takes a few shaky sips and I hand her the cereal bowl. "Eat."

She shakes her head. "I can't."

"Mom, I'm not asking." She lifts a tiny bite to her mouth.

I hear Daniel coming and intercept him at the foot of the stairs. "How's Mom?" he asks.

"She's having breakfast. And you need to eat, too. Then I can walk you to school again."

"No, thank you," he says, like I'm some stranger calling to him from a car. I wonder how long he's going to keep this up.

Walking into school usually feels like dragging myself through quicksand, but today I practically run to my locker. Mercer is waiting there, just as he said he would be. The second he sees me, a grin lights up his face, and I can't stop my own mouth from twisting in response.

"Everything okay?"

"It is now." The casual way he's leaning against my locker stirs a little flutter in my stomach, and I have to fight down the urge to grab him and pull him back out through the doors. Would anyone even notice if we blew off school today?

"How are things at home?" he asks, snapping me back to reality.

"Total shit show."

"Anything I can do?"

"You're already doing it." It's crazy how easily we've slipped into this new way of being around each other. It seems like the most natural thing in the world. I'm sure there are all kinds of reasons why I should be careful, keep my feelings hidden, play it cool, but all I want to do is lose myself in him.

The first bell rings, tearing us apart, and I know I have four class periods to get through before I see him again. They go slowly, but my reward for getting through them is spending a whole lunch period with Mercer.

All those weeks when I was on the outside looking in, I was conscious of every minute as it dragged by. Now I wish lunch period would last all day. The only bad moment is when I see

Skyler in line for the salad bar and feel a sharp pang of guilt. Luckily, she doesn't even look our way before she heads to the other side of the cafeteria, and within seconds, I forget all about her. It's like she never even existed. Mercer and I are back, and better than before. Back . . . with benefits.

Watching him eat his veggie wrap, I can't believe I spent years looking at Mercer, talking to Mercer, and never once thought about kissing him. Now I can't seem to think about anything else.

"Walk you to work?" he asks as we bus our trays.

"That depends. Will there be kissing?"

He laughs, his eyes crinkling at the corners in a way that is both familiar and deeply unsettling. "Is that a trick question?"

"Nope. I just thought I'd mention that there should be kissing."

"Noted," he says, and then heads off to class while I take a moment to wonder what the hell has come over me. I really need to come back down to Earth. And I will, I swear I will. Later.

Later comes about two seconds after I walk through our front door on Friday night. The first thing I see is the bowl on the floor by the sofa, full of fat, spongy cereal. Mom looks even worse than she did this morning. She looks downright disturbing, in fact.

Mission accomplished. My feet are fully on the ground again.

"I've been going over it again and again in my mind," Mom says as soon as she sees me. "I don't know why we weren't chosen . . ."

"What are you talking about?"

"I'm trying to explain why we didn't Depart." Her breath is

ragged, like it's costing her a lot of effort to get the words out. "I promise, we followed all the instructions. I'm just so, so sorry."

I hold up a hand to stop her. "Mom, we didn't Depart because nobody Departed. Except Everett with everyone's money."

"Why are you saying that? You don't know that."

"Because I read the news, Mom! Everyone knows. The NWS was a scam."

For the first time in days, I see a spark catch in Mom's eyes. She looks like a bag lady with her hair all matted, but at least she's finally showing a little life. "That's not true, Rooney. You shouldn't make up terrible stories," she rasps.

"I'm not making anything up! Here!" I grab the laptop and show her the first hit that comes up: "Scam Artist Hunted While Followers Try to Rebuild Lives."

"Read it," I say. "I'm going to make dinner, and then the three of us are going to sit at the table and eat it. You need to come back to the land of the living."

I make some ramen, and as I'm serving it up, the doorbell rings. For a second, I think maybe Mercer begged out of family movie night and came over, but when I open the door, my heart sinks. It's Susan and Roger, one scowling, the other looking apologetic.

"Are you all okay?" Susan demands. "We've been calling for two days, but the phone is disconnected."

"Disconnected? What do you mean?" I pick up the phone, and there's no sound. I check the plug, but everything looks like it's hooked up right. "I don't know what the problem is."

"Where's your mom?" Susan asks. "I need to talk to her."

I point toward the living room. "We were just about to have dinner."

"You two go ahead," says Roger. "Sorry to interrupt you."

They're in the other room for less than a minute before Roger comes back out.

"Rooney, when was the last time your mother ate anything?" he asks.

"She had a little cereal this morning."

"And before that?"

"I'm not sure. I tried to get her to eat, but she wouldn't."

Roger looks at Daniel. "I'm sorry, Daniel. Could you excuse us?"

Daniel looks confused. "Excuse you?"

"I need to talk to your sister privately. Just for a few minutes."

Daniel looks at me and I nod. "Go on upstairs, Bug."

"Why can't I hear what you have to say? I'm part of this family, too."

I shoot him a look. "Please don't give me a hard time, Daniel."

Roger waits until Daniel's door slams, then says, "I'm sorry to be blunt, but I need to ask some questions that may be a little uncomfortable."

"Go ahead," I say warily.

"Rooney, does your mom have any medical insurance?"

"I don't know. Why?"

"Because Susan and I think she needs to go to the hospital."

"The hospital?"

Roger nods. "She hasn't eaten for almost a week. I'm no expert, but if she doesn't get medical help, I think it could be . . . well, very serious."

"So she needs to see a doctor tomorrow?"

"She needs to see one tonight. Susan and I are going to take her to the emergency room. I just wanted to know if she had coverage because our out-of-pocket situation is a little tricky right now."

"What does that mean?"

Roger sighs and rubs his bald spot with both of his hands. "I guess you're going to find out eventually. Has your mother told you anything about her finances?"

"No. I've been helping out since she got fired, and Dad sends her money so she can pay rent and stuff. Why?"

"Because I need you to understand that everything is different now. We're all . . . We have to start over. From scratch."

I shake my head, not understanding what he means.

"Rooney, we're broke. All our money went to the NWS. I didn't sell the house, so we've got that. And I have a little cash that I held on to . . . But I don't know what kind of a safety net your mom has. Your phone service is cut off, which means she didn't pay the phone bill, and I'm guessing she hasn't paid the rent on this house for a few months."

"Guessing?"

"She's not really saying anything. But most people in the NWS stopped paying their bills in the last few months so they could send more money to Everett."

"Damn it!" I charge into the living room, turning the lights up to full. "We need to talk," I say to Mom.

"Not now, Rooney," Susan hisses.

I push past her. "Excuse me, but this is none of your business. I need to talk to my mother. Can you please leave us alone?"

She looks like she's going to snap back at me, but Mom puts a shaky hand on her arm. "She's right, Susan. We need to talk."

"I'll be right in the next room," Susan says, glaring at me. "Make it fast. Your mom is very weak. She needs medical attention."

In the harsh light, Mom looks like death warmed over. She's been wearing the same ratty cardigan sweater and yoga pants for days now, and at the neckline, where the sweater is unbuttoned, her collarbones are sticking out so sharply you could cut yourself on them.

"Roger says you need to go the emergency room. He asked me if you have insurance."

She shakes her head. "I told him I don't need to go."

"That's not what I'm asking, Mom. I'm asking if we have insurance."

No answer.

"Isn't that part of what Dad's been paying for all this time?"

Still no answer. "All right," I say. "What about the phone? Did you pay the bill?"

She takes a shuddering breath and I clench my fists to keep my hands from shaking. "And what about the rent, Mom? Did you pay the rent?"

Silence. "Did you?" I ask, louder this time.

"No," she whispers.

A cold, sick feeling is seeping into me. "Okay, so we owe rent. How many months?"

"A couple."

"What is that? Two? Three?"

"About six."

I lean in closer, hoping I didn't hear right. "Did you say six? Mom, what happens if we don't pay rent for six months? Can Mr. Barrett kick us out?"

She gives the ghost of a nod, sending a tear crawling down her face.

"Are you crazy?" My chest feels so tight it's hard to catch a full breath. "Where were we supposed to live?"

Her whole face crumples. "We weren't supposed to be here anymore!"

There's a scream starting to build up inside me, and I'm not sure how much longer I'm going to be able to keep it down. "Okay, Mom. I'll talk to Mr. Barrett. I'm sure if we pay him what we owe him, he'll be happy. So just tell me: Where's the money that Dad's been sending?"

"We weren't supposed to be here," she says again. "We weren't going to need it. It could do so much more good where it was needed."

In my head, red lights are flashing *danger*. "What do you mean, Mom? What are you saying?"

She turns to look at me, and now she doesn't look sad, she looks scared. "It's all gone. We don't have any money. I gave it all to Everett."

That's when I realize what she's afraid of. She's afraid of *me*. And she's right to be afraid. I don't feel like myself anymore; I feel like I'm watching a movie. In the movie, I'm standing over my mother. The blood is roaring in my ears, so I can't hear anything, not even my own voice screaming at her. I'm grabbing her shoulders and shaking her and she's just lying there, limp and weak, with tears pouring out of her eyes and spit bubbling at the corner of her mouth. I'm screaming, "How could you do this to us? What the hell is wrong with you?" But the only sound I hear is the blood, like pounding waves, in my ears.

I feel big, rough hands on my arms. Susan is pulling me back, putting her body between Mom and me. Roger is pinning my arms to my sides. Is he restraining me or hugging me? I struggle against Roger as Susan pulls Mom to her feet and half carries her past me and out the door.

After they're gone, all I want to do is break things. I want to smash every plate in the sink, set fire to the kitchen table, and take scissors to all of Mom's clothes. Our whole life is smashed to bits. Why should our dishes still be in one piece?

Instead of smashing things, I go out on the porch, inhale big gulps of November air, and wait for the fire in my head to burn out. I stand out there until my teeth start to chatter, and then I go back inside, heat up some milk in the microwave, and try to thaw my frozen hands. I feel bone-tired.

Daniel comes and sits next to me. "Where did you go?" he asks.

"I just needed some air."

"Did Mom leave with Susan and Roger?"

"They took her to the hospital."

"When will she come back?"

"I don't know, Daniel. It may be a little while."

"Are we going to stay here without her?"

For a second, I falter. I could spare Daniel the truth. I could make up a story to keep him from worrying. But he's old enough to know what's going on. He *deserves* to know. At least that's what I tell myself. And so I tell him everything, every terrifying detail. The whole time I'm talking, his eyes are getting bigger and bigger, but I don't stop. Because the horrible, ugly truth is, I want him to be scared. I want him to know exactly how badly Mom screwed everything up so he never trusts her again.

That night, Daniel lets me tuck him in and even sit with him while he falls asleep. It feels so sweet that I'm almost happy, even though I have no idea what we're going to do now.

I'll worry about it tomorrow, I tell myself as I doze off.

Around ten thirty on Saturday morning, Daniel and I are huddled in the kitchen and I'm trying to come up with some kind of plan when I hear footsteps on the porch. "Anybody home?"

Daniel gives me a funny look as I rush to unlock the door for Mercer. "I tried to call, but it wouldn't go through," he says, then catches sight of Daniel. "Oh, hey, buddy. How's it going?"

Daniel doesn't say anything, just turns to look at me.

"Bug, I'm going out for a walk. Just for a few minutes, okay? Lock the door behind me."

"Where are you going?" Daniel asks, sounding much younger than nine.

"Not far. I promise. I'll be right back."

Mercer raises a worried eyebrow at me. "What's going on?" he whispers as soon as we're out on the porch.

"It's bad. Really, really bad," I whisper back. "Not here, okay?" Once we're a few houses away, I tell him everything.

"Holy crap," Mercer says when I'm done. "What are you going to do?"

"I have no idea. I feel like my brain is on strike."

"Do you know if your mom's all right? Or where they took her?"

"No. And I don't care."

He gives me a long look, then pulls me to him, his arms wrapped protectively around my head. "Did you call your dad?" he asks after a while.

"I can't call anyone, remember? No phone service."

"Here," he says, reaching into his pocket. "Use mine."

I shake my head. "What am I supposed to say to him? 'Hey, I know all I ever do is ask you for money, but can I have some money? Like, a whole lot of money?'"

"It's not like this is your fault. He's got to understand that."

"I guess."

"I know it's awkward, but, Rooney, what other choice do you have?"

"None, I guess."

He tries to give me the phone again, but I push it back toward him. "Let me at least try to figure out how deep the hole is first. I need to talk to our landlord."

Mercer looks dubious. "Okay, if that will make you feel better."

"I'd better get back to Daniel. He's pretty freaked out."

"I'll check in on you guys later today," he promises, then climbs onto his bike and pedals off.

"You and Mercer are friends again?" Daniel asks as I shut the door behind me.

I nod.

"So what are we going to do?"

"I'm working on a plan. It's going to be okay." He can probably tell I have no idea what I'm talking about, but he keeps his mouth shut.

I spend the afternoon digging through Mom's papers, trying to find any information about how much money we owe. There are no bills, no records, but I do manage to find our landlord's address. His house is only a few blocks away, so I walk over and ring his bell. No answer.

Daniel and I drift around our house like shadows until Mercer comes back around five o'clock, carrying a bag of groceries. "I picked up a couple of things," he says casually, like it's the sort of thing anyone would do, and I only barely manage not to burst into tears. Daniel looks from Mercer to me, then announces that he's going upstairs.

When he's out of earshot, Mercer pushes himself up to sit on the counter and I slide into the space between his knees. "How did it go?" he asks, nuzzling my neck.

"He wasn't home. I'll try again tomorrow."

"Do you want me to come with you?"

"No. It's okay."

"I think we should talk to my parents," he says.

I break away from him. "No! It will just freak them out."

"But they can help. They'll know what to do."

"I don't want anyone to know. Please don't say anything to them. At least not yet."

He holds his hands up in surrender. "Okay, I won't say anything yet. Now come back here."

Seven

On Sunday morning, I go back to Mr. Barrett's house, and this time he's home. I follow him down a narrow hallway to his bright, sunny kitchen, going over my talking points in my head. I know it isn't going to be easy to convince him to let us stay. I'm not sure it's even legal to rent to someone under eighteen. Still, I've got one thing going for me: I'm not Mom. That has to count for something.

I've barely started my pitch when he holds up his hand. "Just a moment, Miss Harris," he says. "I'll be right back." He disappears into the next room and I hear him rummaging around. Then he comes back and puts a piece of paper covered in numbers on the table.

"I'm sorry, I don't . . ."

"No, of course, I should have . . ." He points to a number at the bottom of the page. "That's the total your mother owes me."

I look at it blankly. "But that's . . . that's more than ten thousand dollars."

He ducks his head apologetically. "That's why I told her you'd need to be out by the end of the month."

"You . . . You told her that?" The walls of the room are shimmering, and it occurs to me that I may be about to pass out.

"I'm sorry, Miss Harris. I gave her all the chances I could."

"I understand," I say, but mostly I'm just trying to get air into my lungs.

"Do you know where you'll go? Is there an address I should forward your mail to?"

"I have no idea," I tell him.

A few minutes later, I'm standing on the sidewalk, my head still spinning. Daniel is waiting for me at home, but I'm not ready to face his scared eyes yet, and I'm already partway to Mercer's house. It only takes me ten minutes to run the rest of the way, and being in motion quiets the buzzing in my head.

Mrs. Phillips answers the door, a strange half smile on her face. Normally, I'd just go upstairs, but she gestures to the den. "Why don't you wait in there, Rooney? He'll be down in a sec."

Mingus is lying on the sectional, and he looks up at me expectantly, his tail thumping the upholstery. I sit down next to him and he leans his chin on my leg until I give in and scratch his head. A minute later, I hear a murmur of voices, and then Merce joins me. "Is it okay that I'm here?" I ask quickly.

"Of course."

"Your mom gave me a strange look. Did you tell her?"

"I told her about . . . us. I haven't told her the rest of it." He sits down next to me and pulls me toward him. "Sorry, Mingus, she's mine."

I keep my eyes on the half-open door. "Your mom . . ." I say quietly.

"Okay," he sighs, putting a little distance between us. "So did you talk to your landlord?"

"Yeah."

"Not good?

"Extra bad. Like, way worse than I imagined."

"Crap."

"Yeah. Crap. I really wanted to fix this, Merce. For Daniel even more than for me. But who's going to rent a house to two kids with no parents and no money?"

"So what are you going to say to your dad?"

"I don't even know where to start."

He links his fingers through mine and strokes my hand with his thumb. "I really think we should tell my parents. They can help us figure it out."

"I don't want to, Merce."

"Why? What do you think is going to happen?"

"I just don't want people knowing."

"But they're not 'people'; they're my parents."

"No. I mean it. Your mom is already giving me fishy looks. I don't want her thinking her son is dating some charity case."

"Oh, are we dating?" he asks, arching his brows at me.

"Well, I mean . . ." The tops of my ears are suddenly on fire.

He laughs. "You can call it anything you want. It doesn't make a difference. I'm yours, whatever people call it."

I've only been gone an hour and a half, but the second I see Daniel's eyes, I can tell something has changed. Since Mom left, he's looked sweet again, trusting, the way he used to. But now

I can see he's not sure of me anymore. I've left him hanging too long.

"Where have you been?" he asks.

"I told you. I went to talk to Mr. Barrett."

"Did it work? Can we stay?"

"I don't know yet, Daniel. It's complicated."

"When is Mom coming home?"

"I don't know. Maybe not for a while. I think she's pretty sick."

"But she'll be all right?"

"Yeah," I say, although I honestly don't know. "She'll be all right."

He doesn't say much for the rest of the afternoon, but by the time we're silently eating PB&Js for dinner, he can't wait any longer. "Are you going to talk to him?" he asks.

"Who?"

"Him. Our . . . dad." The word hangs in the air between us.

"I don't know."

"You have to."

"Is that what you want? I thought you . . ."

"We need help," he interrupts. "Don't we?"

"Yeah. We need help."

After he goes upstairs, I fire up the computer. Luckily, our connection is still working. Of course Mom was still paying that bill: no Internet, no Everett.

"Marina, are you all right?" Dad asks the second his face appears on my screen. "I'm sorry I haven't checked in . . ."

I've been steeling myself to tell him the whole story, but

something stops me. For starters, he looks like he hasn't shaved, combed his hair, or slept in a couple of days. "What's wrong, Dad? Did something happen?"

His eyes widen. "You don't miss much, do you? We had a little scare yesterday. But everybody's okay."

"What kind of scare?"

"The baby was in some kind of . . . distress. They thought we might lose her. They got her stabilized but Carol has to stay in the hospital for another few days, and then on bed rest until she delivers. Apparently, there's some risk of her going into labor too soon . . . Marina? Are you there?"

I'm glad he can't see me. I know my face should be full of concern for Carol and the baby, but right now, all I can think is *Crap! Can't I just catch one break?* "I'm here, Dad. I'm really sorry."

"Thanks, honey. Maybe you and Carol can chat when she's home. She'll probably be pretty bored."

"Sure." I'm only half listening to him. "Listen, you're busy. I'll let you go."

Dad runs his hands through his hair and sits up straighter. "No, no. I want to hear what's going on with you guys. Are things any better?"

I should tell him everything is fine and hang up. He obviously doesn't need more problems right now. But I don't have any idea what to do next. So I pause. Just for a second, but Dad catches it. "Okay, let's hear it," he says. "What's going on?"

"Maybe we shouldn't talk right now, with Carol in the hospital and everything . . ."

He holds up a hand in a *stop* gesture. "Marina. Spill it."

So I do. "Things are a pretty big mess. It turns out Mom hasn't been paying the rent. We're getting kicked out of the house."

"Jesus Christ!" Dad squeezes his eyes shut and rubs his forehead. When he looks up again, his face is dark red. "Honey, can you please go get your mother? I need to talk to her. You shouldn't be in the middle of this."

"She's not here. She's at the hospital."

"Why?" He sounds more annoyed than concerned.

"I guess she didn't eat or drink anything for a couple days. She looked pretty bad, actually."

"So you're there by yourself?"

"Well, with Daniel. Dad, there's something else. It's bad."

"I'm listening." He says it quietly, but I can hear the anger tugging at his voice.

"There's no money left. Mom gave it all away. To Everett."

I hear a sound like a chair scraping the floor. "I have to call you back," he says, and then my screen goes blank.

Five endless minutes pass. When he finally calls back, he's either forgotten to turn on the camera or decided to leave it off. "Sorry, Marina. Can you please repeat what you just told me?"

"Mom gave all our money to Everett."

"Everything? All her savings? And the money I've been sending?"

I nod, then remember he can't see me, either. "I think so."

"And what about your college funds?"

"I don't know . . . she never mentioned any college funds."

"So that probably means yes," Dad mutters.

"Probably."

"Damn it. All right, Marina, I need you to write some things down. Do you have a pen?"

"No, but I'm sitting at the computer."

"Ha! Right," he says, but it doesn't sound like he's really laughing. "Okay. I want you and Daniel to pack suitcases. Whatever you'll need for a couple of weeks. And then stay near the computer so I can call you back once I've booked seats for you. I'm sorry I can't come get you, but I can't leave Carol. Okay?"

He says it all so quickly that I can barely keep up. And then when I don't say anything, he says, "Okay?" again, only louder.

"Sorry, I'm not following," I say.

"The two of you need to get yourselves to New York. You obviously can't stay there alone."

"But . . ." I try to break in, but he's already moving on.

"One of you can sleep in the baby's room, and the other can take the pullout in the office. We can manage that way until the baby comes. And then . . . God, we may need to leave the city. I don't see how we can stay here with three kids . . ."

My head is swirling. "Wait," I try again. "Hang on a second."

"What?"

"I . . . I don't think Daniel and I can come to New York right now."

"Why not?"

Why not? A million reasons. One reason. "Well, we've got school."

"So we'll get you into schools here. I'll make some calls tomorrow."

"But this is my senior year. I can't just transfer somewhere new. And Daniel . . . You can't rip him out of his home." It's all true, and at the same time, not. Daniel and I both have plenty of reasons to get out of Stonebrook. But the one thing that's keeping me here cancels out everything else.

Dad makes an impatient noise. "Marina, you called me because you needed help. Now you need to let me help you."

"But this isn't the kind of help we need." It sounds terrible, ungrateful. Nothing is coming out right.

"What kind of help were you expecting, exactly?"

"I . . . We just need some money to pay the rent."

"Come on, you're smarter than that," he scoffs. "Do you honestly think I'm going to just leave you guys there unsupervised?"

"I can look after Daniel. I've been doing it for a long time."

"I appreciate that, but you need to let me be in charge of the grown-up decisions now, all right?"

"But how can you make decisions for him? You don't even know him!" The sound of my voice is harsh in my ears, but I can't seem to get it under control.

Dad's voice is getting louder, too, and I'm sure his face is getting redder and redder. "I'm still his father," he says. "I'm your father, too, for that matter, so how about you deep-six the attitude and do what I say?"

And then I pretty much lose it. All the built-up worry and fear converts into a hot, molten surge of rage. "You can't just come in out of nowhere and start ordering us around! Just because you're our father doesn't mean we have to do what you say!"

"Excuse me?" he roars. "Listen, I've got a lot on my plate, Marina, and I'm doing the best I can. I'm sorry if it's not *convenient* for you, but you can't just stay there by yourselves. So you're going to need to get your butts on a train tomorrow. Do you hear me?"

"Yeah, I hear you. But we're not going anywhere. Forget I called. We don't need your help. We're fine here." I move my hand to click DISCONNECT, but Dad speaks first.

"You're fine? You're about to get evicted. You want to explain to me what's so fine about that?"

He's right. We're totally screwed and I know it. But right this second, I don't care. "Forget it! It's not your problem!" I slam the computer shut.

My heart is pounding so hard that I don't even hear Daniel until he's almost next to me. "Was that him?" he asks quietly.

I look up at him, panic-stricken. "Yeah."

"Is he coming to get us?"

"No."

His face is stony. "What are we going to do?"

Suddenly, I feel too exhausted to hold my head up. I rest it in my hands, stalling for time. "We'll just keep going like normal. We'll go to school, and you'll hang out at the Connection while I work, and then we'll come home and eat dinner."

"All by ourselves?"

"Sure. We're used to fending for ourselves."

He gives me a long, hard look. "What were you yelling about?"

"He was . . . trying to help, but I didn't agree with the decisions he was making. For us. So I told him that we could make our own decisions."

"You could make *your* own decisions, you mean," Daniel mutters.

"Okay, you're right. I was making decisions for both of us, because somebody has to. I'm responsible for us."

His eyes blaze at me. "You're not responsible. You're just bossy!"

The unfairness of that stings me. "Look, Daniel, what do you want from me? I'm doing the best I can here!" It might as well be Dad's voice coming out of my mouth.

Daniel doesn't say another word. He just turns around and stomps upstairs, and I let him go.

That night, I almost send Dad an email. But every time I start putting the words together to form an apology, they turn themselves into something else. Something that sounds a lot more like the start of an argument. *Maybe things will be clearer in the daylight*, I tell myself.

The next morning, the only thing that's clear is that Daniel is done with me. Any ground I regained after the Departure disaster got blown to hell last night. It's like he's stopped being a little kid overnight, and the sulky adolescent who's replaced him doesn't like me one bit.

He doesn't speak to me from the time I wake him up to the moment I drop him off at school. I want to tell him it's all going to be okay, but the words dry up in my mouth. I don't know how to make any of this okay.

Merce is waiting for me just inside the school doors. He takes one look at my face and puts his arm around me. "Tell me," he says gently.

I do as quickly as I can, knowing we only have a few minutes.

"Okay, I'm calling Mom," he says when I'm done. "Maybe you and Daniel can stay with us. At least for a while." I don't even try to argue. The bell rings and he straightens my backpack strap on my shoulder. "We'll figure it out. I promise."

Three hours later, I feel like I'm about to jump out of my skin. Mercer's already sitting at our table in the cafeteria when I get there. "Aren't you getting lunch?" I ask.

He shakes his head. "Not hungry."

The queasy feeling in my stomach ratchets up a notch. "What did she say?"

"She said you guys could stay for a couple of days if you need to. And she invited you for Thanksgiving."

"A couple of days?"

"Yeah." He laces his fingers through mine. "But she says you have to call your dad back."

My throat tightens. "But he'll make us go to New York!"

He nods gloomily. "I know. I told her that. She says we can't interfere in your family's business."

"Well, I guess that's it, then," I say as the last drop of hope drains out of me. "I need to get a job."

He blinks at me. "You have a job."

"I mean a full-time job."

"You mean drop out of school? That's crazy."

"What other choice do I have?"

"You can call your dad back. You can . . ."

"Go to New York? Finish school there? Is that what you want?" Fat tears well up in my eyes and I brush them away hard.

"Of course not! None of this is what I want! But if it's a choice between dropping out of school and going to New York, it's pretty obvious what you need to do!"

"Not to me." The feeling in the pit of my stomach is spreading to the rest of my body. "I have to get out of here."

Before he can even get to his feet, I storm out of the cafeteria, dumping my sandwich in the garbage as I pass. It kills me to waste food, but there's no way I can eat now.

I almost plow straight into Mrs. Fisher as I make a beeline for the girls' bathroom. "My goodness, Marina, what's the matter?" she asks.

"Nothing." I can feel her eyes drilling into my back as I dart away from her.

I lock the stall and lean against the door. I feel like I'm seeing everything through a pinhole. *Breathe.* My heart is racing so fast it might explode. *I think I'm hyperventilating. Or possibly having a heart attack.* I bend over, brace my elbows on my knees, and try to take slow, even breaths.

What the hell am I going to do?

After a while, my heart stops trying to leap out of my chest, but the sick feeling doesn't go away. I sit through my afternoon classes like a trapped animal. As soon as the last bell rings, I bolt without even saying good-bye to Merce.

eight

I pick up Daniel at school and we walk to the Java Connection in silence. I'm almost glad he's too mad to talk to me, since I'm not sure I could get through a conversation without losing it right now.

"You can sit over there," I tell him after Maddie leaves. "Do your homework." He flashes me a resentful look but sits down and pulls out his books.

I need to start the afternoon inventory, but I still feel like I might pass out. I check to make sure Daniel is occupied, then go into the back room and curl up in a ball on Maddie's sofa. *Maybe we could just stay here*, I think. *Maddie would never have to know. We could shower at school, after gym . . .*

The bell jingles, and I jump up, my heart pounding, and run out to wait on the customer. Daniel doesn't even look up, but I swear I can see rage rippling the air around him.

I go to the back room again and use Maddie's phone to dial Mercer's number, but he doesn't pick up. He's probably in the middle of band practice. "Sorry I ran out on you," I whisper into his voice mail. "I'm kind of freaking out. Come by after practice, if you can, okay?"

A little while later, I'm standing behind the counter like a zombie when the bell jingles again and Mrs. Fisher sails into the shop. "Ah, Marina. I was hoping I would find you here."

Daniel looks up from his book and I do my best to pull my face together. "Daniel, this is my teacher Mrs. Fisher."

He holds out his hand, still too sweet to be rude to a stranger even if he hates me. Mrs. Fisher slips off a glove. "It is a pleasure to make your acquaintance, Daniel." He does a good job of covering it up, but I can tell he's studying her hand. He's probably never seen such dark skin before, not up close anyway.

"Are you enjoying that book?" she asks, pointing to the paperback Daniel's still clutching.

He shrugs shyly. "It's pretty good. It's not important or anything. It's just for fun."

Mrs. Fisher smiles. "Occasionally, even the most serious reader should indulge in a bit of pure escapism. I applaud your choice."

Daniel's cheeks go a little pink and he gives her his old smile. I feel my throat tighten up just as Mrs. Fisher turns to look at me. "Did you want coffee?" I ask, turning toward the machine so she can't see my face.

"No, thank you. I actually came to see how you were doing."

If Daniel weren't sitting right there, I might actually burst into tears and tell her everything. But with him watching me, all I say is "I'm okay."

Daniel and I lock eyes for a long moment. It feels like he's staring into my soul, and finding it pretty disappointing. And then I see his face set: He's made a decision. He turns to Mrs.

Fisher as if she's the cavalry and announces, "Our mother's in the hospital."

Mrs. Fisher looks at me sharply. "Is she all right?"

"I guess so."

"We don't know," Daniel says. "They took her away three days ago."

Mrs. Fisher looks from Daniel to me. "So where are you staying at the moment?"

"Oh, we're just . . . at home," I say.

"The two of you are on your own?"

"Yeah. It's not a big deal."

But Daniel's not letting this chance slip away. "It *is* a big deal," he says. "We're getting kicked out of our house."

Mrs. Fisher pulls up a chair next to Daniel. "I think you had better explain to me from the beginning."

She isn't talking to me, so I just listen while Daniel tells her about the hospital and the house and our total lack of a plan. A few times, I try to interrupt with a better spin, but Mrs. Fisher just nods for Daniel to go on. Finally, the whole story is out, and I have to admit, it really doesn't sound great. I'm sure she's going to yell at me, but all she says is "So what solutions have you thought of?"

"Solutions?" I ask.

Mrs. Fisher puts her head to one side and looks at me. "You are faced with quite a serious problem. I don't imagine you are sitting back and waiting for your landlord to toss your possessions into the street. So what possible solutions have you come up with?"

"Well . . . I talked to our dad last night."

"Your father," Mrs. Fisher says. "Where is he?"

"He lives in New York. With his new wife."

"I see. And what did you discuss with him?"

I hesitate to tell her the whole story since I'm pretty sure she wouldn't approve of me picking fights with our only sane parent. But Daniel looks at me and says, "Good question."

"He wanted us to come stay with him." Out of the corner of my eye, I see Daniel absorb that news. Another strike against me.

"In New York," Mrs. Fisher repeats slowly. "Go on."

"Well, they're about to have a baby, and we're in the middle of the school year, and it just . . . I didn't think it was the best thing for Daniel."

Daniel snorts. "So that's why you yelled at him? Because it wasn't the best thing for *me*? Whatever." Sarcasm is a new thing for him, and it sounds ugly coming from his mouth.

"So where did this conversation leave off? Is your father coming to get you?" Mrs. Fisher asks.

"I don't know. I don't think so. He can't leave his wife right now because she's in the hospital."

Mrs. Fisher turns to Daniel. "You said your *mother* was in the hospital."

"She is. They both are," I explain. "There's something wrong with the baby."

She puts her head in her hands and rubs her temples. "That is . . . unfortunate. So where did you leave things with your father?"

"I'm not sure," I admit. "I sort of hung up on him."

She presses her lips together. "And why would you do that, given the urgency of your situation?"

I look down at my hands. "I know, I shouldn't have," I say. "It's just, he barely knows us. And I didn't think it was right for him to just step in and start telling us what to do."

Daniel makes another snorting sound, but Mrs. Fisher ignores it and looks at me. "My dear, you need to be a bit realistic, and stop sabotaging yourself. Let me ask you: If you were a parent, and you knew your children were in trouble, wouldn't you try to solve their problems the only way you knew how?"

I nod. There's no point arguing with her. I know she's right.

Mrs. Fisher lets out a sigh. "I understand your desire for autonomy, Marina, but this is a serious matter."

"We're all right," I start to say, but so weakly that even I don't believe it, and she waves it away like a cloud of smoke.

"No. This is not all right." Her voice is gentle, but firm and final. "What time does your shift end?"

"Around six thirty."

"Good. Kindly wait for me here." I watch her leave, the fog still swirling around in my brain.

Daniel doesn't say a word to me for the rest of my shift, and I stay quiet, too, tiptoeing around and trying not to do anything to make him even madder. I leave a second message for Mercer, telling him not to come by and that I'll explain later. And then I wait, barely daring to hope, for Mrs. Fisher. Finally, at 6:25 p.m. the door jingles open and she's back.

"I've taken the liberty of locating your mother at the hospital," she tells us. "I'm sorry for the intrusion, but I needed to make sure everything was done correctly."

"What did she say?" Daniel asks. "How did she sound?"

"She sounded . . . tired. Of course, I don't know what your mother usually sounds like."

"Is she getting out soon?" Daniel asks.

"Not for a bit longer, it would appear. She asked me to tell you both that she's sorry. And I have her number now, so you can call her whenever you want. Whenever you're ready, that is," she adds, looking at me. "I'll need to call your father as well, of course."

"Why?" I ask.

She folds her hands and looks at us. "Because, my dear, a teacher can't just take in two children without getting their parents' permission."

I must look stunned, because she starts articulating every syllable even more slowly and carefully than usual. "I know this is far from an optimal solution, but the two of you would be very welcome to stay with me until a better one presents itself."

"We can stay with you?" Daniel asks in a breathy voice that sounds just like Mom's. "Are we . . . is that allowed?"

"Well, it is somewhat unorthodox, but if both your parents agree, it can be arranged."

"When can we go?" Daniel asks.

"Right away," she says. "Let's go pack up your things."

Mrs. Fisher's house is across town. The houses are small, like ours, but seem tidier, somehow, like the people who live here actually love and care for them. As we grab our duffel bags from the trunk, I notice a pile of sticks stacked in a huge beehive shape on the lawn. "What's that?" I ask.

"Ah, you'll have to ask Mr. Fisher," Mrs. Fisher says. "It's one of his projects." She opens the door. "James? Where are you?"

"In here, Aurelia," a man's voice calls back. I've never bothered to think about Mrs. Fisher having a first name before, but Aurelia seems like a perfect fit. It sounds like a name for royalty, someone with a deep, musical voice and excellent posture.

Mrs. Fisher's husband is nothing like I would have expected. And not because he's white—at least, not *just* because he's white—but because he's so different from her. Where she's formal and elegant, he looks kind of thrown together. He's wearing a flannel shirt, patched jeans, and work boots, and his floppy brown hair looks a couple of weeks overdue for a trim.

"You must be Marina," he says, shaking my hand with a surprisingly strong grip. His voice is warm, and a little raspy. "I'm James. Sorry about the calluses."

"That's okay. This is my brother, Daniel."

"Dinner's just about ready," says Mr. Fisher, "but there's no big rush if you want to get settled in first."

"Excellent," Mrs. Fisher says. "We need to make a few decisions." She opens the door to a room off the kitchen. "One of you will sleep here, in my study. That sofa folds out into a bed. And, if you'll follow me . . ." She leads us upstairs and opens a door. As she turns on the light, my first thought is that the room is full of trees. Most of it is taken up by a huge bed built out of branches, with the bark and twigs still attached. They arch overhead in a kind of canopy.

Daniel brushes his fingers against the bark. "It's real!"

Mrs. Fisher laughs. "Do you like it?"

"It's like something from a story."

"Quite right," she says, the way she does in class when someone says something smart. "Mr. Fisher calls this the Brothers
Grimm Room. He'll be delighted that you understood."

So, obviously, I let Daniel have the upstairs room.

At dinner, Daniel and I both take small helpings to be polite,
but Mr. Fisher must see how quickly we polish them off, because
he refills our plates without asking. Daniel seems guarded at first,
not speaking unless someone asks him a question. But the Fishers'
slow, quiet way of talking seems to melt something in him, and
by the end of the night, he's asking Mr. Fisher to teach him how
to use a table saw.

The two of them troop upstairs at bedtime. "Good night,
Daniel," I call after him, but he doesn't answer. Whatever warmth
he's feeling clearly doesn't extend to me.

"Patience," Mrs. Fisher murmurs.

I nod. "Thank you for letting us stay here. We really
appreciate it."

"You are most welcome, Marina."

"Do you mind if I make a quick phone call?"

"Of course not. Use the one in your room."

Alone in the study, I call Mercer.

"Where are you?" he asks anxiously. "Whose number is this?"

"We're at Mrs. Fisher's house."

"What? How did that happen?"

"I'm not sure, honestly. She came to the Connection to see
me, and then she called Mom and Dad and got their permission,
and that was it."

"Seriously? For how long?"

"Until we figure something else out, I guess."

"Your dad isn't making you go to New York?"

"Not yet, anyway."

He makes a sound like a balloon deflating. "God, I was freaking out, Rooney. I went by your house after dinner and there was no one there. I didn't know—"

"I know, I called as soon as I could."

"I didn't know what had happened to you."

"I know. I'm sorry."

"It's okay, as long as you're okay." He's quiet for a while. "So, what's it like there?"

I look around the little room, taking in the colorful rug, the well-worn furniture, the shelves of books, and the three cardboard boxes that hold all my worldly possessions. "It's nice. The Fishers are amazing. I can tell Daniel likes them. But . . ."

"But what?"

"I just . . . I know we're crazy lucky to be here, I really do. But I just feel like a refugee."

We hang up with promises to meet up in the morning, and then I turn out the light, crawl into bed, bury my face in my pillow, and cry until I run out of tears.

nine

I agreed to cover for Maddie during Thanksgiving break, so early Wednesday morning, Mr. Fisher drives me to the shop and I get a little preview of what my life will be like if I have to quit school. By the time my classmates are waking up, I've already hauled the baked goods inside, single-handedly dealt with the coffee rush hour, and still had plenty of time to feel bored and lonely. When Mercer walks through the door, I feel like a prisoner being released from solitary. He doesn't stay long because his mother needs help cooking, but before he goes, he promises to drop by the Fishers' house tomorrow after his family dinner.

Mrs. Fisher comes to pick me up after my shift, all smiles. "James and Daniel have been cooking all day. The smells coming from that kitchen are not to be believed!"

"Daniel's cooking?" As far as I know, Daniel has never even boiled water.

"Well . . . he's assisting. And what he lacks in skill, he is more than making up for with enthusiasm."

"*Daniel* is?"

She seems to understand my surprise. "You'll see. He appears to be settling in very well."

The kitchen looks a little like a crime scene, but Daniel and Mr. Fisher both seem to be having a blast. Daniel even tells me about making sweet potato pie. It's almost like he's forgotten to be mad at me.

"And there's peanut stew for dinner tonight," Mr. Fisher tells Mrs. Fisher. "Just like your aunties made it."

"Ah, you'll spoil me," she practically purrs. There are kids at school who think Mrs. Fisher is intimidating, but I always liked how strong she seemed, the way she held herself as straight as a tree. At home, the strength is still there, but there's a softness, too—a kind of blurring of her edges.

"Will it just be the four of us tomorrow?" I ask once we've cleared some space in the kitchen and sat down to dinner.

Mr. Fisher laughs. "I hope not! We've made enough food for a small army."

"Don't you know how many people are coming?"

"Oh, it will be somewhere between ten and forty," Mrs. Fisher says. "And it will be perfect, whatever it is. Thanksgiving is my favorite American holiday." She wipes her mouth carefully, then looks from Daniel to me. "I was thinking, perhaps you would like to visit your mother tomorrow. We could go in the morning or early afternoon, before people arrive for supper."

"Yes," Daniel says right away. "I want to."

Three sets of eyes turn to me. "I have to work," I mumble.

"I could take you after your shift," Mr. Fisher offers.

"No, thank you," I say as Daniel's eyes harden.

The shop is really quiet on Thanksgiving, which means I have the whole day to sit around and think about what a mess my life is. When my shift ends, I walk to the Fishers' house, wishing I hadn't told them I didn't need a ride. By the time I get there, my nose is running, my fingers are numb, and I'm in no mood for a celebration.

As I open the door, the smells and sounds are so overwhelming that I almost step back outside. The house is bursting with people, and I've never seen so much food in one place.

I squeeze into the kitchen and Mr. Fisher catches sight of me. "Rooney! Happy Thanksgiving! Here, I want to introduce you to my sister, Bonnie."

Bonnie is plump and as wholesome-looking as a bowl of oatmeal. I hold out my hand, but she sweeps me into a pillowy hug. "Nope, I'm a hugger. I'm afraid there's no escaping. Especially on Thanksgiving!"

"I need to check on drinks," Mr. Fisher says. "Get Rooney settled in, okay?"

"Don't worry, Jimmy. I'll make sure she doesn't waste away from hunger."

She steers me toward the dining room, where there are about twenty dishes on the sideboard and a few dozen people happily eating and chatting. "Are all of these people your family?" I ask, trying to be social in spite of my mood.

Luckily, Bonnie has enough small talk in her for both of us. "Oh, gosh no. I suppose you could say they're like family to Jim and Aurelia. But I'm the only blood relation here tonight." She points to some people across the room. "That woman is in Aurelia's book group, I think. The guy standing next to her built Jimmy's website. The two of them seem to collect people wherever they go. They just love to take in strays . . ." She seems to realize what she's saying a second too late, and her cheeks turn bright red. "Oh, I didn't mean . . ."

"It's all right." My face feels hot, too. "I should probably check on Daniel."

"Sure." She looks so embarrassed I immediately feel bad for her.

I make my way through the crowded rooms until I finally find Daniel sitting near the top of the stairs, a plate of food balanced on his knees.

I sit a few steps below him. "Are you hiding up here?"

He nods. "I don't know anyone."

"I know. It's noisy, too. We can just hang out here."

He looks down at his plate. "They had turkey at the hospital. And cranberry sauce." He's probably only talking to me because he feels as overwhelmed as I do. Still, I'm grateful he's talking at all.

"How did she seem?" I ask.

"She wasn't as thin. But she still seems . . ."

It doesn't matter that he doesn't finish the thought. I can picture her as clearly as if I'd been there myself.

We sit there until the doorbell chimes just above our heads. "Maybe I should get that," I say after a minute. "I doubt anyone else heard it."

I push through the crowd to the mudroom just in time to see the door swing open and Mercer peek inside. He holds out a pie to me. "I grew the pumpkin myself."

"You're amazing. I'll put it with the desserts, okay?"

He follows me to the dining room, his eyes getting bigger as he takes in the crowd. "This place is packed!"

"Do you want to meet everyone?"

"Not really," he admits. "I kind of just wanted to see you."

I push him back toward the door. "I'll get my coat." I meet him outside and we nestle into the wooden porch swing. The slats are cold through my thin jeans, but I'd still rather be out here with Merce than inside with all those happy strangers.

"You seem kind of . . . pensive," he says after a while.

"Yeah. I guess I am."

"Well, don't worry about it. It's totally normal for a refugee." He elbows me gently, trying to make me smile. "Too soon?"

"Not actually funny."

"Sorry. But seriously, Rooney, things could be a lot worse. You've got a place to stay, and people looking out for you. And there's a ton of food in that house. You definitely don't have to worry about starving."

"I know."

"But best of all . . ."

"Yeah?"

"You've got a smokin' hot boyfriend who bakes you pies."

I can feel the corners of my mouth tugging upward in spite of myself. "True."

"So, you know, count your blessings. It's Thanksgiving."

I go back inside as Mrs. Fisher is walking into the mudroom. "There you are, Marina. I was just coming to look for you."

"I was getting some air."

She looks over her shoulder toward the still-crowded dining room. "I'm sorry, this must all be a bit much for you."

"No, it's really nice of you and Mr. Fisher to include us. Thank you."

"You are most welcome, Marina. Happy Thanksgiving."

"Happy Thanksgiving."

I wander through the house, looking for Daniel, but there's no sign of him. He's probably gone to his room, and after I eat a little turkey and a slice of Mercer's pie, I do the same.

For the first time since my fight with Dad, I open up Mom's laptop and check my email. There are six messages from him, and two more from Carol. I open the latest one, sent just a few hours ago. "Marina, I just want you to know I'm thinking of you and Daniel. I know we have a lot to talk about. I hope we can do that soon. Happy Thanksgiving. Love, Dad."

I read it a few times, close it, then open it again, my hand hovering over the keyboard until I hit REPLY. I type and delete twelve different responses. Finally, I settle on a simple "Happy Thanksgiving," and click SEND.

DECEMBER

one

"I have some news," Mrs. Fisher announces at dinner tonight. "You have a new baby sister."

The room goes dead quiet as Daniel and I stop chewing, talking, or even breathing.

"You talked to Dad?" I finally ask.

"Yes. He called this afternoon from the hospital. She's a few weeks early, so she's a bit underweight, but otherwise she's healthy."

"And Carol?"

"She's just fine."

"There's something else," Mr. Fisher adds. "Your dad wants to come visit in a couple of weeks." He turns to look at Daniel, who still hasn't said a word. "How do you guys feel about that?"

"Is he coming to get us?"

"To take you to New York, you mean?" Mr. Fisher asks.

Daniel nods. He's as pale as a sheet of paper.

"I think it's best we take things one step at a time," Mrs. Fisher says calmly. "Your father will be here in two weeks, and then we can talk about all the options. All right?"

—

The next day is Saturday, and Mercer and I have plans to study at his house. He picks me up in his dad's car after lunch.

"So guess who's coming to see us," I say as he pulls away from the Fishers' house.

He takes his eyes off the road just long enough to read my expression. "Your dad?"

I nod.

"Just for a visit?"

"I don't know. The Fishers were kind of vague about the whole thing."

"When?"

"Weekend after next."

His eyebrows furrow. "Crap. We'll be in Florida."

"I know." It was my first thought when the Fishers told us last night. Mercer won't even be around to say good-bye if Dad makes us leave with him.

His mom greets me a little too enthusiastically at the door. "Nice to see you, Rooney! How are you?"

"I'm all right," I say, wishing again I hadn't let Mercer tell her everything. "I have a new half sister." I'm not even sure why I tell her, but Mercer's eyes bug out.

Mrs. Phillips congratulates me, and Mercer and I retreat to the den. "Um, any particular reason you skipped that detail before?" he asks as soon as we're out of earshot.

"You're going to think I'm horrible."

"So what else is new?"

"Very funny."

"So? Why didn't you tell me about the baby?"

"Honestly, it's because I forgot. I know it's a big deal, but all

I can think about is Dad's visit. And anyway, having a baby sister, it just feels . . . abstract. Like something that's happening to someone else, not to me. Does that make any sense?"

"Yeah. I get it."

"My whole life just feels unreal to me right now."

"Except me, though, right?"

"Right. Except you."

Even with Mrs. Phillips just one room away, we don't get much studying done that afternoon.

The Fishers have taken Daniel to visit Mom twice in the time we've been living with them. Both times they've asked if I wanted to go along, and both times I've begged out of it. When Daniel sees her, he always comes back all tired and withdrawn, like she's sucked the life right out of him. Seeing him that way only makes me more determined to avoid her. I can't afford to let her drain me dry right now, because my whole life is going to be decided in the next two weeks. Not just because of Dad, but because I'm supposed to hear from Columbia any day now. I'm so stressed out it feels like the tiniest push could send me right over the cliff.

Normally, I'd at least have winter break to look forward to. But with Mercer and his family going out of town, and my promise to cover for Maddie at the shop so she can take her kids skiing, it's not going to feel like a vacation at all. It's just going to be another long dress rehearsal for a depressing real life I never wanted.

I can tell Mercer feels bad about leaving because he's extra sweet whenever I see him. A week after the Dad bombshell we're sitting in his den when he asks what I want for Christmas. "Well, I could use a future," I joke. "Got one of those handy?"

"You got it." He makes a check-the-box gesture in the air. "One bright, shiny future. What else?"

It's not the first time I've thought about it, and the whole idea just makes me anxious. "Honestly? Let's not get each other gifts."

"Why not?"

"Because if you're not going to be here, I'd rather just pretend it's not Christmas at all. And besides, I'm broke. I can't get you anything, so I don't want you to get me anything."

"But what if I want to?"

"Just . . . don't, okay?"

He drops it, but I can tell he's not that happy about it, and I add it to the list of ways I'm not a very good girlfriend.

Two days later he's leaning over my shoulder when I log on to Columbia's website to learn my fate. We both hold our breath until my status appears. And then I slam the computer shut and fling myself facedown on the sofa.

"Deferred isn't so bad," he says, resting his hand on my back. "It's not a rejection. It's just a 'not yet.'"

I barely even hear him. My brain is like a swirling black vortex that no light can penetrate.

The rest of the week is a never-ending festival of suckage. I have to crank out a bunch more applications since I didn't get in early, and every personal essay I write feels like having my skin stripped off. Tell you about a significant experience? No, thank you. An influential person? I'd rather not. My future goals? Are you *trying* to make me cry?

Things at "home" aren't showing much sign of improvement either. I thought maybe Daniel was coming around on Thanksgiving, but when I saw him the next day, he was colder than ever. It just seems so unfair. Around the Fishers, he's as sweet and funny as he always used to be. It's only around me that the wall goes up. I'm not saying he doesn't have a right to be mad at me; I know I've messed some things up. But all I've ever done is try to look out for him. It would be nice if he appreciated that just a tiny bit.

By the end of the week, I'm a wreck. Even Mercer can't get a smile out of me, and the fact that he keeps trying just makes things worse. It's like he refuses to see how bad things really are. And now he's leaving town just when I need him most. By the time Dad gets here, Mercer will be a thousand miles away.

At about five thirty on Friday, the bell jingles and I look up from my textbook. It's a sleety day, the coldest of the year so far, and he's bundled up in a hat and scarf and a big coat. Plus, I wasn't expecting him until closing time. So I don't recognize him right away. And then he takes off the hat and I see his face and feel like I'm going to hurl.

I've spent the last two weeks thinking about what to say to him, trying to find the right balance between apology and declaration of independence. But now, with him standing in front of me, the words all fly out of my head, and I'm left fumbling around in the empty space of my brain, trying to think of something, anything at all, to say.

"Hi, Dad" is what I finally manage to croak out.

"Hi," he says. "Is this . . . Is it okay that I'm early?"

I close my book and stand up but don't walk around the counter toward him. I don't want him to see that my legs are shaking. "Um, yeah, I guess so. We don't have any customers right now."

"Mrs. Fisher told me it's usually pretty quiet around now. I thought maybe the two of us could talk for a minute before we head over to their place." He takes off his coat and scarf and drops them on one of the café chairs.

"Oh, um, okay," I say. *Say you're sorry. Say anything!* "Do you . . . want any coffee or anything?"

"A cup of coffee would be great, thanks," he says.

"The cream and sugar and stuff are self-serve," I say as I hand him the cup.

"Thanks," he says again. "Black is fine." He clears his throat. "Listen, Marina, the reason I came here early is that I wanted to make sure we had a chance to talk on our own. I owe you an apology. Actually, I owe you so many apologies that I'm not quite sure where to start."

"You came here to apologize to *me*?" I blurt out. I'm prepared for him to lecture me, to yell at me, even to pretend our fight never happened. But not this.

"Well, that's one of the reasons, yeah. I came here because there are things I need to fix."

His voice has a tiny catch in it, and I suddenly realize that he's even more nervous than I am. Knowing that he's terrified makes me feel calmer. "Maybe we should sit down," I tell him, and lead him over to the café table where his coat and hat are piled up.

He takes a cautious sip from the hot cup. "I've been replaying that fight in my head for weeks, imagining all the ways I could've pulled us out of the nosedive." He looks up at me. "The thing is, I don't know you very well, Marina. You and I, we haven't spent that much time together since you were little. And I guess I didn't realize how much you had grown up to be like me. I would never let anyone make decisions for me, and I shouldn't have expected you to just sit back and let me start making decisions for you."

"You were trying to help," I say. "I shouldn't have reacted like that."

"I was," he says, "but I didn't go about it in the best way. I can get a little"—he waves his hand in front of his eyes—"tunnel vision. You know?"

"I know what you mean," I tell him. "I get that way, too."

He nods. "Anyway," he says, "things got a little out of control. I was under a lot of stress, but that's no excuse. After I calmed down, I knew I needed to tell you I was sorry. But then, you know, you weren't answering my emails . . ."

Before, it seemed impossible to say the words, but they aren't sticking in my throat anymore. "I'm sorry, too," I tell him. "I just . . . I haven't had a lot of control over my life, you know?"

He nods. "I get that. I shouldn't have come on so strong."

I look at him and realize that for the first time in weeks, my stomach isn't a pit of gnawing anxiety. "Thanks for coming, Dad," I tell him. "I'm glad you're here."

"Me too," he says.

Just then, the bell jingles as the door opens. "Sorry, I'll be back in a minute." I walk over to wait on a big guy wearing a trucker's cap. He asks for the biggest to-go cup of black coffee that I've got and two doughnuts. I tell him it's an end-of-day special and wrap up the last three doughnuts for him. No point in letting one go to waste.

When Big Trucker Guy goes back outside, I carry the coffeepot over to Dad's table. "Want the last little bit before I clean up?" I ask.

He grimaces and shakes his head. "I'd better not. I've already had a few cups today. I'm just so sleep-deprived right now. I can't wait until we get into a more regular routine with the baby."

I hope he doesn't notice the startled look on my face. *God, what is wrong with me? What kind of person keeps forgetting they have a sister?* "How is she doing? And what about Carol?" I ask.

"They're both doing great," he says, his eyes crinkling. "Want to see pictures?" He pulls out his phone, scrolls through some photos and then shows one to me. "That's your little sister."

It's a picture from the hospital, with Carol holding a tiny bundle all wrapped up in a striped blanket. It could be a loaf of bread, except for the red, wrinkled little face and the mop of dark hair. Carol's face is red and puffy and her hair is kind of matted and sweaty-looking, but she looks happy. Really happy.

Dad flicks through some more photos and then shows me another. "Here's one from last night. She's already a little bigger."

I look at the picture and try to see some resemblance to Dad or Carol. She pretty much looks like a baby. "She's beautiful," I tell Dad, since I know that's what you're supposed to say about people's babies.

Dad grins at me. "Yeah, she's amazing, isn't she? Can you believe how much she looks like you?"

"Like me?" I ask. "You think so?" I pull the phone back and take a closer look at the picture. I have no idea what he's talking about.

"Well, not like you today, but exactly like you when you were a baby."

I don't know what I looked like as a baby. Mom was never big on memorabilia, since you couldn't take it to the Next World. "If you say so," I say, handing him back the phone.

"Well, actually, you don't have to take my word for it." He reaches down into his bag and pulls out a small wrapped package. "Merry almost-Christmas. There's a check in there, too," he says awkwardly, "since I know you worry about money . . . But I wanted you to have this."

"Thanks, Dad. Should I open it now?"

He nods and I tear away the paper to reveal a photo book. On the cover is a picture that I immediately recognize, though I haven't seen it in years. It was my favorite picture when I was little: me leaning over Daniel's bassinet, kissing him on the forehead. It must have been taken the day he came home from the hospital. The look on my face is pure rapture, like someone had just given me the best gift in the world. Which, in a way, they had.

"Look inside," Dad says softly as I try to swallow down the lump forming in my throat.

I turn to the first page. A formal, black-and-white picture of a couple in traditional wedding clothes, with "Greta and Benjamin Harris" printed below it. "Those are your grandparents. Do you remember them?" he asks.

"A little. Not like this, though."

"No, of course they were a lot older when you knew them." He flips through the pages, and the photos go from black-and-white to faded color.

"That's you?" I ask, pointing to a cocky-looking boy in a baseball uniform with "Harris" stitched on it. Dad nods and flips the pages again.

"And that's you. At just about the same age that Rosie is now."

I study the picture, trying to see what he saw, the link between me and my new baby sister. But aside from the fact that we both have cheeks, eyes, noses, and mouths, it's hard to find much of a connection.

"Her name is Rosie?"

"Technically, it's Rosalind. After Carol's grandmother."

"Rosalind Harris. That's pretty."

Dad nods. "Rosalind's a lot of name for someone so little, though. So it's Rosie for now."

He pages through the book. Pictures of me as a six-year-old in my dance recital costume. A picture of Dad pulling Daniel on a sled in the park. The picture Carol made us take outside the pizza parlor. And then, on the last page, one of Dad, Carol, and Rosie. "You can always go online and update it with pictures of your friends, or whatever. But I wanted you to have pictures of your family, too. I want you to know where you came from," he says.

"It's perfect, Dad. Thank you." I kiss him quickly on the cheek, and he smiles in a way that makes him look about twenty years younger.

"I made one for Daniel, too," he says. "I wish we could all spend Christmas together. But the baby is so little, and Carol's not ready to travel yet. And with her mom staying at our place, we don't have room for everyone. But at least I can have an early Christmas with you guys."

So . . . he's not taking us back with him. Not yet, anyway. I glance at the clock on the back wall. It's Daniel's turn to meet his father. "We should go. Let me just get things squared away here."

I run through the end-of-day checklist as quickly as I can. When we step outside, sleet is pelting down and the streets look slick and icy. He futzes with his keys and the alarm on a car parked nearby goes off. We both jump at the noise, and he laughs sheepishly. "Sorry, rental." He silences the alarm, then opens the passenger door for me.

We drive slowly through town, the windshield wipers thumping rhythmically. When we turn onto the Fishers' street, I point out their driveway, but he eases into a space a little way down the block.

"Why aren't you pulling in?"

"I just need to collect my thoughts for a minute."

Of course he's stalling. He's scared out of his mind. "Daniel," I say.

"I'm finally going to meet him tonight." He loosens his scarf and massages the back of his neck. "You know, when Carol and I met you for dinner that night, I felt like I was going to go into cardiac arrest. I had no idea what to expect, what you would be like. But this is ten times worse. At least you were already a person by the time your mom and I split up. I don't know the first thing about Daniel, other than what you've told me."

"It will be fine," I tell him.

"I'm going to need your help, Marina."

"My help?"

"Well, maybe 'advice' would be a better word," he says. "It's so important that this goes well. I mean, I know that's not your problem. I'm not, you know, asking you to put in a good word for me or anything. But I sure could use some advice about the best way to approach him. And you know him better than anyone."

"Not really. Daniel and I aren't talking much right now."

"Really? I got the impression you two were so close."

There's no point going into all the reasons why that's not true anymore. "We were. I hope we will be again. But right now, we're not."

"Sorry," he says. "So no advice, huh? No words of wisdom?"

"Actually, yeah, I have one piece of advice."

He looks up at me expectantly.

"You should stop stalling and get out of this car before we both freeze to death."

He laughs. "All right, then. Maybe you're right. Best to do it quickly."

"Like pulling out a tooth," I say.

"Or ripping off a Band-Aid," Dad says. He's quiet for a second, then adds, "Should I be worried that all these analogies sound so painful?"

I give him an encouraging smile. "On the count of three?"

"Let's do it."

On three we throw open the car doors and make a run for the Fishers' front porch. It takes maybe fifteen seconds to reach it, but the sleet is coming down so hard that we're both soaked by the time we get to the door.

He looks at me. "Should I ring the bell or . . . ?"

"I usually just let myself in." I point toward the door handle, which is behind his back, but he doesn't get the hint and move out of the way.

"Oh. You have a key?"

"Sure. They don't usually lock the door until bedtime, though."

"Oh, right. Sure. That makes sense." He flexes his neck and rolls his shoulders like he's about to step into a boxing ring.

At this rate, the two of us will be standing on this porch all night. I put a hand on his shoulder. "Let's go in, Dad."

"Right. After you."

He steps aside, and I push the door open. As I go inside, I can hear him whispering, *"Shit. Shit, shit, shit!"* under his breath.

two

After the cold car, it feels extra warm and bright inside the house. There are voices coming from the kitchen, and I can smell dinner cooking.

We step into the mudroom and pull off our boots. I show Dad where to hang his coat and scarf and then we stand there looking at each other. "Maybe, um . . . I think I'll wait here for a minute while you go in," he says. "I don't want to just walk into their house unannounced."

"Okay. Be right back," I tell him. "Don't go anywhere."

He gives me what is probably supposed to be a cheerful smile but looks more like seasickness. I point at the bench. "Have a seat," I suggest, and then head toward the sound of voices.

As usual, Mr. Fisher is at the stove. Daniel's setting the table while Mrs. Fisher corrects a stack of papers. The scene is so peaceful that part of me wants to turn around and drag Dad away from here. We've all had enough dramarama in our lives. Maybe it's not such a great idea to reunite the long-lost father with the troubled son. But there's no turning back now, so I walk into the kitchen and announce, "Dad's here."

Daniel jumps up. "Where is he?"

"He's waiting in the mudroom. I wanted to make sure you were—"

Before I can finish my sentence, Daniel bolts past me and down the hall toward the front door. He stops short at the entrance to the mudroom. The Fishers are standing right behind me, and the three of us watch as Dad steps out and the two of them look at each other. There's a painfully long pause, with neither of them moving or saying anything. And then they both move at once. Dad steps forward and extends his hand to Daniel at the same instant that Daniel opens his arms and sort of flings himself at Dad. There's an awkward fumbling moment while Dad tries to readjust, but it's too late. The two of them end up shaking hands, like two businessmen at a meeting. "It's nice to meet you, Daniel," Dad says stiffly.

"You too," Daniel mumbles, looking down at his shoes.

And then they just stand there. Dad looks at me, his eyes pleading, but I have no idea how to help them. I'm still trying to get over the shock of seeing Daniel hurling himself at a total stranger. It's like he saw a kid act that way in a movie once, and figured that was how boys were supposed to greet their fathers. Poor kid. What does he know about having a dad?

Mr. Fisher steps forward and holds out his hand. "I'm James," he says. "Good to meet you, Mr. Harris."

"Peter." Dad clasps Mr. Fisher's hand in both of his. "Thank you so much for inviting me into your home."

Dinner turns out to be one of the strangest experiences of my life, and that's really saying something. Once Daniel recovers from the greeting awkwardness, he dives in with a kind of crazed energy I've never seen before. For the next two hours, he basically doesn't stop talking. He tells Dad all about school, what he's reading, the project he's working on with Mr. Fisher in the woodshop. He's like a puppy, wriggling around and licking people's faces, trying to make them love him. The one thing he isn't like, even a tiny bit, is my brother, Daniel.

A few times I look at Mr. and Mrs. Fisher, as if to ask *What the heck is going on here?* but they just shrug and smile.

After dinner is over, Daniel asks Dad to come up and see his room. "Shouldn't we help clean up first?" Dad asks.

"I'll do Daniel's chores tonight," I say, hoping to score a few points, but Daniel doesn't even seem to notice.

Long after the dishes are done, they haven't come back downstairs. Now and then, there's a burst of high-pitched laughter from Daniel, or Dad's lower chuckle, but mostly there's no sound.

"What do you think they're talking about up there?" I ask Mr. Fisher.

"Hard to say," he says softly. "They have a lot of lost time to make up for."

I know I should be glad that Daniel and Dad are hitting it off. But nothing about this feels natural.

"He was acting so weird at dinner, wasn't he?" I say.

The Fishers exchange a look. "Well, he did seem a little . . . keyed up," Mr. Fisher admits. "But we probably need to cut him some slack. It's a pretty bizarre situation, after all."

"It certainly is," Mrs. Fisher agrees. "One can hardly blame him for getting overexcited."

Finally, a good hour after Daniel's usual bedtime, Dad comes back downstairs.

"Wow," I say. "I wasn't expecting that at all."

Dad grins. "Yeah, me neither. The way you described him, I thought he'd be shy. Boy, was I off base!"

I look over at the Fishers again, wondering if someone's going to clue Dad in, but neither of them seems to want to rock the boat.

"I can't thank you enough," Dad tells the Fishers. "I don't think there's any way I can compensate you for everything you've done for my family, but I want you to know, I'm beyond grateful."

Mrs. Fisher smiles at him. "I'm delighted it went so well."

"I'm sorry to have kept you all up so late," Dad says. "I'm going to head to my hotel now."

"Of course. We'll see you in the morning," Mrs. Fisher says.

I walk Dad back out to the mudroom. "So what did you guys talk about up there?"

"We talked about . . . well, pretty much everything."

"Including custody?"

Dad nods, his eyes wide. "Yeah. He didn't even seem surprised. I think he's been worrying about it so much, maybe it was a relief just to have an actual conversation about it."

"So is that it? Daniel's going to live with you?"

"Well . . . No, it's not settled or anything. It's something we need to discuss some more. I'd like to talk about it with both of you tomorrow, if that's okay."

"Sure."

He hugs me good-bye and steps back out into the cold.

Before I go to sleep, I send Mercer an email. "Sorry I've been such a basket case all week. Things went OK with Dad. Still no idea what happens next, but I guess we're going to talk tomorrow. Hope you're having fun in the sun. PS: email is the worst. I miss you."

The next morning, Dad is back in time to help set the table. We stick to chitchat over breakfast, but as soon as the last dish is washed, the Fishers tell us they have some errands to do and excuse themselves.

"So . . ." Dad says when the door shuts behind them.

"So . . ." I echo, feeling my pulse quickening. Daniel looks from Dad to me. He seems a lot more subdued than he was last night.

"I asked the Fishers if we could have a little time alone, because I want to talk to you guys," Dad says. "We have some decisions to make . . . as a family. And I want you to know, the Fishers and I have talked about this, and we all agree that the choice is up to you. Whatever you decide is okay. With all of us." He looks at us in turn. "Understood?"

We nod. I don't know about Daniel, but I can feel my pulse jumping in my throat.

"All right. I've been doing some research into schools near Carol and me." I take in a sharp breath and he glances at me before continuing. "There are some options, but to tell the truth, none of them are perfect. Daniel, there's a school across town that has an opening. If you want, you could go there in January. I'd prefer to find someplace closer eventually, but at least it would be a place to start." He turns to look at me. "The high school situation is trickier. You were right: Schools aren't that keen to take a student for a single semester. But if you want to come, we'll make it work."

He pauses, giving us a second to catch up. "The other option is that the Fishers have offered to let you finish the school year here. We've talked about this a lot, and to be honest, I'm very ambivalent. The Fishers have been unbelievably generous already, and I feel pretty uncomfortable asking two people I barely know to look after my kids. But I know they really care about you guys, and they can give you stability that no one else can right now. So if you want to stay here until the school year is over, you can. And I promise, I won't be hurt or mad or anything." He pauses and looks at each of us in turn. "I mean it. Okay?"

We nod again. I feel Daniel watching me, but he looks away the second I glance at him.

"Okay. I know this is a big decision, and I hate to rush you. But I'm going back home tomorrow afternoon, and it would be good to know by then so I can get the wheels turning first thing on Monday if I need to. Fair enough?"

"Yes," Daniel and I both say.

Dad rubs his hands on his thighs. His palms are probably sweating. I know mine are. "Great. So now that that's out of the way, let's talk about how we're going to spend the rest of this weekend. What do you guys like to do for fun?"

It's a perfectly reasonable question, but Daniel and I both look blank. "Skiing? Museum? Monopoly?" Dad suggests.

"We don't know how to ski," I say.

"You live in Vermont and you never learned to ski," Dad says incredulously. "Honestly, your mother . . ."

"Could we go to a movie?" Daniel asks quickly.

"Sure. Let's check the listings."

Daniel chooses an animated sci-fi flick that's playing at a

mall a few towns away. "What about you, Marina? Does that interest you?" Dad asks doubtfully.

"It's not really my thing. Why don't you guys go, and I'll meet up with you for dinner?" I thought that was what Daniel wanted, why he chose a movie he knew I wouldn't want to see, but the look he gives me makes me wonder if I've gotten it wrong again.

"Okay. We'll be back in a few hours."

Once they're out the door and I have the house to myself, the first thing I do is check my email. Merce wrote back last night a few minutes after I closed the laptop. Just one sentence: "DOES THAT MEAN YOU'RE STAYING?"

Dad picks me up after the movie, and we go to Myrtle's for dinner. Not because it's so great but because the only other option in town is a pathetic pizza place where the crust tastes like supermarket bagels. "This place hasn't changed at all," Dad says, shaking his head in amazement. "I used to bring you guys here for really terrible waffles."

"You did?" Daniel asks. "When?"

"A long time ago. When you were just a sprout."

The waitress dumps a red plastic basket of bread and butter on our table along with the menus. "So what's good here?" Dad asks.

The truth is, it's been a long time since Daniel and I have eaten in a restaurant, even a semi-crummy one like Myrtle's. "I think the pot pie is pretty good," I say.

"Perfect," Dad says happily. "Who doesn't like pot pie?"

We order three pot pies and then Dad tries to get Daniel to tell me about the movie. It's like pulling teeth. Daniel has retreated fully into "I hate Rooney" mode, and I can tell Dad is confused by it. After a while, he gives up and tells me about it himself.

The food comes quickly, and the pot pies are delicious, but the three of us can't seem to get a conversation going to save our lives. "So, Marina," Dad says after a particularly long and awkward silence. "When are you supposed to hear from Columbia? Should be any day now, right?"

The bite I'm chewing turns to glue in my mouth. I manage to choke it down, then take a sip of water before I answer. "I heard on Monday," I say.

They both stare at me. "And . . . ?" Dad asks.

"Deferred."

"Oh, honey, I'm sorry. I wish I'd known."

I put my fork down and wipe my mouth. "Yeah. Sorry. There was just so much going on that I didn't have a chance to mention it."

"So what does deferred mean, exactly?"

"It means they don't want me enough to let me in early."

"But they might still accept you?"

"They might. I won't know anything until March or April."

Dad looks stricken, and Daniel won't make eye contact with me. Suddenly the whole evening feels like a funeral.

"It's all going to work out," Dad says. "If it's not Columbia, you'll go somewhere else. And wherever you end up, they'll be lucky to have you."

I look down at my plate, hoping he'll just let it drop. In the last few days, I've been ping-ponging around between feeling ashamed for not getting in, and feeling something surprisingly close to relief.

Daniel pushes his chair back. "I have to go to the restroom."

When he's gone, Dad covers my hand with his. "I'm sorry you didn't get in early, Marina. But I swear, it will all work out."

"Maybe it's for the best," I say. "There's no money for college anyway."

He tugs at my hand, forcing me to meet his eyes. "Now hold on. I don't want you worrying so much about money. Yeah, it's going to take some work. You'll get financial aid, we'll take out loans, whatever. But we'll figure it out. Okay?"

"Okay."

Dad looks over his shoulder toward the restrooms. "Daniel seems awfully quiet this evening."

"Yeah, that's pretty standard around me these days."

"You know, you say that you and Daniel aren't close right now. But do you know what he asked me in the car this afternoon?"

"What?"

"He wanted to know if I thought you would choose to go to New York."

"Why?"

"Well, I'm no mind reader, but my guess is, his decision depends on your decision."

"He probably wants to know what I'm doing so he can do the opposite."

Dad folds his arms across his chest and leans back in his chair. "I don't think so. I think he's coming around. Just give him time, Marina."

I had planned to wait until tomorrow to tell Dad my decision, but the moment feels right. "I'd like to stay in Stonebrook, Dad," I say, as gently as I can. "I'm really glad that we're talking again, and I want us to be a family—you and Carol and baby Rosie. But I want to graduate with my class. I'm sorry."

Dad takes it in calmly. "Thanks for telling me. I sort of had a feeling." He cocks his head to one side. "Is there something in particular that's keeping you here? Or . . . someone?"

The heat spreads up my neck in a flash. "How did you know?"

"Well, Daniel did mention a friend of yours. I'm not sure Daniel has caught on, but it seemed pretty obvious to me that this wasn't just any friend. So I'm right? Is it serious?"

"I don't know. I'm not even sure what that means. But he's the one thing in my life that doesn't feel all messed up right now."

"I see," he says, a faint smile in his eyes. "So I'd say that's a yes, then." He gives me a long, thoughtful look. "And what if Daniel decides to come to New York for second semester?"

"I . . ." I haven't even let myself think about that. "I don't . . ."

He sees me struggling and stops me with a gesture. "Okay. We'll make it work."

On Sunday morning, Daniel and I go back to Myrtle's with Dad before his flight home. He insists on ordering the waffles, and his face scrunches up as he takes his first bite. "Yep, these are just like I remember. Like sugarcoated cardboard."

"You can have some of mine," I offer. "There's more here than I can finish."

Dad reaches across the table and forks up a bite of my pancakes. "Yeah, those are better. There's a restaurant near us that has amazing pancakes. In the summer, they make them with berries from the local greenmarket. I'd love to take you guys there." He looks at Daniel. "Daniel, I don't mean to pressure you, but Rooney let me know yesterday that she wants to stay in Vermont until school ends. Have you had a chance to think about it some more?"

Daniel nods.

"So . . . have you decided?" Dad asks gently.

"I want to stay here," Daniel says, his voice a whisper. "Is that all right?"

Dad's eyes barely move, but I can see the disappointment behind his carefully neutral expression. "Sure, buddy," he says. "I told you, whatever you decide is okay with me. And you'll come visit, and I'll visit you guys, too. We'll see each other all the time. And then next year . . ."

Daniel looks like he's on the verge of tears. I don't understand why he decided to stay. Maybe it's because he's gotten so close to Mr. Fisher. Or maybe it's because of Mom. Whatever it is, I'm glad. Even when he's barely talking to me, I can't imagine not seeing him every day.

Dad clears his throat. "So that's settled, then. And listen, guys, since we can't all be together next week, I wanted to at least give you your Christmas presents while I'm still here." He pulls out two small boxes and pushes them across the table to us.

"But you already gave us the photo books. And I didn't get you anything . . ." I feel like a big jerk.

"Believe me, this is as much a present for me as it is for you," Dad says. "Go ahead, open them."

Daniel and I pull off the wrapping paper to reveal brand-new phones. "My number is already programmed in there," Dad says. "I got us a family plan."

I feel Daniel watching me and look over at him. He meets my eyes for a few seconds, then pulls the phone out of its little plastic box.

"Thank you," he says.

"Yeah, this is amazing," I add. "Thank you so much!"

Dad smiles. "Honestly, I don't know why I waited so long. I should have gotten these for you a long time ago. Anyway, better late than never. Now we can always be in touch."

After breakfast, Dad drives us back to the Fishers' house. "Well . . ." he says, smiling a little too brightly. "This has been terrific. And I'm going to see both of you soon, right? You'll come to New York and meet your new baby sister?"

"Sure, that would be great," I say.

"Sure," Daniel echoes.

We all climb out of the car and I come around to the driver's side to hug him. "Thanks for everything," I say. "Give Carol and Rosie kisses from me."

Daniel hugs Dad, too, clinging to him for a long moment before he breaks away and climbs the stairs to the Fishers' door.

"We'd both like to stay, if that's all right," I tell the Fishers when they get home a little while later. Daniel and I have been sitting

at the kitchen table, playing with our phones. He's even programmed my number into his, which seems like a good sign.

"I'm very pleased," Mrs. Fisher says. "We both are."

"We really appreciate it," I say. "And we'll do whatever we can
to help out. I can buy groceries and stuff . . ."

She looks at me sharply. "You will do nothing of the kind.
Your father is covering your expenses, and the two of you will
continue to help out around the house. Beyond that, your only
job is to do well in school."

She marches out of the room and Mr. Fisher grins at us. "If
you thought that was bad, you should've seen the way she reacted
when your dad offered to pay rent."

"I didn't mean to offend her," I whisper.

"Nah, don't worry about that. But you guys are our guests
here." He turns to Daniel. "So what do you say, pal? Want to do
some work in the shop this afternoon?" Daniel nods eagerly and
follows him out the door.

I grab my phone and go to my room next to the kitchen. Mrs.
Fisher emptied out the narrow closet for me the week we arrived,
but I've never felt comfortable unpacking. My boxes are still
stacked next to the desk. I open the top one, dump out the jum-
ble of books and clothes that I brought over from our house, and
carefully put them away. When I'm done, the tiny room still
looks kind of cramped and cluttered, and it's still obviously Mrs.
Fisher's office, but it feels a little bit like mine, too.

I plop down on the sofa bed and program Mercer's number
into my phone. "hey" I write. My first text definitely won't be
winning any Pulitzers.

A few minutes later my phone dings. "who is this?"

"it's me Rooney"

"whose # is this?"

"mine! dad got me a phone"

"sweet!!!!!!" He sends a GIF of a dog getting a big bone tied with a bow, and I send him back a picture of a baby talking on a phone. We go back and forth a few more times until he texts, "gtg buy a tree with parents. ttyl?"

"ok"

He sends me a row of hearts, and I send him back a little parade of kissy-faces, and then he's gone.

Maybe it's not great literature, but texting is a whole lot better than email.

But still a whole lot worse than actually being together.

Christmas with the Fishers turns out to be much more low-key than Thanksgiving. Daniel and I make breakfast for them, and afterward we unwrap presents. Mr. Fisher gives Daniel his own set of woodworking tools. Mrs. Fisher gives me a beautiful leather-bound notebook. "For your future writing endeavors," she says as I unwrap it. "Not too far in the future, I hope," she adds.

I give Mrs. Fisher a fat historical novel, Mr. Fisher a cookbook, and Daniel a new drawing pad and colored pencils. Mrs. Fisher scolds me for buying them presents with my savings, but I can tell from the way she handles the book that she can't wait to drag it off to her reading chair. Daniel saves his gifts for last. "I didn't make them all by myself," he explains as he hands them out. "Mr. Fisher helped me." There's a cutting board for Mr.

Fisher, a pair of bookends for Mrs. Fisher, and then he hands me a package. I tear the paper open to find a little wooden box. "You can keep pens in it. Or whatever you want," he says.

I run my hand over it, feeling the warm, smooth wood and the softly rounded corners. It must have taken him hours to make, and I suddenly wish I'd spent more time on his present. The way things have been between us lately, I honestly wasn't sure he'd even give me anything. "Did you really make this? It's beautiful!" I say.

"Daniel has a great eye," Mr. Fisher says. "He's going to be a fine craftsman if he keeps it up."

From the way Daniel looks, I have a feeling those words are the best present he got today.

"So," Mrs. Fisher says when all the gift wrap has been gathered up. "We are going to go visit your mother at her friends' house. Marina, will you join us?" I can tell she wants me to go, but she doesn't push.

Daniel, on the other hand, doesn't hold back. "It's Christmas, Rooney. You should come with us!" He says it like there's some kind of family tradition to uphold, but Christmas hasn't exactly been a highlight of the year since we moved to Vermont. Mostly, it's just a time when Mom gets extra fragile and needy.

"You guys go ahead," I say. "I'm going to stay here." Even if I did want to see Mom, there's not enough family feeling in the world to get me to walk back into Susan and Roger's house after Departure Day.

Daniel gives me a look but doesn't say anything as the three of them leave.

—

It's already dark out when they get back. I've spent the afternoon studying and texting with Merce, and I actually feel a little disappointed when I hear their voices. Still, I make myself walk out to meet them as they're pulling off their coats.

"How's Mom?" I ask.

Daniel gives an angry shrug and goes up to his room. The Fishers exchange a look. "You should probably go after him," Mr. Fisher suggests.

It doesn't seem like such a great idea to me, but I traipse up the stairs and knock on his door anyway. "Can I come in?"

When he doesn't answer, I push the door open. Daniel glares at me from his bed. "So you're not talking to me again?" I ask.

"What do you care?"

Normally, I would try to soothe him, but something about the tone of his voice triggers me. "That's not fair, Daniel, and you know it."

"You don't care about this family. You won't even go see Mom on Christmas!" It's like he's deliberately trying to pick a fight.

"But that doesn't mean I don't care about you!"

Just then, my phone dings and I look down at it reflexively. Daniel jumps off the bed and points like it's Exhibit A in some courtroom drama. "You don't care about us! All you care about is your boyfriend!"

"That's not true!"

"Yes, it is! You don't even care if I stay here or go to New York. You don't care about any of us!"

My whole life, I've looked out for Daniel. I've stood up for him, taken care of him, and never fought with him the way most siblings do. But now, suddenly, I've had it. I'm tired of being taken for granted, of being the bad guy.

"What do you want, Daniel?" I yell. "Do you want me to not have a single good thing in my life?"

He turns away from me and I stomp out of his room. The only thing that keeps me from slamming the door behind me is knowing the Fishers are right downstairs.

JANUARY

one

Mercer finally gets back from Florida the Saturday before school starts, and as soon as his plane touches down, we start making plans for that night.

"I'll pick you up right after dinner."

"Can't wait. Where are we going?"

"Anywhere you want."

All I want is to be alone with him, so our options are pretty limited. We end up in the back seat of his dad's car, a tangle of arms and legs, rumpled, displaced clothing, and frustration. It's too cold out to stay there long, so eventually we make our way back to his house.

Both his parents are in the kitchen when we come in. "Happy New Year, Rooney," his mom says, and gives me a quick hug. His dad is usually more reserved, so I'm doubly surprised when he does the same.

"Happy New Year," I say, casually brushing my hand across the front of my blouse to make sure everything is buttoned.

"Merce told us the good news," his mom says. I glance over at Mercer, not sure what she means. "That you and your dad worked things out," she clarifies.

"And that you're staying through the rest of the year," his dad adds. "Wonderful news!"

They excuse themselves and Mercer wraps his arms around me, his nose pressed against mine. "So listen, I have something for you."

"But we said no presents," I protest.

"Right, no Christmas presents. This is a New Year's gift. Totally different. Anyway, it didn't cost me a cent, so you can't get all freaked out about it."

"What is it?"

"Hang on. Close your eyes." I feel his arms release me and then I hear a sound like a paper bag rustling. A second later, the smell of citrus fills my nose.

"You brought me oranges?"

"Best oranges in the world. From Grandma's backyard. Here, open your mouth."

I do, and he deposits something on my tongue. I bite down and an explosion of sweet juice fills my mouth. It is, without question, the best orange I've ever eaten. It tastes like love.

With my eyes still closed, I wipe a trickle of juice from the corner of my mouth, and I feel him take my hand and lick my finger like a cat. Instantly, my legs go all wobbly. I open my eyes and see he's smiling into my face. "Anyway, you got me a present, too. You're staying."

The Friday of MLK weekend, Daniel goes to New York. Dad invited both of us, but Daniel and I are still barely speaking, which could get pretty awkward in Dad's little apartment, so I bowed out. Mercer's gone for the weekend, too, on his annual family snowshoeing trip.

Mrs. Fisher has been pushing me to write an appeal letter to Columbia, and with everyone gone and school just starting up, I don't have an excuse not to get started. So I spend Saturday trying to explain why I am so much more deserving than the thirty thousand other applicants who want to go there. I've been avoiding it for so long I've almost convinced myself that I hate writing. But once I get started, it's a pleasure to feel my fingers tapping away while sentences fit themselves together in my head. I don't even take a break until Dad calls on Saturday night.

I expect him to be bubbling over with stories about the great time they're all having, but he seems strangely quiet.

"So what have you been up to?" I ask.

"Oh, you know. This and that." He lets out a long breath. "Marina, I could use some advice from you."

"What about?"

"Well, I thought things were going well here. I mean, it's kind of a weird situation, but it seemed like everyone was doing great. But then . . ."

"Then what?" I prompt him.

"Well . . . I walked past Daniel's door last night, and I heard this sound."

My heart sinks. "He was crying?"

"Yeah. I think so. So that's . . . a thing he does?"

"Not that often," I say, feeling disloyal.

"I tried to ask him about it this morning and he went on and on about how happy he is to be here. But then tonight he seemed so quiet and withdrawn . . . If he's feeling homesick or whatever, that's totally understandable. But if he doesn't want to talk about it, I'm not sure what to do. The whole thing is all just . . ." He sounds worn-out, and sad.

"Just what?"

"Just . . . familiar," he says. "Uncomfortably familiar."

"Because of Mom." I know exactly what he means.

"Yeah. I guess I hadn't realized that Daniel's so much like her."

"Why did you marry her?" I ask, only realizing as the words come out of my mouth how wrong they sound.

"Wow, you don't beat around the bush, do you?"

"You don't have to tell me if you don't want to," I say, embarrassed.

"I married her because I loved her."

"Yeah, but . . ."

"Not really what you were looking for?"

"Well, I was hoping for a little more . . . specificity."

"So where do you want me to start?" he asks.

"From the beginning, I guess." I get my pillow and blanket out of the closet and toss them on the couch. Then I lie down and balance the phone on the side of my face. "Like, maybe where you met."

He sounds surprised. "Your mother never told you?"

"After we moved here, she almost never talked about you."

"Ah," he says. "Of course. Well, we met in college. In a biology class."

"Biology? I figured her more for the poetry type."

"Marina, your mother has a degree in environmental science."

"She does?" I ask, wondering if somehow I've misheard him.

"She won the science award for our year, plus, she got this really prestigious fellowship."

"Fellowship . . . ?"

"You honestly don't know any of this?"

I shake my head and catch the phone as it slides onto my neck. "Uh-uh."

"It was a big deal. She was working with a team in Antarctica, taking ice-core samples."

"Mom was. *My* mom?"

He chuckles. "I know. I guess it must be pretty hard to reconcile."

"Like almost impossible. So what happened?" I ask.

"Down there?"

"Well, yeah . . . and with the two of you?"

"I don't know, exactly," he says slowly. "Something just . . . changed for her. She dropped out of the study. She came back and moved in with me in New York. I had this terrible little studio apartment, and I was barely earning a living. But she said she wanted to get married, have a family."

"So that's what you did?"

"Eventually, yeah. She loved her work, so when she wrote to tell me she was walking away from it, I assumed it was just a temporary thing. Maybe I should have tried to persuade her to stick with it, but I was so sure she'd change her mind."

"But she didn't?"

"Nope. She gave it all up." His voice sounds far away. "We got married, and then you came along. And then we had Daniel, and . . . Well, you know what happened next."

He sounds like he's done talking, but there's still so much more I want to know. "I do and I don't. I know *what*, and more or less when. But I don't really know why."

"The why . . . that's always the hardest one, right?" I cradle the phone to my ear, waiting. "The truth is, I don't think I can give you a reason. I only have theories."

"Your theories are about the best lead I've got right now," I say.

"I guess that's true." He blows out a long, tired breath. "Look, Marina, there are plenty of ugly things I could say about your mother. But I want you to know that I loved her like crazy back then. You probably don't remember the good times, but we had a lot of happy years together. And when she was in a good place, emotionally, there was no one I wanted to be with more."

My mouth actually drops open and I sit up on the couch. "Why?"

Dad laughs. "Well, it didn't hurt that she was beautiful. Those eyes, my God . . . But honestly, it was her intellect. She wasn't just bright. She was . . . incandescent. All of your smarts, that GPA of yours? You better believe that didn't come from me. That was all her."

"So what happened? When did she turn into . . . this? Was it Everett?"

"I don't think it's that simple. Your mother was searching for something. And then she happened to find Everett. But if it hadn't been him, it probably would have been someone or something else. She needed answers, some way to make sense of it all. After she came back and we had you, she seemed better for a while. But then she had such a hard time being pregnant with Daniel. It seemed like she was always crying."

As he says it, I can picture Mom in the old apartment. She's holding Daniel all wrapped up in a blanket, and there are tears running down her cheeks. I always thought it was because I had done something bad.

"It wasn't like she woke up one day as a totally different person," he says. "It was a couple of years where the balance just kind of shifted. She went from someone who was bright and interested in the world and had a few bad days, to someone who couldn't cope at all. It got to the point where she wouldn't even talk about the work she did at the South Pole. Even mentioning it would send her into a tailspin."

"She just stopped talking about it?"

"About that and everything else that was real. But it all happened so gradually. And even when things got bad, there'd still be a good day every now and then, and I'd remember the way she used to be. So I held on for a long time. Maybe too long."

"I never knew any of that," I say. "I do remember the good times, though. I remember you guys laughing. But I remember her crying, too."

"I wonder . . ."

"What?"

"She had so much sadness inside of her. And Daniel was inside of her, too, you know? I wonder whether he somehow absorbed it from her. Maybe I should have done more to protect him from that."

"Do you think she's . . ." I've been throwing the word *crazy* around for years to describe Mom, Everett, everything about my life. But now, suddenly, it doesn't feel safe to say it out loud. ". . . mentally ill?"

He takes his time answering. "Looking back on it now, it's pretty clear there was something wrong. Something . . . chemical. Depression or . . . I don't know. Maybe your mom is just more sensitive than most."

Like Daniel.

"Well, anyway, that was all a long, long time ago," he says, his voice turning brisk. "All we can really do now is deal with what's in front of us."

"Right," I say, still reeling from this deluge of new information.

"So. No advice about Daniel, huh?"

"I don't know," I say, racking my brain for something that might help. "I think the crying is worse when he spends too much time in his own head. Maybe if you just keep him really busy, with you and Carol and the baby . . . ?"

"Thanks, Marina," Dad says. "I'll give that a try."

After I get off the phone, I sit in my room for a while, just thinking. It's so hard to imagine Mom as a science whiz, but it's even harder to picture the two of them, young and in love, just a few years older than I am now. There's something beautiful about knowing they loved each other, but it's a sad kind of beauty. They once meant everything to each other, and now they can't stand each other.

How does that happen? And how do you stop it?

The beginning of a dull ache is taking hold in my chest. I need to get out of this room and away from these thoughts. The lights in the kitchen are already off; the Fishers must have gone up to bed. Outside, big white flakes of snow are falling, drifting slowly like feathers. Staring out the window, I feel like the only person on Earth.

I wander upstairs and stand outside Daniel's room. The door is open a crack and I put my hand on it, hesitating, then push it open. I'm not sure what I'm looking for, exactly, just some kind of connection, something to fill the chasm of loneliness that's torn open in my chest. I breathe in the woody smell of the branches Mr. Fisher used to build the bed. I rub my thumb against its frame, feeling the roughness of the bark, then slide my hand down to the soft quilt. Daniel's been sleeping under this quilt for months, but it still has the smell of someone else's house. I reach for his pillow, holding it up to my nose. It's faint, but I can just make out a whiff of Daniel there.

I sit on his bed in the dark for a while, holding his pillow and breathing in its scent. I close my eyes and rock back and forth, which is comforting, but also makes me feel a little like a crazy person.

That thought is enough to stop me cold. I know I'm nothing like Mom. But Dad's description of her . . . what? Depression? Feelings of hopelessness? It feels just a little too close to home to me.

As I put the pillow back, my hand bumps into a stack of books and a few of them fall on the floor. I snap on the light and pick them up. I don't recognize any of them. They must be books Mr. Fisher lent him, or that he took out of the library. It's been a long time since Daniel told me what he was reading.

Then one catches my eye. It's the one about Easter Island from last fall, back before everything fell apart. When I pick it up, the smell of our old house fills my nose, and my head is flooded with snapshots from all the years we spent there.

Daniel's not coming home for two more days. As long as I put the book back by Monday afternoon, he'll never know the difference. I turn off the light and take it downstairs with me.

I need to sleep, but my brain won't quiet down, so I pick up the book and breathe in its scent again, hoping it will work some kind of sedative magic. No dice. I flip through it, like it will give me some clue to what Daniel is thinking and doing and feeling right now. It falls open to a section of black-and-white photos and, tucked between the pages, a few folded sheets of paper.

I immediately recognize Daniel's pencil sketches. He's drawn a row of giant stone figures lined up on a cliff, just like in the picture on the facing page. But there's something different in Daniel's version. They aren't just staring up into an empty sky. They're staring at a kind of fancy airplane flying overhead. I guess Daniel was trying to give them a reason for looking up. The idea makes me smile.

The next page has a bunch of separate sketches of those same figures. Only, instead of being cut off at the torso, each one has a different lower body. One has tentacles like an octopus, another has legs like a person but with wheels where the feet should be. A third has a tail like a snake. The drawings are strange and a little creepy, but also kind of fascinating, even beautiful in a way. I can see that Daniel was concentrating hard when he did them, and they're full of strange and amazing details.

I flip to the third page. More of the same, but there's something else, too. At the bottom of the page, Daniel has written HWARAL in neat block letters.

The word is like a cold hand on my neck. I flip back and look at that airplane again. Now that I'm really looking, it's obviously not a normal airplane. Daniel's drawn the stone figures on Easter Island looking up at a spaceship.

Easter Island . . . I reach for Mom's laptop as though I'm in a dream. It's not easy, now that the NWS website has been shut down, but after a little searching, I manage to track down a bootleg video of Everett's Town Hall lecture. I never want to hear that voice again, but something's tickling my brain, a fragment of a memory, and there's only one way to catch it. I click PLAY and hold my breath.

There's Everett, walking on stage in his expensive suit. The suit he bought with our rent checks, I know now. He starts his speech, and I listen closely, waiting for the moment that will unlock that memory. It doesn't take long.

"Easter Island. Stonehenge, the Plain of Jars, the Nazca Lines, all unexplained for so long," I hear him say again. "Now, in the light of the Writings, they resolve into obvious human attempts at communication on an interplanetary scale. The people of Earth were trying to reach the Hwaral. Perhaps they were trying to summon them back."

I can picture Daniel up in his room, watching this speech over and over, his brain stuffed full of Everett's words, Everett's visions. He must have been so excited when he thought he'd solved the mystery of those giant stone figures. *They were aliens*, I imagine him telling Max. *The Easter Islanders made them to tell the Hwaral to come back.*

I can feel the yearning in those drawings, the longing to believe in something more magical, more hopeful than regular life. Daniel put all of his heart and faith into those ideas of Everett's because what was happening in the real world was too scary. And all I did was tell him not to worry.

I tuck the drawings back in between the pages, and then I turn to the first chapter and start reading.

Right away, the writing draws me in. It's exactly the kind of brisk, vivid storytelling that Mrs. Fisher was always trying to coax out of us. For the second time today, I remember how much I loved writing for the *Sentinel*, working with Mrs. Fisher to polish and hone my words until they shone like diamonds. I wolf down page after page, knowing I should turn out the light, telling myself I'll stop at the end of the next chapter.

It's 2:00 a.m. when I finally close the book. The rest will have to wait until tomorrow. I'm working a Sunday shift and I have to be there in four hours.

I wake up still thinking about the book, and know right away that my day is going to be all about finishing it. Even while I'm foaming milk and toasting bagels, I can't stop thinking about it. Not because of the story but because I feel like I've discovered a code for unlocking Daniel, for understanding everything that's escaped me all this time. When he first told me about these people chopping down all their trees, I didn't understand why they mattered so much to him, or why he was so wrapped up in something so distant, so long ago, when we had such big problems here and now.

Now, reading the book myself, I feel like maybe I finally understand what Departure meant to him. And if I'd only done a better job of listening, maybe he wouldn't have followed Mom, and the two of us would still be a team.

I finish the book late Sunday night while the Fishers are watching a movie in the family room. When I turn the last page, I feel gutted. But there's something else, too. Daniel is coming back tomorrow, and I think I finally know how to break through to him.

Monday is the longest day of all. I don't have to be anywhere, and I can sleep all morning if I want, so of course I'm wide awake at 5:00 a.m. The Fishers don't come down until after nine, and by then I'm starting to feel like I might burst out of my skin. After breakfast, Mr. Fisher heads for his workshop while Mrs. Fisher makes a beeline for her reading chair. I'm too fidgety to read or work on my appeal, and there's no one to talk to. So I do nothing. I stare out the window and will the time to pass.

The clock on the living room wall goes so long between ticks that I think it must be broken. A patch of sun inches across the floor, and my mind jumps back to Susan and Roger's living room and waiting for November 17 to be over. Was that really only two months ago? It seems like a lifetime. I don't even feel like the same person who was in that room. That person believed she was almost at the end of a long road. But now I'm standing at the beginning of a different road, and I hope with all my heart that it leads to something better.

Finally, in the late afternoon, Mr. Fisher comes in to grab his car keys. "Are you heading out to get Daniel?" I ask.

"In a few minutes, yeah. You want to come with?"

I can't wait to see Daniel, to tell him everything I've been thinking about, but these aren't things you blurt out in a waiting room. Plus, I know Daniel will be happy to see Mr. Fisher waiting for him. I don't think I could survive if he looked disappointed to see me standing there next to him. I shake my head.

"Okay. See you in a couple hours," Mr. Fisher says gently.

Mrs. Fisher is still in her reading chair, her quilt neatly tucked around her legs, her book on her lap. I wish I could be as peaceful as she is, but I'm too nervous and in-between-y. So I watch the patch of sun moving across the floor, and I watch the cars outside the window, and I wait.

two

Finally, around five thirty, a car turns onto our block, and the headlights swing into our driveway. I wait, my heart bumping against my rib cage, until a distorted image of him swims into view through the warped glass door panels. He trudges up the steps, hauling the duffel bag that's almost as big as he is, and then he's standing there, tiny and rumpled in his down jacket, squinting against the hallway light.

"Hi," I say, hoping that one syllable can somehow convey all my sadness and remorse.

"Hi." His one syllable doesn't convey much.

Mr. Fisher puts a hand on Daniel's head as he passes. He catches my eye, lifts his eyebrows slightly, and heads straight for the kitchen. I silently thank him for giving us space.

"Welcome home," I say, hoisting his duffel bag onto my shoulder while he pulls off his coat and boots.

"I can do it," he says, but it's a pretty feeble protest.

"It's all right. I want to carry it." He follows me upstairs, his socked feet barely making a sound, even on the creaky boards.

"Can I come in?" He nods and I drop the duffel bag on the rug next to the bed, waiting for some sign about what to do next.

Daniel stands with his hands stuffed in his pockets. "How was the trip?" I ask, perching on the edge of the bed. "Did you have fun?"

He's hovering by the door like he hasn't made up his mind to stay. "We went to the Freedom Tower and Times Square and the Natural History Museum." His voice is so flat, he might as well be telling me he ate a tuna sandwich. He closes the door and leans against it. "I'm going to move to New York as soon as school is over."

I nod, hoping he'll say more, but he just stands there, looking at the floor. This isn't going to get any easier if I wait. I just have to take the plunge. "Daniel, there's something I need to tell you. While you were gone, I read your book. The one about Easter Island."

He glances at his bedside table. "Why?"

"Because it mattered so much to you. And I want you to know that I understand now. I totally get why you were so upset, and why you wanted to Depart. I'm sorry I didn't take it seriously back then. But I get it now."

His scrawny shoulders hunch. "It doesn't matter."

"Of course it matters. Anything that's important to you matters to me."

"But it's not important to me. Not anymore." He finally steps into the room and starts pulling laundry out of his bag. "Departure was just a lie. And I can't think about Easter Island anymore."

"Why not?"

"There's not enough space."

"What do you mean?"

He sits back on his heels and spreads his hands in front of him. "I don't have enough space in my brain to worry about that now. There are too many other things to worry about."

"What other things?" I ask.

"Like getting through the rest of this year. Like going to New York. Like not drowning."

"Drowning? Daniel, what are you talking about? How would you drown?"

"I don't mean drowning-drowning. I mean . . . being drowned. By New York."

I slide off the bed and lean against it, my feet inches away from him. "Didn't you like New York?"

"I hated New York."

It's such a strong word coming from him that it sends a little shock wave through me. "You did? Why?"

"It's like . . . being inside a video game, but not a fun one. There are too many people, and they're all bumping into you, and the cars honk all the time, and it's never quiet."

I'm an idiot. Of course Daniel felt overwhelmed in New York. His favorite place is the reading room in the library, and he's never been anywhere but Stonebrook. "Why didn't you just tell Dad it was too much?"

"I didn't want him to know."

"Why not?"

He looks at me miserably. "I need him to want me there. I can't be a problem."

"But, Daniel, that's crazy. You don't have to put on a big show for him . . ." An image of him at dinner that first night with Dad pops into my head, and my voice trails off.

"He has to like me!" he insists. "I need someplace to live, and Dad is my only option. He lives in New York, so that's where I'm going. Anyway, I have to go someplace where people won't know about . . . last year."

"Has it been really bad? At school and stuff?"

"Nobody talks to me," he says quietly.

"Nobody? What about Max?"

He shakes his head. "Only the teachers. Everybody else just makes fun of me. And there's one kid who shoves me every time he passes me in the hall."

I want to kick myself. "I'm sorry I've been so wrapped up in my own stuff. I've been a pretty crappy sister lately."

"It's okay. I haven't been the best brother, either."

"So . . . does that mean you're not mad at me anymore?" I ask, hoping I'm not pushing my luck.

He gives a half shrug. "I guess not."

Warm relief floods my body and I wonder what he would do if I threw my arms around him right now. I settle for resting a hand on his knee, and I'm grateful that he doesn't flinch away from me. "I'm so glad, Daniel."

"I thought about you a lot this week. Because of Dad."

"Why? Did you guys talk about me?"

"He just reminded me of you. He looks like you. And he kept saying things I could hear you saying. It was nice." He says it simply, but it still makes my heart twist in my chest.

"What did you think of Carol?" I ask.

"She's nice. Really different from Mom."

"Yeah. I guess Dad didn't want to make the same mistake twice."

Daniel's eyes flick up to mine, and I worry I've said the wrong thing. "I guess," he says.

"And what about Rosie? What's it like having a baby sister?"

"Half sister," he corrects me. "I only have one whole sister."

And then I can't help myself. I scoop him up and hug him with all my might. At first he's stiff, but then his shoulders relax and his head drops onto my shoulder. I don't ever want to move again.

After a while, he asks, "Do you know why I'm going to be okay in New York?" His voice is muffled by my shoulder.

I shake my head.

"Because you'll be there, too."

I pull back to look at him. "What do you mean?"

"You'll look out for me," he says.

"But what makes you so sure I'll be in New York?"

"You're going to Columbia. You have to."

"But . . ." I start to say, then bite my tongue. I can't let him down again. I'm just going to have to make it true. "But not right away," I finish. "I won't be there until the fall."

"That's okay," he says. "It's only a couple months." He leans back against the bed. "You know, Rooney, since I stopped being mad at you, maybe you should stop being mad at Mom."

Before I can respond, there's a soft knock on the door. "Come in," Daniel calls, and Mr. Fisher pokes his head in.

"You two ready for supper?"

"We're ready," Daniel says. Then he looks at me. "Right?"

Daniel doesn't say much at dinner, but it's so different from the silences of the last few months. The relief makes me giddy, and it takes a lot of effort not to pelt him with silly questions just to keep him talking to me. By the time dinner is over, he can barely keep his eyes open. "You go upstairs," I tell him. "You look like you're going to pass out on your plate."

303

He gives me a small, sleepy smile. "Thanks, Rooney. I'll clear the table tomorrow." He comes around behind my chair. "Night," he says, and kisses me before he disappears.

"Well," Mrs. Fisher says, beaming at me. "That is quite a change."

I know there's a big, dumb smile on my face, but I can't help myself. "Yeah. We had a good talk."

"That's great, Rooney," Mr. Fisher says. "I'm so glad."

"Me too," I say. "And there's something else. Something I could really use some help with."

"We are all ears," says Mrs. Fisher.

"I need to write a bulletproof appeal to Columbia. And then I need to fill out all the financial aid stuff. And I think the deadline is pretty soon."

I can tell from the way the corners of her mouth are twitching that Mrs. Fisher is trying not to look too pleased. "I'll take dish duty," Mr. Fisher says. "You two get busy."

After the Fishers have gone to bed, I call Dad. He sounds half asleep when he answers. "Sorry, did I wake you?"

"Oh, yes and no," he says, yawning. "I feel like I'm semicomatose most of the time these days. Anyway, I'm glad you called. How are you? How's Daniel?"

"He seems . . . He seems like Daniel." The words themselves are trivial, but I think he'll understand what they really mean.

"That's terrific, Marina," he says. "I had a feeling that iceberg was starting to melt." He yawns again. Time to get to the point.

"So I wanted to ask you something. I started my financial aid applications tonight. Could I send you some forms and stuff to fill out?"

That seems to wake him up. "Of course! Good for you, Marina. So . . ." He clears his throat, and I can tell he's about to bring up something uncomfortable. "Have you . . . talked to your mother about this?"

"No. Why would I?" I ask, too surprised by his question to be polite.

"Well, I just . . . I figured you'd need to get her financial information, too."

"What information? We already know she's stone broke."

"Well, right, but they probably still need to know the specifics. And besides . . ."

"Besides what?" I ask suspiciously.

"I just think you should tell her you're okay," he says.

"Why?"

"Well, she *is* still your mother."

"Technically, yeah, but . . . so what?"

"Marina." His tone is severe. "You don't want to become someone who throws people away, least of all your own flesh and blood. I know she made mistakes. Big ones. But she'll never stop being your mother."

"I don't get it, Dad," I shoot back. "Why would you defend her? You of all people?"

He lets out a sigh, and I picture him rubbing his forehead. "I know. It must seem strange. But spending time with Daniel this weekend, I feel like I saw a different side of things. Maybe she hasn't been the best mother ever, but the two of you turned out pretty great. And I know I can't take any credit for that. Being a parent, it . . . it's not that easy."

"Being a parent? I know more about that than she does!"

I know I'm being a brat, and I fully expect him to call me out, but he doesn't. "I don't blame you for being angry at her. I was angry at her for a long time myself."

"But you're not anymore?"

There's a long pause before he says, "I guess I'm not."

Two nights later, Mrs. Fisher and I download Dad's completed financial forms. "Everything appears to be in order," she says. "So now it's time to bite the bullet, as they say."

"What if I filled out the forms for her?" I ask, only half kidding. "It's just going to be a bunch of zeros anyway. No income, no investments, no cash in the bank . . ."

Mrs. Fisher doesn't even humor me with a smile. "I'm afraid you can't risk misstating anything. You're going to need to call your mother."

"Ugh." I know she's right, and she knows I know it.

"I'll fetch her number for you, then," she says, pulling her phone from her purse.

"Can I ask a question?"

"You may." She underlines the correction with a lift of her eyebrows. "There, I've texted it to you."

"I was wondering," I start, then falter. For all Mrs. Fisher's warmth, for all the kindness she's shown me, there are certain things I've never asked her about, an invisible line that I haven't dared to cross. But after everything that's happened, it doesn't seem right to know so little about her. "Do you have a family? Besides Mr. Fisher, I mean."

"Of course I do."

"Where are they?"

"They are back in Ghana. Where I grew up."

"They didn't come here with you?"

She shakes her head, and I can tell from her expression that the line has officially been crossed.

"That must have been hard," I say. "To leave everyone behind."

"It was very difficult indeed. But I knew it was the right thing to do. I was given an opportunity that no one else in my family got."

"What kind of opportunity?"

"A ticket to a better life. I received a full scholarship to an excellent school here in the States."

"Wow. You were lucky."

"I also worked extremely hard. But yes, I was exceedingly lucky."

"Is that why you became a teacher?"

She looks thoughtful. "In large measure, yes. I liked the idea of helping people reach their potential, just as my teachers had helped me."

"And is that why you took us in? Daniel and me?"

She nods slowly. "I suppose it is."

My phone dings as the text message comes in and she starts to get up, but I stop her. "Thank you. For taking us in, and for taking such good care of us."

"It has been our very great pleasure, Marina. You and Daniel have become like family to us. Now, hadn't you better get on with it?" She rests her hand on my back for a second, then sails out of the room.

When I finally call the number she gave me, Roger answers, his voice as calm and tired as ever. "Hi," I say. "It's Rooney. Is my mother there?"

"Oh! Yes, she's here. Hang on!"

After a minute or so, a whispery voice asks, "Rooney?"

"Yeah, Mom, it's me."

"Are you all right?" Even over the phone, the panic in her voice sends me into a full-body cringe.

"We're fine," I say. "There's nothing wrong."

"Oh, thank goodness! I just thought . . ."

"That I wouldn't call otherwise. Yeah, I know." I can hear her breathing, ragged and fast, on the other end of the receiver. "Are you crying, Mom?"

She gives a tiny sniff. "I'm sorry, Rooney. I'm trying not to."

"Why are you crying? I told you, we're fine."

"I'm just . . . I'm so happy to hear your voice."

"Okay, well . . ." I fight the urge to hang up. "I just need some information."

"Anything," she says.

"I need to know about money." There's a long pause on the other end of the line. "For college," I add.

Mom lets out a shrill little squeak. "Did you get into Columbia? Mrs. Fisher told me you applied. I don't know when you found the time, or how you figured it all out on your own . . ."

"Mrs. Fisher helped me. And no, I didn't get in. Not yet." I sound like a robot. I wish talking to her didn't turn me into someone so unlikable. "Anyway, I have to fill out a bunch of forms. They need to know all about your finances."

"Do you mean the . . . the college fund? Rooney, I don't even know how to say this . . ."

"No, I already know that's all gone. They need to know your income, that kind of stuff."

"Well, I'm . . . I don't have any income yet. I haven't got a job. But I've started looking. I'm sorry, Rooney . . ."

"It's fine," I say. "It's better, actually. The less income you have, the more financial aid I'm eligible for."

There's a sound like a strangled laugh. "What?" I ask.

"Nothing. It's sort of . . . funny, isn't it? The best way for me to help you is by being completely useless."

She sounds like she's about to lose it. "Well, okay, that's all I needed to know. I just need you to sign some stuff," I say.

"Rooney, wait. Will you give me one more minute?"

"I don't have much time, Mom. I have a lot of homework to do." It's a dumb lie, but I doubt she'll notice.

"No, I know. I just . . . I know you must hate me for what I did. But you and Daniel will always be the most important thing in the world to me. I just need you to know that."

"I don't hate you, Mom." I say it too grudgingly, but at least I say it.

"You don't?"

"No."

"Oh, Rooney. Thank you. Thank you for that."

MARCH

one

When Mrs. Fisher picks me up tonight, she's listening to public radio as usual, but she turns it off when I climb in. Driving home, she asks me questions about my day, but she doesn't seem like she's really listening to the answers.

"Is something wrong?" I ask her. "You seem kind of distracted."

"I'm sorry, you're right," she says. "I heard something on the news just now."

"What was it?"

She pulls over and turns to look at me. "They've located Everett Nichols."

Ba-doomp goes my heart. "Is he . . . Where did they find him?"

"Apparently, he's been hiding on an island in the Caribbean under an assumed name."

"Are they sure it's him?" I ask.

"Yes. They've taken him into custody and they're planning to extradite him for trial in the U.S."

My thoughts are racing. "Did they say anything about the money?"

Mrs. Fisher shakes her head. "It was a very short piece. I was trying to decide whether I should even mention it, since there are so many questions that can't be answered yet."

We listen for the rest of the ride home, but the whole time they're just talking about the stock market.

"Where's Daniel?" I ask Mr. Fisher as I run inside.

"He's in his room, I think. Is everything okay?"

"I'll be right back," I tell him. "Could you turn the radio on?"

I barge into Daniel's room without even knocking. "You should come downstairs," I say. "They've found Everett."

We listen all through dinner, but there's no mention of Everett on the radio. After dinner, Mrs. Fisher pulls out her computer and we do a search. The first article that comes up is headlined "Con Man Nabbed in Island Nest." It's just a short piece, only about a paragraph long, and doesn't tell us anything more than we already knew.

We click on a few more articles, but they're mostly just people's reactions to the news. It's kind of shocking how many of the Next Worlders think the reports are part of a government conspiracy, or were planted by the Pope. You would think by now they'd realize Everett conned them. I guess some people never learn.

"We may have to wait until tomorrow, or perhaps longer, to get details," Mrs. Fisher says after we've read every article.

Even so, we keep refreshing the searches until Mr. Fisher comes in from his workshop.

"C'mon, Daniel, it's past bedtime," he says.

They disappear upstairs, and I keep searching until Mr. Fisher comes back downstairs. "Still nothing?" he asks.

"Uh-uh."

"Daniel wants you to come talk to him. Don't keep him up too late, okay?"

I go up and sit next to the bed. "Hey, Bug. What's up?"

"Do you think Mom knows? About Everett?"

"I don't know."

"I think we should call her," he says.

"But, Daniel, it's almost ten o'clock. You have to be up for school."

"I don't mean right now. Maybe tomorrow night. We should make sure she's all right."

I don't want to get him all riled up, so I just say, "We'll see."

He pulls lightly on my sleeve. "I know you're still mad at her. But maybe this is a reason to not be anymore."

"Daniel, why is this a reason not to be mad? Even if they do find the money, how does it change anything? She still did what she did!"

Daniel looks up at me through his eyelashes. Mom's eyelashes. "It's not for her, Rooney. It's for you."

"For me?"

"It's a lot of work, being mad at people. You need your energy for other things."

Once again, he's knocked the spit right out of me. "Who told you that?"

"Nobody. I just figured it out," he says. And then he scrunches down under the covers and turns out the light.

An hour later, I'm still hitting refresh, hoping for more news. It feels like things should be more different, somehow, now that

Everett's been found. Everyone else is asleep, but I'm full of an itchy kind of energy that makes me want to run around and howl at the moon.

I pull the phone out of my backpack and call Mercer. "Did you hear the news?"

"No. What?"

"They found him. Everett." I quickly fill him in on the few details I've got.

"That's it? What happens now?" he asks when I'm done.

"Who knows?"

He's quiet for a while, then asks, "Do you think your mom knows?"

"I don't know! I don't care. Why are you even asking me that?"

He laughs lightly. "Easy there, slugger. I was just wondering."

"Sorry. I just feel like the whole world is nagging me about talking to her right now."

"Can I say something you don't want to hear?"

"Can I stop you?"

"Nope."

"Then I would love to hear whatever it is you have to say."

"I just think, if the whole world has the same idea, then maybe—just maybe—that idea could be worth considering."

There's a mocking edge to his voice that doesn't sit well with me. "Oh, right. Like when the whole world thought the Earth was flat. Good point."

"Okay, fine," he sighs. "I'm just saying . . ."

"What?"

"Look, you have a right to be mad at your mom. She made

some giant mistakes, and she screwed up your life. I totally grant you that."

I can feel it coming. "But?"

"But she's also the only mom you get. And if you don't find a way to love her anyway, you're going to spend your life with a big hole in your soul where your mother is supposed to be."

"But . . . You know what she's like. You're supposed to be on my side." I try unsuccessfully to banish the quiver that's creeping into my voice.

"I *am* on your side," Merce says firmly. "Why else would I bother to say it?"

Over the next few weeks, the senior class gets buried in an avalanche of college acceptances and rejections. Mercer gets into Vassar, and then Swarthmore, his two top choices. I can see how excited and relieved he is, but he plays it down around me because I'm still waiting to hear from Columbia. They got my appeal two months ago, and the silence has been deafening.

"We should celebrate," I tell him. "I'm really happy for you."

"We'll celebrate when we both have good news," he says. "It won't be long. I know it."

A few days later, posters appear all over the school announcing the theme for the senior prom. "Seriously?" I groan.

Mercer laughs. "No, come on. What could be more perfect than an Arabian Night to Remember?"

"In Vermont?"

"Totally! Harem pants and ski jackets! It's gonna be awesome!"

I look at his face, suddenly unsure of myself. "Wait. Do you . . . want to go to prom?"

"Do you?"

"I asked you first." When he doesn't answer right away, I poke his shoulder. "What? Say it."

"No. It's nothing."

"It's definitely something."

He sighs. "Look, I know you. I know how you think. You would never spend money on a dress you're only going to wear once. Plus, you aren't really friends with anyone in our class. So prom is just stupid to you."

"But?"

"But this is the only senior prom we're ever going to have. And yeah, I kind of want to go. I want you to wear some insane dress, and maybe even let people see your legs for once. And I want to dance and hang out with my friends and make fun of the lame decorations and the cheesy band. And it kind of sucks, you know? That you never want to be part of anything that's happening at school. Or even have any kind of fun."

"That's not true. I have fun."

"When do you have fun?"

"I have fun when I'm with you. See, isn't this fun? Arguing about prom in front of my locker?"

For once, he doesn't smile back at me. "I'm just saying, you've spent this whole year being stressed out all the time. It's been one thing after another. But the year's almost over and there's nothing to be stressed out about right now. So why can't you let go for one night?"

I can feel the muscles in my jaw tightening. "Is this about me, or is it about you?"

He looks me straight in the eyes. "Actually, for once it's about both of us."

"For once?" I swallow hard. Suddenly, I get the feeling we're not just talking about prom anymore. "Are you mad at me for something?"

He exhales sharply. "No, I'm not mad at you. I just don't need everything to be a crisis all the time."

"It's not. Not all the time."

"Rooney, every time my mom asks how you are, the answer is 'worried,' 'stressed out,' or 'panicking.' Literally every time."

"Well, don't tell her that!"

"Then what am I supposed to tell her?"

"Don't tell her anything. It's none of her business."

"Gah! Just stop!" Mercer whacks my locker with the palm of his hand, and the bang echoes through the hallway. A group of freshmen walking by jump at the sound and Mercer mutters an apology.

"What the hell, Mercer?" I hiss when they're out of earshot. "What are you so worked up about?"

"My mom isn't allowed to know how you're doing? That's crazy, Rooney. It's like being in a relationship with a fugitive. Are you going to spend the rest of your life in hiding?"

"Don't you think that's a little dramatic?"

"No. Actually, I think you're a little dramatic. Why do you always assume everyone is so focused on you and your damage? Everyone's got stuff to deal with, Rooney. You're not the only one.

Maybe if you came out from under your rock every now and then, you'd see that."

His words slap me in the face, leaving my cheeks red and stinging. And even after all the day's classes are over and the last bell has rung, I can still feel the burn. Mercer has the longest fuse of anyone I know. So even though I don't really understand why this bothers him so much, I do understand that I need to do something about it.

Which is why, two nights later, I find myself sitting in the front row at the spring Jazz Band concert, right next to Mercer's parents. It's probably my imagination, but I could swear the entire room is looking at me and wondering what I'm doing here. I sit up straight and hope my back tells them, "I belong here just as much as any of you." When Mercer's mom asks me how I'm doing, it may just be small talk, but I make good and sure to tell her that everything is great. I probably overdo it a little, but I figure I have a lot of history to overcome.

As soon as the concert starts, I know that coming here was the right move. I've been to plenty of Mercer's concerts over the years, but what I'm hearing tonight sounds completely new to me. Although, to be honest, I don't know whether it's his playing that's different, or just the way I'm hearing it. I used to think the oboe sounded sort of like a duck. It still does, a little, but it sounds sexy, too. Like a really sexy duck. He has a big solo during the third number, slow and bluesy, and the waves of sound coming from him make my whole body vibrate. At one point, his mom catches me looking at him, and I see her stifle a smirk. After that, I try to do a better job of controlling my facial expressions.

At the end of his solo, his parents and I applaud like crazy.

And then Skyler Jamison stands up, her hair glowing golden under the stage lights, a look of calm concentration on her face. I've barely seen her since November. The truth is, I've avoided running into her because I was afraid to see my own reflection in her eyes. I don't want to have to think of myself as someone who goes around stealing other people's boyfriends.

She raises the flute to her lips and starts to play, her fingers fluttering as fast as a bird's wings. It's just her, the bass, and the drums, filling the auditorium with this incredible groove. She's not looking at any sheet music, and I doubt anyone wrote the notes she's playing. They're just part of her, and for the few minutes of her solo, everyone in the room belongs to her completely. She is unbelievably good.

When the concert ends, Mercer and I have a few seconds alone, and I try to tell him how it felt to listen to him. But then I see his parents coming. "I'll tell you more later," I say.

"You'd better," he says, grinning.

"I'll be back. There's someone I want to talk to."

I have to wait a little while because there's a crowd five people deep around Skyler. When I finally get to the front, I can see the surprise on her face.

"You were amazing!" I burst out. "I had no idea you were that good."

She laughs lightly. "Um, thanks?"

"Do you think we could talk for a second? In private?"

She looks around. "Well, my parents are here, so . . ."

"Just for a second. I promise."

She follows me to a corner, still holding her flute case, and looks at me expectantly.

"I just . . ." I start. "I wanted to say that I'm sorry."

She raises her eyebrows but doesn't say anything.

"I feel rotten about the way I treated you. It's not an excuse, but I was going through a rough time. And I felt like I was losing Mercer to you. And then you were so nice about everything, and I never said anything to you."

"It's okay," she says, smiling ruefully. "I wasn't that nice."

"But you told Mercer he belonged with me. That was . . ."

"I was hoping he'd tell me I was wrong," she says, and then laughs again, this time a loud guffaw that shakes her whole tiny frame. "You win some, you lose some, I guess!"

A movement catches my eye. Someone is waving to her from a few feet away. "I should let you go," I say. "Great job tonight."

"Thanks," she says. She starts to walk away, then turns back to me. "Did you get into Columbia?"

"Not yet. Still waiting."

"I'll keep my fingers crossed for you. Maybe we'll run into each other in New York. I'm going to Juilliard."

"That . . . That would be great. Congratulations," I say. And I actually mean it.

APRIL

one

"I have questions."

"Questions?" She sounds nervous. Not surprisingly.

"Yeah. There are things I want to know." It's been a few weeks since they located Everett. I've probably picked up the phone and put it back down again at least a dozen times since then. I'm still not sure what's stopping me from hanging up this time.

"Of course. I'll tell you anything you want. But could we do it in person?"

"Why?"

"Oh, Rooney, I know I don't have the right to ask anything of you. I just . . . the phone is so impersonal. If we're going to have a conversation that matters, I want to be able to see your face."

"Fine, Mom. You can come by the Java Connection tomorrow afternoon."

"I wouldn't be able to get there before seven," she says, her voice hesitant. "Isn't your shift over by then? I could take you to dinner. Anywhere you want to go."

"I can't afford to eat out, Mom. I need to save everything for college."

"Oh, no! Of course I didn't mean for you to pay . . ." She stops talking, probably because she's thinking the same thing I'm thinking. I've been paying my own way for years. "I have a job, Rooney. I'd like to take you out."

I'd honestly given up hope of her getting a job. When I've thought about her, I've pictured her like an invalid, lying on Susan's sofa, drinking milky tea, too weak to do anything for herself. "Where are you working?"

"I'll tell you all about it when I see you. So is that all right? If I get there around seven?"

"All right. I'll meet you at Myrtle's."

"Yay!" It's like she can't even hear all the suspicion and hesitation in my voice. "I'll see you tomorrow night!" I'm about to hang up when she says, "Rooney?"

"Yeah, Mom?"

"Thank you."

I don't know if she's thanking me for calling, or for agreeing to meet her, or what. "Okay," I say. "See you."

She's always been late for everything, if she remembers to go at all, but when I get to Myrtle's, she's already waiting by the hostess's stand. I think she's going to run over and try to hug me, but she just stands there, smoothing her skirt with her hands.

The first words out of my mouth are "You cut your hair." My whole life, Mom's long braids were as much a part of her as her tiny hands or waist. Now her wavy hair is trimmed short in a perky little bob.

Her hands shoot up to the back of her neck. "Do you like it? I still wake up and wonder why my head feels so light."

326

"It looks nice."

Now she does move to hug me, but I turn my body a little and she ends up just lightly touching me on the back. As she lowers her hand, I see something register in her eyes, a thought clicking into place. It isn't the hurt look I had braced myself for. More like a mental note.

She steps back and says, "You look wonderful, Rooney."

I look down at the crumpled khakis and button-down shirt I wore to work, and notice a coffee stain. Of all the things she could have said, as usual she's found the one that makes the least sense. I shrug and look around for the hostess. "Why didn't they seat you?"

"Oh, I didn't want to choose a table until you got here. We can sit wherever you like."

"It doesn't matter, Mom. I don't care where we sit." I know she's trying, but somehow that just irritates me more.

The hostess walks us over to a table in the back.

"Oh, this is perfect!" Mom claps her hands together like little butterfly wings. "Thank you!"

The hostess raises an eyebrow at me, then leaves us alone. "So where are you working?" I ask. "Did they take you back at the day care?"

Mom tries to tuck a stray wisp of hair behind her ear. It immediately pops out again, but she doesn't seem to notice. "No, I got a job at the university."

"The university? What are you doing there?"

"I'm assisting one of the professors. It's mostly administrative for now, but I'm hoping he'll let me help out in his lab over the summer."

"And you're still living with Susan and Roger?"

"For now. They've been so wonderful to me. But in a few months, I should have enough saved up to get my own place. There's a little garage apartment near them. Just tiny, but . . . there would always be room for you or Daniel to stay. If you ever wanted to visit, I mean . . ."

I look down at my place mat to escape her searching eyes. "So you know that Daniel's moving in with Dad?"

"Yes." She says it so simply that I look up in surprise. Her eyes are bright, but her face is calm. "I think that's going to be just wonderful for him. And for your father, too."

She nods as I gape at her. "We have a lot to talk about. But you said you had questions. Do you want to go first?"

Out of nowhere, an old, old memory comes into my head. I'm standing in Central Park, no more than four or five years old. I'm holding a shiny rock, and Mom is explaining that the sparkle comes from a type of rock called mica. I'm asking her question after question, and she's telling me about Manhattan schist and pointing to the huge slabs of stone all around us. It seems like she knows everything about the world, like there's no question she can't answer. How long has it been since I've felt that way about her?

"Dad told me you were this brilliant scientist. If that's true . . . why did you ever believe Everett?" I ask.

She closes her eyes, and I think maybe she won't answer. But then she opens them again and says, "Rooney, that's a really good question. I want to explain, but it's going to take a little time. Is that all right?"

I cross my arms and lean back in my chair. "I'm listening."

"Did your father tell you anything about my work?"

"He said it was something to do with ice in Alaska or something."

"Antarctica. We were taking ice cores," she says. "We'd drill way, way down and pull out this tube full of the history of the planet. It was just amazing. You could see every year as a layer in the ice, and each layer told a story about what that year was like. Once you understood how to interpret it, it was like reading the Earth's whole life story."

She looks at me to make sure I'm following, then goes on. "But the trouble was, the data was painting this terribly bleak picture. When you looked at the cores, you could see exactly where the industrial revolution happened and humans started filling the atmosphere with carbon. And from that moment, you could see the temperatures rising. It was just as plain as day. And it was hard not to get sad about that. And then there was the whole polar bear problem."

"There were polar bears?" I ask, trying to imagine my tiny mother confronting a giant white bear.

"No, not in Antarctica. Penguins, though," she says, and her eyes light up for a second. "Oh, I loved the penguins!"

"But you said polar bears," I say, wishing she would just stay on track for once.

"I meant in the news. The same phenomenon we were studying was impacting the polar bears in the Arctic. The ice pack that they relied on to get to their food was breaking up because it was so warm. So they were starving to death."

"But I don't understand what that had to do with you."

"I know, I'm not explaining it well. It was just . . ." She picks up her napkin and twists it until it curls in on itself. "It was on my mind. The work we were doing had implications in the world. And those implications were . . . well, they were hard to live with."

The waitress comes and takes our orders. "Go on," I say as soon as she leaves.

"My supervisor on the project was this giant, burly Swede named Lars. He used to say to me, 'Sentiment is the enemy of science, Anneliese.' So I really tried to think like a scientist, to keep a clinical distance. But there was no way to ignore the fact that the planet—the whole beautiful, miraculous world that contained every living being that I cared about—was dying. The polar bears were just the . . . well, the tip of the iceberg. So I could spend the whole day analyzing and intellectualizing, but at night, alone in my room . . . Well, my heart was just breaking."

Her eyes dart up to mine, like she expects me to interrupt her. I do want her to get to the point, to tell me about Everett, but I want to hear this story, too. Ever since Dad told me about those early years, I've been trying to piece together some new picture of Mom. "Go on," I say again.

"Well, all this time, your dad was waiting for me to come home. I was falling apart and I thought the only thing that would save me was to be with him. So I ran away. I ran back to him, to New York, and I thought everything would be all right."

She takes a long, deep breath and lets it out slowly, her eyes far away. "Rooney, I need to tell you something, and I really, really hope you can understand it. I wanted my life to have meaning. I thought being a mother would do that for me. And having you and Daniel was the greatest joy of my life. But . . ." She starts to reach for my hand, then checks herself and folds her hands back in her lap. "But it was the biggest mistake of my life, too."

For a second, I stop breathing. *Who says something like that to their own kid?* But then the answer comes to me: *Mom does.* Looking into her searchlight eyes, I can see how hard she's working to be honest with me, to tell me her whole truth. It's a strange gift she's trying to give me. But that's Mom for you.

"Wow," I say at last. "That's . . . a lot to take in."

"I know it must sound terrible to you. But being a mother . . . no one can prepare you for how it feels. You're completely responsible for these perfect, precious, helpless creatures. I couldn't stop worrying about you, because I knew, deep down, that I should never have brought you into this world."

She takes a long drink of water, and I wait, not wanting to break the flow. "Your dad . . . he hates me now, and I don't blame him. But in those days, he just wanted me to be happy. So when I first heard about the Next World Society, and started reading about Balance, I think he was glad that I wasn't so worried anymore. You understand, back then, Everett hadn't started talking about the Hwaral yet. That came later."

Finally, she's starting to get to the point. "I didn't know that," I say. "So he kind of lured you in?"

She shrugs unhappily. "I guess it must seem that way. It's still hard to accept that it was all deliberate. His vision seemed so beautiful, and so logical. If humans could just learn to live in Balance, everything would be all right. We could make the world whole again. It seemed like a solution to this terrible, selfish thing I had done by having you and Daniel. Do you understand?"

I nod. I'm not exactly sure I do, but I want her to keep talking.

"A few years later, Everett revealed the Hwaral to the inner circle. And that caused a big, big rift in the NWS. For a long time, I didn't want to tell your father about them. I knew he would have such a hard time accepting it. But I desperately needed him to, because that was the only way we could all stay together."

"So when you finally told him, that's when the fighting started." I've learned more about Mom and Dad in the last ten minutes than I've known my whole life, but I still don't have an answer to my question. "But, Mom, why would you believe such a ridiculous story? Aren't scientists supposed to be all about, I don't know, evidence and stuff?"

She stares off over my shoulder, shaking her head slowly. "Rooney, I don't have an answer that will satisfy you. By then, I trusted Everett, because I thought he had the solution I'd been looking for. Maybe there was some part of me that didn't want to question it too closely. I needed it all to be true. Because if it wasn't true, we were all doomed on this poor, dying planet. And I was going to lose everything. I was going to lose you, and Daniel . . . and your father, too."

"But you did lose him. You chose to leave him. Didn't you?"

"In the end, I did leave him. I thought it was the only way to save you and Daniel. But it hurt like I had torn out a part of myself. I never stopped loving him. And every time I looked at you, I saw his eyes, judging me, hating me, even. Rooney, I need to tell you something else. Something I haven't admitted to anyone. Is that all right?"

I nod, wanting and not wanting to hear what she has to say.

"In November, when we didn't Depart . . . ?" She winds the napkin around her hand, exactly the way she used to wind her braid. "I was sure it was my fault. I asked everyone to let go of their ties to the Earth, and I tried. I tried to let go of my ties. But I couldn't do it. I could never let go of your father."

It seems like she's reached the end of her story. I sit across from her, trying to reconcile this strange, surprising woman with the mother who destroyed my life.

"You know, there's an odd kind of power in having your deepest fears come true," she says after a while. "You think it will be the worst thing that can ever happen to you. But in a strange way, it frees you."

"From what?"

"Well, from . . . from fear, I guess. From that feeling that you're waiting for the other shoe to drop. When you're finally at the bottom, there's nothing left to be afraid of. For so long, I was terrified of losing you and Daniel. Everywhere I went, every day, my mind was full of terrible visions. When you were a little girl, I would watch you on the subway platform, and I'd picture you falling onto the tracks. It didn't matter how far you were from the edge. There was just this movie playing in my head. Sometimes I'd have to grab you and run out of the station. People must have thought I was out of my mind." She gives a little laugh, high and birdlike, and I imagine she's probably right.

"I worried so much about losing you that I started doing all kinds of things to try to protect you. The NWS was just one of those things. There were so many others. Little rituals I'd do every day that were supposed to keep you safe. And then . . . I couldn't save you. All my plans turned out to be for nothing. And not only that, but I lost you. The thing I feared the most happened. And it was awful. It really was. I thought it might kill me.

But it didn't. And once I saw that I could survive that and go on living, I realized maybe I was stronger than I'd ever thought."

Before I called Mom, I wrote out all my questions in my old reporter's notebook. As I go through them now, putting little mental check marks next to them, there's one big one left. I had planned to ask why she didn't let us go to Dad's wedding, why she cut us off from him. Back in September, I was sure I could never forgive her for that. But now, even without asking the question, I feel like I have my answer. On one level, it isn't good enough. It will never be good enough. What Daniel and I lost can never be replaced. But on another level . . . I know I was wrong about not forgiving her. Never is a long time.

After dinner, we walk out of Myrtle's together. It's a warm night, and I can see the Big Dipper above us. "Well, I'll see you around, I guess," I say.

I brace myself for the good-bye hug, but she just fishes in her purse and pulls out a set of keys. "Can I give you a ride home?" My eyebrows shoot up and she lets out a nervous giggle. "I got my license. About a month ago."

"Wow. That's . . . hard to imagine," I say, and she laughs again.

"I know. I'm not that good at it yet. I mean, I'm super safe. I just go too slowly for everyone else on the road." She jingles the keys in front of me like she's playing with a cat. "Want to see?"

I shake my head. "I think I'll walk. But thanks." It's nice out, and I have a lot to think about. She's working hard not to look disappointed, and I have to give her props for the effort. "Maybe another time."

"Really?" Her face brightens. "Do you think we could do this again?"

"Yeah, sure," I say. For some reason, my old impulse to crush her isn't kicking in.

She opens her mouth to say something, then seems to change her mind. "That would be so nice. Good night, Rooney." She climbs into an old blue car with a big dent in the fender, then looks up and sees me watching. "That wasn't me. I swear, I bought it that way!"

"Sure you did," I say, smiling.

Mom getting out of the parking lot isn't the smoothest thing I've ever seen, but she does manage not to hit anything. I give her a thumbs-up as she drives off, then turn and start walking toward the Fishers' house. I'm halfway there before I realize Mom never once said "I love you" tonight.

two

I don't tell Mrs. Fisher the whole story when I get home, only that things went okay. I want Mercer to be the first one I tell. But two days later, while Daniel and Mr. Fisher are working out in the shed, I tell her everything. All about Mom's time in Antarctica, and how she joined the NWS, and even what she said about wishing she'd never had us.

"So how do you feel about all of that?" Mrs. Fisher asks when I'm finished.

"Honestly? I'm not sure. Part of me is still mad at her for ruining our lives. And I don't think I'll ever understand how someone can be so smart and so stupid at the same time. But . . ."

"But?"

"I had this dream last night. About Daniel." The feeling of the dream is still so intense that I almost can't describe it without getting sucked back in. "We were walking across a frozen lake. I was holding his hand, but then the ice started cracking and breaking. And then . . . the piece Daniel was standing on started floating away from me."

I take a breath and Mrs. Fisher hands me the Kleenex box. "I could see his iceberg getting smaller and smaller, melting away, but I couldn't reach him," I say, blowing my nose. "It sounds silly when I describe it now."

Mrs. Fisher shakes her head. "No. It sounds terribly frightening. And it sounds to me as though you understand a good deal about how your mother felt."

I stare down at the crumpled tissue in my hand. I don't know that I'm ready to forgive Mom for everything, but Mrs. Fisher is right. I do feel like I understand her now. More than I ever did before, anyway. "You know what the problem is with Everett?" I ask, giving my nose a hard rub.

"What?"

"He was a liar, but not everything he said was a lie. He lied about the solution, but not about the problem."

I'm sort of hoping that she'll deny it, that she'll say that every word out of Everett's mouth was pure fiction, but she nods. "That's true."

"So you . . . you think Mom's right? About the planet dying?"

"I wouldn't use those words." She speaks slowly, carefully. "Let us say that I have grave concerns."

"But if you feel that way, how do you live your life? Why do you bother trying to teach us? To make things better?"

She spreads her hands out palms up on the table. "Because I hope I am wrong."

"That's it?" I groan.

She takes her time answering. "I am not a prophet, Marina. I don't know what the future holds. So while I fear the worst, I keep looking for reasons to be hopeful. I live my life in the best way I can, and hope that it's not too late to turn the tide."

Something clicks in my head. An echo of a long-ago conversation. "So it's Pascal's Wager?"

She raises her eyebrows at me, looking a little pleased, I think. "Yes, I suppose in a way it is."

"You're saying that . . . you can't know whether it's too late to fix things? All you can do is . . . act like it's not? Hope for the best?"

"Well, it's not enough just to hope; you have to *do*."

I rest my forehead in my hands, feeling overwhelmed, and she pats my shoulder. "Marina, I'm not telling you this is your problem to solve. It is no more your problem than any other human's. I am merely telling you that you have power. There are things you can do, if you choose."

"But what can I do? I'm not a politician, or a scientist, or a teacher or anything. I can't change the way things are."

A smile lifts the corner of her mouth. "That's true. All you are able to do is write. And clearly, writers cannot change anything. Never, in the history of mankind, has a mere writer persuaded anyone to act." She holds up a finger and gazes up in the air. "Ah, wait a moment. Perhaps I'm remembering that wrong . . ."

"Fine," I tell her. "I get where you're going with this."

"Bright girl."

I close my eyes, and the image of Daniel drifting away is there again, just behind my eyelids. "But what if . . . what if I try, and it's still too late? What if I can't change anything?"

"Then you won't be any worse off, will you? I'm sorry, but that's the best I can offer. There are no guarantees." She waves a hand in correction. "No, that's not quite right either. There's one thing that's guaranteed. If we all do nothing, then I think we can be quite certain that nothing will change."

It takes another three days before I sit down and open Mom's laptop. Staring at the blank screen, wondering where to begin, I remember middle school, and Mr. Bradford writing the 5 Ws on the board. The Who, What, Where, and When have always been easy. They've been the facts of my life. But the Why . . . That's been the slippery one. Now it's finally in my grasp.

Once I get started, my fingers can't keep up with my brain. I've always been a careful writer, choosing each word deliberately, but now I just let the words pour out of me. I don't stop and reread, I don't edit. There will be time for that later. For now, all I can do is get out of the way and let the story tell itself.

A few days later, I hand a slim stack of printed pages to Daniel, and then I go back to my little room and try not to chew off all my fingernails while I wait for him to read it. The desk is littered with photos and articles I've printed out as reference. As I gather it all up, I notice a phone number written on the back of an NWS pamphlet. I've been swimming through a sea of memories this week, but for some reason, this one has escaped me until now. I don't want to dial the number, but I know I have to. The story still isn't complete.

"Hello?"

"Anjelica?"

"Yes?" The voice has none of the energy or warmth that I remember. It's the voice of a stranger. I think about hanging up, but my number is in her phone. I can't un-call her now.

"It's Rooney. You know, from . . ."

"Oh my gosh. Rooney! How are you?"

"I'm good. How are you?"

"Oh, I'm okay," she says in a way that makes it instantly clear that she's not.

"So . . . what are you up to?" I say into the dead air. "Did you go back to school?"

"No, I'm waiting tables. And Alice needs a lot of help around the house, so that keeps me pretty busy."

"Alice?"

"Yeah. I moved in with her after . . . well, after Fred passed."

It takes me a few seconds to register what Anjelica's said. "Wait, did you say . . . ?"

She takes in a hissing breath. "I'm sorry, I just assumed you knew. He died three days after Dep . . . after the heart attack."

For the first time since it happened, I let myself think back to the terrible scene at Susan's house. "I'm so sorry," I say. "I guess I've kind of been . . . you know, just trying to keep my head above water here. I didn't know what happened to everyone else."

"Yeah. It was awful. He never regained consciousness. Alice didn't even get to say good-bye."

I barely knew Fred. He was just a nice old guy who was around during a couple of really bad days in my life. So I don't understand why my eyes are suddenly swimming. "Is Alice all right?"

"She's alive. I guess that counts for something, right?" The words themselves aren't so bad; it's the defeated tone in her voice that rattles me.

"Where are the two of you living?" I ask.

"In her house."

"She didn't lose it?"

She makes a sound like a laugh with all the funny sucked out of it. "No, that was her one piece of luck. They tried to sell it before November so they could give the money to Everett, but it was so run-down, no one wanted to buy it."

"What about your family? Have you talked to them since November?" I ask, looking for some kind of bright spot to focus on.

"We're . . . I guess you could say we're taking a break from each other." She breathes a long, hopeless sigh. "It's ironic, right? The thing that drew me to the NWS in the first place was how much I cared about my family. I thought what Everett was promising was the only way to keep them all safe. And now they won't even talk to me."

She sounds completely tormented. I've spent the last few months putting as much distance between myself and the NWS as humanly possible, but for her it feels like November 17 was yesterday. "You still think about it a lot, huh?"

"All the time," she says. "I feel like what's-her-name, that Greek girl."

"Greek girl?" I don't remember any Next Worlder with a Greek name.

"Yeah, you know. She could see the future, and she wouldn't shut up about it. And she just drove everyone crazy?"

"Cassandra?" I guess, remembering one of Daniel's old mythology books.

"Right, her. Sometimes, I get so frustrated I just want to scream at people for the trivial nonsense they spend their time on. Even people who mean well, they focus on poverty or social injustice or endangered species . . . it's like treating the symptoms but ignoring the cause. We can't solve any of those other problems unless we get the planet back in balance."

Maybe I shouldn't have called. I thought it was something I had to do, but now I think I've just made things worse for her. I desperately want to get off the phone, but I feel like I'm abandoning her. Again. "Would you . . . want to talk again sometime?" I ask.

There's a long pause on the other end, and I'm half expecting her to say no. "I'd like that," she finally says. "I don't have a lot of people I can talk to right now."

"I'll call you next week. And don't give up on your family, okay? I bet they'll come around, after they've had a chance to cool off."

"You really think so?" she asks.

I don't know. But if I can forgive Mom, it seems like anything might be possible.

A little while later, there's a tap on my door and Daniel comes in. He puts the stack of paper on the desk and sits down next to me.

"What do you think?"

"I think it's perfect."

"You do?"

He nods solemnly. "What did Mrs. Fisher say?"

"I haven't shown it to her yet. I wanted you to be the first one to read it. And I won't show it to anyone else unless you say it's okay."

"You should show it to her," he says. "And Mom, too."

Three days later, it's Mrs. Fisher who's looking over my shoulder as I log on to Columbia's website. At the last second, I squeeze my eyes shut. "I can't look. You tell me."

The room is dead quiet for much too long. It's bad news. I know it. I'm going to end up working in a coffee shop for the rest of my life. Mrs. Fisher puts a hand on my shoulder. "You're really going to want to read this yourself."

I force my eyes open and stare at the screen. "Dear Miss Harris," I read aloud. "Congratulations! We are pleased to welcome you . . ."

I hear a muffled shout from the kitchen, where Daniel and Mr. Fisher are pretending not to eavesdrop.

". . . to the class of . . ." That's as far as I get before they burst into the room and Daniel jumps on me. The two of them are whooping and cheering, and the whole time, Mrs. Fisher is sitting perfectly still, a huge, satisfied smile spreading across her face.

"I believe a celebration is in order," she says when they stop shouting. "Ice cream? Shall we invite Mercer to join us?"

"Yes, please," I say. And then I look at Daniel. "And let's invite Mom, too."

MAY

one

About a week before prom, the entire senior class simultaneously loses its mind. No one can talk about anything else. After a while, the teachers give up and the whole school day turns into one endless discussion of who's going with whom, what everyone's wearing, and the best strategies for smuggling booze into the after-party. Mercer and I have carefully avoided any mention of prom since the scene by my locker, but I can tell he's still touchy about it. Luckily, I've got a plan.

"So what do you want to do tomorrow night?" he asks on Thursday. "Movie?"

"Actually, I have something else in mind," I tell him. "Do you think you can borrow your dad's car?"

He looks at me curiously. "Probably. Why?"

"Just trust me. Oh, and wear something swanky."

On Friday night, Mercer comes to the Fishers' door, wearing a suit that must belong to his dad. It fits him surprisingly well. "Nice fedora," I tell him.

"Thanks," he says, whipping it off his head with a flourish. "Nice . . . everything." Mrs. Fisher and I had to work pretty hard to assemble an appropriately glamorous outfit for me, but even I have to admit the end result isn't half-bad, especially since she let me borrow her favorite pair of four-inch stilettos. Mercer's eyes travel approvingly from my head to my toes, and I silently resolve to show my legs more often.

He walks me to the car, then holds open the passenger door for me. "Madame . . ."

"Thank you, kind sir."

As he pulls away from the curb he asks, "Where to?"

"On a magic carpet ride," I tell him. "Take a left here."

Pretty soon we're pulling into one of the little parking lots at the back of the park. I take his hand and lead him along a dirt track that branches off from the main walking path. "Welcome to your prom night," I say. "Close your eyes." I lead him another ten paces forward, stepping carefully in my high heels. "Okay, breathe in. No, through your nose!"

He takes a deep breath and a smile spreads across his face. "Lilacs? Did you know they're my favorite?"

"Of course I knew," I tell him. "And thanks to you, I also know that if you put them in a vase, they'll be dead in a day. So you're just going to have to enjoy them here."

"That's all right, I don't mind."

"Okay, so that takes care of your boutonniere." I pull out my phone and hand him one earbud while I insert the other in my own ear. "Now for the cheesy band . . ."

The first song on the prom playlist I downloaded from the school website starts to play. *"Midnight at the oasis,"* a woman's voice croons in my ear. *"Send your camel to bed . . ."*

We both burst out laughing. "I can't believe this is a real song," I say. "Want to skip to the next one?"

"Come on, this is a classic!" He pulls me to him, wrapping an arm around my waist and clasping my right hand in his.

"Check out the decorations," I say, looking up into the sky. The last hint of blue is fading, and a crescent moon is just rising over the trees. The Milky Way is directly overhead, little pinpoints of light twinkling in the velvet darkness.

"Nice effect. Very realistic," he says.

"Well, this is a very classy operation. Now, tell me the truth: Are you still wishing you were with the rest of our class?"

"Not even a little," he admits.

"So if I told you we were going to the party at Chris Jennings's house later . . . ?"

He pulls away slightly so he can look me in the face. "Are you sure? The whole class is going to be there."

I shrug. "Why not? When you look this good, you shouldn't hide under a rock, am I right?"

"So right," he says.

The song ends, and now a man begins to sing. *"Fly me to the moon and let me play among the stars . . ."*

A hazy memory flickers into my head. "Oh, I know this one." As we turn in a slow circle, I can see another couple, young and laughing, turning in their own slow circle. They dance in a cramped living room while their tiny daughter laughs and claps in delight. *"In other words, hold my hand,"* Mercer sings along with the recording. *"In other words, baby, kiss me . . ."*

I do, long and unhurried, lips meeting lips, tongues moving in their own slow dance, warm and wet and dark, until the song is nearly done and the past is back in the past.

"In other words, please be true," he sings softly into my ear.

"In other words," I whisper back, "I love you."

JUNE

one

On graduation morning, I wake up early and lie in bed for a while trying to figure out how I feel. It isn't any one thing, more like a swirling mixture of emotions. Mostly, there's relief and excitement, but right below the surface, there's a little dread, too. I just want everything to go smoothly today.

And then, buried down deep underneath all that, I can feel something else, something that's harder to put a name to. Something that feels a little bit like sadness, but different. It's not regret, exactly. It's the feeling of letting go of a part of me, or a time of me. A word swims into my head, and I let it float, giving it a little poke now and then to send it drifting away from the corners. *Nostalgia*. It's close. What exactly I should be feeling nostalgic for isn't so clear, though. Any sane person would be glad to finally be moving on. But now that I'm almost on the other side, there's a part of me that doesn't want to cross over, not quite yet.

I'm not ready.

As soon as the thought comes into my head, I give it a hard shove. Not ready? I've been ready since the day I came to this town. It's time to put on my big-girl pants and get this day started. I throw the covers off and get out of bed.

By the time I've showered and dressed, there's still no sign of Daniel. I go up to his room and knock lightly on the door. "You almost ready, Bug?" Mr. Fisher is making a special graduation breakfast, and I don't want to keep him waiting.

Daniel opens the door. His hair is sticking up all funny, and he looks like he hasn't gotten much sleep. "I'll be down in a sec," he says.

"Did you have fun with Dad and Carol?" They had dinner with the Fishers last night while Mercer and I went to our class's pregraduation celebration at Myrtle's.

"Yeah," he says without much enthusiasm. He doesn't seem very excited about seeing them. Maybe he just doesn't want to say too much, because it's supposed to be my day. But I know he's still worried about the move to New York, and I wish there was some way I could help him feel even a fraction of my excitement.

I put my hands on his shoulders and wait for him to look me in the eyes. "It's all going to be okay. From now on, we're in this together. We're going to New York and we're going to take care of each other, and I'm never going to lose track of you again. I mean it."

"I know," he says, looking down again. "It'll be okay."

I want so badly to say something that will make him feel better, but the truth is, I don't know that he's going to like New York any better than last time. I don't even know that it's going to be better than Stonebrook. I'm just hoping it will be. I try to smooth down his hair, but there's one piece that doesn't want to lie flat. I think about licking my hand to flatten it out. Maybe I could even get a laugh out of him. But in the end, I just give his shoulder a squeeze. "See you downstairs."

While we wait for Daniel to come down, I check my phone. There's a text from Mercer saying he'll meet me in the auditorium at ten fifteen. And there's another text from Anjelica. "Congrats!!!" it says. "C U after the ceremony. Remember to enjoy it!"

The morning is overcast, but by the time we reach the high school, most of the clouds have burned off and it's starting to turn sticky. "Very warm for June," Mrs. Fisher observes as we pile out of the car. "Too warm," Mr. Fisher agrees, shaking his head. I hug both of them, then Daniel, and tell them, "I'll see you in a little bit." I walk through the empty, echoing hallways to the gym, put on the slippery nylon gown and the weird square cap, and look around for Mercer, but he's not here yet. So I sit on the bleachers and wait for the rest of my class to come filing in.

Every time someone walks through the door, I say their name to myself. I know their faces, the way they flip their hair, the clothes they wear, but so little about who they really are—what they think or feel. This morning's not-quite-right word swims into my head again. Am I nostalgic for my classmates? For what might have been?

Across the room, there's a clump of girls milling around. They're the ones who were always outside smoking before school and during lunch. Usually, they all wear the same uniform: ripped jeans, black eyeliner, surly glares. But today they're laughing and talking excitedly in their purple graduation gowns, like they've completely forgotten to act cool around the rest of us. At the edge of the circle, one of them is looking back at me. Brandi Chilton. Razored burgundy hair. Crooked front teeth. I can't remember even laying eyes on her since the night of Eric Wurtzel's party. So why is she staring at me?

Just then, Mercer walks in, and I wave to him. He climbs up next to me on the bleachers and grabs my hand. "You ready?"

"Born ready," I say, straight-faced. "You?"

His eyes dart sideways. "Burnout heading your way," he whispers.

I turn, and there's Brandi walking up to us. For some reason, I break into an instant sweat. As if anything anyone could say today could hurt me.

"Hey, Rooney," she says, and I'm equally surprised by the raspy sound of her voice and the fact that she knows my name. "I liked that thing you wrote in the paper. About your mom and that wacko cult and everything."

"You did?" I almost changed my mind five times before I let Mrs. Fisher print it. Eventually, I told her she could run it in the final issue of the year. By then, I figured, even if there was a huge backlash, I'd only have to get through a few weeks of torment. But in the end, most people still treated me exactly the same as before. The mean ones were no more or less mean after it came out. The ones who had ignored me kept right on ignoring me. And, thank God, the nice ones kept right on being nice. Still, there were a few surprises.

"Yeah. That was all true, what you wrote?" Brandi asks, jutting her chin at me.

I nod. I've got nothing to hide anymore.

"I never knew any of that about you. That's messed up."

She's looking at me so intensely it's making me squirmy. "Yeah. Well, you know, it's all in the past now."

"Still, it was pretty badass to write about all that."

"Um, thanks."

"Cool." She glances over her shoulder to where the rest of her crew is standing, staring at us. I think she's going to walk back over to them, but she turns to me again and crosses her arms tightly over her chest. "I could kind of relate. My mom's a junkie," she says.

It takes every ounce of self-control I have to keep my eyes from bugging out. "That's . . . terrible," I manage to say.

"Yeah. Well, good luck with college and everything. Keep writing." Then, without another word, she goes back to her friends.

Out on the football field, all the families are seated in the bleachers. Their faces are a blur as we file out past them, and it's not until we're seated, listening to Amanda Chen's valedictorian speech, that I finally pick out Daniel's face in the crowd. Once I've spotted him, everyone else snaps into focus. Mom is sitting on his left, and Anjelica's next to her. Not two feet away from Mom, on Daniel's right, Dad is sitting next to Carol, who's holding Rosie. And Mr. Fisher is sitting next to her. Seeing them all together, all these fragments of my life, is so disorienting that I forget where I am and just stare. They're all too busy watching Amanda to notice, except Mom. She's looking straight at me, and when our eyes meet, she gives a little, uncertain wave.

The rest of the ceremony passes in a sweaty haze. As the sun beats down on us, I wonder why they don't make graduation gowns out of breathable fabric, and wish I had something to blot my sweat mustache with. After Amanda, it's the principal's turn to exhort the graduates. I tune in every now and then to catch some platitude about leadership or hard work, but mostly I'm adrift in my own thoughts. And then, suddenly, everyone is on their feet, and we're marching toward the podium in alphabetical order.

When I finally hear the words "Marina Harris," my feet step forward as though someone else is moving them. I shake a few hands, accept my diploma, and that's it. I'm free.

I feel completely numb. Not happy. Not sad. Not even relieved. Just empty. And then I look over to the chairs where the teachers are seated and see Mrs. Fisher looking at me. Her face is glowing like a thousand-watt bulb. All the teachers are clapping politely, but she's thumping her hands together so hard that I can hear the sound of it above everything else. And then she rises majestically to her feet and gives me a one-woman standing O.

"Okay, guys, just one more!"

Everybody groans, but they humor me and squeeze in for one last photo. I already have a bunch of great ones, but they don't need to know that. Taking picture after picture is just an excuse to make them stay this way, all of them with their arms around one another, smiling and laughing. I want to burn the image onto my brain so I never forget it. It may never happen again, but here and now, I feel like I know what it means to have a family.

I finally let them go, and they drift across the Fishers' backyard, little groupings forming and re-forming. I wander among them, eavesdropping, soaking them in. Anjelica and Mercer comparing notes on their veggie burgers. Mom admiring Mrs. Fisher's brightly printed dress. Dad helping Mr. Fisher at the grill. Daniel holding Rosie so carefully as Carol shakes her noisy bunny. I'm eating it all up, making a meal of it, when Anjelica sidles up. "Congratulations, Miss Graduate."

"Thanks. I'm really glad you're here."

"Me too."

"How are things going? You seem better. More like yourself."

"I guess I feel more like myself. I got a new job. Working for an environmental advocacy organization."

"That's great! What are you doing for them?"

"Social media, mostly. Trying to raise awareness. I don't know how much difference it will make, honestly, but at least I'm trying to make things better, you know?"

"Have you talked to your family?" I ask as gently as I can.

She looks away. "No. I keep hoping, but I guess they're still not ready to turn the other cheek."

"Sorry," I say, wishing it wasn't such a useless word.

Out of the corner of my eye, I notice Mom and Dad standing in a corner by the fence. They look like they're having a pretty intense conversation. I strain my ears, hoping to catch a word or two, but they're speaking too quietly. I wonder whether I need to go break things up. The last thing I need is for the two of them to get into a fight and ruin the day. "Hey, will you excuse me for a sec?" I ask Anjelica. "I need to check on my folks."

"Of course," she says. "I should probably get going anyway. I have to be back in time to make dinner for Alice."

"Oh, no," I say. "Can't you stay any longer?"

She shakes her head. "You should be with your family, anyway." She pulls me in and gives me a big hug. "Don't be a stranger, okay? Text me when you get to New York and let me know how it is. I'm going to have to live vicariously through you until I can get back to school."

After I close the gate behind Anjelica, I walk over to where Mom and Dad are still talking. They stop when they see me, but not before I hear Dad say, "I'll tell her," in a low voice.

"What's up?" I ask as they exchange guilty looks.

"Oh, nothing," Dad says. "Nothing you need to worry about."

I try to catch Mom's eye, but she won't look up from the ground. "I should go," she says.

"Are you sure?" I ask. "Mr. Fisher made brownies."

She shakes her head. "No, I should be getting back. But there's something I'd like to give you."

"I should check on Carol and the baby," Dad says. "Good-bye, Anneliese."

Mom reaches out and grabs Dad's hand. She holds it in both of hers. "Thank you, Peter," she says.

"What was that all about?" I ask after Dad walks away.

"I'll let your father tell you," she says. Then she hands me a long, thin box. "Here, this is for you. I'm sorry I can't give you more."

"You didn't have to get me anything," I say. I start to open it, but she holds up her hand. "Save it for later. I don't want to take you away from the party."

"Okay," I say. "Well. Thanks."

"I'll just go thank the Fishers. Congratulations, Rooney. I'm very proud of you." And then she's gone.

That night, after the guests have left, after the dishes are scraped and washed, after Merce and I have taken a long, slow walk around the block, after the Fishers and I have devoured the last few bites of brownie and I've thanked them one more time for everything they've done for us, I hug them both good night and head to my little room off the kitchen.

Mom's present is sitting on the desk, next to the tassel from my graduation cap. The box is made from some kind of silver cardboard that looks old. As I lift the lid, a familiar smell fills my nostrils. I close my eyes and inhale, my nose practically touching the brittle cardboard. And then, in an instant, it comes to me. The top drawer of Mom's dresser in our old apartment, where she kept all her "treasures." I can see it as clearly as if I were standing in the room. A tarnished turquoise necklace. A box like this one, holding an old-fashioned charm bracelet that she told me had belonged to her mother. And a little stone bear carved from a white rock. A polar bear.

I carefully push aside the white tissue paper until something peeks out. It's my mother's watch. The one her parents gave her. The one she took off on November 16, and probably never put on again. I turn it over in my hand, amazed at how feather-light it feels. The band is so tiny it will never fit around my wrist. On a hunch, I poke my finger back under the tissue paper and find three extra metal links, never used. And then my finger touches a piece of paper. I lift out the little card, and see Mom's spidery handwriting: *For my brilliant girl. I wish I could give you back the time we lost, but this will have to do. I love you. Mom.*

AUGUST
AGAIN

one

The blue car is barely big enough, but luckily, I don't have much stuff. I let Daniel sit in front first, and then we switch places after lunch. The route we're traveling is still familiar a year later, and I keep remembering odd little details. The way Alice fussed around Fred as he carried their heavy suitcase. Anjelica squeezing into the back seat to sit with me . . . In so many ways, I don't feel like the same person who made that trip.

As the city comes into view, Mom points toward the skyline. "Not much longer now. How are you feeling?"

"Good," I say. "Nervous. But good. Both hands on the wheel, please!"

She laughs. "Come on, I'm doing great!"

"You're doing fine," I admit.

Almost before I'm ready, we're driving through those same big gates that Anjelica and I stood outside of. They're open wide today so all the students can move in. Inching along College Walk, we're in a sea of blue. Blue balloons everywhere, blue banners, and students in blue T-shirts. As soon as we park, three of those T-shirts surround the car. "Are you a freshman?" a girl asks.

I nod.

"Awesome! You can go straight to registration." She points to a huge white building, all marble and columns. "We'll take care of your stuff."

"We don't have to carry anything?"

"Nope. What's your name?"

"Marina Harris," I say.

"Nice to meet you, Marina. I'm Jen. Welcome to Columbia!"

Seconds later, Jen and her blue-shirted crew have pulled all my shabby cardboard boxes out of the trunk, and Mom, Daniel, and I are walking toward that white palace to make it all official.

My dorm is a big, anonymous-looking building right on Broadway. Cars are zooming past and the sidewalks are swarming with students. Daniel flinches when a taxi horn blares, and I take his arm and escort him across the street. "You really like this?" he asks, his eyes wide.

"I really do." I feel like I haven't stopped grinning since we drove through the gate.

My resident adviser is waiting for us as we get off the elevator. "You have a little time before convocation, but don't wait too long," she says. "You want to get good seats!"

It takes us all of twenty minutes to unpack. The last thing I unwrap is the little wooden pencil box that Daniel made me for Christmas. "I'm putting it right here on my desk," I tell him. "So every time I write something, I'll think of you."

Just then, my phone bloops. Dad is downstairs. "Be right down!" I text back.

Convocation starts with horns playing some kind of fanfare and an endless stream of people marching past, carrying flags. There are men and women in gowns in all different colors, with velvet stripes on their sleeves and crazy hats. Everyone's cheering for them like they're astronauts or football players or rock stars.

Sitting on my folding chair, with Mom and Daniel on one side of me and Dad on the other, I let the speeches roll over me. I don't worry too much about catching every word. I know that what they're really saying is "Welcome home."

"Do you want us to stick around?" Dad asks when it's done. "Meet your roommates, or . . . anything?"

I shake my head. "No, you and Daniel should get going. Carol's waiting for you."

"You sure?" Dad asks, his forehead wrinkling with concern.

"Positive. Call me when you get home, okay, Bug?" I pull Daniel into my arms. "Call me sooner if you want," I whisper.

"See you in a few days, sweetie," Mom says, giving him a long hug. "I'll be waiting for you at the gate when you get off the plane."

The morning after graduation, Daniel and I had one last breakfast with Dad and Carol before they headed back to New York. We shared a big booth, and Carol let me hold Rosie and feed her little bites of soggy pancake. Anyone looking at us would have seen a family like any other family, laughing, joking, not a care in the world.

Toward the end of breakfast, Rosie started to get fussy, and Carol and Dad exchanged a look. "I'll take her for a walk," Carol said, catching a sticky little fist before it collided with her chin. "You guys take your time."

Almost as soon as she was gone, Dad's expression changed. He glanced over at Daniel. "I think it's time," he said. "Right?"

Daniel nodded, his expression just as serious as Dad's.

"What's going on?" I asked.

"There's something we need to tell you," Dad said.

"Promise you won't be mad," Daniel said.

"Okay, I promise," I said, even though a sour feeling was rising up in my stomach.

"I'm not moving to New York. I'm going to stay in Vermont with Mom," Daniel said.

"Right," I said. "Very funny." But he didn't crack a smile. I turned to Dad, and he nodded. "You're serious? Why would you do that?"

"Because I belong in Vermont," Daniel answered. "Just like you belong in New York."

I shook my head. "But we were going to be a team. I was going to look out for you."

"I know," Daniel said. "I'm sorry."

I turned back to Dad. "I don't understand. Why would you let this happen?"

"It was my idea," he said quietly.

"Your idea? Why?"

"Because I did what you said," Daniel said. "I told Dad how being in New York made me feel."

Just then, Carol came back holding Rosie on one hip. "Hey, Daniel, I could use a hand with her," she said. "Would you mind?"

He started to get up, but I put my hand on top of his. "Are you sure this is what you want? You really want to live with Mom again?"

He nodded. "It's not going to be the way it was. She's better. And I'm still going to see all of you. I'll come visit. And you can come visit us, too."

I let go of his hand and he followed Carol outside.

Dad and I looked at each other. "Can you tell me something . . . anything that will help me make sense of this?"

"It's what he wants," he said, spreading his fingers in front of him in a helpless gesture.

"Is it Carol? The baby? Is it just too much for you guys to take on right now?"

The shocked expression on Dad's face looked genuine. "You think it's because we don't want him?"

"I don't know what to think."

"Carol and I are crazy about Daniel. We'd turn our lives upside down to have him with us." He pinched the bridge of his nose like he was trying to smooth away a sharp pain. "Look, I know your mom doesn't have the best track record. But she's getting help, and she really is a lot better. You've talked to her. Does she seem the same as she was before?"

I couldn't get used to Dad defending her. "If she's so different, why didn't she tell me herself? Why did she get all squirrely at the party yesterday and run away instead of talking to me?"

"That was me, too," he said, wincing. "She wanted to tell you, but I asked her to let Daniel and me do it."

"She should have told me herself," I grumbled, not ready to let it go.

He looked at me seriously. "People deserve second chances, Marina. What your mom did . . . She did all the wrong things, but she didn't do them for the wrong reasons."

"I know, it's just . . ." For as long as I could remember, Daniel had been the reason I got up in the morning, the reason I did well in school, the reason I went to work every day. How was I supposed to go to New York without him?

"He's not happy in New York," Dad said, gently interrupting my thoughts. "I don't know for sure that he'll be happy living with her, but it's what he says he wants, at least today. And if he changes his mind, he knows we'll be here for him."

That evening, Daniel and I sat in his room. Once he turned ten in the spring, he'd finally decided he was too old to be put to bed, but every now and then, he was still willing to make an exception.

"Are you mad? About me staying?" he asked.

"I promised not to be," I reminded him.

"Sad, though?"

"Yeah. Sad." The word stuck a little in my throat, and I coughed to cover it up.

"We'll still have the family plan. We can talk all the time."

"That's true." We sat there for a few minutes, listening to the night sounds outside his window. Then I got up, pulled my phone out of my pocket, and dialed his number.

"Hello?" I could hear a smile in his voice.

"Hey, it's Rooney," I said, closing his door behind me.

"Hey. How's college?"

I had to pause for a second to steady my voice. "It's great. How's your new school?"

"It's good. Everybody's really nice. Nobody knows about last year. And it has a huge library."

"That sounds really good."

"Yeah. It does."

I listened to him breathing until finally he said, "Good night, Rooney."

"Bye, Daniel," I whispered.

"Do you want to get something to eat? Maybe we can find a slice around here," Mom offers after Dad and Daniel leave.

"No, it's okay. You should probably get going." Her driving has gotten better, but she's still not great in the dark. And since she refused to spend money on a hotel room, she's got a long drive ahead of her.

As we walk toward the car, I can feel time flooding past me, unstoppable, about to take her away. All I've wanted for so long was to get away from her, and now, with my escape almost complete, I desperately want her to stay. She's just a foot away from me, and it feels too far.

When we reach the car we stop, hands dangling awkwardly at our sides. I was prepared for a river of tears, but her eyes are dry. Even more surprising, there's a stinging feeling in mine, and my throat feels raw. "Is there anything at all that I can do before I go?" she asks.

"I have everything I need."

She smiles. "You really do. Rooney, I'm just so amazed by you. You grew up so well." She doesn't grab my hand and squeeze it, but I'm pretty sure she wants to.

"You too, Mom."

She laughs at that, a lilting whoop of delight. "Let's take a picture. Two grown-ups!"

She holds her phone out and tries to bring us into focus. I have to bend down a little to get in the shot, but she doesn't lean in to me. I can feel the sliver of space she's left between us, her hesitation. *It's all right*, I want to tell her. *I forgive you.*

"My turn." I take out my phone and then I pull her in to me until there's no distance between us, until I can feel her molecules touching mine. I look at our two faces on the screen, and it's like I can see a whole alternate reality. A different mother, a different daughter, a different history. One where all the mistakes, all the foolishness, all the anger are wiped away and there's nothing left but love. "Just one more," I say. She looks at the camera and I lean in and kiss her cheek. *Click.* The photo captures the look of surprise and happiness in her eyes.

And then time lurches forward. "Well, I guess this is it." She climbs into the driver's seat, carefully buckling her seat belt.

"Drive safely," I say.

"I will."

"Call me when you get there. And don't forget to take rest breaks. And eat something!"

"Yes, Mom." She rolls her eyes at me, and we both laugh. I step back and swing the door shut, then immediately want to yank it open again. I want to curl up in her lap so she can stroke my hair the way she did when I was little. But I don't move.

Without taking her eyes off me, she lifts up a hand and touches her cheek. Her fingers float over the spot where I kissed her. She holds her hand there, like she's sealing in the kiss, and her eyes get brighter until a tear slides down her cheek.

Without taking my eyes off her, I lift my hands up and clasp them to my chest, just over my heart. I don't even care that my own cheeks are wet. I don't wipe the tears away.

We stay like that as the seconds stretch out into infinity. And then she brushes her fingers under her eyes and starts the engine. I don't run after her as she drives away. I don't shout, "Don't go!" I watch the car as it passes the big gate and turns right onto Broadway.

I check the little silver watch on my wrist. Fifteen minutes until orientation. I walk to the library and sit on the steps, dwarfed by the massive building. Alone in the crowd, I pull out my phone again and lose myself in that last picture. The kiss on Mom's cheek, the smile in her eyes.

When I've memorized every detail, I flick the screen and begin to scroll through the pictures, going backward in time. The selfie I took on my last day at the Java Connection. Mercer in his garden, holding a giant tomato out to me. Everyone together on graduation day. Mercer and me in our caps and gowns. Mr. Fisher and Daniel working in the shed. Mrs. Fisher in her reading chair, smiling like the Queen of Somewhere . . .

I don't have a "normal" family. I probably never will. But all the people who matter to me are with me as I sit here. They're holding me in their hearts, and I'm holding them in mine. And maybe that's where Balance really begins. With everyone taking care of each other the best they know how.

It may not be enough.

But it's a start.

Acknowledgments

This book would not exist without the help and support of so many people, but especially:

My parents, Deborah and Andries, and my sisters, Elisa and Lori, who celebrated and commiserated with me every step of the way.

My early readers, Timo van Dam, Mirea Klee, Francesca Levett, Ioana Petrou, Matthew Levett, Mark Jamison, Cory Jamison, MacKenzie Cadenhead, Gustie Owens, and Crissa Carlotti, who said ultra-smart stuff in the most loving way.

The friends and family, too numerous to name here but no less loved, who cheered me on through the dark days.

Caitlin Fross, Rebekah Metz, and Neil Rhodes, who told me things I couldn't just Google.

Kari Sutherland, who chipped away a whole lot of rock to reveal the sparkly bits inside.

Paula Allen, who provided wise counsel at so many junctures along this bumpy road.

My agent, Marly Rusoff, who must be a magician because she pulled a rabbit out of a hat, and Elaine Berg, who introduced me to her.

The phenomenal team at Scholastic, and most especially my editor, Anamika Bhatnagar, and associate editor, Megan Peace, who continue to amaze me by loving Rooney and Daniel as much as I do.

My Big Person and my Medium-Sized Person, who are always in my corner and make me want to be better.

And you, who trusted me with your time.

Thank you.